Pra

"Buchman changes up the game plan here… His meticulous research is once again duly noted, as are the action-packed mission scenes and the passionate love story between the phenomenal lead characters, with the romance being equally as breathtaking as the action."

—*RT Book Reviews*, 4.5 Stars, Reviewer Top Pick

"As usual, Buchman skillfully balances the romantic and military aspects of his story, populating it with memorable characters and pulse-pounding action."

—*Publishers Weekly*

"The pacing and technical details are superb (this is a Buchman book, after all)… Buchman cannot write a bad book, and this, possibly his best yet, is another great example of what military romance should be."

—*Booklist*

"Buchman has catapulted his way to the top tier of my favorite authors…*Target Engaged* has everything I need to keep me enthralled. A sexy alpha male who's an honest-to-God good guy…a kick-butt heroine engaged in some heart-stopping advent███████ ██ ██e hero, and off-the-chart stea██████ ██████ █████ █omance."

███ *esh Fiction*

"M. L. B██████ █████████ ████ ██ favorite authors…h██

███ *Reviews*, Reviewer Top Pick!

Also by M. L. Buchman

HEART STRIKE

A DELTA FORCE NOVEL

M. L. BUCHMAN

sourcebooks
casablanca

Published by Sourcebooks Casablanca, an imprint of Sourcebooks, Inc.
P.O. Box 4410, Naperville, Illinois 60567-4410
(630) 961-3900
Fax: (630) 961-2168
www.sourcebooks.com

Printed and bound in Canada.
MBP 10 9 8 7 6 5 4 3 2 1

Chapter 1

RICHIE GOLDMAN EASED BACK INTO THE DARKNESS.

Most of the Bolivian farmworkers were sitting around the nightly campfire, eating their *salteñas*—meat-, veggie-, and quinoa-stuffed pastries. He'd learned to pretend that their food didn't agree with him. It gave him an excuse to duck into the trees frequently, though he'd actually learned to enjoy the local food almost as much as a good New York pastrami on rye.

Some of the farmhands were idly chewing on a strip of *charque de llama*; the llama jerky lasted forever despite the jungle heat. Others chewed on coca leaves—little more than a low-grade stimulant in that form, and it grew in lush abundance all across the hillside above their camp. Refined cocaine was too valuable for mere farmers, but chewing the leaves was practically a national pastime. Street vendors had piles of them in all the cities.

Richie had tried it, thinking it would help him fit in, but found the taste so astringent that he had no problem just tucking it in his cheek and only pretending to chew. Others on his team had found similar tricks. Only Duane had flat-out declined, but his formidable silence made it so that he wasn't an easy man to question. The locals let him be.

Once out of the firelight, Richie met up with Duane. That left the other three members of his Delta Force team—Chad, Carla, and the team leader, Kyle—still at the fire making sure that no one followed them into the darkness.

He and Duane spoke softly in Spanish about nothing in particular as they strolled along the edges of the coca fields they'd been working for the two weeks since their arrival. A thousand hectares, almost five square miles of coca plantation in this farm alone. They'd been building up to this one for six months; it represented almost five percent of Bolivia's coca production. They'd be gone in a few more days.

And that would be the last day of this farm's existence.

Only two more measurements to take. They strolled the edge of the field like a pair of *hombres* walking off the day. Their feet were nearly silent on the rich dirt. To one side was thick jungle, with no two trees alike. A massive kapok, a spindly palm, and a fig tree that was bigger than the Goodyear blimp sitting on its butt were crowded together. Beneath them were banana, rubber, and a hundred other small trees he couldn't identify in the dark, but the rich, loamy scent was lush with life. The leaves rustled, whether on the light breeze or due to some passing band of monkeys, he couldn't tell. To the other side, there lay row upon neat row of man-tall coca bushes with their thick leaves ready for harvest.

When they reached the southwest corner of the main field, Richie ducked down low while Duane kept watch. He pulled a GPS tracker out of his boot, checked that he had a valid and stable reading, then recorded the numbers. He slipped it back into his boot, and once more they were just two shadows strolling the line.

The two of them had originally bonded during the six-month training course for The Unit—as Delta Force operators commonly referred to themselves. They had discovered a shared inner nerd over various triggers for different types of explosives, which was Duane's specialty. *Being* the team's chief nerd was Richie's specialty.

Duane's deeply laconic nature made for a very lazy conversation, a rhythm which Richie had come to rather enjoy. It felt as if they blended better into the night that way—the occasional bat flitting by with a quick *brrrr* of wings, the dry grass rustling against their calves, and two guys down on their luck sharing quiet commiseration.

Kyle and Carla were a couple now, and it was rare to have a conversation with one and not the other. And *any* conversation involving Carla was more like a debate match than a conversation. The lady was intense. Amazing, beautiful, and incredible…but intense. And Kyle and Carla's relationship was like that too. Richie had never seen anything like it, had never imagined it was possible. When the two of them were together, the day became brighter. His parents had always been his ideal of a good relationship, which was solid and stable, but Kyle and Carla made it look like a heck of a lot of fun too. For the first time, Richie was forced to recalibrate the standards of what he hoped for from his own future.

Chad, on the other hand, talked about women and nothing but. He thought women were great sport, and if he hadn't been so successful with them, Richie would have discounted half of what he said. Chad somehow always ended up with the hot women and seemed to leave every one of them smiling; his successes were short-lived and he claimed that's the way he wanted it. He just didn't have the greatest conversational range on other topics.

Duane was the one most like Richie on the team. They came from professional backgrounds; they both had grown up in nice neighborhoods with good schools, corporate executive fathers, and involved mothers— Richie's was a housewife who did a lot of entertaining in support of Dad's job; Duane's was a family-law attorney. It was almost like he and Duane were related, separated only by New York versus Georgia respectively and an entirely different hereditary line.

"I don't know, brother," Duane was saying. "How did Chad sweep up Mayra?" They spoke Spanish for both the practice and to protect their cover story.

It wasn't typical of them to discuss women, but Mayra was the hottest, most-built Bolivian beauty they'd seen in the eleven coca farms they'd worked over the last six months. Their Delta team had been quietly roving the countryside, posing as itinerant workers—ex-pat Americans down on their luck. Their assignment had been to blend in, precisely map each field's location, and then move on with no one the wiser.

"Chad makes it look so easy." Richie didn't exactly envy Chad's insane success with women. It was too slick, too casual, and too easily forgotten. But he wouldn't mind having at least a few of those skills himself for when the right woman came along—so she wouldn't pass on by before he could untie his tongue.

"Maybe he is hung like horse," a voice said out of the

darkness. Rolando faded into view, a battered AK-47 over his shoulder catching the moonlight and an even more worn radio at his hip.

"You got patrol tonight. Sorry, *amigo*," Duane said more easily than Richie could have. Rolando was one of the most dangerous of the coca farm's guards. The others joked that he loved his gun more than his mother.

"No big deal. But I was *mucho* close to spreading Mayra." He held up two fingers so close together the moonlight couldn't slip between them. "Like so before he come along." Then he shrugged. "Maybe when he gone."

With Rolando it was hard to read if that meant he was expecting them to just leave or if Rolando was planning to accidently shoot Chad some night soon. Richie reminded himself to tell Chad to watch his back around Rolando—not that Chad was easy to surprise. He might be a complete womanizer, but he'd also grown up on the wrong side of the Detroit streets.

The first option was unlikely, because once a person came to work on a coca farm, it was very hard to leave. There were hundreds of booby traps set around the perimeter of the fields. They were intended to keep raiders and government men out, but the lethal wall was not far into the jungle and it did just as effective a job of keeping the workers in. The main road in and out was always heavily guarded, except for a few minutes around sunrise a couple days from now, which is when the Delta team would be leaving.

They traded some more sympathy with Rolando, all agreeing that it would help if Chad wasn't such a good guy as well.

Richie knew better.

Chad was one of those guys who was everyone's friend and most people assumed that's all he was. But he had also come by his nickname, The Reaper, because he was a stone-cold killer when he needed to be.

Richie and Duane continued their walk, leaving Rolando to watch the night. They stopped and chatted with two more guards before reaching the one corner of the field they hadn't had a chance to exactly locate yet.

"Anyone?"

He and Duane stood for at least ten minutes, talking about the backbreaking work of tending the vast plantings—which in truth wasn't as tough as a typical day of Delta training—and watching over each other's shoulders.

Duane finally shook his head in answer to Richie's earlier question. They were alone.

Richie knelt quickly and pulled out a small, high-powered radio, unfolded a tiny parabolic dish antenna, and aimed it upward. He checked his watch, shifted the antenna to point toward the constellation Virgo, and pinged their full set of GPS data coordinates up to a satellite that should be in that vicinity. By using a directional antenna and sending all of the data compacted into a single short burst of information, their signal should be undetectable.

Many coca fields were heavily protected from above as well; acre after acre of camouflage nets hid the cash crop. Others, like this one, were hidden so deep in the mountains that it was easier to find them from the ground, following leads and tips rather than aerial photos.

Ten seconds later a "squirt" pinged back from The

Activity—America's most clandestine military intelligence agency in Fort Belvoir, Virginia. Another coca field had been accurately located and recorded.

Richie glanced at the return message quickly, checking that it unscrambled cleanly. Then swore when his eye caught on the last line.

"What?" Duane whispered.

Richie sent the "message received" squirt back, collapsed his little setup of equipment, and scanned the message fully before putting away his gear.

"Six hours," was all he said. "All the way out."

"Aw, *mierda*!" was Duane's response.

The living room was a complete shambles. It reeked with the bitter sting of spent powder, though not enough shots had been fired to cloud the room with smoke. The room was chilly, threatening to freeze the sweat on her forehead. The midsummer North Carolina heat hadn't penetrated the thick concrete-block walls—which were painted in a rich brown, creating the worst visibility conditions for the exercise.

Staff Sergeant Melissa Charlene "The Cat" Moore did her best to keep the pure glee of the entire experience out of her expression as her three-person team moved through the room finishing the job—and over the last six months, they had become *her* team. She'd fallen in as the natural leader despite being the only female.

Six months ago she had been the one sitting on this same worn couch, for which too much fake blue leather had died decades before. There were mismatched armchairs, a battered entertainment center, dining table, kitchen in the corner…the whole nine yards of a well-worn modern family great room.

There were three types of occupants.

The first were seven armed terrorists—all now dead with two shots each to the chest or three in the pelvic region for those wearing armored vests. As they'd fallen, they'd knocked over chairs and lamps. One had slid down the wall and taken a pair of cheap paintings with him. The woman in the kitchen with an MP5 machine gun had flailed back into a dish cabinet with a clatter far louder than the silenced weapons used by Melissa's team. It was immensely satisfying, even if all seven terrorists were mannequins.

The lights came back on and Melissa flipped up the night-vision goggles attached to the helmet that covered her blond hair. Her Kevlar vest was weighed down with a wide array of hardware, most of it spare magazines for her rifle and handgun. After so much training, it felt unnatural whenever she took it off rather than when she strapped it on.

The second type of occupants in the room remained paralyzed with shock. They were the five members of the most recent group to make it through the Delta Force Selection Process and had played the role of being hostages. They still sat in their chairs as if they'd been bolted there. Melissa barely managed to suppress a very un-Delta-like giggle.

She knew from personal experience that despite being trained soldiers, getting over that shock would take them at least a minute—more than long enough for her to complete her tasks and clear out. For that amount of time, her team could do practically anything they wanted, perhaps even pick the new recruits' pockets. She recalled that she'd certainly been in that level of shock when it had been her turn half a year before.

It had taken her team under three seconds to neutralize the room.

The shock of the "hostages" had many sources, the amazing speed and brutal application of force by the rescue team being the worst of it. Nothing in military training, not even Ranger School, could prepare a soldier for the ferocity a Delta team could unleash.

Mutt had breached the room's steel door with a large explosive charge and Jeff had killed the lights in the same moment.

Melissa then slid in a flashbang. It had done exactly as its name implied, releasing a blinding flash and an explosive percussion as loud as that of an M33 frag grenade but causing none of the damage.

Then their lightning attack with suppressed, night-vision-scoped rifles had capped off the mayhem.

Live ammo fired at much closer quarters than any other Army shooter would dare had riddled the bad-guy mannequins—rounds passing so close by the hostages' heads that it almost trimmed their hair.

That was the ultimate shocker to soldiers who thought they were already good but hadn't faced a Delta-style room clearing before. There was a whole other world of "better" that these new recruits had never encountered, despite a minimum of four years of military service.

There were only five "hostages" in the room. The monthlong test of the Selection Process to apply for admission to the 1st Special Forces Operational

Detachment-Delta training was brutal. This class had started with ninety-eight applicants.

Her own Delta Selection class had shrunk from a hundred and twenty-two applicants down to six who had passed. Only three of them had made it through the six months of the Delta Force's Operator Training Course, and Mutt had been from the prior class but torn out a knee halfway through his first try at OTC. Of her own class, only she and Jeff had made it through from the group of six who'd passed—two injury drops who would be back next time and two couldn't-hack-it drops.

That was the third group in the room—she and her two classmates. With the completion of this exercise, the three of them were the newest graduates of the OTC and full members of The Unit.

With a quick hand signal, she had Mutt and Jeff sweeping the room for hidden explosives and booby traps.

Melissa "The Cat" circled the couch and used her silenced Glock 23 handgun to drop an extra "security" shot into the forehead of each terrorist mannequin. Never just presume they were dead—she'd been trained to make sure they were never getting up again, no matter what help arrived how fast. A .40 S&W round into the brainpan guaranteed these mannequins were never going to sell trendy, overpriced clothes again. She considered dropping two shots into the MP5-wielding female lying among the shattered dishes. She was wearing a horridly clashing blue miniskirt and an orange blouse—which now had two neat holes in it where 5.56mm NATO rounds had punched into her chest. But the extra shot was against protocol—save the ammo; you never know what is coming next. Maybe save the round for whatever member of the training cadre had dressed her that way. Melissa sent just the standard single round into the Styrofoam brainpan—a silenced spit from the weapon and a sharp *thwap* from the mannequin's plastic skull.

Once she'd done the last of the security rounds and Mutt and Jeff had signaled an all clear, they began clearing the weapons that had been in the terrorists' possession.

Six months ago, when her own class had been the ones on the couches and chairs, she'd been nearly catatonic with shock—and desperate with need. In a few blazing seconds, the arriving Deltas had shot every terrorist and not harmed a single recruit. No prior intel on the number of terrorists, hostages, or their positions.

Now she knew how they did it. The Unit—though it was easier to think of herself as Delta—trained exhaustively to deal with the unknown. Hostage rescue was but one of a hundred skills they practiced endlessly.

Half a year of brutal training, learning how to walk, then run, then run backward, all while becoming absolutely lethal shots. The Unit didn't waste rounds during training. Unlike most outfits, they never delivered a hail of bullets—except when it was called for. Instead, every single shot counted, was aimed and placed with an accuracy practiced until it was instinctive. But while doing that, the fewer than a thousand operators of The Unit's entire combat personnel still shot more training rounds than the two hundred thousand jarheads of the Marine Corps.

Of the five "hostages" who had survived this round of Delta Selection, there was one woman—only the third to ever qualify for The Unit. She was the first to recover;

spotting Melissa, the woman shot her a cheeky grin of *Oh yeah, sister!*

Melissa offered an infinitesimal nod in return before gathering the last of the weapons and heading for the door. She wondered what the first woman of Delta had felt when she'd spotted Melissa on the couch. She certainly hadn't smiled back. Or nodded. Or even blinked.

Carla Effing Anderson.

The first woman of Delta.

She'd been too chill to offer even the tiniest bit of encouragement to Melissa.

Of course Melissa had been in near-terminal shock. She'd thought that she was the first woman to make it into The Unit—right until the moment Carla led in the room-clearing strike team.

One moment her class had been having a tactics discussion with Colonel Michael Gibson.

Then the room had gone dark, the door blown, the flashbang, and twenty-four shots went into eight terrorist dummies.

In less than four seconds, the terrorists were "dead," and Carla Anderson had simply materialized a meter in front of Melissa. Even *Star Trek* transporters didn't work that quickly. Melissa still had no idea how she'd done it.

And all through OTC, Melissa had heard nothing but "Carla always this…" and "Carla always that…"

Crap! She was sick of it.

What was worse, Melissa didn't hear it only from the training cadre. Mutt, real name Tom Maxwell, had gone through Delta Selection and half of OTC with the famed Carla Anderson before blowing out a knee and having to drop back to Melissa's class. He'd clearly been impressed as could be by the woman and had been real slow about learning when the heck to shut up. He'd finally backed off when Melissa had threatened to knee-cap him in the other knee. In answer, he'd shot her a grin and said, "Exactly what Carla would have done. Except she wouldn't have warned me first."

Melissa had always lived up to only one standard since her brother's death—her own. Granted, following in the footsteps of Carla Effing Anderson had pushed her harder, but it had also ticked her off. If she ever met the woman, Melissa was going to kick her butt just on general principle.

Last out the door behind Mutt and Jeff, she paused for one final glance back into the room.

There was a fourth type of person in the room, just one.

Colonel Michael Gibson, the most senior and scariest operator of them all. He'd stood unflinching during their entire raid as rounds flew close by either side of him. He was a bird colonel, yet he still fought out on the front lines. There wasn't anyone else like him—definitely not in the room, probably not anywhere in The Unit. Which meant he was the top warrior anywhere in any military.

No matter how many were in the room, he would always need a category of his own, commanding abso-lute respect by the simple fact of his presence.

"These are the graduates of the class before yours," Gibson informed the latest selectees/freed hostages in his surprisingly quiet voice. His words earned him the same gasps of surprise it had elicited from her own class six months earlier. "Operator Training Course will begin the day after tomorrow at oh-six-hundred. Get some sleep."

And they'd need it too. Fresh from the single most harrowing part of the entire month of Delta Selection, the Commander's Review Board, she'd been hammered and desperately wanted to let loose a bit. But her body had been wiser and she'd slept most of the thirty-six hours between the end of Selection and the start of OTC. And he hadn't been kidding about needing sleep. That oh-six-hundred formation, after only one day's break, had been the start of a twelve-hour day of shooting skills requiring immense concentration.

The newbie woman recovered enough for a question to cross her face, though it was another ten seconds before it connected to her body and her hand shot up. Unlike Melissa's own fair, blond, and built physique, she was a sleek-figured brunette with skin just dark enough that it wouldn't peel at the first exposure to sunlight each spring like Melissa's.

Gibson nodded at the newbie in that slow, this-had-better-be-good way of his.

"How many women in The Unit?"

More than Melissa had been able to articulate six months ago when Carla Anderson had magically materialized a single foot in front of her.

"Two, now. You will make three. Feel free to inspect the results of this team's attack," he addressed the rest of the group. Then the Colonel did one of his fade things that was so fascinating to watch.

As the five new graduates of the Selection Process rose to inspect the carnage that she, Mutt, and Jeff had wrought on the seven terrorist mannequins, Gibson moved at exactly the same speed they did, even using gestures common to them and nothing like his own daunting self. To them it would feel as if he was just one of them, milling about the room, trying to understand how the attack had been executed; except he wasn't. He moved across the room without drawing their attention, then shooed Melissa out the doorway and into the corridor beyond, with no recruit the wiser to his seemingly magical disappearance.

Gibson always reminded her of someone, but she could never pin down who. They'd seen him only rarely during OTC; typically he was still forward deployed despite his age and rank. But he'd been there for her Commander's Review Board, her graduation, and now her achieving full operator status. She didn't recognize his face; she had an exceptional memory for faces. But still he was irritatingly familiar, irritating because she couldn't pin it down and there was no way they could have possibly met before.

He had showed up one other time, during the fourth month of their training. By that point her class was totally down with the basic Delta skills. They were convinced that it was just a matter of honing them from that point on.

They'd shared a pretty cocky, *we got this* attitude… until the silent Colonel showed up. Their class, still six people at that point, had been sent to track Gibson in a tiny five-acre plot of woods. Not even overgrown, it should have been a cakewalk.

They didn't find him.

But he found them.

None of them even saw a teammate go down.

And none of them had seen the man who took down all six of them; to drive the lesson home, he hadn't been gentle. With their due humbling and numerous bruises handed out, he'd spent a week showing them how to do the same. After that, Delta training had shifted—no longer about honing what they knew, it had become about discovering what they didn't know.

A quartermaster was waiting for them in the corridor. While the recruits' voices slowly came back to life in the shoot-room, her team turned in their weapons, signing everything back in.

She felt practically naked without the HK rifle over her shoulder and the Glock handgun strapped over her solar plexus.

Been through a lot of changes, girl. And she'd bet there were a whole lot more to come.

———

Sunrise was less than an hour off when Chad jostled his shoulder.

Richie hadn't been asleep and barely managed to suppress an oath as Chad shook him hard enough to wake the dead—his idea of humor. Richie noticed that he was a little more cautious with Duane, who often woke with his knife half-drawn. Kyle and Carla were already at the hut's entrance.

Kyle had taken one look at the order and, in minutes, outlined a plan of how they were going to exit the farm with hopefully minimal exposure and risk. The guards they were anticipating would be off duty and the patrol timing would be wrong, but Kyle's plan was as solid as they could get with what they knew.

No way would Richie be missing this place. Dirt floor, woven grass mat, and a thatched roof that could really use some thatch before the next rainstorm but wasn't going to get it.

He felt sorry for the laborers. Some of the farmers were about to have an even worse season than the last one. At a big site like this, they were little better than slaves. Once the coca was gone, they'd be free, but with no assets and no working farm crop. In the coca business, locals just weren't part of the profit equation.

Rolando and the drug lord's other armed guards Richie liked well enough, but had less sympathy for.

The Delta team slipped out into the darkness, just a hint of the blue in the sky that was already washing out the fainter stars. They passed the farmers' huts and were almost to the road leading out of the camp.

"Where are you going, *amigos*?" Rolando, his AK-47 no longer over his shoulder but now in his hands.

"Hey, buddy." Chad started forward, but stopped and tried to look stupid when Rolando flicked off the safety.

Carla stepped forward with an easy sway of her hips. Her dirty blue work shirt unbuttoned far enough to reveal that her assets weren't all that much less impressive than the fabled Mayra's.

Rolando's eyes dropped to her cleavage.

She moved a hand up to his chest. With a little flick of her wrist, she revealed the long KA-BAR military knife she was holding and rammed it up under his chin and into his brain.

Rolando twitched once.

"That's for trying to ram it up my backside without asking."

"He what?" Kyle snarled, but Carla didn't waste any time answering. If there was ever a woman able to defend herself, Richie knew it was Carla Anderson.

Then Rolando collapsed to the ground and his finger must have snagged on the trigger. A single 7.62mm round gave a loud crack and zinged off into the trees.

"Shit!" the whole team said pretty much in unison.

With their clandestine departure blown, Chad swept up the AK-47 and fired a security round into Rolando's forehead.

In seconds, they were fifty meters away and moving fast. Kyle had Rolando's sidearm and Carla had a subcompact Glock 27 that she'd produced from somewhere—where was one of the questions Richie suspected he'd be better off not asking. Still, it was an interesting problem because they'd all been checked on arrival as being unarmed. Richie had pre-buried his GPS and satellite gear in the jungle, carefully crossing then recrossing the mined perimeter before they'd come into the camp so that he could retrieve them once the team had been accepted.

The two guards at the main gate were half-awake when they stumbled to their feet. They went back down fast and Richie and Duane now had AK-47s as well. Chad stripped them of a pair of Makarov handguns, tossing one to Richie that he caught midair.

There was an old Jeep parked by the gate, but neither of the guards had a key. It was probably back in the open, on Rolando's body. Chad started hot-wiring it while the rest of them stood watch.

Then Richie heard it. Distant at first, but building fast. The four-engine gut-thumping roar of a loaded 747.

"Come on, Chad," Carla pleaded. "Get us out of here."

The Jeep's engine roared to life and they piled in.

Duane tossed his AK-47 to Chad and dove into the driver's seat—he was the best driver they had. He'd been working up the sprint-car circuit toward NASCAR when he'd taken his detour into the military.

Kyle and Richie dropped two more armed guards who came rushing from the huts, half-dressed and scared awake.

Duane raced the Jeep out of camp along the road, praying for no booby traps.

Then the largest tanker plane in the world descended and began its run.

The 747, converted for firefighting, had been put into deep storage in the Tucson desert when its owners went out of business. The CIA had found another use for the massive plane, which now began its dump of twenty thousand gallons—over eighty tons—of defoliant across the exact coordinates that Richie had sent to them just six hours ago.

His Delta team had been to twelve coca farms in the last six months. And the 747 tanker had visited each in turn. Twelve farms that wouldn't produce a single leaf of coca anytime soon.

"Down," Chad shouted.

They all ducked and hung on as Duane rammed the heavy wooden outer barrier at thirty miles an hour. It blew apart. A four-by-four shattered the windshield and Carla knocked the remains of the glass clear with the butt of a Chinese QBB machine gun she'd acquired somewhere along the way before turning it around to shoot a guard who'd been standing well clear of the gate.

Richie kept an eye out to the rear, but no one was following. If they were, they'd have a long way to go. The team had been pulled out of Bolivia. They were being tasked to a new assignment.

That was fine.

After six months training together and another six in the field, it was the last line of the message that had worried them all.

> *Proceed to Maracaibo, Venezuela. Acquire*
> *new team member.*

———

Colonel Gibson led Melissa and her team down the dark central corridor of the hostage rescue training building. She could still hear the amazed voices of the newest class as they attempted to reconstruct the shoot-room attack.

The building had six doors along this concrete hallway—six doors of hell.

The doors had started out as a bewildering array of challenges that she would never understand. Over the last six months she'd been sent through each one of the six so many times that it no longer mattered which one they entered, with how little preparation; there would be no surprises that she couldn't take in stride.

An airliner, a cave-and-tunnel system, an elaborate multistory shoot-house in which the walls and stairs were never in the same place twice, even the one where Gibson was now leading them, the bridge of a ship. Through the last door on the right stood an airplane-hangar-sized space with the upper three stories of an oceangoing vessel standing in its center, complete with a flybridge sticking out to either side like wings.

The white steel tower had given her endless hours of trouble; big ships were designed with far too many sharp corners and narrow ladderways for the bad guys to use to their advantage. The training cadre had helped them beat it, but it had been so much harder than it looked, even tougher to take down cleanly than an airplane filled with passengers.

As a former museum technician, she had to admire each of the sets that The Unit's training cadre provided. When she was in the scenarios, they were incredibly believable. Radar scopes swept, instruments lit, televisions displayed—everything authentic right down to the questionable fashion sense of the mannequins. To add to the authenticity, they often did the raids with Simunitions rather than live ammo. In those situations, armored training cadre shot back.

Melissa had worked at the Royal BC Museum in Victoria, British Columbia, for three years before she'd decided to use her dual citizenship to sign up for the U.S. military. At the museum she'd helped build elaborate sets that had to stand up to millions of visitors a year yet still be interactive and intriguing. The cadre's set dressers were of an equally high caliber.

In moments Gibson and their team were all seated in thoroughly believable command chairs of a cruise ship's main bridge. Last time she'd fought her way aboard, it had been configured as a container ship. The set was battered, but the training cadre did a fine job of putting it back together despite stray gunfire and the occasional application of explosives. Thankfully the museum's tourists hadn't been quite that aggressive.

Colonel Gibson sat in the helmsman's seat, looking greyhound fit, his dark hair and light eyes a startling contrast when you noticed them, when he wasn't being invisible. He was dressed in the same ACUs they were—Army Combat Uniform and boots—nothing to distinguish his superior rank or vastly superior skill.

She'd always felt a little uncomfortable around him and could never quite be still when he watched her. She realized that she was fooling around with the switches on the communications officer's panel and pulled her hands into her lap.

A smile quirked at the corner of Gibson's lips, which was wholly impossible, and then it was gone, so she knew she'd imagined it.

"Well done," Gibson began. "Three Delta against seven terrorists, very well done."

And suddenly Melissa felt about three meters tall and, like Alice in Wonderland, wondered how she still fit in the room. She reached out to slap a high five with Mutt, who sat in the radar tech's chair beside her.

"Gosh, Colonel. You sure know how to make a girl's head spin."

His smile was wintry.

Then she pointed at Mutt and Jeff. "I mean, just look at them." They were clearly feeling the same effects she was from the rare compliment.

That earned her the first laugh she'd ever heard from the Colonel. Mutt stuck his tongue out at her. When she was foolish enough to turn her back on him, he tugged on her short French braid. Jeff merely sighed.

The three of them had plagued each other from the first day. They'd tried to tag her as M&M because, "Melissa Moore, you gotta know you're total eye candy." She might be, but she'd walked more than a hundred other top soldiers into the ground to get here.

Most men who'd tried to bed her called her The Ice Queen because she froze them out. She had a dream of finding someone who brought the heat and the heart, not just fun but someone who would be a keeper. She had that dream as a young girl…she'd had a lot of stupid, naive dreams back then.

In vengeance for M&M, Tom Maxwell and Sem Jaffe became Mutt and Jeff.

Worse for them, she'd made sure that M&M didn't stick and that Mutt and Jeff did.

She'd left behind Charli from her middle name Charlene, because that had been her brother's nickname for her. The name had died with him. Her middle initial was turned into "Cat" because she could sneak up on anyone, except Gibson. And just as cats sometimes had too many toes, she had too few. She'd lost two toes and her brother to an ice storm during a winter climb up Washington State's Mount Rainier. *Shut it out. Shut it out.* Even after five years, the memory still hurt like a knife.

"Mutt and Jeff."

Melissa The Cat wanted to purr when Gibson called them that.

"We need you on fireteams based out of Saudi Arabia. Are you ready for that?"

"Sure," they chimed in together. They were always doing that, which is why her tag for them had stuck so well.

She'd be up for that too. Her Arabic was poor—okay, dismal—but she knew from experience just how fast she could fix that. There wasn't anyone in The Unit with less than three languages fluent and several more at least serviceable.

"Good." Gibson nodded. "Your flight leaves in forty-five minutes. You have time to shower, pack your gear, and get to Hangar Seventeen. Go."

There was a stunned second or two as they realized that they wouldn't all be deploying together. They'd known that was unlikely of course, had talked about it, but it was still a shock. For six months of OTC plus the additional month of Delta Selection with Jeff, the three of them had rarely been apart. They'd become her friends. Her team. They had, as the saying went, gone through hell and hell together.

There wasn't a third second of hesitation—The Unit's operators were trained to adapt rapidly.

Maxwell and Jaffe offered her high fives; instead she gave each of them a hug.

"Now she lays some flesh on us," Mutt quipped. Jeff was quiet as usual, but gave her a good hug *and* a high five. Then he whispered quietly to her, "Kick ass, sister."

Not trusting herself to speak, she nodded and they were gone.

The shock of their departure left her in the lurch, like she'd leaned up against a wall that had always been there and suddenly it wasn't.

Colonel Gibson was silent, waiting patiently in his helmsman's chair.

She did her best to school her nerves into a calm state—wasn't working, so she shot for a calm*er* state and made it only partway there—before sitting down. Not quite sure how, she'd landed in the captain's seat. Now that she was in it, the chair felt odd, wrong, too big and too important. Hell, she'd only graduated OTC a dozen minutes ago and already her two closest friends were up and gone out of her life. The military was like that, but it didn't make it any easier.

Melissa forced her attention back to Gibson and shot for casual to hide the lack of calm. "So, what's the deal, Boss?"

He glanced at his watch uncertainly.

Nervous? The most highly trained soldier in any military in any country was nervous? Oh man, this was going to be so bad.

"I have—" He cleared his throat and started again. "You are fluent in Spanish?"

He must know that she was from her file. "*Ja, ich spreche Spanisch. Auch, Italienisch und Französisch*," she answered in flawless German.

No smile. Not even a hint that he could. He had actually laughed with her not a moment before; Melissa was sure he had…fairly sure. She knew he wasn't about to confess to being her father, because Mom and Dad were living happily on their houseboat in Victoria Harbour on Vancouver Island in Canada.

"And you can fly planes."

"Small ones, sure. I can even take off a helicopter without crashing, if I have an instructor beside me." Melissa and her brother had gotten their private pilot licenses together, and she'd had a few rotorcraft lessons for the fun of it. She'd kept her private pilot's license current more in his memory than anything else.

So what the hell was going on? Why was he asking her things he must already know? And she could still read the nerves on him. She tinkered with the captain's command board, wondering what it would take to navigate out of this moment. That switch there? Or the darkened map display? Key in a new GPS coordinate and go, full throttle outta here.

"I have recommended that you be assigned to our top South American team."

"Sounds *muy bueno*," she agreed cautiously.

"Good. Your transport is in one hour, Hangar Three."

He rose to his feet and headed for the door.

She took a deep breath and jumped in. "What's the other shoe, sir? The one you don't want to drop."

He stopped with his back to her, hands braced on the door.

Melissa held her breath, could feel the fear squeezing in on her—a place dark and bitterly cold. A feeling she had struggled with often on particularly long and lonely nights.

"I'm sorry." Gibson turned to face her, his face carefully controlled, then whispered, "I'm sorry that I couldn't save your brother."

Though he looked at her for a long time, Colonel Michael Gibson was gone long before she could recover from the shock.

At least now she knew why she both had and hadn't recognized him. On a bitterly cold and cruel mountain five years ago, Colonel Michael Gibson—as unrecognizably swathed in as much mountain gear as she had been—had saved her life. Saved it and completely changed it.

—⁓—

"*I* didn't ask for anyone else." Carla "Wild Woman" Anderson was on a roll. The same roll she'd been on fairly continuously since the orders had come in.

Richie kept his head low, pretending to concentrate on sorting out their radio gear. He'd spread it across one of the hotel suite living room's rosewood coffee tables and then propped up the tablet computer to catch up on the news. The remains of his chili-laced hot chocolate had long since cooled from breakfast. But he sipped at it anyway to try and appear thoughtful.

It must have worked, as she headed over to the window to stare south once more as if she could divine who was flying in from five miles away.

The room was something of a shock to his body with its broad clean windows, luxurious furnishings, and stunning view of Maracaibo, Venezuela. Hot showers and efficient room service only made it all the stranger. The suite had five bedrooms, but as Carla and Kyle shared one, there was a spare.

An ominous spare, as they knew someone was inbound to occupy it. Kyle had gone out to the airport to meet him, and his buffering effect on Carla's temper was much missed.

Richie was just hoping they were done with their six months posing as itinerant Bolivian coca plantations laborers. Nothing to connect their team with the large, unmarked CIA and Colombian planes that flew low overhead in the middle of the night and blanketed the plantations with defoliant. They'd destroyed over four thousand hectares of coca that would never be processed into cocaine, though that ten percent felt like such a small dent in the estimated sixteen thousand hectares in cultivation. Thankfully, one farm didn't talk much with the next, so no one in the camps knew to ask how the intel for the planes was so perfect despite rough terrain, camouflage nets, and remote locations.

His problem, and he suspected half of Carla's—as she stormed into Richie's bedroom again because he had the best view of the airport—was that he was sick of the Bolivian fields. So much of it had been scout work. It was time for a little action.

Now the team had been directed to a quiet hotel suite along the waterfront in Maracaibo. Then they'd been told to plant their asses and wait.

Carla wasn't good at waiting, except when actually on a mission, and then she had the patience of a sphinx. But now, in a room that she insisted was too beige, looking out at a city that was too crowded and a river that was too wide and a sky that was…

Richie didn't mind the waiting. With most of the last six months out deep in the field, he was behind on a dozen different fronts of his normal news gathering. The Russians were testing a new microwave "gun" that could fry a drone's electronics from ten kilometers away. The Air Force had retired the A-10 Thunderbolt…again— even though they still had nothing to replace it. Heckler & Koch had a new modification for the HK416 rifle, a softer bolt return that should make it even quieter. He couldn't wait to try it—he looked up the mod but couldn't see any way to fabricate one in the field.

There was a cool article about DEVGRU on one of the military blogs intended for veterans and their families. It was really impressive how few facts they had right; half of the images were just standard SEAL teams and two clearly showed Marines. SEAL Team Six, as DEVGRU was still incorrectly known despite shedding that name thirty years before, continued to be a media sensation—which left The Unit to continue operating nicely in the dark. Of course the rare articles about The Unit were even farther off the mark than this one about ST6, which was even more satisfying.

"Did you ask for someone new?"

He'd missed Carla's return. She now stood close beside the dining table where Duane and Chad had an intense game of Truco going over the last dregs of breakfast. The card game really needed four players, but having no one else willing to join in didn't stop them. The Colombian forty-card version of contract rummy was cutthroat and anything but quiet—a skill they'd all honed on the coca farms.

She broke their concentration, which was hard to do. Chad and Duane always played with an intense mano-a-mano combativeness—especially when they were trying to ignore one of Carla's rants.

"Huh?"

"What?"

Carla snarled at them.

Richie watched out of the corner of his eye. Duane didn't look like he came from a well-to-do household like Richie's; instead he looked like he came from a boxing ring. He was a good-looking guy, at least the ladies all seemed to think so, but he just looked that tough. And he was leveraging that with a dark scowl of concentration at the moment.

Chad was the opposite. He wasn't called "The Reaper" for his charming Iowan personality and farmboy looks, but rather for the hundred-percent thoroughness he wrought on any who crossed him—a survival skill honed by the Special Forces Green Berets.

"You two are useless," Carla snapped at them.

They both gazed at her blankly for several long seconds, grunted at each other, shared a shrug of confusion, and turned back to their game. It was well timed; she appeared to buy it.

Richie couldn't help himself; he watched Carla as she stormed back and forth across the room.

It was a mistake.

"What are you looking at, Q?"—a moniker he'd been tagged with long before Delta. Which was too cool, because James Bond's technical support wizard totally rocked. Richie had done okay identifying with Desmond Llewelyn, except that the guy had been old the day he was born. Richie had never clicked with John Cleese, but Ben Whishaw was awesome. Too thin and scrawny to go Delta, but still way cool. Richie checked online—no new trailer on the next film yet.

Besides, how was he supposed to not look at Carla? She was the first woman of Delta. She had long dark hair, a Bond-girl body honed fit by The Unit and half a year in the field, and features and skin tone that harkened back to her Cherokee ancestors. She was magnificent, way out of his league, and the most dangerous member of their team—with the possible exception of her husband.

Except Kyle wasn't here at the moment to keep Carla from taking it out on the rest of them.

"I didn't make any requests." Richie recalled what

he could of his handling-a-hostile-witness training. Not a witness, but definitely hostile in her current mood. Duane and Chad had chosen the dangerous tack of ignoring her. Yet it seemed to be working for them, perhaps because of the added variable of being members of her team, so they knew she wouldn't hurt them without greater provocation.

Richie didn't think the dumb-silent act would work for him, so he'd try interaction. *Agreement with a witness may put them at ease, leading them to think that you are there to help them.*

"It is puzzling though," he tested carefully.

Carla stopped pacing and faced him directly, her dark eyes black with her anger, fist clenched where the butt of her sidearm would normally be.

Her attire was completely incongruous with her mood. She wore a light blue sundress that would fit in at the hotel and the local city streets, but still it looked damned strange on her. He was used to Carla in worn camo pants or jeans, boots, and a ratty T-shirt. The dress did look weird on her, but it also looked great. Once again he was left to wonder if he'd ever find someone so amazing for himself.

"The five of us"—Richie nodded around the room— *offer the witness a supporting statement as if you are helping them. It is most effective when it is information they already possess. They will take their prior knowledge of that information as an internal recognition that they are the ones in control of the situation*—"we were kept together after OTC graduation six months ago."

Duane and Chad were eyeing him carefully from behind their cards. Ready to leap to his rescue if needed? More likely wanting to see just how much Carla might hurt him. Richie decided he was on his own and ignored them.

"It makes it hard to see why they'd bring in another person," Carla finally spoke.

When the witness first speaks, you have developed a basic rapport. Pause to see if they will continue. Be prepared with another statement of support if they don't. If they do, it will indicate a growing level of trust.

"If," Carla bit at her words, "they try to put someone in charge other than Kyle, I'm going to murder them."

Richie laughed in surprise.

Duane and Chad both came out from behind their cards now that Carla had finally revealed what was eating at her.

"What the hell, Q?" Suddenly Carla was right in his face and the pretty part of her now mattered much less than the dangerous part.

Breaking an initial rapport abruptly will increase a witness's hostility by a factor of two to five times depending on the severity of your breach.

"Sorry." Richie held up his hands defensively. "I just didn't really expect our hostile-witness training to work on you. Now we get why you're upset."

"Hostile what?" The last word wasn't a steam-whistle shriek, but rather low and dangerous. Then—the moment before Richie thought Carla was going to jump over the low coffee table and throttle him—she covered her face and screamed into her hands. She dropped back into a floral-brocade couch that completely clashed with her dress and groaned.

"Hey, Carla," Chad spoke up. "Anyone tries to replace Kyle, I'll send them down the garbage chute."

Richie smiled—their second live mission as a team had required them to climb up one.

"I'm being a bitch, aren't I?" Carla looked deeply chagrined.

"No more than normal, honey." Duane made a rare dry comment.

"Sorry," she mouthed at Richie.

He shrugged an easy acceptance. Carla's rants rarely lasted long and they always had a reason behind them. It was one of her strengths in the field. Their cover would start to shred and Carla would just let herself go off, creating the perfect distraction and convincing the bad guys of her own authenticity right down to the core. Because she really did care that much. The bad guys just couldn't read their own doom in her rants.

"Hostile witness?" Her wry tone brought some heat to his cheeks.

"Well, it worked."

She tried to scowl at him but ruined it with a smile.

Then she bolted to her feet when there was a *scrape-tap-scrape* on the hotel room's door. Long-short-long, *K* for Kyle in Morse code. Had he been knocking under duress, it would have been *tap-scrape-tap* for the short-long-short of *R* for Reeves. First initial was an all clear; last initial was a danger signal. He knew better than to unlock the door with his own card key under any circumstances.

Still, Chad and Duane slipped hands down onto their sidearms before nodding to Carla to open the door.

Melissa stood in the cheery lemon-and-sky-blue hall of the luxury hotel and still couldn't make sense of how she'd gotten here. She was supposed to be joining a top Delta team, not wandering around a luxury hotel. Something was going wrong and her instincts were saying, "Run!" but she had no idea toward or away from what. The perfect clarity of the last six months— actually, the last five years—had been shattered in an instant by Colonel Gibson's parting comment.

Five years ago her brother had talked her into the fatal winter climb of Mount Rainier. An unidentified man had hiked solo across the glaciers atop the peak during a raging winter storm and saved her life, though it was too late for her brother. It had turned out that even if the balaclava-masked rescuer had been standing right there at the first moment, it would have been too late for him.

Then her rescuer had disappeared.

All she'd ever found out was that his first name was Michael.

She'd been airlifted from just below the peak, blind from the blizzard, by a U.S. Army helicopter piloted by a Captain Mark Henderson. He'd offered to track down her rescuer and later reported he hadn't been able to. He was a lousy liar, which told Melissa that he'd succeeded but couldn't reveal who it was. Someone secret.

The helicopter had told her that her rescuer had been from the U.S. Army, so she'd joined. Not in hopes of ever finding Michael, but in learning the skills to pay back as he had. Her parents had been aghast. Before the climb, she'd been firmly on track for a very comfortable career in the museum's exhibits department. Afterward, she became an Army soldier, and not a Canadian one.

The higher she'd progressed in the United States Army, the more she'd learned about what sort of man her rescuer must have been. She'd gone 101st Airborne, then almost gone for Green Beret. But in the end, the sheer audacity of a man doing a solo winter climb on Rainier and succeeding in rescuing her by calling in Army air support made her reset her sights. She'd gone for Delta Force and made it.

And, much to her amazement, she'd ultimately been right. Only the very best Delta operator on the planet could have saved her from those hellish conditions alone. And he had been—Colonel Michael Gibson.

What's more, during training, he must have known it was her. And now he'd sent her here—the thick-carpeted hallway of a luxury hotel in Venezuela.

She inspected the man who'd fetched her from the airport acting completely as if he was an ordinary citizen. While transferring at Aruba, someone had insisted on selling her an "I (heart) Aruba" T-shirt that she didn't want. He'd closed the sale when he'd told her, "Wear it when you get off the plane, pretty lady. It will work wonders for you." And then he winked at her. So, the T-shirt was the identifying mark for her contact at the Maracaibo airport. She'd fought it on, at least a size too small—maybe more but avoided mirrors because she didn't want to know—and done her best not to feel totally humiliated.

Melissa had felt as stupid as could be stepping off the plane in Maracaibo, the only tall light-blond person of either gender on the flight, in a sea of actual returning tourists—almost exclusively of smaller stature and Spanish-dark. Though dozens of them wore Aruba-worshipping T-shirts. Voluntarily.

In Maracaibo, a hard-bodied man had breezed

up, given her a hug as if she'd known who he was. Otherwise, the embrace was completely appropriate to the circumstances, but no more; decent guy not even trying for a grope.

He greeted her with, "Hey, sis! How was the flight?"

No one had called her "sis" since her brother died. She couldn't even manage a mumbled response on the blessedly short drive back to the hotel. She could hear that he was trying to be pleasant, then eyeing her oddly when she didn't respond. Gracious, she didn't even understand the words though they sounded like English, which made her feel like even more of an idiot than the T-shirt did. Unit operators were not supposed to feel like idiots, especially not in the first twenty-four hours after graduation. It wasn't really fair.

But it didn't take a genius to pick out what he was from the first moment. Kyle Reeves—she knew once her "brother" had introduced himself—blended into the crowd a little too perfectly. Whereas she hadn't blended in at all. But she knew. One Delta operator could pick out another just by how their eyes moved and how they shifted through a crowd, always scanning for potential threats and vigilant to have an exit at their back.

"Like the T-shirt. Fred always did have a sense of humor," he said as they waited for the hotel door to be opened.

"Fred?" The disconnect only worsened, as that had been her brother's first name, but at least she could understand his words now.

"Fred Smith." He glanced away as the peephole darkened with someone looking out at them. "He's an alphabet man."

"Fred Smith," she managed. Not her brother. Instead, an alphabet agency man, probably a CIA spook, who had sold her a T-shirt to make her stand out more in a crowd than she already did. And the jerk had made her pay for it! If she ever met him again, she'd squeeze him until she got her money back for making her feel so stupid.

Kyle Reeves stood at ease beside her…except she'd come to suspect that nothing was "at ease" with Reeves. There was a readiness about him. He had a lively smile, a quick wit, and appeared to live on the balls of his feet, ready every instant to spring into action.

As if she needed another sign that this was for real.

The door locks began to rattle open.

Reeves wasn't tall, little more than her own five-eight. He wore a maroon-and-white jersey—"Venezuela's national soccer team colors," he'd told her—and had dark-haired good looks. He fit right in at the airport, and he fit right in beside her in the hall. Handsome enough to make her think some thoughts she definitely wasn't going to be thinking.

She, on the other hand, stood out like a runway beacon with her height, blond hair, and white skin. Operators weren't supposed to stand out. Though there were enough foreign tourists in Venezuela that it wasn't totally horrid; it just wasn't good. What idiot had assigned Melissa to—

The hotel door swung open…and there she was.

There was no mistaking Carla Anderson. She might be in a sundress rather than combat clothes, but her dark beauty and that same impossible poise she'd exhibited in the shoot-room six months ago were completely present. She also displayed a scowl of complete distrust that would have made Melissa feel even more disoriented if that was still possible.

"Hey, Wild Woman." Kyle stepped forward and kissed her.

Which actually did manage to create a new degree of disorientation for Melissa. She'd never seen a Delta-Delta relationship before. Of course she was only the second woman to make the grade, and she sure hadn't had one. She couldn't imagine any other unit that was crazy enough to let such a thing happen so openly. Next thing you knew they'd be repealing gravity.

The Wild Woman looked as if she wanted to attack Melissa.

"Ease off." Kyle backed Carla into the hotel room with his hands around her waist.

Carla neither stumbled nor stopped glaring.

Kyle tipped his head to invite Melissa in from the hall. Once in the room, luxury suite or not, she knew she was in the right place. Now that they were together, she recognized the room's occupants as the graduates of the prior Operator's Training Course class. Individually she might not have, like she hadn't recognized Kyle at the airport. But together they were such an incongruous bunch that you couldn't miss them.

There were three other guys waiting, two at a table, one on a short couch. There was a second, longer couch that showed signs that Carla Anderson had been sitting there alone, a couple of tasteful armchairs, a big-screen television, and a sweeping tenth-story view of Lake Maracaibo and the five-mile-long bridge that crossed it just south of the hotel.

Then it struck her.

They had gotten to stay together after OTC, while Mutt and Jeff—who she'd been missing during the entire flight down—were now on the other side of the world. That pissed her off almost as much as the discovery that she'd been assigned to Carla Anderson's team.

Two of the three guys stumbled to their feet when she entered; they'd been playing cards at the dining table which had the remains of a large breakfast shoved off to one side.

The smooth one, a blond guy who looked about as dangerous as a farm-boy hamster, was already heading in her direction with a woman-eating smile.

The quiet one, darker and sleeker than his blond friend, reached across the table they'd been sitting at and peeked at his opponent's cards. He smiled slightly before setting them carefully back down exactly as he'd found them.

And the… Melissa couldn't quite tag what the third one was just by looking at him.

The guy sitting on the two-person couch surrounded by a small pile of radio gear and a tablet computer simply gawked at her. He looked like he was about twelve with his mouth hanging open like that. He had straight, light brown hair and lighter brown eyes. Melissa had to remind herself that if he wasn't Delta, he wouldn't be in this room.

Then he closed his mouth and suddenly he looked far more the part. He also aged from a ridiculous twelve to the seriously good-looking boy-next-door in his late twenties. He didn't look like a typical Delta— the overly serious, intensely dedicated hard-ass. He looked like a…nice, decent guy. So what the heck *was* he doing here?

"I remember you." Carla had sidestepped Kyle and was once again right in front of Melissa, effectively blocking her last step into the room. "You're from the new class."

Melissa nodded sharply. After graduating yesterday and traveling overnight, she was ready for a fight. "And you're the bitch from the class before mine."

Carla quirked up an eyebrow.

"Darn it! Sorry." That was a bit much, way too much for her. "Didn't mean to say that."

But the four guys burst out laughing, even the nice one, and oddly, Carla's scowl shifted easily to a considering smile.

Melissa couldn't make sense of it as Carla held out her hand. Her shake was as solid and powerful as any guy's.

"Just remember that and we'll get along fine."

———ᵥᵥ———

Richie watched the new arrival as Chad did one of his smooth, so-glad-to-welcome-the-pretty-lady moves. He always envied Chad that skill. Despite being Scandinavian blond, he could charm his way right into a Bolivian coca operation run only by darker-skinned, darker-haired natives as if he was their long-lost cousin.

Richie managed to talk to pretty women; he just always completely mucked it up. So this time he'd keep his mouth shut.

But the new arrival was really something. He'd noticed her during his own graduation exercise, sitting on the couch and looking more like a model than a soldier.

Even in the eye-blink moments of time after they'd cleared the shoot-room, he'd been aware of her intense, blue eyes and light, blond hair that hung almost to her shoulders. It was straight but fluffed out with just enough curl to catch every hint of light. It was longer now, pulled back in a short French braid.

His team had unleashed havoc in the shoot-room and this woman—her name went by in an introduction and he missed it, crap, typical for him—had watched with open eyes and an eagerness to do the same things his team had just done.

Richie had recognized the hunger of it because it rang so clearly inside him. It wasn't about the battle for people like them; it was the challenge.

People like them.

What did he actually know about her? Yet he knew he was right. There was a drive—all of The Unit's operators were driven or they wouldn't be here—but the drives were all different. Carla fought; Chad and Duane hammered; Kyle outsmarted. And Richie...

He'd never tried to define it for himself.

He...played. Not that he didn't take the job seriously, but the last year had been the most fun of his life.

Prior to Delta, Richie had always been the outsider. Sure, he'd been valued as the top technician back with 82nd Airborne's combat engineers, but all his time in Eagle Battalion he'd never really fit in. Once he'd proven that he was a good enough soldier to make The Unit's grade, he'd simply belonged.

That first time he'd seen the newbie, she'd been

wearing the ubiquitous black T-shirt and gray-green camos of most Special Operations Forces.

Now she was clad in what he guessed were fashionably tight jeans, which looked amazing, and a white T-shirt at least two sizes too small, which was right off the charts incredible. It clung to every shape, showing off her complete fitness and perfect curves. A little too short, it kept offering intriguing flashes of her flat stomach, and the "I (heart) Aruba" was stretched across her chest to the limits of the thin material.

She gave Chad the brush-off, not something Richie had seen many women do. Of course, that would only egg him on, but Richie liked that about her.

She, Kyle, and Carla moved from the entryway, farther into the suite's central living room.

"You guys have it rough." She looked around the room.

"Pacific Northwest," Richie said without thinking. "Say something else."

The blond looked down at him strangely. "I'm not a puppet ready to perform."

"Washington State, west side of the mountains. No, that's not quite right. Say something else."

Her blue eyes narrowed and suddenly he could see the dangerous, Delta operator side of her. Perhaps not as wild as Carla, but there, deep behind that incredible face. "How the heck did you—"

"I was wrong. You're too polite. Canada. British Columbia. Vancouver Island, though it's pretty well buried, probably by the years of military service."

Her jaw went slack as she stared at him.

"Q does shit like that." Chad punched him in the

arm hard enough to hurt, communicating a clear *Shut up, Man!*

Richie ignored him.

"You're the team geek." She nodded as if he somehow fit into place.

"Proud to be. What are you?"

She laughed. "I'll be damned if I know."

It was a sudden, simple laugh, not angelic or calculated. It was the honest kind that happened around the dinner table with family. It also made him decide something.

"Here." He moved his gear farther down the coffee table he'd been using for a desk then shifted so a spot opened up between him and the arm of the two-seater sofa. His tablet computer had a classified Unit-internal report on a new stealth drone, so he closed that just in case she wasn't cleared for it. "Have a seat. It will protect you from, you know"—Richie nodded toward Chad who was still hovering—"man-apes."

She nodded agreeably and dropped down beside him.

Chad didn't counter the insult or even offer a riposte. He just looked at Richie as strangely as if he'd grown another head like Zaphod Beeblebrox in *The Hitchhiker's Guide to the Galaxy.*

It would be cool to have a second head, kind of like an outboard processing unit. But he knew he didn't. So it didn't explain why, not just Chad, but all of them were looking at him like that.

Honestly, he'd spoken to women before.

Chapter 2

"NO, SERIOUSLY, I DON'T KNOW WHAT ROLE I FILL IN A team's structure." And Melissa felt even more awkward for repeating it. She'd been trained well enough to walk into a city alone, extract or remove a target, and disappear with no one the wiser. But her only specialty in OTC had been coercing a group of nonconformists to function as a well-oiled machine. As that was clearly Kyle's role in this team, she decided against bringing that up.

Outside of that one skill, she could use explosives, but she wasn't a breacher. She could easily cover for a med or comm tech, but she'd never been focused on either. Mutt had been a hell of a breacher and Jeff a top paramedic. All Delta were good shooters, but she wasn't a sniper. She was... Melissa honestly didn't know.

"I speak four European languages."

"Including Spanish, I hope." Carla sighed from where she sat with her back against one arm of the other sofa with her bare legs draped over Kyle's lap. "Or you're gonna be a real pain in the ass."

"*Sí*." Melissa kept it short and sweet.

"Richie has seven." Carla put it down as a challenge.

"Four," Richie corrected her. "Six if you count both English and bad English."

"Bruce Willis, *The Fifth Element*." Melissa knew the reference.

"Wasn't that a great movie?" Richie's smile went brilliant and for a moment she wondered just how alone he'd been to light up so. Or was that something he simply did in the joy of a moment? Either way, she could definitely relate to the movie. Then they both looked around the room and the four others were looking at them blankly. He leaned in close. "Don't mind them. They're total heathens when it comes to good film."

Calling *The Fifth Element* a good film was something of a stretch, but it had been filled with any number of good one-liners.

Richie started tapping out the diva's aria with a couple of small screwdrivers on the coffee table's surface.

"I made it through OTC yesterday," Melissa continued to the room at large. "Which means I haven't slept in a seriously long time."

That got her groans of sympathy and a little drum roll finish from Richie.

"I'm a good shooter, but not the best."

"That would be me." Carla made it sound like a brag. But by the others' nods, Melissa could see that it wasn't.

"She was afraid you were coming in to take over the team," Richie told her. Mr. Techie was acting as interpreter for what was going on. While it was odd, she appreciated knowing the subtext of the dynamics, and she was especially glad she hadn't mentioned her typical leadership role. "She's also much nicer when she hasn't been caged up in a hotel room in a city for a week."

"It's been less than twenty-four hours," Chad offered with a hard-suffering sigh. "It only feels like a week." He was being outwardly charming, but he was so transparent that she wondered if he ever succeeded with his act. Were women really that desperate?

Hopefully she hadn't ever been.

Far stranger would be Carla Anderson having even a sliver of nice. Melissa would believe that when she saw it. "I'm a good hiker in any terrain."

"That's me again."

Melissa was starting to take Carla's jibes personally and had to remind herself that Carla had admitted she was a bitch. Well, Melissa might be Canadian, but she could bitch right back.

"Number One in every hike or march event from the first day of Delta Selection."

"That," Kyle said and patted his wife's knee to stop her before she could speak, "would be me."

"Except once," Carla insisted.

"Except once," he agreed. Kyle was as amiable as she was prickly. Did that balance them out to make them one complete person, or were they always bro and bitch to the team?

"I walked his ass into the ground on the forty-miler."

Melissa looked at her again.

The forty-mile, rucksack hike.

It was the final exercise of Delta Selection before the Commander's Review Board. After thirty brutal days of endless hikes and orienteering, it all came down to that moment. An individual—with a bloody heavy pack— crossing forty miles of mountainous, trackless forest at night with a compass and a flashlight. After thirty days of tests and challenges thinning the class, that one hike had still cut the remaining quarter of her class in half again. And it had nearly killed her to hold her lead. Her strength wasn't actually hiking under a heavy load; it was that all of her years of backcountry hiking had made her exceptional at orienteering. Add that to her ability to visualize a topo map like a museum exhibit laid out before her, and she never wasted a step.

Carla was not that tall a woman and her legs weren't long and sinewy. Below the hem of her dress, they looked like the legs of a workout queen, not someone who had walked everyone else into the ground on such a brutal hike. That meant a lot about what had driven her to succeed.

Carla being a cast-iron bitch probably covered it.

"That's impressive," Melissa finally offered, not knowing what else to say.

"Warned you." Carla tapped her own chest. "Total bitch."

"And mind reader," Melissa agreed as pleasantly as she could.

Richie snorted out a laugh.

Melissa didn't mind that Richie had shaved Chad off for the moment. He'd saved her from being truly rude to a new teammate. But Carla was really testing her resolve on that point.

"Got a name?" Chad asked from where he'd returned to the dining table and was fooling around with the cards that Duane had managed a look at upon her arrival.

"I already told you my name—Melissa."

She saw Richie repeat it a few times subvocally, as if memorizing it deep, like it was important.

"Not that. What did they call you, honey?"

She glared at Chad. "You try *honey* again and you'll find you have trouble walking for a while."

"I could get to like her," Melissa could hear Carla saying softly to her husband.

But Melissa had something else she had to straighten out at the moment and didn't dare look away from Chad.

He was grinning in a wolfish way that he seemed to think was amiable and charming. He tried again. "So, what did they call you...sweetheart?"

"The Cat. You won't hear me coming, and I'll scratch your eyes out."

"Ooo, I'm so scared." Chad pretended to cower.

Duane rolled his eyes at his buddy. At least he could see how much Chad had misread his own charm.

She was just about to move in for the kill—

"But why 'The Cat'? The name had to come before the description," Richie asked her with simple curiosity, missing all of the dynamics of the moment.

Melissa was ready to unleash The Cat on someone— Chad for being a jerk, Carla for being a bitch, or Kyle for being so content with the mayhem the other two were trying to unload on her. At this point, she'd even take a swipe at the silent Duane for not speaking up at all.

But she couldn't take it out on Richie; he'd actually been nice to her. She took a deep breath, looking for steady even if calm was long gone.

"This guy in my OTC class named Jaffe had a cat with too many toes. I have too few."

"Cut them off during a pedi?" Carla tossed out, but it was more of a tease than a jibe, and Melissa let it pass.

"Lost them during a winter hike just below the summit on Mount Rainier during an ice storm."

"Shit, man." Duane spoke for the first time. "I've been up there. That's harsh."

"Same storm I lost my brother."

It was finally too much; she hadn't meant to say that. The anguish, so carefully suppressed, had built up inside her and her exhaustion and the stress of this unknown situation had caught up with her. She turned to face Carla Effing Anderson.

"You happy now, bitch?"

But Carla's face had gone white despite her dark complexion. She swung her legs free of Kyle's lap and leaned forward.

After a long moment, Carla spoke in a whisper, "The worst pain in the world." She didn't make it a question; she knew.

Melissa swallowed hard. Of all the stupid things to have in common with Carla Anderson: The Unit and a dead brother.

All she could do was nod her agreement. It had changed her entire world. If not for that, right now she'd happily be working at the Royal BC Museum and playing auntie to her brother's kids.

―⁂―

Richie looked down at his hands. He knew that this was exactly the sort of moment when he was supposed to know what to do with them—reach out and console the woman beside him. But how did you do that when she was a Unit operator?

She wasn't crying, which would have made it easy to offer a gentle pat like James always did with the wimpier Bond girls.

Instead she looked…hard, like Melina Havelock in *For Your Eyes Only*. The pain was there, right on the surface for all to see, but she had it a hundred percent in control—he sat close enough to see that her eyes weren't even tearing up. Melissa The Cat stared across at Carla with conflicting emotions crossing her face, like she was pissed and sad at the same time.

"Uh…" Richie didn't know what to do with the sound now that he'd made it.

There was a sharp knock on the hotel door that shattered the tableau. Not a coded tap, but the sharp rap-tappa-tap-tap of "Shave and a Haircut." Carla and Melissa both jerked like they'd been slapped.

Chad and Duane were already on the move back into their rooms. They'd be out of sight with weapons drawn in case force was needed. Richie swept his radio gear and computer into a sack he'd kept handy and kicked it under the couch.

He brushed his fingertips across Melissa's shoulder, partly to get her attention and partly because he wanted to. There was a shock, like one of deep recognition. She felt…amazing, even from that light brush.

She spun to face him in surprise—whether at the touch or if she felt the same thing, he couldn't tell.

"There are a pair of silenced Glock 23s behind the sofa cushion you're leaning on," he whispered. Then he stretched his arm along the back of the couch. It would look as if they were a couple, but it placed his hand ready to plunge down and grab a handgun if needed.

Melissa studied him for just a second, shook her head more like a wet dog than a surprised cat, and nodded. In that instant, Richie was overwhelmed by the blueness of her eyes. There was a depth there normally reserved for dark-eyed women. Her eyes said, "I've seen some shit," then they turned calm and cool as the operator clicked into place.

As Kyle rose to his feet, checking the room with a single glance before heading to answer the door, Melissa did the strangest thing.

She turned and leaned back against Richie's chest as if they were indeed a couple.

Strategically, it was a good move. First, it provided her with a natural reason to turn and fully face the entry-way that had been off her left shoulder. Second, it would look casual to anyone who entered. And third, it placed her hand close beside his, just above the hidden guns, without inhibiting his own line of fire.

And fourth, it totally overwhelmed him. If brushing his fingers along her shoulder had been a shock, having her lean back against his chest was a body blow. She was warm…hot…radiating, as if she was a part of his own bloodstream or nervous system or something. It felt as if she'd always been there, and if he were to place his arm around her waist instead of hovering it over a hidden Glock 23, they'd be just as they were meant to be.

Her head rested back against his shoulder, brushing half of his face with her hair. It was soft and smelled of shampoo and plane flights—also of icy mountaintops and warm fires on a dark night. He buried his face in her hair and breathed her in.

"Hey!" She tried to twist around to look at him and impacted his nose with her temple.

"Ow! Crap!" His eyes crossed at the sudden flash of pain.

"God damn it!" Carla was swiveling in their direction to see what was happening and had her own pistol drawn.

That, in turn, had Melissa grabbing for her hidden weapon.

Chad and Duane rolled into the room with the HK416 assault rifles raised to their shoulders and seeking a target.

Richie heard the distinct *snick* of the HKs' safeties coming off.

Everyone was holding a weapon except for Richie, who was holding his nose.

Kyle stepped back in from the short front hall and stopped. A tall thin man peeked over Kyle's shoulder. He looked familiar, but Richie's eyes were still watering and he couldn't see clearly.

The man surveyed the tense situation.

"I don't think they're glad to see me."

———※———

"You beast! I should shoot you!" Melissa sat bolt upright when she recognized the new arrival.

Richie grunted when she rammed an elbow into his gut to leverage herself upright, but right then she was too angry to care.

The man peeking over Kyle's shoulder had changed to wearing a loose, white, button-down shirt, khaki shorts, and Birkenstock sandals, but it was the same tall frame, thin face, and reddish-blond hair. There was no mistaking him.

Everyone in the hotel room turned to look at Melissa, and she decided that her next best step was to lose the weapon. She stuffed it back behind the sofa cushion.

"Any particular reason?" Kyle asked carefully. The others were being slow to stow their own weapons.

Brazen it out, girl. Besides, you've taken enough crap this morning.

"This is the jerk who sold me this stupid 'I (heart) Aruba' T-shirt, insisting that I needed to wear it for you to find me." She couldn't believe she hadn't seen through his ploy.

"You look damned good in it too," the man replied.

"She does, doesn't she?" Kyle was smiling, in clear cahoots with the stranger in some guy-ness mode that tempted her to pull the handgun back out from behind the cushion.

Kyle apparently recognized the look. With a half-amused expression, he stepped aside as if to say, "Hey, go ahead and shoot him if you want to."

"I want my twenty dollars back is what I want"— though the weapon was still tempting. "I can't believe you made me pay for it."

"No returns, Ms. Moore."

She growled to herself for all the good it would do her, "Maybe I'll just take it out of your hide."

"You'd look great out of it too," a whisper sounded from very close beside her ear; it tickled. Richie.

She waited to see if he'd figure out what he'd just said.

Carla was shaking her head. "He won't get it unless we tell him."

"I won't get what?"

Melissa turned to really look at Richie, carefully so as not to smash his nose with her temple again.

"What did I miss?" Then he got it. "I didn't mean—" And he blushed scarlet. "I meant in any shirt. You have a sports bra on anyway. I can see it right through the thin cotton—Darn it! That's even worse, isn't it?" When the blush hit his ears, he mumbled, "Shutting up now," and clamped down on his tongue.

Melissa looked over at Carla. "How in heck did someone that sweet get into this outfit?"

Carla's laugh was bright and sparkling, completely belying the rash of attitude she'd been unloading on Melissa since the moment she'd walked through the door. "Beats the shit out of me. When you figure it out, let us know."

"Yeah, do that." Chad was passing close behind the sofa. He leaned over to put Richie in a headlock and gave him a hard knuckle rub on top of his head, clearly unhappy about his own inability to target Melissa.

She shot an elbow over the back of the couch, intentionally aiming just an inch or so to the side, but still Chad doubled partway over in surprise and clapped one of his hands protectively over his crotch.

"You, however, Melissa The Cat," Carla said, "have just proven that you totally belong. Now back the fuck off, Chad."

And just that fast, he did.

Melissa reassessed. Kyle might be the group's leader, but clearly no one messed with the Wild Woman.

Then Carla turned to face the new arrival. "Hi, Fred. Haven't seen you since the last time we started a drug war."

Melissa blinked. *Started* a drug war? Not fought the War on Drugs but—

Richie leaned in again, narrating. "Cartel de los Soles in Venezuela and Sinaloa out of Mexico; we kinda set them up to hate each other, which wasn't all that hard. We also deep-sixed thirty tons of cocaine that was on some submarines while we were at it."

"I heard about…" she tried to remember, "…the Navy intercepting a submarine, singular, with ten tons of cocaine aboard, not thirty."

He shrugged easily. "Duane destroyed and sunk the other two. It was fun; I'd never driven a submarine before. Spent two days running submerged before we gave that one to the BGBs—the Big Gray Boat boys."

"Stupid squids," Chad grumbled. "Gave all the credit to DEVGRU."

"I told them we were Seal Team 6," Duane admitted.

"Really?" Richie sounded very pleased. "Cool, Duane. They got a bunch of press for it. All over the place."

"Feeding the frenzy, bro," Duane agreed.

Even Chad looked mollified that more press attention had been misdirected away from The Unit.

Melissa's briefings—there were many of them in OTC—had tracked a new and escalating drug war lighting up between the Venezuelan and Mexican cartels that had come out of nowhere six months ago and disrupted deliveries ever since. Street prices of cocaine were soaring because a quarter of the annual supply had been intercepted and the war had stopped another quarter of the shipments.

"You guys did that?"

"This team did."

"It was righteous," Duane agreed in a tone befitting a southern preacher. Then he grinned. "It also totally rocked."

"Sure," Kyle answered in a dry tone as he returned to sit beside Carla. "If you don't mind dying."

That got him a laugh around the room from the team, though no one was explaining and Carla didn't look very happy about it even though she'd joined in. Melissa guessed it had gotten ugly and everyone on the team had thought he'd died. But Fred, the new guy, also looked left out in the cold on the details, so Melissa didn't mind as much.

"Do you have a real name?" She decided it was time she started taking some control of her new situation. She'd already had enough of being the outsider.

Also, she had to distract her own attention from how good it had felt to lean back against Richie, before she almost busted his nose. That it had been a long dry spell—the Unit's Operator Training Course didn't leave much spare time or energy—didn't begin to account for how good he'd felt. He might look the nerd, he might *be* the nerd, but leaning back against his chest she'd been able to feel his strength and fitness. The only one to keep his cool and not reach for a gun had been pure Richie, seeing the whole situation even though he couldn't see. No matter what first impression he gave, he belonged.

"Fred Smith. Honest." The guy dropped into an armchair beyond Melissa's end of their small sofa, but didn't relax. "Case Officer Smith, not Agent Smith, you know. *The Matrix* came out the year I joined the agency. And as much as I wanted to be Neo, I really could have done without the whole Agent Smith thing. At least I have better hair than Hugo Weaving." Smith's hairline wasn't receding. As a matter of fact, it was long enough that he could use a haircut.

"The real problem?" Carla looked over at Melissa. "*Agent* Smith is a gregarious and pleasant CIA man, which shouldn't be possible."

"Still owes me twenty dollars," was the best retort Melissa could come up with.

"We'll corner him and beat it out of him later," Carla offered.

"Deal!" Melissa agreed and they nodded at each other in mutual alliance. Melissa felt as if maybe she'd just signed a deal with the devil she didn't know, but it didn't feel bad either.

"So why are we all here, Fred?" Carla might be wearing a flirty sundress, but she was all business.

Melissa liked that about her too. Crud! Another thing she and Carla Anderson had in common. And suddenly the whole scene made sense, like a museum exhibit where all of the pieces finally fit. The team had been on hold awaiting her arrival, with no idea of what was coming next. And if they weren't working for the CIA, they were certainly about to be in a project with them. Now if only she knew what she was doing here. She was the one piece on display that belonged the way a Picasso painting fit in an exhibit about Etruscan art— not at all.

"I suppose that's the end of the pleasantries." This time Fred leaned back and propped his Birkenstocked feet on the coffee table, suddenly at ease with a mission discussion. He'd been more tense pretending to be casual, which made her hate him a little bit less.

"We wanted to know how you feel about flying."

———※———

"Flying?" Carla shrugged. "What kind of dumb question is that?"

And Richie blinked in surprise. It wasn't a dumb question at all. Of course Delta operators flew in airplanes all the time, and jumped out of most of them.

"He doesn't mean flying; he means flying."

"Richieee." Carla rolled her eyes at him. "What the hell are you talking about?"

"Not me." He nodded toward Smith. "It's what he's talking about. Flying."

It sounded as if Carla was grinding her teeth.

He knew he wasn't being as clear as could be, but Smith explained before Richie could figure out how to correct himself.

"I'm talking about piloting a plane."

Richie pointed at Smith and nodded to Carla. "What he said." Then he noticed that his pointing hand was just inches in front of Melissa's nose. "Oh, sorry." He pulled it back.

Melissa grinned at him like he was being too sweet again. He was a Unit operator. Delta Force. A member of the most kick-ass military outfit there was. *Sweet* rankled deep and he didn't—

"Call the Air Farce," Chad suggested. "The CIA must have some pull with those jokers."

It was the sworn duty of every service to look down on every other service they could. That was one of the things that Richie liked about being Delta—they got to tease everybody else while very few soldiers outside The Unit or DEVGRU even recognized an operator, never mind would dare teasing one if they did.

Chad and Duane had restarted their card game, only paying indirect attention to the conversation. But Chad appeared to be losing badly, which was unusual for him, so his attention must be drifting. Maybe because he was still thinking too much about Melissa.

Richie didn't want Chad thinking about Melissa

Moore. He didn't want *any* other guy thinking about Melissa. He tried to recall if he'd ever been possessive about a woman before and couldn't come up with one.

"Don't want the Air Farce," Fred replied as pleasantly as if they were at one of Richie's mom's cocktail parties. "The Company needs Unit operators on this one. Preferably ones already deeply familiar with the South American drug trade. Which means this team. So, who here knows how to fly?"

Richie raised his hand, as did Melissa a moment later.

And that was it.

It was a surprising moment for Richie. He knew he was the oddball of the outfit. Electronics, computers, figuring out how to drive a narco-submarine when nobody else knew…that was his niche in the team and he was glad to fill it.

Yet here he had a skill, a—he searched for the right word, a, uh—military-type skill that none of his original teammates did. It just felt…weird. Carla could do everything better than most people, and Kyle could do anything…but both of their hands remained down. Just he and Melissa… He did his best to quash the idea of the two of them flying a little biplane together over the Grand Canyon with a dog poking its nose out into the wind. *Stupid!* That's how he got around women. That's why he—*shut it down, Richie. Back to the problem.*

During the Operator's Training Course, they'd all been taken out for orientation flights on small airplanes and helos—enough so that they would stand a chance of not crashing one in an emergency. They'd spent far more time figuring out how to disable them than pilot them. He hadn't realized that he was the only one of the team who had already known how to fly.

"Are you current?" Fred asked.

"Yes," he and Melissa answered in unison. They turned to look at each other then turned back to face Smith.

"We are," again in unison.

Carla burst out laughing.

Melissa turned to look at him. "Cut that out," she hissed.

"It's not intentional. I just—"

"I know." Her voice little more than a whisper. "Just…stop it."

He nodded and she turned back to Smith.

Richie had thought it was fun and funny that they were doing that. Apparently Melissa didn't. Not even a little.

"What are your certifications?"

Melissa turned to look at Richie.

He shook his head.

But she kept her lips firmly pressed together.

Finally he spoke, "Beech—" at the same moment she said, "Cessna—"

He shrugged an apology and she looked away.

Carla was still snickering at them. Richie wished she'd stop; it was getting on his nerves.

"Cessna 172," Melissa said clearly. "Instrument rating. And about fifty hours toward my commercial one. Also some seaplane time on a de Havilland Beaver."

Richie kept quiet, wondering if it was safe to speak yet.

"Go already." She didn't turn to face him but he could hear the irritation.

"Beech Bonanza V35," he kind of blurted it out. "My dad's plane," he tried to explain to her back. He didn't want her to be upset that his experience was in a somewhat more advanced aircraft. Even if both were small, single-engine planes, a Bonanza was a much hotter aircraft than a 172. Like a Lexus versus a VW beetle. One of the old ones. Though having seaplane hours was very cool and he was a bit envious of that.

"VFR and IFR—that's visual flight rules license," he explained for the nonpilots on his team. "Which means you can fly when you can see. And an instrument rating which means—"

"You can fly when you can't see," Chad cut him off. "We get it, Q."

Richie ignored him. "I have a lot of hours, just never did the commercial training. Dad's an IBM salesman for high-end systems. He used to take me with him during summer sales calls—he flew himself place to place all over the northeast. He let me take over most of the flying. I did the necessary ground school but I never wanted to be an air jock for a living, so I didn't do the commercial coursework. Sometimes I still go out with him when I have leave and we…"

Everyone in the room was smiling at him.

"What?"

No one answered.

"What?" he whispered it to Melissa's back, hoping maybe she'd explain.

She turned to look at him, then patted his knee. "You worry too much." At least there was a smile on her face, though he wouldn't mind it if she looked less amused.

Chapter 3

"THAT HAD TO BE A RECORD," MELISSA GROANED as she climbed out of The Company's spiffy Cessna 560XL, which had no relation to her little Cessna 172 back in Victoria. The 560 was a comfortable business jet that was a vast improvement over flying coach or military. The CIA didn't have it so bad.

The mid-July heat and humidity of the Florida panhandle hit her like a sucker punch, far harder than it had in Venezuela two thousand miles closer to the equator. She wanted to stagger under the weight of it—the soup they called air was so thick that it was painful to breathe—but if she staggered in her present condition, she'd be as likely as not to go down. It would help if she'd slept more than three of the last forty-eight hours, but she hadn't.

"What record?" Richie asked as he climbed down beside her.

"This morning I was on a whole new continent and I was only there for one meal." And now she was in the roasting hell of Florida's summer heat pounding off the pavement; everything more than a dozen steps away transformed into a shimmery mirage. The Gulf of Mexico, just a mile to the west, didn't offer any cooling breeze, like the Pacific Ocean brushed across Victoria Harbour. Instead, it merely added a salty bite to the scorching heat.

"You're just a modern jet-setter," Richie agreed happily and Melissa managed to resist poking him in the ribs. He'd said that he was glad to be out of waiting mode in that hotel room.

She wished she was passed out *in* a hotel room. At the moment, a patch of pavement wouldn't look so bad to lie down on, if it was out of this inferno.

The Company's plane had whisked the two of them from Maracaibo to the U.S. Coast Guard Air Station Clearwater on the panhandle's inside coast in under three hours. Now it had dropped them off in front of a line of big hangars. Across from them, blinding in the sunlight despite her sunglasses, were four monstrous fixed-wing C-130 Hercules in white livery with an orange stripe, and a row of Sikorsky Black Hawk helicopters in the same colors—Coasties called them Jayhawks, probably for their bright plumage. As a Delta operator, even during training, she was used to flying on the Night Stalkers' versions of the Black Hawk, which were all painted pitch-black without even a unit designation on their sides.

The flight had taken almost the same amount of time she'd been in Venezuela.

It wasn't quite that bad. She'd landed at eight a.m. and hadn't left until after lunch, which was still ridiculously short for a new country and a new continent. She didn't feel like a jet-setter at all; she felt much more closely related to a dirty dishrag.

Over lunch in Venezuela she'd gotten to know the team a little. Most of it had been strictly social, rather than any mission recaps, as Fred had led them out to the hotel's patio restaurant for lunch. At least the view had been good, overlooking the five-mile-wide outlet to the massive Lake Maracaibo.

Richie had sat to one side of her, which had continued to frustrate Chad, and surprisingly, Carla had sat to the other. Richie had continued being thoughtful but awkward. Carla, even more surprisingly, had become polite and a little bit reserved. The change was so dramatic that Melissa hadn't known what to make of her but had been too exhausted to pursue the matter.

"We were going to start your training here in Maracaibo," Agent Smith had explained, "but decided that was too obvious. So we'll finish it here." And then he hadn't elaborated at all.

After lunch, still stuck in the "I (heart) Aruba" T-shirt because they kept moving her along faster than her brain could catch up and send her somewhere to change, she'd been returned to the Maracaibo airport and flown out to Clearwater, Florida.

She'd slept for the two hours of the flight and felt as if she could use a couple dozen more. Actually, she wished she hadn't slept at all. That wholly insufficient amount of sleep had given her body a chance to report how exhausted she truly was. Now it was complaining bitterly about having to move around again.

The pilot came down behind them and pointed them toward the farthest hangar, of course, shimmering in the heat rising off the long stretch of asphalt. At least she hoped the heat was blurring the air and not melting the landscape like some Salvador Dalí painting.

"Why are we here again? I can't remember."

"That's because they didn't tell us." Richie reached out and easily plucked her duffel off her shoulder.

The sudden lightness almost did send her to the ground, as she staggered against a weight that was no longer there. If she hit the tarmac, she'd probably fry like an egg by the way the late afternoon's heat was re-radiating off the surface. She grabbed the duffel back—Melissa always carried her own load.

Richie looked a little bummed, Mr. Helpful stymied in his quest to be Mr. Way Too Helpful. So she gave him a pleasant, "Oh." Then thought to expand it with, "That explains why I can't remember."

"I can conjecture."

"Go for it," she said, because her mind certainly wasn't working on such matters. However, it *was* busy noticing that, despite being the tech guy, Richie had lifted her duffel easily. No matter his long and lean build, he was Delta strong. The Unit's Selection Process and Operators Training Course didn't favor the bulky. Wide-shouldered Chad was the largest man she'd ever seen in Delta and even he was barely six foot. But just because Richie was slender didn't mean he could have survived the training if he wasn't powerful. It was just…unexpected.

"The rest of the team is still in Venezuela. No word about breaking us up, so we're headed back."

"Doesn't matter to me. I haven't actually been anywhere long enough to care in a while. A long while." She was rambling. "Maybe since my brother died." That was twice in one day; she typically didn't mention him that often in a year. Definitely time to shut up.

Richie bit his lower lip to cut off whatever he was about to say.

She wished he wasn't wearing his sunglasses against

the late-afternoon light so that she could see what he was thinking. But she was wearing hers too, so they were even.

"They want pilots," Richie explained. "And we're headed into trouble."

"How do you know about the trouble?"

He paused while a departing jet shattered the afternoon stillness.

"We're Delta," he said simply once her ears had stopped ringing.

"Right." She nodded in agreement. This wasn't the Operator's Training Course any longer. "Keep going. You're on a roll so far."

He stopped her at the edge of the hangar's inviting shadow, just five steps from blessed relief from the sun's blaze as if he didn't notice it.

"What?"

"Our team has been exclusively deployed to South America and solving the drug issues as close to the coca source as possible."

"Okay, which means what?" She was far too tired to put it together. "Wait a second." Some part of her brain was working, and she didn't like what it was telling her. "You think—"

"Best bet is that we're here for a brush-up course and then you and I will be flying drug-runner planes above the Amazonian jungle."

"That's crazy!"

One of the helicopters whined to life behind them, probably headed out for a pre-dinner beach patrol.

But it wasn't *totally* crazy. It was hard to remember that she'd crossed over from trainee to operator. It had only happened yesterday, and she still hadn't caught up with the new way of thinking yet.

"I'm not even licensed to take paying passengers between safe little American airports."

Richie grinned at her and turned for the shadows.

"Neither am I. But I don't think the drugs will mind."

―⁓⁓⁓―

They did let Melissa sleep—for six hours. Richie had tried protesting that she needed more, but his attempts to protect her fell on deaf ears.

He, however, hadn't slept a wink. They'd been assigned a hotel room just off Clearwater Air Station's field, overlooking the runway. Nothing fancy, a single room with two queen-size beds. When he'd started to protest, he'd been told that no one had told them the trainees were differently gendered and it was the only room available unless one of them wanted to sleep in the barracks at the airport.

Melissa had been past caring she was so tired.

Richie had cared a great deal because all of the thoughts he was having about Melissa The Cat Moore were wholly inappropriate for a fellow soldier.

She'd face-planted onto the bed and hadn't wiggled even a toe when he unlaced and pulled off her boots. At first he was glad that she'd landed facedown, because that T-shirt was killing him. Then he started noticing all of the other nice shapes he shouldn't be noticing and went looking for a blanket to spread over her before he got any stupid ideas.

He'd gone for a 10K run, found a weight room, and pumped iron for an hour, then showered. By the time they were due back on the base, he still hadn't slept a wink. And he'd spent the entire time Melissa had been in the shower and changing with his back to the closed bathroom door. Why did they make the things so damn thin that he could hear her every motion through them?

A quick meal and thirty minutes later, they were airborne for a nighttime flight over the brilliantly lit landscape of the central Florida panhandle. He took the right-hand copilot's seat and Melissa sat as pilot. She looked cute even in the big headphone and boom-mic rig of the intercom and radio.

And he needed his head examined.

They were in a Beech Baron. It felt familiar; it was essentially the twin-engine version of his dad's Bonanza. There were more controls and instruments for the second engine, but the rest of it was familiar. It was a six-seater, including the pilot, and as comfortable as most Beechcraft planes were. He'd always found the Cessnas and Pipers to be less cozy and more noisy.

Close behind them sat an instructor who hadn't identified his rank or his branch of the military. He was just Vito Corrello.

"Priest," Melissa had tagged him immediately, showing that she was less out of it than he'd thought. Father Vito Cornelius had been the priest and wise man in *The Fifth Element*—well, the wisest of a not very swift lot.

Vito the pilot hadn't reacted when they'd called him that, which told Richie plenty. Their trainer had to be from the U.S. Army's Aviation Center of Excellence at Fort Rucker. If he was Coast Guard or Air Force, he'd probably have been much friendlier. But because he was Army and they were Army, he would feel honor bound to be a complete hard-ass. And being from Fort Rucker's ACE, he would be doubly so.

He was.

They were barely out of the pattern and clear of the airport when Vito told them to cut the left engine's throttle to simulate a failure.

Richie reached out, taking a moment for a quick look at Melissa in the soft red light cast by the flight instruments setup for nighttime flying. She offered an infinitesimal shrug, so he pulled back the power.

Neither of them had been at the controls of a multi-engine airplane before so they didn't know what to expect.

The Beech Baron stumbled. As if it had caught its left wing in the weeds though they were two thousand feet up. It twisted to the left and then headed into a leftward roll—which would be fatal at their low elevation.

"Copilot!" Vito snapped out loud enough to make Richie jump in his seat. "Feather the prop."

Richie had to think for a moment to remember that meant him. He reached out and yanked on the appropriate lever.

"Pilot! Right bank. Right rudder. Retrim."

He could feel Melissa's instant response through their shared control yokes.

"You, copilot. Get that engine checked out and restarted."

Richie went through the standard protocol for if it had been a single-engine plane while Melissa fought the plane back into normal flight. Fuel—the tanks had plenty. He checked that the "Fuel Boost" switch was on because that sounded promising.

Switch the magnetos—unlike a car, small airplane

engines had two sets of electrics for firing the spark-plugs, just in case one failed. *No change*.

He checked engine temperatures, which thankfully had a green range on the dial and the needle was in it. He found a de-icing switch and toggled it on—shouldn't be a problem at low altitude in the Florida summer, but you never knew. He went through every step he could think of before answering: "Loss of engine appears to be solely due to shutdown of throttle."

"You missed something," Vito The Priest snapped. "What is it?"

Richie had already done everything he'd ever been trained to do on a single-engine plane. When he reached for the manual that was lying across his lap from the startup and takeoff, The Priest shouted at him to use his brain instead. What was different about a two-engine plane that he didn't get?

Seeing nothing in the cockpit, he tried looking out into the darkness at the plane's engines for a clue.

"About time," Vito snarled.

Richie looked at Melissa. What had he done? He hated looking stupid in front of her, but again, she shrugged.

"Okay," he admitted. "What did I just do that I was missing?"

Instead of some sharp reply, the trainer spoke calmly over the intercom. "In a single-engine aircraft, you're used to the engine being directly in front of you, mounted in the nose of the airplane. You would automatically see any bad fire or heavy smoke. In a multi-engine plane, with the engines mounted on the wings, you need to turn and look at the engines. A simple visual inspection."

Simple, once you knew about it. And now drilled in deep by the instructor's initial harangue.

"Restore the engine. Here." Vito The Priest handed Richie a pad of Post-it notes after he did so. "Place these over…" and he began listing off instrument dials. It was an easy way to simulate the failure of an instrument—cover it so that the pilot can't read it, then they have to fly on what systems remain visible.

Except Vito kept listing them until most of the panel was Post-its.

"Now take us out over the Gulf." Using the compass—the only directional aid still uncovered—they turned west for the Gulf of Mexico.

Richie worked to add the habit of occasionally looking left and right to keep an eye on the engines. As Melissa turned the plane, he caught a bright flare off the right wingtip.

Reds, blues, greens.

The colors burst in the night sky as if their wingtip was exploding!

"What the—"

"Disney World," The Priest said drily.

Then the perspective shifted. Not inches, but rather miles off their wingtip, Disney World was having their nightly fireworks show.

Melissa had never flown a plane as powerful as the Beech Baron, and it was a total thrill ride. It was near midnight and she was flying at two hundred feet, practicing engine-matching technique—when the two engines ran at slightly different speeds, it set up strange harmonics in the airframe.

The Gulf's night air was so clear that she could see forever. The lights of coastal cities danced all along the horizon. Small fishing boats were plying the waters, leaving wide phosphorescent wakes.

If she nudged one of the throttles even the tiniest bit out of sync, an irritating thrum was set up that soon pounded against her eardrums as if—

"Crap!"

All of a sudden, one of the distant cities had jumped closer.

Way closer!

She slammed the throttles in her right hand hard against full power, synchronization be damned. Left wheel, left pedal, and pray.

The plane was agile and twisted hard, clearing the massive oil derrick with plenty of room to spare, as long as you were measuring it in feet and inches rather than yards or plane wingspans. Once well clear, she leveled the plane, eased back the engines, and circled back for a closer look.

The Christmas-tree-bright drilling platform had multiple hundred-and-fifty-foot cranes, a helicopter platform, and a massive central derrick. She couldn't do more than gawk as she flew a couple laps around it. Her heart rate was still higher than the derrick.

"Wondered when you'd notice," was all The Priest said to her and went back to instructing them on engine adjustments.

She gave it one last look and turned back to the lesson. Now that she'd seen one of the big rigs, she spotted dozens and dozens of the thirty-story-tall structures planted broadly across the Gulf like the sparse bushes a chintzy landscaper would put out in front of new tract home.

Then she'd discovered container ships, less well lit, lower to the water, but far longer.

The one cruise ship had been easy to pick out—lit up like a twenty-story-high amusement park.

Her hands had shaken for an hour afterward, making her landing less than clean.

Once they were landed and out of the plane, The Priest then led them along the line of U.S. Coast Guard C-130s. They were massive, four-engine cargo planes. She'd jumped out of plenty of Hercules, as the C-130 was known, but…

"We don't have to fly one of those, do we?" Melissa tried to decide if she was excited and terrified. She settled on the former. She'd jumped out of them any number of times, but felt a new appreciation for their huge size. Four stories tall, a hundred feet long, and with an even bigger wingspan. Each monstrous engine had a four-bladed propeller and each blade was taller than she was. To pilot something that big—

"At thirty million dollars each, I would guess that the drug cartels have very few aircraft like that. They also aren't very…" Vito's tone was drier than desert air, "…subtle."

"But we don't get to fly them, do we?" Richie sounded as eager to fly one as she felt.

"The Coast Guard prefers their planes to remain undamaged."

Melissa tried to tell if Vito The Priest was joking or not. If he was laughing, it was only on the inside.

He led them past the last plane, out through a security gate, and over to a long, two-story building made with five-foot bands of red-and-white brick. As they passed through the security gate onto the lawn surrounding the building, she could see that he was leading them toward an aircraft parked on the grass—a display aircraft. Approaching from behind the plane, it didn't look that big, but with each step closer, it grew. The night, even here with streetlights around them and both of her feet on the ground, was messing badly with her depth perception. By the time they walked beneath its wing, fully two stories above her head, she was feeling very small.

"However," Vito spoke for the first time since she'd spotted the craft, "you might be asked to fly this one. The USCG retired the Grumman HU-16 over three decades ago, but these are still plentiful in the fleets of marginal and third-world markets. They can carry four tons over three thousand miles and don't need an airport to land in."

"I've never flown a seaplane," Richie commented.

That's when Melissa focused on the monster before her. It had a wide belly that looked like a boat hull and the wings had pontoons the size of Zodiac Special Forces boats hanging from them.

Melissa nudged Richie with her shoulder. "And all you can think to say is that you haven't flown a seaplane before?"

"Well I haven't." Richie waved at it as if it wasn't bigger than the Victoria Harbour houseboat she'd grown up in.

"I also haven't ever flown a 747," Melissa answered him. "And no, I'd rather not try one of those at the moment. I have flown seaplanes, but they were little ones. Maybe the size of this one's wing pontoon."

She'd started in standard planes. After work, she'd hop on her bicycle and race out to Butchart Gardens where her brother was an arborist. They'd bike together for the last few kilometers to Victoria International and go flying. Afterward, they'd race the thirty klicks home along the Galloping Goose Trail.

They'd worked out a complex scoring system of who cycled fastest and how few corrections they'd received from their flight instructors to determine who had to shell out for gelato. The two of them would come zooming into the heart of Old Town, Victoria—fast, furious, and sweaty on their bikes—and spook the tourists ambling down the street with their Hudson's Bay bags.

On their fateful climb up Mount Rainier, they'd talked about taking seaplane lessons.

Her brother hadn't survived to take them, so she had taken them in his memory. There had been more tears than joy each time she'd climbed into the de Havilland Beaver floatplane and taken off out of Victoria Harbour. His dreams had always been simpler than hers. They'd each buy a houseboat to either side of their parents', raise families, and work and play in Victoria. She'd always been the one pushing every limit she could find.

Yet she'd been the one who worked in the provincial museum and he was the one who'd suggested the winter climb on Mount Rainier. That alone should have warned her somehow.

Despite the inner conflict, she'd always been thrilled by that moment of skipping the seaplane off the wave crests of the second-busiest marine runway in North America just the moment before taking the air.

A de Havilland Beaver could be comfortably parked

under the wing of this monstrous Grumman HU-16 Albatross parked on the front lawn of the USCG headquarters building. At least the plane looked like it belonged there.

But the more this night progressed, the less certain she was that *she* belonged. She hadn't joined the Air Force. Her training in military weapons had been done over four long years before she'd even been allowed to apply for The Unit. And a Unit operator trained more hours in a typical two-week stretch than she'd ever flown...total.

Now she was looking up at this monster plane, well aware of the irony of an albatross around her neck and the plane model's nickname.

She had a private pilot's license with a floatplane certification in a single-engine aircraft. Why were they throwing her at this monster aircraft with wholly insufficient training?

"This doesn't make any sense."

Once she'd said it aloud, she knew she was right.

"Richie." She snagged his arm and pulled him aside. When Vito The Priest turned a curious glance her way, she pointed at his feet. "You. Stay!"

Then she towed Richie over to the fence line.

"What are we doing here? We're not trained military pilots. And don't shrug at me as if this was somehow normal."

Richie started to shrug then apparently thought better of it. "We're Delta. Normal went out the window long ago."

"That doesn't explain that." She waved a hand at the massive plane.

He looked over at the plane, which even at a distance loomed above them.

"Well?"

Richie did shrug this time. "Since I fielded, I've sailed a seventy-foot yacht, stolen a Venezuelan federal police boat, bribed customs officials, driven a narco-submarine sixty feet underwater for two days with no idea if I could resurface it, and infiltrated Bolivian farms where I spent a lot of time working as an itinerant laborer in the fields."

"Say what?" Melissa wasn't sure she'd ever been on a farm. She'd ridden her bike through farming country between downtown Victoria and the airport for flight training. The farms had looked pretty enough, though she suspected that was only because they were at a distance. Up close they smelled like cows and hard work. "Farming as a Unit operator?"

"And calling in defoliant airstrikes on the coca fields."

Melissa clutched her fingers through the cyclone wire fence, rough with rust and sea salt.

Richie continued, "I never thought I'd do any of that from the relative safety of The Unit's shoot-house. Kyle and Chad were Special Forces. Carla was 4th Infantry and Duane was 75th Rangers. None of us were ready for it when it hit us. Twenty-four hours after OTC graduation we parachuted into a drug lord's hacienda fortress and took it down hard. OTC was prep school, but no matter what they do, it's just enough training to keep us alive when we hit the real world. It sure didn't prepare any of us. I guess we didn't have time to think about it, so we got our baptism fast. I've learned that if I roll with it, it generally all makes sense later."

Melissa stared at Richie. He had the even temperament of a top soldier; reminded her of a particular major in the 101st Airborne who she'd seen on the sly for a while. Bennett took things as they came with an easy level of acceptance she'd never really understood. He'd had other issues—like thinking that if they got serious she'd be the one leaving the military, that and being something of a yawn in bed—but she'd liked the man even if she hadn't understood any of his attitudes.

She planned every step of the way. Perhaps it was the rock and ice climber in her.

Yet here was Richie, showing calm acceptance. Somehow he made it sound rational to simply learn what came next when it finally presented itself without worrying at it beforehand. And what did she know? She'd been out of training for barely twenty-four hours.

"I was way out of my depth on that first mission, but I had one distinct advantage."

"What was that?"

"I had Kyle and Carla in the lead, like Q going along with Bond and the kick-ass Bond girl. I was way out of my depth coming from the 82nd's combat engineers, so I just copied them and did the best I could. All you've got at the moment is me—Q. Wish I could offer you more than that."

Melissa tilted her head either way to loosen her stiff neck.

"Richie?"

"Yeah?"

She brushed a hand along his cheek. Not because it was appropriate—it totally wasn't—but because it felt so good.

"Richie, this girl is going to count herself lucky that you're the one I'm riding beside."

He looked at her in wide-eyed shock.

"We good?" She nodded toward the waiting Vito.

Richie shook off his paralysis and hit her with another one of those super-smiles of his. But there was more to this smile. This time it included the man who had buried his face in her hair and sighed with pleasure.

Her body gave back an answering sigh, though she kept it quiet. Richie was so easy to like and to trust. Maybe too easy. Which was odd for her, as she was very slow to trust anyone.

As they turned back to face The Priest, Melissa did her best to ignore the part of her that wondered if he was better in bed than Major Bennett had been.

Unit Operator Melissa The Cat looked forward to finding out.

Chapter 4

PRIEST VITO LED THEM THROUGH THE ALBATROSS seaplane inch by inch, outside then in. When they arrived in the cockpit, he had them sit in the command seats; Melissa was deeply thankful that Richie was sent to the pilot's seat this time. The plane was poised to look out over rolling lawn and a big highway exchange with an overpass. From up here in the cockpit, the land looked far below, as if they were flying already.

The seats were heavy gray steel and the instruments looked primitive in comparison to the Beech Baron that had been their first plane this night. But once she got past the foreignness, it wasn't that different. The engine controls might be mounted in the ceiling above the windshield, but they were still pitch, throttle, and fuel mixture. The steering wheels looked more like a WWII jeep's than an airplane's: hard plastic, too thin to be comfortable, circular except for the top third which had been cut out so that it didn't block the view of the instruments.

For three hours Vito ran them through drills on the parked and silent aircraft until she could find every control and breaker in the dark…while blindfolded… and whistling "The Devil Went Down to Georgia." And at the end of those three long hours it felt as if they'd been flying through a hurricane without ever leaving the grassy front yard of the Coast Guard station. She'd hit the wall and couldn't absorb another fact.

"Here." Vito handed them each a manual about a mile thick. It had an exciting title: *Multi Engine*. "You'll want to get through most of this before tomorrow. You'll be multi-engine certified by end of week. We won't get you type-certified in most aircraft, but we want you to be able to survive a flight in almost anything."

And then he walked away.

"Serious hard-ass."

"Not exactly the fatherly type," Richie agreed.

As they walked back across the lawn and toward the hangars where they'd left the motor-pool car they'd been given, Melissa thumbed through the manual— maybe it was only an inch thick. The dawn light was coming up just enough for her to see the manual clearly. Tons of fine print and a kajillion graphs; might as well be a mile thick.

She flapped it at Richie. "Please tell me they're just kidding me."

"You're just sleep deprived."

"Sleep deprived, plus I almost rammed an oil rig."

"Yeah," Richie agreed, "that was something. Nice job not killing us by the way."

Melissa chewed on that the rest of the way back to the car. How much had Richie seen in the last six months that being only seconds from death wasn't worth more than a stray comment? Or was he still quaking in his boots and simply hiding it?

She strongly suspected the former.

Well, if he had learned to face death, so had she— high atop a mountain of ice. She had waited for hours to be rescued, tied to the mountain, unable to reach her brother; his safety line had run through her harness and she'd been the one anchored to the ice. Hoping hour upon hour that the wind's howl was masking his calls of reassurance from deep in the crevasse but, even at the first, knowing that was a lie. And soon realizing that her own rescue was equally a lie.

A lie until the moment she'd been snatched back from an icy sleep by Michael Gibson and an Army helicopter that had flown into the heart of the storm. That was the last time she'd allowed herself to give up on anything.

All the changes of the last forty-eight hours had simply stirred it all back up again. Melissa shoved it all into her past. Maybe, just maybe, this time she could finally leave it there.

At the car, she called to Richie, "Toss me the keys. I'll drive."

Without any "guy" stuff, he handed them over and headed for the passenger door.

"Hey," she called.

He turned back to look at her from just a few steps away.

A part of her wanted to put him in the "little brother" slot, even though hers had been older than her by a year. But Richie refused to go there in her head.

Either he was too damn good-looking or too nice. Or too Delta. And with the way their few brief contacts had felt, he definitely wasn't going into that "little brother" pigeonhole.

He'd been right there for her from the first moment she'd stepped into the hotel suite in Maracaibo. All through tonight's flights—both the real one in the Beech Baron and the phony one sitting in the parked monster of a seaplane. He'd ridden the controls with her every step of the way. She'd been able to feel every nuance of his touch through the connected flight controls just as thoroughly as she'd felt them when she'd leaned back against his chest.

Even now, he stood close and simply…

"How much longer are you going to wait?" she asked him.

"For what?"

"You aren't that naive."

She could see Richie calculating, that Q brain analyzing rapidly. Maybe he was that naive. Maybe he—

His process complete, some light went on.

She half expected his jaw to drop in surprise. She'd never had a guy gawk at her the way he had when she'd arrived in that stupid Aruba T-shirt.

But he didn't this time. His eyes did widen for a moment, and then he smiled at her. "The nickname is Q, not James Bond." A tease from Richie, his first.

"Which means what? Doesn't Q ever get the girl?" Now she was the one being surprised. She'd known Richie for less than twenty-four hours. Twenty-four hours, two continents, and three plane flights if she counted the jet up from Maracaibo. Being forward wasn't her style at all. Being the one who asked…well, this was the twenty-first century.

"Never." But his smile wasn't going away.

"Poor Q." Asking Richie…that should have been the biggest surprise of them all—but it wasn't. Not from the first moment when she'd leaned back against him and felt more right then than she had with any other man in her past.

"How about," Richie started, "I wait long enough to *not* be standing in the middle of an Army base?"

"This isn't the Army; nothing here but a bunch of Coasties."

"Well, we wouldn't want to shock them, would we?"

She could feel the wall coming down and the moment slipping away. Melissa could feel the protective shield of ice that she'd built up around her recrystallizing. Whatever the moment had held, it—

Richie took a slow step toward her and brushed a finger down her cheek. Such a simple gesture, it should have been meaningless, but it lay there on her cheek like a line of fire. Not wildfire, but rather a warm fireplace on a cold night.

"What are—"

"Shh," he whispered and leaned in to brush his lips over hers. It was the gentlest of kisses—it bore no more weight than the fingertip that had brushed her cheek. But neither was it merely a test. Richie didn't offer a question with his kiss, nor a desperate hunger. Either of those she would have known what to do with.

Instead, the kiss was sweet, as she'd expect from him. But it was also complete unto itself, as if of course he'd be kissing her. He made it the most natural thing in the world.

Not knowing quite what else to do with the kiss, Melissa The Cat purred. Heck, her entire body felt ready to do the same though their only contact was the lightest of touches along her jaw and their lips.

"Sure you want to drive?" he whispered.

"Bet your bum," she replied.

"Definitely Canadian," Richie remarked and turned back to the passenger side car door.

She circled the car and decided that maybe she'd show him a thing or two about polite when they arrived back at the hotel.

Richie rode shotgun for the short drive back to the motel.

He watched Melissa drive, without watching her. She drove the way she flew, clean and precise. He'd felt how her hands had moved through their joined dual controls and tried to imagine he could do better…and couldn't.

It wouldn't have surprised him if Carla had done that, though her style would be totally different. But that there were two such competent women…well, anywhere, was no end of a surprise. He'd met smart women or strong ones or pretty ones…all he'd had to do to find that last type was to go to any soldier bar in any level of uniform.

The pretty ones flocked!

A couple years ago, before joining The Unit, he'd gone to his five-year high school reunion with his full dress uniform, his brand-new Airborne patch, and three stripes on his arm. His buddies had no clue what to do with that. Spackenkill High was almost exclusively IBM brats, the company's original and still-primary plant was less than a mile from the school. Almost everyone he knew had gone on to college and a whole section of his friends were in grad school or working at the plant.

But the geeky guy who was the head of backstage tech in the high school theater had become the ultimate magnet for women who flocked to the uniform.

Melissa didn't flock to the uniform; she was the uniform. To make The Unit took strength, skill, *and* brains;

and a level of determination that no civilian could ever comprehend. That she was knock-out beautiful was just impossible, but still true.

The hotel was only a mile away, at the other end of the airfield. It didn't give him much time to think, but he spent it thinking hard.

He wanted to touch Melissa. To see if that incredible feeling, that even the least contact with her caused to ripple through him, promised more.

But he also wanted her to remain on the team with him. He wanted to be near her like no one before. If they started too fast, it was likely to end just as fast. He had observed that numerous times.

He remembered the electricity that had crackled between Kyle and Carla from the first second. It had been impossible to miss. Yet he knew that they hadn't so much as touched throughout the entire month of Delta Selection. The change in both of them when they finally did had been dramatic. And though the two of them had lived together through much of OTC, and they'd all fought together in Venezuela then Bolivia, it was only last month they'd traded vows.

Chad had stood best man. He and Duane had shared the "men of honor" role for Carla, figuring the two of them together had some chance of handling her. It had been a small, quiet ceremony in the same beautiful church in the heart of Maracaibo where he'd been drugged and Kyle had been kidnapped. He'd loved how it brought everything full circle. And Carla had looked astonishing in her wedding dress.

He'd never seen a woman who so outclassed other women—until Melissa Moore had stumbled into the hotel suite, blinking tiredly and wearing an over-tight "I (heart) Aruba" T-shirt.

Two questions, Richie.

One, do you want her?

More than Bond had ever wanted any of his many girls, except maybe Vesper Lynd in *Casino Royale*. Because that had been serious. Tracy didn't count. Because even if Diana Rigg had been hot, the fact that she'd said yes to Lazenby's Bond wholly disqualified them.

Two, what are you going to do about it?

Bond offered no answers.

So instead he'd go Delta—make it up as he went along.

Chapter 5

MELISSA HADN'T PROTESTED MUCH WHEN RICHIE steered her into the hotel's restaurant for breakfast; she'd been famished.

Any adrenaline that had carried her through the night had been spent by the time they'd reached the room. Eight hours of broken sleep in four days didn't begin to cover it. Richie had tucked her in, kissed her on the nose, and she'd been out.

Now she was awake, hungry again, and very frustrated. For one thing, she was alone in the room. For another, when she looked again, she was still alone in the room.

Showered and dressed, she started with the restaurant, then the weight room. She finally found him under the shade of a cloth umbrella at the side of the short pool. A low cyclone fence with those plastic slats separated the bare cement from the parking lot packed with cars baking in the sun. A Coast Guard Jayhawk helo ripped by close overhead, masking any possible sound of her arrival or approach.

Richie's hair was still wet, as if he'd just been swimming laps.

And he was gorgeous.

Brain boys were not supposed to be gorgeous; it was against the rules. She'd come up to him from the side. He was intently studying the flight manual they'd been given. Okay, she'd feel guilty about that later. He wore scant swimming trunks and nothing else. A towel was draped over the back of the chair; his T-shirt was balled up on the table next to his sunglasses.

One thin strip of cloth away from naked, it was easy to see that he was just as powerful as Chad in his own way. Muscle rippled across his shoulders as he turned a page. She could have traced out his leg muscles through the smooth skin. No knife slices, no bullet holes, his body was pristine and stunning. She was glad there weren't any women lying in the half-dozen plastic loungers scattered around the pool—they'd have been all over him in a second.

"Planning to stand out there in the sun until you burn to a crisp?" he asked as soon as the helicopter's roar had diminished enough to be heard. She could see it banking hard to the south and moving off in a hurry. Just because Cuba was opening up didn't mean that there weren't still desperate refugees braving the crossing to Florida in crappy watercraft.

He didn't turn to her, but of course she couldn't sneak up on a Delta even with the departing helo's noise. He'd probably known the moment she'd walked through the hotel's side door into the pool area.

She would have had the roles been reversed.

Wouldn't she? Had she missed something in training?

He reached out to tap his sunglasses resting on the table and she saw his-and-her tiny reflections in the curved surface. "Trick I learned from a SOAR pilot."

Okay, in the future, she'd know if he came up behind her.

"Pretty slick, Slick." Melissa circled around to the

chair across the table from him but still in the wide umbrella's shade. Two minutes standing in the after-noon sun and she could feel her brain cooking.

He marked his place with a small piece of paper rather than dog-earing the page the way she would have, then slid on his sunglasses.

"So, what have you learned?"

"That you smile in your sleep."

"I'm just a happy gal." Though Melissa did wonder what dreams she'd been having that she didn't remember.

"I didn't know if you'd want lunch or breakfast." He waved toward the door that had just opened behind him, despite his sunglasses no longer resting on the table to reflect his environment.

She hadn't heard the door open, but she'd seen it... which meant that Richie had seen her reaction to it. *Twice slick, Slick.*

"So I ordered one of each. Asked them to serve it when you passed by."

"Out of the whole place, how would they know it was me?"

"Easy. I told them to look for the most beautiful blond they'd ever seen."

Melissa tried to think of a good answer, but she still hadn't by the time the waitress propped her big tray on the edge of the table.

"Breakfast or lunch?" Richie asked as if he wasn't messing with her brain at all. Which he totally was, intentionally or not.

"Uh, breakfast."

The waitress set a big plate in front of her with an omelet, hash browns, and bacon. Coffee and orange juice.

Richie was served a burrito about the size of his head and a massive lemonade.

The waitress was gone and Melissa still felt like she sat in a fog. Q was no longer present at the table with her. Richie had somehow transformed into…himself, she supposed. But it was as if she didn't recognize the handsome soldier even though she'd been admiring him plenty.

"You actually told them that?"

His smile was luminous. "Couldn't think of a better way to describe you."

No arrogance. No cockiness. It was as if he was speaking simple truth, like laying out the known factors of an upcoming mission.

"Richie?"

"Yeah?" He dug into his burrito.

"What the hell happened to you? Where's my too-sweet genius boy?" Like he'd been hers to begin with.

"I…" He blinked at her in surprise. "…don't know. I never say stuff like that, do I? But it just came out. It's true—and not like me at all." He turned to look after the departed waitress and then back at her. "You're doing strange things to me."

Rather than admit that he was doing strange things to her too, she changed the subject.

"So"—she nodded toward the book that he was at least halfway through—"tell me what you learned."

And just that simply, he switched modes and did. The comfortable geek returned as she began working on her omelet—better than average for hotel fare. He told her about drag factors in single- versus dual-engine flight on a multi-engine aircraft. Induced versus parasitic drag trade-offs and varying P-factor forces.

While he grew excited by what he'd learned and dove deeper and deeper into the tech material, the hard-bodied soldier didn't disappear as he had back in Maracaibo.

That his T-shirt was still bundled up on wire-mesh table next to his lemonade was allowing her an eyeful. And the suspicion that he would not have been quite so excited to explain this to anyone else gave her a charged feeling that she was unable to ignore.

The more he continued in his rich, confident tone—comfortable in his role as analyst of information and teacher of knowledge—the more some long-forgotten girlie part of Melissa Moore—the museum carpenter living in her family's houseboat—listened right alongside Melissa the Delta Force operator known as The Cat.

Listened and was rapt.

—◊◊◊—

"I talk too much, don't I?" he asked as they rode the elevator back up to their room. It was a pretty standard hotel affair, dark-brown veneer paneling, a darkly mirrored ceiling so that the elevator didn't look so small but average people didn't freak out when they saw themselves standing there upside down in a small box apparently twice as tall, and a handrail for those less steady on their feet. Not a whole lot to look at other than the woman standing beside him. Richie couldn't believe that he'd spouted off about multi-engine flight for close to two straight hours. He'd finally stopped when the sun had shifted toward setting into the Gulf, indicating they were due at the airfield soon.

"For a Unit operator, probably," Melissa answered.

"Damn it!" Richie leaned back and pounded the back of his head against the wall of the elevator. "I'm sorry. I just get excited by something and… Chad's always telling me to shut up. Though Kyle and Carla never seem to mind, I do sometimes catch them sharing one of those laughing looks. But I—"

And Melissa turned to face him, clamped a hand onto the handrail on either side of him. She stood between his feet and used her grip to pull her body up against his. He still only wore his swimming shorts; despite the hotel's chill air-conditioning, he'd continued to carry the T-shirt low by his waist, hiding the reaction his body had been having to her all afternoon.

Now she leaned against him and there was no hiding anything. Not with the way her legs—that he'd very much admired because she'd been wearing shorts as well—rubbed against his. Not the way her breasts pressed against his chest through the thin cotton of her tan T-shirt. Though being military issue and therefore far thicker than the Aruba one, it still showed her off splendidly. One of the reasons he'd babbled for two straight hours about airplanes was so that he didn't spend them staring at her breasts. Or her face. Or her eyes, once she'd shed her sunglasses.

"Now might be a good moment to stop talking," she murmured, their faces mere inches apart.

The elevator dinged and he glanced up at the indicator above the door. "Eleven, that's our floor."

She sighed and moved away, ready for the door to swish open.

Talking too much again, Richie.

So he grabbed her wrist, tugged her back against him, and, ignoring the door, kissed her hard. Kissed her the way he'd wanted to since the first moment he'd seen her.

She didn't even hesitate. She leaned into him and wrapped her arms around his neck.

His own arms simply fit around her. No overreaching, no awkward gaps. Melissa fit in his arms as if custom-made to the lengths of his radius, ulna, and humerus bones.

His hands too, from scaphoid to distal fingertips, cupped perfectly about her waist and cradled her upper vertebrae and cranial... He lost track of what he'd been thinking, simply lost in the taste and texture of her kiss, of the astonishing nerve signals sent by every instance of bodily contact between them.

He'd always figured himself fated for some hometown girl in an unknown but distant future. Instead he was in Florida, kissing a Canadian turned Delta Force operator, whom he'd met in Venezuela. Richie didn't know when his life had gotten so exotic, but he was enjoying every second of it.

Melissa felt incredible, smelled better, and, he realized in the first few moments, was the best kisser he'd ever had the opportunity to assess.

Again, there wasn't "fire," like all those novels his mom read. He'd tried a couple—maybe more than a couple during his raging puberty years—some of those women were very steamy writers.

Melissa's kiss was too solid, too rich, too deep to be described as fire.

It was more like the end of Delta training, having shot

a rifle so many times that it was no longer familiar, but rather integral.

Familiar yet new.

As if they'd kissed a thousand times before, yet it was their first real kiss and felt that way.

The kiss lasted forever. It lasted—until the door dinged and began to close.

Melissa slipped out of his arms, caught the door, then smiled wickedly.

Part of their training had included knowing which brand of elevator closed how quickly, useful information in a firefight. He glanced up at the manufacturer's loading plate. On this model, the doors held open unattended for three point four seconds and took one point five to close as installed by the factory. That could be varied, but few bothered to change the standard settings.

He leaned there against the elevator's back wall and tried to make sense of the fact that so much was possible in less than four point nine seconds. No matter how he calculated it, it wasn't.

Yet Melissa stood there in the hallway, grinning in at him.

"Come on, flyboy. Gonna be late for class."

"Uh-huh."

She turned and sauntered out of sight, hips swaying. If she'd had a tail, Melissa The Cat's would be arced high in the air in that happy question-mark thing that cats did.

Three point four seconds later, the door closed on him and he was down to the eighth floor before he managed to hit a button. The elevator was headed for the lobby, so he got out on eight.

He entered the stairway, the concrete steps chilly against his bare feet, and began the walk back up to eleven.

Chapter 6

THEY STARTED AT A LINE OF AIRCRAFT THAT MELISSA hadn't noticed last night. It was behind the main hanger. Along the fence line were numerous planes parked too tightly together for everyday use. There was her Cessna 172, looking much the worse for wear. Pipers, Beechcraft, more Cessnas, a sleek little Learjet. Singles, twins, seaplanes, even a big DC-3 tail dragger that she half expected a team of smokejumpers to be diving out of with their parachutes and axes.

"What's all of this?" She shrugged a men's button-down shirt she'd stolen from Richie over her T-shirt. With the sunset, the temperature had gone from blistering to merely obnoxious. She missed seeing Richie only in his bulging shorts, but he looked pretty damned amazing in the black T-shirt and jeans that matched her own.

"Seized aircraft," Vito The Priest answered. He too wore nondescript khakis and a dark T-shirt. They could be three off-duty military personnel or three casual tourists. "Sinaloa, the Mexican cartel, tends to run the smaller craft mostly off the Yucatan. Venezuela has to cross the Gulf of Mexico to reach us, so they favor the bigger and more powerful equipment. Smaller planes out of South America don't have the range to reach us directly—they're mostly used for hopping over to Aruba or up to Honduras or Mexico, so we don't see Venezuela's small planes here, but they have a lot of them."

"Are we going to fly all of those?" Melissa eyed the long line of aircraft.

"Doing anything else for the next three nights?"

"Three nights? I thought we were here for…" *Huh!* No one had said for how long; at least now she knew.

"Why always at night?" Richie asked.

"Flying during the day is easy." He led them to a big Beech King Air, a ten-passenger twin turboprop—the Beech Baron's big sister. "Running drugs during the day is stupid, too easy to spot. Drug flying is done low and at night, typically with insufficient or malfunctioning equipment."

Which, Melissa now understood, explained the Post-it notes all over her flight instruments and flying low enough to ram an oil derrick.

Courtesy of Richie's careful analysis and lecture, she kept up easily as The Priest rattled question after question at them. His final grumpy assessment of "Not bad. Do better tomorrow" must be his idea of high praise, because he said nothing nice about her piloting at any time during the rest of the night.

It's not that she was bad; The Priest also didn't find anything to criticize. Richie was simply a better pilot than she was. He had more than twice as many hours as she did, but that wasn't all. His analytic brain could react faster than her instinctual one. She always had to *do* in order to learn; Richie only had to think to learn.

He'd clearly thought through how to kiss a woman. He put more attention into kissing her than most men had into bedding her. And the results showed. Damn but that man was a pleasure. And his paralysis in the elevator hadn't done her own ego any harm.

She was going to have to teach him a thing or two about continued engagement of a willing target though. They'd been in the room at least ten minutes together, changing from pool garb into more appropriate clothes for the night's flights, and he hadn't grabbed her once. Sure, they hadn't had time, but he could have at least tried. What was up with that?

It was easy to see that he was still thinking about her. Even jeans didn't hide his continuing interest, yet he'd been the perfect gentleman. She'd finally caught up on her sleep, so they'd definitely be taking care of that… after tonight's lessons.

The Priest worked them up and down the Florida coast. Once convinced they could both avoid oil derricks and fishing boats with ease, they followed a clear route a half mile out from the last line of towering condos, working strictly on the planes themselves. He rotated them through plane after plane, simulating failures and dumping an unending stream of performance characteristics. Some planes were easy and they were gone and back again in fifteen minutes and right on to the next one. Others were more touchy and they might spend a whole half hour in.

Any attempts at small talk with The Priest to interrupt the battering stream of aircraft data utterly failed.

"What do you do when you aren't teaching beginners how to fly?"

"Teaching non-beginners how to fly better."

Maybe they should have called him The Monk.

And chatting with Richie while the three of them were on a single intercom wasn't going to happen. So she just flew.

And she got better.

Engine failures became second nature. The Florida winds were steadier than Victoria's. The Pacific Ocean often sent battering winds that were ripped up and twisted by the hills and bays of Vancouver Island. The winds here were steady and light—and The Priest lectured them endlessly on the storm variations and how to fly through them. Her comment that she was surprised that he hadn't arranged a hurricane for them to learn in had earned her a bright laugh from Richie and ten seconds of solemn silence from Vito Corello before he returned to his lectures.

"Light twins lose altitude when you lose an engine; their second engine is not powerful enough to climb. You get to drive to your crash," The Priest intoned. "Avoid them if you can. You are better off in an engineless box kite like a Cessna than the lead brick of a light twin. The problem in a light twin is that one remaining engine does give you safety choices, only not nearly as many as you think. I'd rather have you panicked and figuring out how to get your plane down."

Normal twins could still fly and even gain altitude under most conditions after losing an engine. Some flew exceptionally well. The big DC-3 was so well designed that when they lost an engine, she could almost hear the old aircraft thinking, "Huh. What was that? Am I missing something? Oh well," and continuing on with a shrug of its vast wings. The plane rapidly became a favorite of hers.

"Why did they ever stop building these?" she asked as they skimmed low over a mangrove swamp. She felt like a huge, swooping gull.

"Because they're idiots." It was the first, and only, personal response she'd elicited from Vito Corello.

Low-altitude flying was the next challenge, and exactly the opposite of what FAA instructors wanted a small plane pilot to be doing. All of her carefully trained, private-pilot instincts told her to fly at least a thousand feet over cities and five hundred over countryside or water.

Vito kept forcing them down to two hundred feet, then a hundred. The DC-3 had a wingspan of a hundred feet—fifty to either side. Which meant a steep-banked turn would put the wingtip far too close to trees and highway road signs. Tall buildings became an issue, as did radio masts, even tall, whip antennas on yachts. Suddenly oil rigs and cruise ships were the least of their worries.

"Why so low?" Melissa's hands hurt with how hard she'd been holding onto the control yoke as they cruised over water and land.

"At seventeen miles from a Coast Guard cutter, you break onto their radar screen at about two hundred feet. Florida has a lot of coast, and they can't put a cutter every forty miles, so they keep moving and don't advertise their positions. At a hundred feet, you cut their range to twelve miles. At fifty, down to eight. Staying low is your best defense."

She reluctantly brought the DC-3 back to the airport and they moved on to another plane—a seaplane this time. The first night—after she'd almost eaten the oil rig—they'd had a couple of hours in a small seaplane called a Lake, which was even littler and more fun than the DHC-2 Beaver she'd flown in Victoria as a teen. It had a boat hull, sat low in the water, and had an engine sitting on top like a miniature lighthouse turret. They'd practiced takeoffs and landings, first in the harbor, then on the ocean.

This time The Priest led them to a much bigger plane and, thank god, sent Richie into the pilot's seat. She didn't know if she'd be up for another low-level flight at the moment.

It was a de Havilland DHC-6 Twin Otter—the big brother of the Beaver. The Beaver had six seats and the Twin Otter could carry twenty. The Twin also, like its name, had two large engines on its high wings. She knew from flying beside them in Victoria Harbour that the Twin Otter was an amazing STOL craft. Short take-off and landing was something of a trademark of the de Havilland planes.

This had made it a favorite of every environment from Vietnam War jungle airstrips to the Australian bush. She and her brother had sometimes fantasized about the latter as they rode the tiny water ferry from their family's houseboat in West Bay to downtown.

"What do you say, Charli?" She still missed her brother calling her by her middle name. "Let's get type-certified and go find us some roos to chase across the bush." He had the worst fake Australian accent ever, and she'd trade in anything at this moment to hear it again.

Instead, she inspected the aircraft more closely and did her best to be objective. The Twin Otter was smaller than her newest buddy, the DC-3, but it was a floatplane with small wheels sticking out of the huge floats for landing on runways. That made the bottom of the door roughly level with her head because it was parked on land. The door at the rear of the main cabin was a side-by-side affair, each half opening to the side to make a four-foot square entry—clearly meant more for carrying cargo than people.

Richie paced along the pontoon floats that were twenty-five feet long and almost two feet in diameter. The tops were flat and broad enough to stand on comfortably. He rapped his knuckles against the side, and it gave off a hollow ringing sound like an out-of-tune bell. By the way he did it in three separate places, she could only assume that he was assessing the structural design, thickness of materials, who knew what else.

Melissa was used to being the smartest in the room. At the museum, she could always see how a space would feel before it had been fully designed. Could explain problems about the experience they were trying to create before her far more seasoned coworkers. With Richie, everything was measured, calculated, and comprehended. The only thing he appeared the least bit dense about was her.

It was kind of fun, riding in his blind spot. Was it all women or just her? Or maybe it was people in general. He didn't seem to be reacting in any discernible fashion to Vito The Priest's chilliness or Chad's "friendly" abuse.

The Twin Otter was surprisingly like the much smaller Beaver in that it felt more like a pickup truck than a refined aircraft. In her little Cessna that she'd flown off Victoria International's paved runways, you pulled the doors closed with the ease of a passenger sedan and twisted the small locking lever.

In the Beaver and Twin Otter, you slammed the door like a pickup truck and cranked the lever into place. It even sounded like a truck with a slam and a rattle of metal.

Which was especially appropriate for this particular

plane. There was no separation between the two pilot seats, the six passenger seats in two rows close behind, and the big open area for cargo.

She pictured it full of bales of illegal drugs and disreputable smugglers. Then she sighed. If Richie was right, that would soon be them. Melissa wished that the future would hurry up and get here. She was getting tired of all the waiting and, after six months of OTC, was beyond sick of training.

After the standard familiarization tour and pre-flight, they took off into the night sky from the paved runway, retracted the gear, and then Vito instructed them to land almost immediately on Old Tampa Bay. They went back and forth, bay to airport to bay, alternating who was at the controls until there was no question about landing in water with wheels down or back on land with the wheels up. Then Vito put them through their paces up and down the coast until it was as familiar as the DC-3 or even her old Cessna.

It was an intense, visceral relief that echoed through every aching cell of her body when they parked the big, twenty-passenger plane close by the line of other confiscated craft just as the sky was breaking dawn.

Vito leaned forward between the pilot seats in the echoing silence interrupted only by the pings of cooling engine metal. "No flight tonight. Take today off and finish the manual, get some sleep. Tomorrow during daylight hours, we'll work on long, over-water flights. Think about the two primary problems. First, on a long water flight, there's nothing to look at but water and sky; it's very easy to lose focus and low altitude doesn't allow for mistakes. Second, how do you gauge distance above the water? Your altimeter is pressure based, which means if you move into a new weather system, it becomes inaccurate, so you can't trust it."

Then he turned on his heel and walked away.

———————

Richie fooled with the control yoke for a minute. It felt good in his hands, familiar. Like the Delta Force shoot-rooms, each plane's training layered onto the ones before until it was only the quirks that separated each type—the underlying patterns and skills were all the same.

He also knew that the moment he climbed down, he was going to be all over Melissa. And he didn't want to do that. He didn't want a quick tumble with her.

Liar.

He absolutely wanted a quick tumble. But he also wanted more and that wasn't going to happen if they simply went back to the hotel and fell into bed together.

"A whole day and night off," Melissa said softly, apparently aghast at such a luxury. He carefully didn't look over at her sitting beside him but could see that she was shifting uncomfortably. He'd guess that things were moving both too fast and not fast enough for her as well. He felt all out of balance perched high up in the air in a parked airplane.

"We could…" Richie's throat was dry at the thought of Melissa naked beneath him. Some crappy, barely-off-base hotel was all wrong for such an incredible event.

Think. Distract yourself.

And he recalled that first flight and the fireworks off the wingtip.

"We could go to Disney World."

"The Magic Kingdom." Melissa laughed, at first in surprise, but then in relief. So he'd guessed right for a change.

"A princess makeover for you," he said, imagining her in a form-hugging Elsa gown, her hair as light as *Frozen*'s heroine, which was even now back in her typical French braid, sounded like an exceptional idea.

Then he grimaced.

"Why do the Disney princes always end up in tights?"

"Oh, trust me, Richie," Melissa said in her low The Cat tone. "There are many, many reasons. Maybe we'd be better off at Space Mountain."

"Or we could hit Harry Potter at Universal."

"Get a butterbeer at the Leaky Cauldron."

"Buy wands together. Whose would you get?"

"McGonagall's, of course."

Richie would have bet on Hermione's. "Why?"

"Maggie Smith totally rocks. Transformations. Changing into someone other than myself."

He turned to look at her as the sound of sudden pain tightened her voice to husky, like it hurt to speak. The predawn light was coming through the forward windscreen and lighting her face with a soft glow. She stared studiously out the window, watching the first of the morning Coast Guard patrol planes do its run-up, taxi into position, and finally take off on the nearest runway—yet another good reason not to run drugs during daylight hours. The roar of its four big engines was muffled by the Twin Otter's fuselage.

"Bet you'd go for Dumbledore's wand," she said without turning.

"It's too much. I may be Delta, but that would be like bragging about it." That earned him the smile he'd been hoping for. "As a kid, I always liked Neville."

"The nerd, of course."

"Hey, he kills Nagini the snake with a sword. That's my kind of nerd. Why do you want to be different? You look pretty damn spectacular to me."

She didn't answer, and suddenly Harry Potter didn't seem like the answer either.

He considered pushing her on the personal transformation thing, but he barely knew her, no matter how much it felt as if he did.

"I heard there's some good blue hole diving in Florida." She planted the subject change solidly between them, telling Richie he'd definitely been right about not pushing at the moment.

He considered her suggestion.

Being Delta, they were both trained as Combat Swimmers. Not the full two-month SEAL Combat Diver course, but water was the big thing for those Sea, Air, and Land types. Still, a Unit operator was a better diver than almost any sport diver.

A dive sounded good.

And he'd never gone down into the underwater limestone caves of a blue hole. Actually, he'd never even seen the darker blue patches in the ocean except in photographs.

But he remembered from a *National Geographic* article that the best blue hole diving...

He began the engine-restart procedure on the Twin Otter. With the long-range tank some long-ago drug runner had installed, they had plenty of fuel.

"What?" Melissa looked at him in surprise.

"Blue hole diving sounds like a great idea."

"And we're going to fly there?"

"Sure." He set the throttle to idle and the props to forward. Fuel boost pumps on. Engine start switch, battery voltage only fell to eighteen volts which was a good sign. The engine began ticking over.

"You're stealing this plane?"

"We are. Besides, the plane was probably stolen by the drug runners before it was 'stolen' by the U.S. Coast Guard. We're just the next in a long line." Light-off and the engine temperature gauge began climbing.

"We're stealing this plane," she made it a statement.

"Uh-huh." He definitely liked the *we* part of that. The generator light popped on and he released the start switch.

"In a multi-engine aircraft without an instructor."

"We're Delta." Which meant they could do whatever was needed, and often whatever they wanted.

"Cool! Where are we going?"

"It's a surprise."

"And the nerd disappears again."

Richie thought about that as he turned on radios and nav gear. It wasn't about control. Melissa made him want to surprise her; do something special for her at every chance.

Why would someone so perfect feel they needed to change? Maybe they should have gone to Disney World for that transformation into the *Frozen* princess. Melissa as the ice princess came to him so clearly. What would it take to melt her frozen heart? He didn't even know if Melissa's was frozen, but...

He was clearly losing his mind, thinking in circles

again. The external geek might go away, but the internal one never shut down. Except for four point nine seconds in a cheap elevator when his brain had imploded and Melissa's kiss had completely overwhelmed him.

Once he had the plane ready, he talked to the tower as if this was a perfectly normal flight. Once cleared, he taxied to the runway and took off into the sunrise. He aimed them due east across the Florida panhandle. It was such a pleasure to fly in daylight that he might have once again been over the gently rolling hills that surrounded Duchess County Airport, New York, rather than the cluttered flatlands of Tampa, Florida.

"I thought we'd get in some of that low-level water flying practice The Priest was talking about."

She looked down at the land passing beneath them.

And he knew in that instant he'd given her too much of a clue. It didn't really matter, because he'd have to call in an international flight plan shortly or he'd attract some very bad attention from the Coast Guard themselves.

He'd give her five seconds to figure it out. They'd done all of their over-water practice on the Gulf of Mexico. The nearest water on their present heading was the Atlantic Ocean a hundred and thirty miles away.

It didn't take her five seconds; it took her less than three.

She let out a totally girlie squeal of delight that ricocheted painfully within his headset, his ears caught in the crossfire.

"You're taking me to the Bahamas to go diving!"

"Only the best for my Elsa."

"Elsa?" Then her tone shifted in a flash from ecstatic to…flash chilled. "Like in *Frozen*? What the hell? I kiss you like that and you call me the Ice Queen? Well, you can just forget about it, buddy. Turn this goddamn plane around."

"Whoa there! I'm not calling you the Ice Queen." Richie really hadn't meant to say "Elsa" out loud. But it was clear that he'd struck a serious nerve. He'd never heard her swear before.

"Then you'd better explain pretty damn fast before I clobber you and fly myself back. And if your body just happens to fall from a great height into the Everglades and gets eaten by a crocodile or alligator or whatever they have there, I'll declare no knowledge."

"They actually have both. The Everglades is one of the few regions where the two species coexist. And they aren't just different species. They're also different genus and family. You have to go all the way up to the order Crocodilia to find their common ancestry which is probably an archosaur. That's like going back up to Primates for chimps, lemurs, and humans to—"

"Goddamn it, Richie! Stop changing the topic."

"I wasn't. You said…"

The Cat didn't hiss over the headset. It was more of a grizzly bear snarl; an animal which only shared kingdom and phylum—Animalia and Chordata—with crocs and gators. Though he decided against pointing that out.

He shrugged but continued flying east. "I haven't been able to get the image out of my head since I thought it up."

"Melissa the Ice Queen?"

"No, how could you even think that about yourself? But I can't stop picturing you in Elsa's clingy blue-green gown with sparkles all over. She was merely hot. You'd look amazing. Maybe Ilsa would be better. Ingrid

Bergman in *Casablanca*. The hair is wrong, but you've got to grant she's one of the great film beauties of all time and that role was the ultimate. That totally works on you, especially as we're headed into such foreign lands. Oh, hey, and Bogey's character is Rick Blaine. Rick—Richie. Get it?"

Melissa went silent. He risked a glance, and he would judge her expression as merely puzzled.

"What is it?"

"A lot of guys call me the Ice Queen—the light hair and skin." Then her voice turned softer and bitter. "That and because I won't screw every guy who thinks he deserves it."

"Ice? You?" He had to laugh. "Only if they're completely blind. So I won't use Elsa again. *Ilsa*, you sizzle! And in a dress like Elsa's with your hair down?… Whoo! Just the idea of it. Whoo!" He didn't know what else to say.

After a silence that spanned dozens of miles over the heart of the Florida panhandle, she leaned over and pulled aside the earpiece of his headset.

He braced himself for an ear-splitting shout.

Instead she spoke in a breathy whisper that tickled his ear.

"I'd look great out of it too."

His training kept the big plane on an even flight, but he had no training concerning what to do when his mind rammed full speed into such heavy turbulence.

Chapter 7

THREE HOURS LATER, THE PLANE WAS FLOATING alongside a small resort's dock on Cat Island because Richie had said he just couldn't resist. And Melissa hadn't been about to argue. She was certainly as pleased as a cat.

They were sitting down to split a sausage-and-pepper omelet and an order of Bahamian cinnamon French toast. It wasn't all that different from the breakfast she'd had a dozen hours earlier next to the Clearwater hotel pool, but it tasted about a thousand times better.

The setting was part of it. To the north lay the pale blue of submerged reef and the long reach of palm-covered Cat Island. Just on the other side of the pencil-thin island was the great drop-off to the distant limits of the true ocean floor—six thousand feet of water that didn't get shallow again until it hit Africa.

Out to the west and north, a few more islands dotted the horizon, so low they were mere suggestions of palm-dark shading. Only directly behind them lay the thick palms that passed for a forest on Cat Island. Small huts and a lodge were nestled in among the bare trunks.

The occasional gull soared overhead. Smaller birds prowled the trees and the surf splashed onto the bright sand a few dozen steps from their table.

She'd obviously died and gone to heaven.

The more immediate local scenery was also

incredible. The instant they'd come ashore, they'd raided the resort's small store. All they'd brought with them were the standard: money and passport. The military ID that no soldier was ever without was in her secure locker back at Fort Bragg. It wasn't the sort of thing you carried as a Delta Force operator.

Richie had bought shorts and once again shed his T-shirt; wearing nothing but dark red shorts, sunglasses, and a bright gloss of sunscreen. He had looked good at the poolside beneath the Clearwater runway's flight path. Wearing the same on the edge of a white sand beach with the Atlantic morning breeze riffling through his light brown hair, he looked incredible.

The other female patrons were eyeing him, some surreptitiously, others flat blatant.

Too bad, ladies. This one is taken.

And he was.

By her.

Which was even stranger.

"Did you set out to confuse me?" The question was out before she thought about it.

"Depends. How am I doing?"

"Far too well."

"Good thing or bad?"

Richie, always measuring. She ate some of the cinnamon toast off his plate even though there was a slice of it on hers. "Not sure, but good, I think."

"Cool!" And there was her mild-mannered nerd again.

She wasn't sure which unnerved her more, Q or the soldier. Or was it the unconsciously potent combo of the two?

"Now I have to think of what to do next?" he asked.

"You're on a streak. I don't want to break it." Besides, her own thoughts at the moment were very one track. "Anything specific in mind?"

"Taking the plane out to some remote, uninhabited island and making love to you for the rest of the day and right into the night."

And completely taking her breath away in the process. One of them had finally said what they'd both been thinking. Now that it had been said, it didn't get more manageable but rather the exact opposite.

"It's an idea anyway," he hedged.

"And we aren't doing it because…?" Melissa certainly couldn't answer that question for herself.

"Calories for one thing," he indicated the sumptuous breakfast laid out before them. "Another—"

"You've got a list, don't you?"

"Do I?" He did that inward-focus thing whenever some fact surprised him.

"Always."

"Oh." He looked a little worried. "Is it annoying?"

"Not particularly, just very you."

"Oh, okay. Let me know if it tips over to the dark side."

Darth Richie. "Deal." She could get to like this. Most men lived by their gonads; Richie lived by his brains. But a slightly evil version of him was a very enticing image.

He focused on his breakfast.

"What's the rest of your excuses as to why we aren't racing to the nearest uninhabited island? How much longer *is* your list?"

"Only two items." He studied his plate carefully.

"Okay. Give. But they better be good ones."

"I promised you diving. And I think we really should

go. Not just because imagining you swimming along a coral reef is even better than witnessing you flying an airplane."

"You just want to see me in a bikini."

"You have a bikini?" That got his attention away from his plate.

"Uh-huh. Bought it in the resort's gift shop. Wearing it right now."

His eyes tracked down to her T-shirt and shorts, but he managed to recover pretty quickly. Then he followed it up with a big grin. "Okay, a dive is now a very, very high priority for me."

"What's the other reason?" Melissa couldn't remember another time she'd so enjoyed teasing a man. "Better be a good one; that private island sounds awfully good."

She didn't get the blush from him this time.

Instead, he slipped off his glasses and leaned forward until she could see the hint of green hidden in his blue eyes. He suddenly felt dangerous, unpredictable.

Techies nicknamed Q had simple blue eyes and tousled hair.

Delta warriors had hints of green in their eyes, and the winds that had started in the great deserts of Africa toyed with his hair. He also projected a personal power that set off every single one of her body's proximity alerts.

"It's a good reason." His voice was deep and smooth with all of the soldier's confidence and none of the genius-boy's caution.

She swallowed and tried to ask, but no sound escaped her throat. Beneath his close scrutiny, all she managed was a tight nod for him to continue.

"The first time I make love to you, I want it to be in

a bed. I also want it to be somewhere I won't be interrupted by surprise visitors, weather changes, or anything else. I want a long stretch of hours that are only ours."

And now she knew exactly why she was already staking her claim on this man.

Then he leaned back and slid his sunglasses back on. "That's why I really think we should go diving first."

"Huh?" It came out as little more than a gasp. She'd missed something.

"Because once I start making love to you, I have no intention of stopping anytime soon."

Oh. No, she hadn't missed a thing.

It wasn't a blue hole, but the reef around Cat Island was plenty amazing. Especially to a guy who'd gotten certified in hard surf and cold, muddy waters with crappy visibility by a bunch of Special Operations trainers intent on drown-proofing their victims.

Unlike during his Combat Swimmer training, this water was aquamarine—the perfect match for Melissa's eyes behind the mask that made them seem even bigger—and visibility was measured in dozens of meters.

With her training and her lean Delta muscles, she didn't swim; she flowed beneath the water. And the dark green bikini didn't favor her body by being skimpy. Instead it clung and looked twice as sexy as half the material would have.

A guide led them past fan and sponge corals along sandy bottoms. They startled a Nemo fish—bright-orange-and-white striped—who defended his anemone by bumping repeatedly against Melissa's dive mask when she got too close. A half-dozen green sea turtles, each a meter across, scooted by to get out of the way of a two-meter loggerhead who gazed at them thoughtfully with deep wisdom.

And all Richie could do was gaze at Melissa with no wisdom at all. He'd never wanted a woman the way he wanted her. He wanted to hear her laugh—which would be awkward as they were currently a dozen meters down and had regulators stuffed in their mouths. He wanted to be near her. Not even to touch, though that too, but just because he liked the proximity.

He swam up beside her and took her hand.

He'd never been a hand-holding sort of person. And though he now suspected his mother might be, that definitely wasn't Dad's style. And Richie had done his best to be as much like his father as possible. But there was a simple rightness to holding Melissa's hand.

They spooked an eagle ray, dark brown with white polka dots, that rippled its meter-wide wings as it rose off the sandy bottom and flapped its way off with its long sting-ray tail trailing behind it. A cloud of exotic fish swirled in its wake: blues, golds, greens, big, small, quick, sedate...

The guide was good and found them everything from seahorses to reef sharks.

But most of it was a blur and Richie didn't know how much he'd remember, other than the way Melissa had flowed through the water, her legs impossibly long from bikini bottoms to flippers. Her body... Well, he was just dying here, despite the harness and tanks that masked much of her form.

When they finally ran the tanks dry, having spent

well over an hour on a thirty-minute tourist bottle, as they'd learned how to truly conserve air while diving, Melissa spit out her regulator and pulled at their clasped hands until they broke the surface.

"When did that happen?"

"Oh, a while back." Richie was quite amused that something that had so consumed his attention had gone by Melissa unnoticed and unremarked.

"Weird."

"Why is it weird?" Richie thought incredible, not weird. Had he done something wrong? With any woman, that was a safe first-order assumption on his part, but he didn't want to be that social-klutz of a guy around Melissa.

"Because"—she shook her hand free of his and then dragged her mask back onto her forehead—"I don't do that much."

"If that makes it weird, then I'm in trouble. Personally, I've never done it before at all." And he was in way more than trouble if he didn't get her somewhere private soon.

———

"I got you a present."

"You did?" Richie lit up like a little boy.

"It's nothing really." Melissa had only remembered it the moment she'd climbed back aboard the dive boat. She dug around in the small bag she'd left aboard. "I just saw it at the gift shop and thought it would be a way to say thank you for bringing me here."

She held it out and Richie reached for it just as a wave rocked the boat. In an instant, it was gone into the water.

"Damn!"

"It isn't impor—" But Richie was gone over the side after it.

There wasn't a chance that he'd find the little thing in thirty feet of water—but Richie resurfaced hand first with her gift held high.

He clambered back aboard getting her all wet again with the warm Bahamian water.

"It really wasn't that impor—"

"Are you kidding me?" He looked at her aghast. "A gift from my Ilsa is as important as it gets."

She tried to process that as he bent over to study it. Richie had a way of making her feel special, not just the soldier part of her either. Melissa had never felt so…feminine before. Yes, her features attracted men, and she'd offset that by being the best fighter she knew how to be.

"It's a replica of a Spanish doubloon, pirate treasure," she explained to hide her sudden discomfort. He was making too big a thing over it. But that wasn't what was bothering her. It was that, instead of feeling he was being too clingy, she was feeling charmed that he cared so much about a souvenir shop gift.

"A four escudo gold doubloon." He turned it over and over in his fingers, ignoring the water dripping onto it from his hair.

"A cheap copy."

"Kind of obvious." He tugged on the black cord that had been looped through a hole so that it could be worn like a necklace. "But otherwise it's a good copy. This would have been a colonial one, seventeenth century by the form of the Spanish seal that was used. In the sixteenth century the cross of the church was—"

She kissed him, figuring it was the only way to stop the lecture. It was a wet kiss that tasted of salty seawater, like an intriguing spice on a luscious, rich meal.

The guide, apparently having enough of such antics, restarted the boat's noisy engine and in moments they were hanging onto the bulwarks as he skimmed them back toward the resort.

Richie did take a moment to slip the medallion's cord over his head. The flash of gold, about the size of a half dollar, bounced and spun against his beautiful chest.

She had to look away before she jumped him right in the boat, guide or no guide.

Melissa had never been to the tropics before, never seen marine wildlife like that. She'd felt like she was swimming inside an aquarium the whole time, that sort of magical place where anything was possible.

And as the dive boat ran them back toward the resort, she supposed that anything was. She'd gone swimming with the handsomest man she'd ever met. He also kept being kind and considerate. She already felt closer to him than any friend in her past.

That was the biggest surprise.

Her big brother had also been her best friend until she'd lost him to the ice. The Royal BC Museum of Victoria, British Columbia, had a small, tight-knit, exhibits department—a couple of carpenters, a metal fabricator, and few others—but she'd never grown particularly close to any of them. She and her brother had met the department manager during a winter hike on Elkhorn Mountain—the tallest peak on Vancouver Island. Elkhorn was ironically within a meter of being half as high as Mount Rainier, which had ultimately cut their brother-sister team in half.

When one of the carpenters went on maternity leave, the manager had invited Melissa in. When the woman hadn't come back, Melissa figured she'd found her life's career. She'd enjoyed the work and the people, but that was as far as it ever went.

Then the ice storm atop Mount Rainier had changed everything.

So, Melissa had gone military.

Started in the U.S. Army. One in seven was female. If she'd stayed with her original unit, she might have made some true friends, but she kept moving around.

First Airborne, which put her in the one-in-thirty-seven category of front-line females, greatly decreasing the number of women whom she might have been friends with.

After that, Delta, where she was one of the two women out of eight hundred operators. Just her and Carla. Most men didn't want her there any more than Carla did—though she'd mellowed quite a bit after the we-both-lost-our-brothers thing.

Chad had seen her as a target, Kyle as a wait-and-see. If Duane had an opinion, he was keeping it to himself.

But Richie wanted her in a way that wasn't confined only to the bedroom. She remembered his rapt attention as he instructed her from the *Multi Engine* manual. Each time she'd proven that she could keep up with him, he'd gotten more, rather than less excited. When flying, he deferred to her seaplane skills easily, with no ego that she could detect. And there was no ignoring his true joy at her simple gift.

He was willing to accept her as she was.

As to the *more* that he wanted, the physical, she

shouldn't be so willing to share. They were still unproven to each other in the field. Any disharmony their personal life caused could shatter into chaos once they deployed into the field.

Yet somehow Carla and Kyle were making it work… despite Army regulations to the contrary.

The dive boat jounced over hard waves as they rounded the southern point of Cat Island and the resort swung into view.

But they were both proven; they were both Delta. Sure, Richie had six more months in the field, but could it really be that different from the OTC? So far, it had just been some flight training.

In the last forty-eight hours she'd flown nine different models of planes, mostly at night, mostly below minimum FAA regulation limits. And she was about to crawl into bed with a man for the first time in over a year. Closer to two.

The boat eased up to the dock and Richie leaped out lightly to set the lines. Every motion was easy, fluid, and strong.

No, she wasn't going to crawl into bed with him.

She was going to dive in.

Richie would have been thrilled with a twin-sized bed in a cinder-block room.

It was the off-season and the clerk had promised him one of their nicest rooms at a reasonable rate. It was open just the one night between two rentals, so everyone came away happy.

He had stopped at the gift shop and bought her a

matching doubloon that now dangled enticingly above her breasts. Then he swung through the restaurant and preordered the Angus beef and Bahamian lobster surf-and-turf for two for later.

"We'll be needing the calories," he whispered to Melissa as he led her across the stone-paved courtyard toward their private bungalow under the gently sway-ing palms.

When he swung open the door, he'd been ready for the worst. Instead he found screened windows that allowed a gentle, palm-scented breeze to waft at the brightly-patterned curtains. The walls were sunshine yellow and the spread on the king-size bed was a stunning wash of coral red and ocean turquoise. It had an ornately carved headboard adding to the feel of exotic luxury. The carpet was thick beneath his feet and Melissa…

She stood close behind him, peering over his shoul-der. "Ooo! Fantasy," she whispered—that same tickle against his ear that reminded him she'd look even better out of her clothes than in…not that the bikini, or the dress shirt that she wore over it, unbuttoned with the hem that landed high on her thighs, represented all that much cloth.

Richie was trying to decide how to ease into the moment…perhaps wait for Melissa to take the lead if she wanted it.

But his body had other ideas.

He pulled her against him so that he could kick the door shut, though not before he hung out the "Do Not Disturb" sign. Even the thin bits of cotton that were between them was too much.

No luggage to unpack, just a bag with their pants and

T-shirts…and a new box of protection—torn open and half its contents rammed into his shorts pocket. He dropped the bag and scooped her up. He held her in his arms and twisted around to fall backward onto the bed with her on top of him, still cradled close.

"I'm salty."

"I'm Richie. Pleased to meet you."

"No, I mean I should shower."

"Sorry, I can't wait that long," and he slipped her shirt off her shoulders and down to her elbows.

She shrugged it away. "Your loss. I bet the shower in this place is big enough for two."

"We'll find out later." He unclasped the catch on the bikini top and slipped it off her shoulders. Above her slender waist, she now wore only the small gold medallion.

"You're supposed to be kissing me when you do that."

"Okay." He tipped her back in his arms and kissed her breast. She hadn't been kidding—she looked magnificent out of her top.

Melissa wrapped her arms around his head and pulled him in tighter. And he lost himself in heaven.

When he laid her back on the bright bedspread, the powerful colors emphasized the icy whiteness of her skin, the palest gold crown of hair framing her face, and the frosty blue of her eyes. But her skin was warm, her eyes darkening with heat, and her embrace eager.

A Delta never lost control. Emotions never ruled. They were the clean-kill squad of elite counter-terrorism. They were sent in to rescue, but they weren't much for carrying handcuffs on their missions.

Richie maintained control of absolutely nothing from that first moment she lay there before him. He wanted to catalog this moment, just as when they had been swimming and he had recorded her every movement in his memory and even now could barely recall any of the marine life they'd come to see.

He wanted to be gentle, kind, tender. But that thin resolve was shredding as he looked down at her magnificent form. In moments it would break free and he would ravage this willing woman.

Sliding his hand down breast, ribs, and hip, he hooked a finger in the bikini bottoms.

Melissa raised her hips to aid its removal.

There was a distant pounding on a door.

He ignored it. He wanted to—needed to see all of her.

The pounding grew louder. It was on their door.

Melissa turned from studying his face to glancing over at the distraction.

"Go away," he called out in a voice so hoarse and thick with need that he barely recognized it as his own.

"Sir. You must come quickly!" There was an urgency behind the shout. The desk clerk.

She lowered her still-covered hips and he took a moment to brush his hand back up her length, trace his fingers along the doubloon medallion resting between her breasts, and brush a thumb over her lips.

"Remember where we were."

Melissa nodded mutely, the look in her eyes almost keeping him in place.

The pounding renewed. "Your plane, sir."

With a nasty curse, he pulled away and stalked to the door, still wearing his shorts. Why were they bothering him about some slipped tie line or a misplaced dock bumper?

He cracked open the door, blocking any view back to the bed with his Ilsa on it, waiting for him.

The resort's clerk stood well off to the side.

Four Royal Bahamian Marines were arrayed in a spread across the small courtyard outside their bungalow. Two had shouldered M4s pointing directly at his chest. The other two had HK UMP submachine guns and were watching along either side of the building.

Through the trees he could see their plane floating quietly at the dock. And one of the country's few large patrol boats—all fifty meters of it—was waiting offshore. Its deck guns were aimed shoreward. The hotel's other guests must be sequestered somewhere out of sight.

"Ilsa, honey," he called back over his shoulder. "You might want to put your gown back on."

—⁓—

Melissa didn't know whether to weep or laugh.

Three hours later, they'd traded a luxurious bed built for two for side-by-side cells. They'd given her back her pants and T-shirt from the plane, but the concrete was chilly. The sole source of warmth was where their shoulders touched through the bars. They were the only prisoners in this section—a line of three steel-bar cells in a concrete cube. The Bahamians probably considered them as too dangerous to be in with the common drunks.

The laughter won out.

"You really know how to show a girl a good time, Q."

Richie grunted at her. He'd done little else over the last three hours.

They'd been seized and questioned while the Twin Otter was practically torn apart looking for drugs. Sometime after a missed lunch, they were dragged back to Nassau. Curiously, as the only ones qualified to fly the plane, they had made the flight as pilots—with three armed guards stationed in the passenger cabin.

Richie had managed to get his one phone call before they took his prints.

USCG Clearwater Air Station's liaison officer had denied any knowledge of a person named Vito Corello. The officer had admitted that the Twin Otter belonged at their field but was currently missing.

Richie's request that the arresting officer call Fort Rucker, Alabama, had gotten him nowhere. They didn't even know Vito's rank, or if that was his real name.

The plane was what had started the whole mess. They'd stopped at customs on the north end of Cat Island upon entering the country. It had taken a while, but their computer system had eventually spit out that the aircraft belonged to a drug lord named Andres Estevan. The Royal Bahamas Defence Force had come looking for them.

Richie's comment at the beginning of the questioning, saying "He's dead," had been ill-timed.

"Our records do not show that. How do you know about a major drug runner's death? Are you the one who killed him? Did you take over his operation?"

Richie had clammed up after that for what good it did them. And that left Melissa to wonder if he had.

She waited until they were truly alone and whispered, "Estevan? You?"

He shook his head.

She wondered how he'd known about it then.

"Kyle."

Oh. That explained it. Except… "Not Carla?"

"No. Not for lack of desire though."

And that left Melissa with a lot to think about. Despite the Operator Training Course and now flight training, she had yet to be in the field as an operator. Her last military action had been a 101st Airborne deployment that had earned her a lot of ground action in Afghanistan over a year ago. With the drawdown of the wars, the personnel remaining in-country had been pressed twice as hard.

Her new Delta team, assuming she got out of this prison cell, had done some serious black ops. It rankled that she hadn't had a chance to prove herself yet, to live up to the standard of a team that killed drug lords. Maybe even started intercontinental drug wars.

All she could do was sit on her hard bench and feel useless. The next step would happen when their prints came back, and in the meantime, as mundane as could be, her stomach was rumbling.

"I could use some lunch."

Richie looked at her between the cell's bars that separated them. His gaze narrowed as if he couldn't understand her words.

"That omelet and cinnamon toast is long gone."

He shook himself out of his apathy. "I'm worried about what happens when two operators' prints pop up on Fort Bragg's systems."

"I'm worried about my empty stomach."

Now he was practically squinting. Then, with a sharp nod of concession, he rose and went to the jail cell door and shouted for the guard.

Oddly, she was as touched by that as by almost anything else during this crazy day. He wouldn't have done it for himself, never would have thought to. But for her, there wasn't even a question. If she wanted dinner, he'd face down the Royal Bahamas Defence Force for it right from his prison cell.

His efforts earned them each a heavily escorted trip to the vending machines and five dollars to spend. He just set his meal beside him on the narrow bench and looked down at the floor again.

"Mmmm," she teased him as she chewed. "Dry roast beef on soggy white bread, my favorite."

"I'm so sorry, Melissa. I should have figured—"

"Shut up, Richie. If I'm Ilsa and you're Mr. Rick, we can at least say, 'We'll always have the Bahamas.' It's not quite Paris but that's got to be good for something."

The officer who'd done all the talking between phone calls and fingerprints came to stand in front of the cells. He didn't move to unlock them.

"Your prints came back." He held up a sheaf of papers.

"Shit!" Richie hung his head even farther.

"Dishonorable discharge."

Richie's head popped up in surprise.

No, the Army couldn't have. Melissa didn't think they could do that without a general court-martial. And definitely not so fast. Getting the "double-D" took forever and required hard proof of a heinous crime.

"Seems that you have a whole history of drug running, starting with Army medical supplies."

Oh. Melissa was glad she'd kept her mouth shut.

She could read Richie well enough to see the initial shock and then how quickly he covered it with a noncommittal shrug. She was in Delta now, but being a member of The Unit wasn't something that ever showed up on public records—not even for queries between military units. The Pentagon still officially denied The Unit's existence to this day.

So they'd given Richie a fake dishonorable discharge and he was sharp enough to catch onto that right away.

"And you, lady. A supply sergeant dealing illegal arms under the table. Do neither of you have any respect for the uniform?"

Melissa considered pointing out that his own sandals, shorts, and light khaki shirt weren't exactly the most formal of attire. Instead, she conjured up a pained look in Richie's direction as if she was sorry she'd gotten him into something.

"We found no evidence of drugs or guns on your plane. USCG Clearwater has sent someone to retrieve it, but they are not pressing formal charges for its theft. You are to be released shortly and have six hours to be out of the country. If you can't find a flight, I'd suggest you start swimming."

The officer turned and was gone.

Richie was back to scowling at the floor.

"Six hours?" she asked.

He nodded.

"Is that enough time to get that Bahamian lobster and Angus beef thing you promised me?"

Richie looked at her cross-eyed for a moment, then he laughed. He leaned back against the cell wall and just howled with it.

This time when he looked at her, there was a warmth in his look that reminded her of what they had been on the verge of doing the moment before they were arrested.

"Ilsa, honey," Richie paraphrased a fair Humphrey Bogart imitation. "I think this is the beginning of a beautiful friendship."

"Friendship? Feh! I want some good food or else I'll tell everyone that in addition to being a lame-o of a drug runner, you're a total welcher on your promises. You promise me good food and great sex, and what do you deliver? I ask you. Dry roast beef"—she waved her half-eaten sandwich in his face—"and a cold jail cell doesn't cut it."

Richie looked at her through the bars, his face just inches from hers. "Trust me, I fully intend to deliver on both accounts."

"Good."

"Especially the latter."

"You better." She left the threat hanging.

—◆◆◆—

As they left the police station, Richie was wondering if they had enough cash for two plane tickets and the meal. He definitely owed her. The whole idea of stealing the plane and whisking her off to the Bahamas had been his in the first place.

The desk officer had been less than polite when Richie had inquired after a nice place for a late lunch.

"Maybe we should have opted for Disney World," he mumbled as they stepped out the front doors. Three stories of cool brick and concrete opened onto a narrow lane baking with the early afternoon heat. They'd arrived in the Bahamas at seven this morning, been diving by eight, and arrested by ten. It was now two and he hadn't slept in two days. What he really needed was a hotel room, but he was more than ready to be gone from this country.

Straight across the one-lane road was a parking lot for visitors and the police cruisers. To the left was a busy commercial street that probably had a decent restaurant. To the right was a small park with flowering shade trees—each bloom the size of his head.

And sitting on the bench under the nearest tree was…

"We definitely should have gone for Disney World," he told Melissa.

"No way you could have talked me into an Elsa gown. I'm merely warning you of that." Melissa slipped her hand into the crook of his elbow. Now they looked like any average tourist couple. She turned them toward the park; showing her Delta training, she too had picked out the man waiting in the shade.

"Would have been fun to try."

"Better luck next time, Richie. Besides, you got me into a bikini. Can't think of any man I've ever done that for."

"But I didn't get you out of it." They crossed the street.

"Partway."

"Doesn't count as I didn't get to take advantage of it, though you were right about looking even better out of your clothes."

"Then you'll have to try again, won't you?"

And they came to a stop in front of Vito Corello beneath the brilliant red blooms of a Royal Poinciana flame tree.

"Well." He looked up at them as if in surprise—not

a chance. "What was your maximum altitude on the flight over?"

"A hundred feet," Richie grumbled at him.

"Determined how?"

"We used three different methods," Melissa explained. "Radar, angle to horizon, and angular distance between successive waves to maintain altitude."

"Good. I'd say that means that your training is over."

"Hello to you too." Richie tried not to be angry. He didn't mind, he really didn't, the mess he'd walked into. But he felt awful that his treat for Melissa had backfired so badly. "Do you have a real name?"

"Yes," Vito The Priest replied without elaborating.

Richie sighed. Some things were harder to get used to than others in the black ops world.

"You have a flight clearance for the next thirty minutes." Vito dug into his pocket.

"No. I'm taking Melissa out to dinner."

Vito tossed him a set of keys. It took him a moment to recognize them as the keys to the same Twin Otter that had been confiscated when he was arrested.

"Sure you are. In Aruba. I'd recommend the scallops Florentine on black fettuccini at the Flying Fishbone. It's about ten miles south of the airport." He pointed at the keys. "Fully fueled and the duffel bags that you left at the hotel in Clearwater are aboard." Vito looked at his watch. "You have a reservation at the Flying Fishbone in seven hours and it's a six-hour flight. I'd suggest you hustle."

Richie opened his mouth to protest.

"Reservation is in the name of Anderson."

Carla. Richie shut his mouth.

Vito turned away, then turned back and shook their hands. The smile on his face suddenly bright and sincere.

"Damn fine job, you two. I had real trouble following you from less than ten miles back. You need to watch your six more carefully. They're not expecting you to be Special Operations pilots, just unrespectable drug runners, but you need to be more aware of what's coming up from behind you—not that you would have seen me. I'll make certain that the FAA gets the floatplane and multi-engine certs on your civilian records. We'll back date them, of course, for authenticity's sake. It's been a pleasure." Then he turned and headed away, whistling merrily to himself.

Richie and Melissa looked at each other; her expression matched his own bewilderment. And that laugh that Melissa had impossibly dragged out of him while they sat in their side-by-side jail cells bubbled up once more.

"They want us out of their country so badly." Melissa offered a smile that belied her aggravated tone as she fisted her hands on her hips. "Fine!"

"Yeah!" Richie agreed imitating her stance. "We'll never run our drugs here again!"

A policeman on the way to the station from his cruiser looked at them aghast, and then hustled toward the station.

This time Richie caught Melissa's bright laugh in a kiss.

Ice Queen, hell! She melted against him with an undeniable heat. And while they hadn't made love, he'd certainly had those amazing curves imprinted on his mind.

The kiss fired through him and left them both gasping for breath.

"C'mon!" Melissa managed with an impressive amount of vocal control.

He couldn't speak at all after a kiss like that.

"Let's get out of here before that officer comes back with reinforcements and we miss dinner too."

He grabbed her hand and they rushed toward the police impound docks floating just a few blocks away. But it was hard to keep his feet when all he wanted to do was hold onto his Ilsa for as long as she'd let him.

They'd been aloft less than twenty minutes when Richie spotted what he was looking for and took the plane back down.

"I thought we were going to Aruba." Melissa looked up from the last of her conch fritters, ketchup-lime-Tabasco dipping sauce, and soft panny cakes that they'd grabbed from a street vendor on their rush to the dock.

"We are. Just have to make a quick stop first."

She checked their GPS location. "Hey, we're still in the Bahamas. I thought you couldn't wait to get out of this country."

Richie kept his reply down to an "Uh-huh" of agreement, so that he didn't give anything away, and settled the plane down on the rolling waves with the ease of several dozen water landings all in the last twenty-four hours.

She was craning her head about trying to see where he was heading. "Where are we going?"

"Nowhere." He slid to a stop and cut the engines. Unbuckling the seat harness, he headed back into the rear cabin. "Come on."

He could feel her staring at his back in confusion. Knew he had her completely lost. No sound of her following him yet, so he grabbed a couple of blankets and tossed them out on the cargo deck. He swung open the double rear door to let the warm Bahamian breeze into the cabin. The turquoise water spread for miles in all directions. He could see clearly down to the sand and coral a half dozen meters below the planes pontoons. He knew it wasn't a luxury hotel bed and they didn't have much time, but he hoped—

Melissa crashed into him from behind and drove him to the deck, pulling the hem of his shirt up over his head.

He'd forgotten what she'd said about being stealthy as a cat.

He managed to roll onto his back and dragged his shirt off the rest of the way so that he could see her.

Sitting on his midriff, proud as a peacock, sat Melissa The Cat Moore and she was grinning down at him.

"We don't really have time," he started to explain, "for a deserted tropical island, but I thought that maybe we could—"

"Shut up, Richie."

"—because I want you more than…" And then his words did run dry.

Melissa peeled off her T-shirt and bra in one smooth pull. Once again she was clothed only in a four escudo doubloon coin and her pants. The gentle rocking of the plane on the low waves had the medallion swinging back and forth between her breasts like a hypnotist's watch. And he was wholly hypnotized by this woman.

"I—"

"Did anyone ever tell you that you talk too much?" She was grinning down at him.

He thought of a good rebuttal, then traded it in on dragging her down against him.

She laughed as he did so. Then, when they finally lay skin to skin, they both sighed.

Her kiss tasted of conch fritters and dipping sauce. Her skin still tasted of the sea. And her moan sounded softly through the plane's cabin, even quieter than the lap of the waves on the pontoon.

Finger-brushing out her French braid, he was soon lost in a golden shroud of her hair.

She began brushing her chest side to side against his. She broke the kiss and they both dragged in desperate breaths for air.

"Not a word, Richie."

As if he could speak at the moment. He was lost in her wonder of sensation. There were no words that could describe them, that could capture this moment in time. His heart was running so fast that he was unable to supply it oxygen fast enough. What he had first thought was merely lust was rapidly being converted to heat.

Melissa's fair skin was already flushed and when he dug his fingers into her back muscles, she groaned, a vibration that passed between them chest to chest more strongly than mouth to ear.

He hadn't slept in days and yet had never in his life felt so awake. He floated beneath Melissa much like the airplane did on the softly rolling sea.

Unsure quite how he lost his pants, he'd never in his life forget the moment when she slid down his body and pressed him between her breasts. In a helpless, desperate need for more, he arched against her. A remote corner of him thought that helpless might not be the best possible state for a Unit operator. If there was an attack right now, he'd be toast.

Actually, there was an attack right now, and all he could do was run his hands into his attacker's hair, massage the nicest set of shoulders he'd ever felt, and feel her triumphant smile against the center of his chest.

He wanted this to last all day, all week, but if Melissa kept doing what she was doing to him, it wouldn't last more than a few minutes. He knew they didn't have time and he didn't care, but he did care about prolonging such a perfect moment.

———⁓———

Melissa was discovering the pure pleasure of absolute control over such a body. She had Richie writhing against the cargo deck. Since when had a man ever been so beautiful? So sculpted that he belonged in a museum? His eyes practically rolled back in his head as—

With a move so smooth and powerful that she never had a chance to counter it, Richie flipped their positions. The man she had thought helpless beneath her now lay beside her, pinning her in place with no more than the light pressure of one hand.

The eyes she'd thought gone blind now studied her with an intense brown darker than wooded hills at sunset, a shade between umber and hickory.

With a brush of his thumb over her lips, he marked where he had left off back at the resort. Then he traced her face with light fingertips as if memorizing every shape. Down her neck. She lay her head back and closed her eyes, allowing herself to enjoy his light ministrations.

His hand traced down between her breasts and came to a rest on her flat stomach. She could feel her skin quivering beneath his touch. She hoped that her gentle geek wasn't always this gentle a lover, but it was so soothing that it was hard to compla—

When his mouth closed on her breast, all the tension that had been rising inside her released in a desperate, arching need. Her hard gasp was part sensation and part shock at the suddenness of the change that she felt wash over him as he feasted upon her. He kept her there, vibrating like a harp string, as his hand continued its explorations.

Where had this come from?

Melissa had wanted Richie. In the Maracaibo hotel she'd thought he was cute, quickly amended to handsome and cute. Over the last few days she'd come to know and appreciate the gentle genius. This man silently driving her body toward madness was an unknown to her.

Her eyes shot open when he cupped her solidly—not hard, but as if he was going to hold her there and never ever let go.

Richie was gone. A dark-eyed warrior was watching, studying her from just inches away. Those laughing, light brown eyes had gone nearly black, so intense she couldn't bear to look into them for long. She pulled him back down to her breast and allowed her body to drink in all he could give her. She went from arch to thrash faster than a plane skipping one wave to the next.

The waves rocking the plane felt like they were abruptly hurricane force and then the storm broke over her and all she could do was wrap her legs tightly over his hand and hang on. No man had ever given her so powerful a ride.

———~~~———

Richie watched Melissa spasm and thrash and he wanted more. He wanted to draw it out and discover what her soldier's body could take.

Take.

The word lodged somewhere in his consciousness. He needed to take this woman, the amazing, beautiful spectacle of the ultimate female form.

He found his pants, cast aside. Foil packet in the pocket. Sheathed himself as he kept her right where he wanted her, pinned in place by only his tongue as he tasted her. She tasted of glory.

Richie needed to drive in, to pound, to possess.

But instead his body found the gentler rocking of the plane. He entered her, not in one satisfying plunge into heat, but rather in small stages, letting the rhythm of the sea slide them together.

And that's how they rode the waves their first time, together. A long, slow, almost agonizing descent that shattered any experience he'd ever had before.

She cried out when her release slammed into her. That cry, that exaltation of absolute triumph, echoed deep inside him and carried him over the crest as well. He had no voice to give it, but as he lay down upon her, wrapped in arms and legs inseparable as his or hers, he knew that triumph was but a small shadow of how he felt about Melissa The Cat Moore.

Chapter 8

MELISSA COULDN'T STOP SMILING AS SHE FLEW THE Twin Otter toward Aruba, threading her way between Cuba and Haiti. *Flying over the bright blue seas to piracy we go, way-hay.* She knew she was mixing Gilbert and Sullivan operatic metaphors, but her body was humming with music.

Even as brief as their time had been, Melissa couldn't recall a more incredible bout of sex. Maybe it was because of the long dry spell, but somehow she didn't think so. She glanced back over her shoulder into the cabin and couldn't help smiling at the scene.

No, it wasn't just the long gap. Her gorgeous warrior still lay on the blankets in the center of the cargo bay, sprawled naked and so exhausted that even the jouncing takeoff hadn't woken him. If only she could fly such cargo every time.

If she'd had a chance, she might have gone back to hold up a mirror to see if he was still breathing. She tried to count back and wasn't sure if he'd actually slept since she'd met him. She was tired, but they were a legitimate flight with a filed flight plan, so she was flying up at ten thousand feet instead of a hundred. Much less concentration was required when you weren't constantly less than two seconds from a fatal crash.

They were half an hour out of Aruba when the sun started setting. The horizon turned yellow then orange as the sun journeyed down into the wine-dark sea—my but she was getting poetical all of a sudden if she was fishing up *The Iliad* now. But the sunset reminded her so much of the sunsets over Victoria Harbour as she rode the little water taxi home from the museum, so the poetry shouldn't be a surprise.

Many evenings, she and her parents would sit out on the tiny porch built onto the roof of their houseboat and look out over Victoria Harbour. Neighbors would be close by on their own tiny balconies…it was a neighborhood in miniature. No one lived more than a narrow dock away from the next house. Yet the head of the pier, where the nonfloating world began, might as well have been on another planet for how little impact it had upon them.

The sun would drop down over the low hills of West Victoria, sailboats that had nosed out for a quick evening sail would ghost across the harbor, silent except for brief snatches of laughter. The occasional seaplane would choose its lane, crank up its engine, and roar aloft before some jet skier could slip across its path.

The sudden pang of loss was so deep that it hurt, and she rubbed a hand against the center of her chest. She'd left so much behind. Her brother, her home, her schooling. Even her career in the museum's exhibit shop had been disassembled and left for another to build.

But when she did rub her palm there, she felt the silly little gold-plated doubloon medallion. And she recalled that he'd ignored the pounding on their hotel room door long enough to trace his fingers over where it lay between her breasts and brush a thumb over her lips. He hadn't gone for a last grab and squeeze; he hadn't touched her breast at all. Instead, he'd let her know that it was her he was seeing, and not her body.

She knew her body wowed guys, but they were easy. It had certainly grabbed Chad's attention. Despite being arrested and photographed, she'd bet not a single officer could have described her face afterward.

But Richie was different. Well, that was something of an understatement; Richie was exceptionally different on a dozen fronts. But one of those was his habit of looking her in the eyes and at least acting as if he saw her.

Her hand brushed again over the medallion. No, he didn't act as if he saw her rather than her body—he actually did. No matter how much their first experience together had been about need and their bodies, she could still picture his dark eyes watching her intently as he took her body to places it had never imagined existed.

The sunset reminded her so much of home...and she wanted to share it with him. Home had always been a very private place. Just her family. It hadn't even included herself very often since her brother's death. The impossibly empty gap had been too hard on both her and her parents.

But still she wanted to share it with Richie.

She considered letting him sleep, considered leaving him there in the middle of the cargo bay all naked and glorious for the customs inspector to find. The image of a "product safe for import" stamp applied to Richie's heel tickled her.

Though she'd done her own inspection of him after he'd kissed her and rolled to lie on his back close beside her. Altogether a very pleasing package. Even in repose he looked strong. And in his sleeping smile she saw little of the genius boy and a lot of the man who had so perfectly ravaged her body.

But they were coming into Aruba shortly, and she wanted help with navigation and the radio work as well.

"Richie," she shouted back into the cabin.

Not so much as a wiggle.

"Richard Goldman!"

Nothing.

Then she remembered the pilot's cabin PA. She found the switch, set the volume to maximum, and flicked on her mic. Because he was such an old movie buff, she couldn't resist shouting.

"The Russians are coming! The Russians are coming! Everybody to get from street!"

She couldn't hear him over the noise of the plane, but his head popped up in alarm, looking in every direction but hers. When he finally did look in her direction, over the length of his sprawled naked form, a bright smile lit his face. She looked away before she could be tempted to land the plane and go back to tackle him again.

A minute later, a clothed Richie dropped into the seat beside her without so much as a kiss or a shoulder squeeze.

"Good morning." She did her best to sound arch.

"Uh-huh," was the grunt she received in response.

"Have a nice nap?" Which was about all it had been; five hours on a severe sleep deficit.

"Uh-huh."

"Any synapses going to start firing soon?"

"Uh-uh." He rubbed at his face. "Not unless you're actually real and this isn't a dream."

"What are you talking about?"

"This old plane. The sunset. A tropical island on the horizon. And you smack in the middle of it all. Reality never looked this good." Then he leaned over and kissed her hard on the shoulder.

"And I thought I was the one feeling poetical." She tried not to feel pleased by the compliment, but he'd given it so simply that she couldn't ignore it. Plenty of guys had sweet-talked her or tried to. Maybe if a few more had tried to talk sweetly to her instead, she wouldn't have gained the reputation of being the Ice Queen.

"Huh," was his noncommittal response about his abilities as a poet.

"There. I feel better now. Are you sure you're a Delta operator? You strike me as way too considerate."

"Okay. I can cut down on that."

And she laughed. She couldn't help herself; it just slipped out. She hadn't laughed this much since her brother's death. As a matter of fact, thinking back, she wasn't sure that she had laughed at all since then until she met Richie.

Together they circled down to Queen Beatrix International Airport in Aruba, remembering to extend the wheels out of the floats so that they could land on the runway.

The customs official was courteous…far more than the departing Bahamian official had been. "Welcome to the Kingdom of the Netherlands."

"Excuse me?"

The official smiled amiably. "Always surprises foreigners. There are three islands in the Dutch Caribbean. We're our own country but part of the Kingdom of the Netherlands."

He eyed them curiously when he did a search on the plane's registration. "Andres Estevan of Maracaibo? Six months deceased. I think you will want to be updating the registration."

"Is that something you can help us with?" Richie asked casually.

Melissa was about to protest at how unlikely that was, but the official offered an odd grimace that she couldn't quite read. Usually she was good at reading people.

"It is difficult, sir. Different departments, you understand."

"Of course I do." Richie shook the man's hand and Melissa almost missed the transfer of a couple of hundred-dollar bills. "Anything you can do would be appreciated."

Melissa caught up. A customs official worked on one of the primary drug smuggling routes into Europe. He knew Estevan's name and also about his death. How much money had this man made in the past from turning a blind eye to such trade?

"Well, I can make no promises, but if I can contact the proper authorities for you, who should the registration be changed to?"

"Carla Ander—" Richie glanced at Melissa. "Make that Melissa Moore." And he gave the standard drop box that had been assigned to his team. It was a secure P.O. box in Denver that would autoforward to their commander at Fort Bragg.

Another hundred followed the first two.

"I will talk to a friend."

They shook hands like two men closing a business deal.

Richie scooped a hand around her waist and guided her off the field toward a taxi stand.

"Why would I want to own an ex-drug runner's plane?"

"Why not? The government is just going to scrap it. Besides, if someone checks ownership, I want us to look legitimate. Or at least partly so."

"Sure, like that's going to work. The moment they look, they'll see that the prior owner was an eminent—"

"And dead."

"—drug lord."

"Which will make us even more legitimate. I hope that the Coast Guard has reported the plane as stolen. That would be even better." Clearly Richie had been putting together a lot of the pieces as they'd descended into Aruba.

"Give."

"I want to wait. See what the rest of the team has been up to."

"And if you're right?"

He pulled her close, so that they were walking joined at the hip. "If I'm right, this is going to be a lot of fun."

She knew that was the nerd part of his brain talking about the upcoming operation, but the way he felt against her, the way he was holding her, she was also counting on the warrior feeling the same way about the two of them as well. It had been a long time since sex had been really fun.

———

Richie's thoughts were fractured. He slipped his hand into the back pocket of Melissa's slacks as they walked and tried to remember ever holding a woman so closely—certainly not in public.

As they climbed into a taxi, his attempts to piece together the exact assignment that a Spanish-speaking Delta team and a Twin Otter were going to be assigned to dissolved into a need to nuzzle Melissa's neck. She still smelled salty. Next time he'd opt for the shower first, but he liked the scent of the sea on her. He'd always think of her that way.

"Are you a nymph?"

"Is your reference to the slutty or the Greek?"

"My golden Ilsa of the Cat Island reefs."

"Greek then, and hogwash," Melissa teased him.

"Mixture: three parts Greek, one part slutty." He knew he'd never said such a thing to a woman before.

"And nine-tenths hogwash," but she sighed when he kissed her.

And he groaned that there wasn't a hotel room in their immediate future, because he hadn't had nearly enough of this woman yet. Maybe he never could.

Chapter 9

"WOW! LOOK AT YOU TWO." CHAD THUMPED RICHIE on the shoulder hard enough that Melissa was surprised that he wasn't knocked out of his wicker chair.

Melissa didn't know what there was to see about them. They'd been waiting about a beer's worth at the restaurant. There'd been a palm-wood table—lustrous in the candlelight—set for seven, awaiting for them in an amazing locale. Twenty or so tables were right out on the beach and theirs was closest to the water and offered an uninterrupted view of the ocean. Waves lapped just a few meters away. Palm trees lined the beach and small candle lanterns lit the tables. It was one of those tropical paradise settings like they always had in the movies. It was her second such spot ever, also her second one today—a Bahamian beach shortly after sunrise and an Aruban one not long after sunset.

Melissa could definitely get into this aspect of a Delta operation. And she'd wager that she needed to savor them as they were probably few and far between. Richie's description of five months tromping from one Bolivian coca farm to another had sounded far less idyllic.

While waiting in this tourist poster place, she and Richie had been talking over the day's adventures, marveling that at this time last night they'd been practicing touch-and-gos on Old Tampa Bay in Clearwater.

Perhaps they'd been leaning a bit closely together; it made it easier to talk over the Caribbean band playing under the trees. She was fairly sure that steel drums had nothing to do with Aruba and a lot to do with Jamaica, but the band was good, so she didn't mind. She wouldn't mind doing a little dancing later.

"You two do look awfully cozy." Carla dropped into the chair to Melissa's other side that Chad had been pulling out to sit in himself. She wore a different sundress, lemon yellow this time, and it looked fantastic against her skin—a dress color that Melissa couldn't even get close to without looking like she had jaundice. Kyle sat beside Carla, and Duane took Richie's other side, forcing Chad to the far side of the table, which was fine with her. She had no experience to judge his fighting skills, but she'd just as soon he kept a little more distance.

"Matching medallions," Carla whispered to her privately. "Very sweet."

"Fair copies of seventeenth-century four escudo doubloons, or so Richie informs me."

And they shared knowing smiles. The line was so very Richie, and they both knew it. It made her feel even closer to him, so she slipped her hand into his.

A quick cascade of looks worked its way around the table. And though Richie put on a tough-guy, don't-mess-with-my-girl expression, she was close enough to see his blush in the candlelight. Her warrior-geek. Not separate, not as distinct as she'd first thought. She'd thought it was similar to a split personality, but now wasn't so sure.

She could feel the heat rising to her own face and searched for a subject change. The last empty seat provided it.

"Who's the seventh?" she asked Carla to give Richie a moment to recover.

"That would be me!" Fred, the cheery CIA agent, dropped into the last chair between Kyle and Chad.

"Good." Melissa looked for a bright side to go with her opening response. She was exhausted from the day and the flight and growing even more frustrated about not getting her arms and legs around Richie. Agent Smith's arrival meant there wouldn't be a break anytime soon. Then she found her bright side. "At least we know who's picking up the bill."

Agent Smith frowned but everyone else cheered at Melissa's suggestion.

"Glad you're back." Carla leaned in. "He's been running our asses ragged."

Melissa had assumed the rest of the team had been lazing about Maracaibo for the three days—only three?—that she and Richie had been gone.

"I know the feeling," Melissa groaned in empathy.

And Carla's smile was again warm in return.

That's when Melissa knew she was screwed. After six months of despising Carla Anderson's merest existence, it was weird to discover that she liked her.

Chad, on the other hand. He was staring at her across the table. For just an instant she saw a wholly different expression on his face. The smooth charmer was gone. In its place was a dangerous, suspicious bastard who trusted nobody, least of all her. Every team had to have a bad egg, but why did he have to target her? Then the look was gone and he was all Mr. Smarm again, leaning in to whisper something to Duane.

Duane's gaze flicked in her direction, even as he was

listening to Chad. His neutral expression didn't change in the slightest, but his look lingered on where her hand was still in Richie's, then he looked away.

Well, she'd fought her way through similar situations a hundred times in the lower ranks. No one ever believed that a pretty blond could outgun and out-nasty them. So far, she'd proven every single one of them wrong. Her awkward attachment to Richie added a new factor, but she was Delta and the battle didn't scare her.

Bring it on! She aimed her thought at Chad. *I dare you!*

His look shifted dark again for just an instant as if he'd heard and accepted the challenge.

This was going to be epic, and not in a good way.

No one else at the table appeared to have noticed the final exchange, they were all teasing Agent Smith about being nothing more than a desk jockey.

Richie squeezed her hand tightly and, when she turned to him, he brushed a light kiss over her lips that made her want to melt. She wasn't a hand-holder and the only men who'd ever wanted to kiss her in public were doing it as a power display to other guys. Richie, she somehow knew right to the core, had simply wanted to kiss her.

To hell with Chad!

Not the best thing to be thinking while kissing her man, but it was the best she had.

Case Officer Fred Smith was explaining why they were here.

The others looked surprised, but Richie had already put it together. With his expectations confirmed, he tuned Fred out. Bottom line, they'd be back in it by tomorrow morning; that was the only piece he'd been missing—the timeline.

Something else was going on around the table, a lot of somethings. He knew that social dynamics weren't his strength, but he focused on them.

One, Melissa had reacted to something and reacted hard. He could feel it through their joined hands. When he'd kissed her—there was no way he'd ever get enough of doing that, and if he didn't get more than that soon he'd go stark raving mad—there'd been a hardness there. It had melted in moments, which meant it wasn't directed at him, but it had been there at the start of the kiss.

But two, she'd relaxed during the kiss, which she wouldn't have if the threat had been imminent.

He surveyed the area in zones exactly as he'd been trained. The immediate team around the table was a known quantity. They had lived in each other's pockets for over a year now, so there was nothing here. Fred Smith was also a known.

The waitress who came for their orders had a strength of waiting tables, but a softness that belied being undercover military. She was very pretty and wore no ring—he gave Chad a fifty-fifty chance with her; then Chad lit up that smile of his and the odds shifted rapidly to seventy-thirty. Richie ordered the scallops Florentine per Vito Corello's suggestion because it saved him having to look at the menu.

He widened the scope of his study. The couple dozen tables scattered along the beach were still filled despite the late hour. Ten at night, the slow tropical sunset had finished a while ago, yet the restaurant was in full swing. The waves, broken by an outer reef, merely splashed quietly against the low, rock breakwater that defined the edge of the dining area.

Young palm trees scattered among the tables were wrapped in cheery strands of white twinkle lights, offering good visibility among the candlelit tables. Tourists, wealthy locals, honeymooners, more tourists, girls'-night-out…it was easy to catalog every table. Not a single one of the other restaurant patrons paid his table the slightest attention except when Carla's or Melissa's laughs sounded particularly brightly. That and the four women at the girls'-night-out table, but it was easy to see what they were thinking when they looked toward his team. Not a source of danger.

Beyond that stretched brightly lit waterfront from other restaurants and souvenir stores down the beach with few interspersed patches of darkness. A distant threat seemed highly unlikely in the current situation. He and Melissa hadn't been followed; he'd checked their backtrail a half dozen times on their way to the restaurant. Often over Melissa's shoulder while they'd been fooling around in the backseat, but still their backtrail was clean.

Melissa apparently had been doing the same when they'd been turned the other way in the taxi, a fact she'd communicated with admirable subtlety with a simple shake of her head. The rest of the team would have done the same—it was a deeply ingrained Delta skill, so deep there was no real way to switch it off. Agent Smith was their only possible hole there because who knew what training the CIA gave to a case officer who wasn't a field agent. Richie hoped it was sufficient.

Finding no external threats, he focused back on the immediate zone for things that might have triggered Melissa's reaction.

That Carla clearly liked Melissa made Richie smile all on its own. Carla was the smartest person about other people he'd ever met. He'd observed that her rapid judgments were consistently more reliable than a month of his own study. Richie was always trusting someone he shouldn't, whereas Carla trusted no one who hadn't earned it ten times over.

Richie hadn't doubted his attraction to Melissa. Been surprised by it. Been shocked beyond wildest geek-boy fantasies that it was returned. But to have Carla confirm that Melissa was as wonderful as he thought made for a comfortable feeling. It also made him just that much more attracted to her. The candlelight caught in her hair, which was down and brushing over her shoulders. And the dark blue, sleeveless blouse he'd helped her pick out—from among the "I (heart) Aruba" T-shirts at a nearby market stall—made her eyes shine.

She and Carla had their heads together and were talking happily about something. He tried to tune in but could only catch snatches. Ah, their Bahamian arrest and incarceration told in grand-story style. There were other things that had Carla glancing over at him and smiling at him with a warmth she'd never displayed to him before, but he couldn't hear those at all.

Duane and Chad had picked up on the table of girls'-night-out ladies. The women were dressed up high—beach style but very well tended. Richie demoted the waitress back to forty-sixty against and felt a little sorry for her.

Thirty-seventy after he saw Chad's non-reaction when she arrived with their food. Personally, he thought Chad's meter was off; Richie liked the look of the waitress more than the studied beauty and over-eager expressions of the group of women. Then he noticed that Duane, on the other hand, in his own quiet way, was charming the waitress. Perhaps that was what the two of them had been whispering about earlier—Duane asking Chad to clear the field so that he'd have a shot.

When the waitress leaned in to deliver his meal, Richie whispered quietly to her, "His name is Duane. He's quiet, but he's a great guy."

The waitress studied him closely for a moment, then flashed him a smile with a, "Thank you, sir. Hope you enjoy your meal."

Moments after she was gone, Melissa leaned in and kissed him on the cheek.

"What?"

"You're just such a great guy, Richie. I honestly don't know what I'm going to do with you."

"Well, whatever it is, I doubt we'll have a chance to do it before six a.m. tomorrow."

She grimaced and nodded.

No chance this meal was going to break up before midnight. He'd had five hours sleep in the last three days; she'd had about eight in the same time span. They both knew that they'd need every second of sleep they could get tonight, which left him with no way to deliver on the hours of attention he'd promised.

"Sorry," he whispered.

"At least you finally got me a good meal." She stuck

her fork into a large shrimp dripping with a bleu cheese–shiitake sauce.

That's when he realized that she was left-handed. He ate his meal with his right hand, she with her left. They could still hold hands while they both ate.

How cool was that!

Chapter 10

THE FLIGHT TO MARACAIBO TOOK LESS THAN AN HOUR IN the old floatplane.

Richie flew as pilot this time, and Melissa was fine with being copilot as she was still groggy.

After dinner the night before, they'd made it to the hotel, taken one look at each other, then collapsed onto the bed fully clothed. She'd remembered curling up against him with her head on his shoulder and her hand resting on the doubloon he still wore beneath his shirt. The next thing she knew, the phone was ringing with a harsh wake-up call, and they were stumbling downstairs for breakfast. She still didn't feel awake despite the tea and food and now an hour in the air as copilot. She'd never quite made the crossover to the American habit of coffee—especially not with how the Army brewed it—but she'd welcome a jolt right about now.

As Richie started the descent, she glanced back at their passengers.

In the first row of the two that remained, Carla and Kyle shared one of the side-by-side pairs of seats. She was asleep on his shoulder, which still didn't jibe with Melissa's image of Carla Anderson. The woman had a reputation of steel, something Melissa had certainly experienced upon her arrival in the Maracaibo hotel room an age and a half ago. But she looked so soft and feminine asleep against Kyle's shoulder. The two were now dressed in worn camo pants, black T-shirts, Carla had an aged bandana tied about her throat, and they wore heavy boots that might have once been Army boots.

The rest of them were similarly dressed. Chad and Duane were crashed out in the second row of seats. Chad had taken the pair behind Kyle and Carla; Duane stuck in the single seat across the aisle. Typical Chad. Both were looking much the worse for wear even if their clothes were fine. She would put money on the waitress being happy this morning, but she wondered if the dressed-up girls'-night-out ladies would ever try such a stunt again.

Chad looked so…pleasant when he was asleep. She wagered on hair-trigger reflexes, so she didn't suggest maybe they should roll him out the cargo door and into the Caribbean Ocean while they had the chance.

Kyle noted her attention, looking up from a well-thumbed Stephen King novel that he'd been pretending to read—he was on the same dog-eared page he'd been on when she'd last looked back early in the flight. He nodded to her as if to say, "I trust you with the flight. Good job. Welcome to the team."

She returned the nod carefully. How did the man communicate so much so easily? No wonder he was the team's leader; it was impossible not to respect him. And the rumors about Kyle Reeves among the training cadre said The Unit hadn't seen a soldier like him in years.

Mister Kyle.

All the things they could have called him, and that was the name they'd planted on him. It spoke volumes.

Wild Woman certainly fit Carla. Duane The Rock and Chad The Reaper both made perfect sense. She could see the easy violence that lurked just beneath Chad's surface.

Then there was Q…which didn't begin to describe her feelings about the man flying the plane. It also didn't describe the man—did his team really see so little of who he really was? Q was only a small portion of him. But he also wasn't *Casablanca*'s dark Rick any more than he was the goofy ice merchant Kristoff in *Frozen*. Besides, Kristoff had loved Anna, not Elsa.

Melissa shook her head to clear it.

She was obviously losing it if she was trying to cast Richie as some movie hero.

The poor old Twin Otter looked even more battered on the inside than the outside. The drug runners had used her hard and the Coast Guard had certainly never fixed her up. Mechanically, she was sound as a rock though.

"We need to name her," she said over the intercom without preamble.

"*The African Queen*?" Richie was, typically, completely in tune with Melissa despite the lack of clues she'd given that she'd meant the airplane.

"Too Humphrey Bogart. *Enterprise*?"

"Possible," he agreed. "We could stencil NCC-1701-TO for Twin Otter along the fuselage. But…" And his voice took on that teasing tone that told her he was about to say something that at least he thought was very clever.

"What?"

"She is a floatplane."

"She is," Melissa agreed carefully.

"There's only been one other truly famous floatplane," he teased.

But it was enough of a clue that she got it.

"*Spruce Goose*," they said in unison.

"Except she's metal, not spruce," Richie, of course, had to clarify.

"True."

He clicked on the radio. "Maracaibo flight control. This is the *Tin Goose*, tail number YV-triple five-R. Requesting entry into the pattern for landing."

One thing about Richie. He could always make her laugh.

Richie was surprised by the airport every time he came to Maracaibo—and flying as pilot of the Twin Otter, he had an unprecedented view.

In a country he knew to be mostly filled with lush jungle, the airport had a barren and desolate feel. At the midpoint of its lone runway, a central terminal building had Jetways to service a half dozen jets and room to park half a dozen more.

To one side of the terminal was a large hangar for military aircraft which held only a few aircraft and a pair of helicopters. He wondered how many of even those few aircraft still functioned—an air force was very expensive to maintain in both dollars and skilled manpower.

The thing that wasn't obvious from the ground was an area close behind the military hangar. It was a jumbled parking area where a dozen small jets and many little planes had been pushed together in an area that might normally service one or two passenger jets. It unnerved him, an unusual sensation for a Unit operator. How many of those were seized drug-runner aircraft and what had become of their pilots? Suddenly the *Tin Goose* stopped being such a lark and he wondered what had happened to the crew that had flown her to the States. And how many had died right here and had their plane stuffed into a forgotten corner of this airfield.

To the other side of the terminal was a well-maintained parking area which boasted a number of sleek private jets in pristine condition. Didn't take much to figure out who owned these: drug lords and oil barons—Venezuela was awash in oil with more proven oil reserves than even Saudi Arabia. Number One reserves in the world and *not* friendly to the United States.

Beyond that stood lines of decrepit hangars—a warren that grew worse and worse the deeper Kyle directed them into it. Toward the far end most of the hangar doors looked rusted or broken open, which didn't matter as the aircraft within were often in worse condition.

At the far end of the last row, Kyle could easily pick out their hangar. It was big enough even for the tall Twin Otter. It looked no less disreputable than the hangars around it except for two factors.

It had doors that looked as if they worked, and there was a large and shiny new padlock keeping them closed.

Once Duane and Chad had jumped out and opened the doors, he could see a pair of immaculate, late-model, black Toyota Forerunners were parked inside the hangar.

He killed the engines, went through the shutdown, and then they pushed the plane back into the hangar, the wings easily passing over the top of the tinted-window SUVs. They rolled the big doors shut and the interior was cast into dark shadow. It was so dim that even removing his sunglasses revealed little detail.

Tiny shafts of sunlight snaked in through rust holes in the hangar's side walls, making blinding pools of brilliance and casting the other shadows even deeper.

"Man"—Richie looked around—"I feel like a drug runner already." Because that was the plan.

They had a former kingpin drug-runner's plane that they'd just "stolen" from the U.S. Coast Guard. They'd just come in on the well-flown Bahamas-Aruba-Maracaibo drug route. High-security hangar in the most remote corner of a relatively quiet airfield. Top vehicles.

They were definitely going to draw the wrong kind of attention, which is exactly what they wanted to be doing.

"Was our trip to the Bahamas just to setup the mission?" Melissa asked from close beside him. She sounded pissed. By the dim light filtering in through all of the cracks and rust holes in the hangar's side cladding, he could see that her looks matched her tone.

"I don't think so. I don't think anyone even mentioned the name of the country before I thought of taking you there. As far as I can tell, it's something that we did that just happened to come out to our advantage. Our Bahamian arrest record will be there for anyone who cares to look, but I don't think Vito or anyone set us up."

"And you didn't either? This isn't some Richie-Q-genius operation where you saw what was going to happen twenty moves ahead of everyone else?"

He glanced around to make sure the others were busy elsewhere at the moment, then took her arm.

She tried to pull away, but Richie held on because she didn't try very hard.

"Please believe me when I tell you that I had very, very different plans for that night."

"Promise?"

He wished he could see her more clearly. But they were in the dim shadows and she was backed by sunlight patches, making her little more than a dazzling silhouette.

Her voice was suddenly so tentative, not something he'd heard before. It was as if the Ice Queen had just let down some barrier that he hadn't known was even there. He wished he could see what that looked like but he couldn't.

He brushed his thumb over her lips, to remind himself of that moment, their last before the arrest when she had lain mostly naked and very willing on the bed before him. "I promise."

"Okay." She blew out a breath hard. "I'm not good at trusting men...but okay."

He wanted to ask why. It was like she didn't trust herself about what was happening between them, which, at the moment, was no more than a lot of unassuaged lust. Which made no sense at all. In Richie's experience, women—especially military women—knew exactly what they wanted and how to get it. Melissa—being Delta like Carla—had that in a quadruple dose. Some niggling voice inside him said not to push, again. Better yet, change the subject. He didn't usually think of such things before he spoke, but he'd learned to trust that quiet voice the few times it showed up around Melissa.

"There's something else you said."

"What?"

"The twenty moves ahead of everyone else thing."

"Yes, what about it?"

"Do I really do that?" he asked in his most innocent voice.

"Do you what?" Her last word came out as a shout that echoed about the inside of the dim hangar and got everyone else's attention. "You don't know that you're the smartest person in any—"

Then she caught on that he was joking.

Too close for a punch, she side-fisted him square in the chest.

Right on the doubloon that hung there, which kind of hurt.

Which hurt quite a bit.

But it was totally worth it.

He could hear Chad whispering to Duane, "And when did he grow a sense of humor?"

Richie had a sense of humor. He knew he did. Because he could remember every single time he'd made Melissa laugh.

Even when he didn't intend to.

―⁓―

Melissa stood in the shadows as Richie moved off to inspect the hangar and did her best to reel herself back in.

Never show weakness.

That's what a woman had to do to survive in the military. Showing any hint of weakness, caution, or hesitancy was seen as an instant target for military jerks. They waited for the least sign of a woman not being good enough and pounced on it. Another guy could screw up repeatedly and get away with it, but a woman couldn't do it once without being labeled a burden or danger to the unit.

A hundred times she'd thought that she should have

gone Canadian military. But a hundred and one times she'd remembered the man atop the mountain. And later, finding Michael Gibson had done nothing to diminish the images she'd built up in her head. The man was scarily impressive.

Richie was equally impressive in his own way, and she'd wager that she'd discover he was even more competent, rather than less, as she learned more about him.

But he also caused her to show vulnerabilities that she didn't like having revealed. She'd heard her own voice and how it had sounded as she begged him to promise that what she'd been feeling in the Bahamas had been real.

She didn't grow attached to men, especially not military men, and definitely not so quickly. But that one moment before the Royal BDF knocked on the door had been the most romantic of her life. It hadn't been just about sex. It had been about a man who thought of her and her heart first. How could such a small gesture have been so important? Yet she could still feel where his fingers had brushed over her lips and promised they were only at the very beginning of what was to come.

No weakness, she admonished herself and turned to inspect their new setup.

One glance around and she couldn't help muttering, "Well, that sure doesn't work."

"What doesn't?" Duane stood close beside her in the shadows; he'd somehow moved close without triggering her Delta training.

She studied him, trying to read what he was thinking. He had a good face, solid and friendly. But not expressive. His reserve ran miles deep, making the man an enigma. However, Duane didn't radiate the hatred that Chad sent her way at every opportunity. He stood with his arms crossed over his broad chest—not in denial or rejection, but rather as if he was simply more comfortable standing that way.

Melissa waved about the hangar.

"What's wrong with this picture?"

Duane studied the space, slowly turning a full circle. A frown crossed his expression and he turned a second circle. "What am I missing?"

"I worked for three years in a museum building exhibits. You have to get out of your own view because you know too much. You have to think like a patron coming to the exhibit for the first time and present a believable world. Create a context for them to subconsciously accept. Now imagine you aren't a Delta operator but a client looking to hire a new outfit to transport your deeply illegal product."

The frown cleared from his face and he grunted. Then he snapped his fingers, a sharp sound that echoed inside the steel hangar.

Melissa could see everyone's heads pop up from wherever they were occupied around the space. He circled a finger in the air over his head, indicating he was a rally point. In moments the whole team was gathered around them. They were all looking at Duane.

Then, rather than speaking—of course—Duane simply pointed at her.

All eyes turned on her. Chad's ire, Richie's curiosity, Kyle's and Carla's waiting patience. She glanced at Duane again and he offered an infinitesimal nod in her direction. So she took a deep breath and resisted the urge to back away.

"You're all too clean." It sort of blurted out, but it was a place to start.

They all started looking at each other in surprise.

"We're supposed to be a desperate paramilitary operation, on the edge, willing to take whatever risks are necessary. Right?"

"Right," Richie confirmed before anyone else. Any started protests died. Clearly the team trusted Richie's assessments implicitly. His genius commanded that much respect in the group. What she'd spent hours piecing together and only completed with Richie's help, he'd seen as a single gestalt with only the clue of their sudden flight training. And the others accepted him completely in the resident genius role.

"Do we look like a desperate paramilitary group?"

The team looked down at themselves then at each other in surprise, but they took no actions.

Melissa sighed. She pulled out the rag that she'd stuffed into her back pocket. She'd used it to wipe down the landing gear and the lower engine housings. A white cloth would reveal oil or hydraulic leaks far faster than a mere visual inspection. Earlier, she'd found a loose grease fitting and it had left a thick brown stain on the cloth. She turned and smeared it on Richie's shirt.

Then she pulled her knife out of its sheath on her thigh and turned to the next team member. It was Chad.

Don't hesitate…

…so she finished the motion. Plucking a fold of his shirt clear of his skin, she nosed the blade into the fabric.

She thought hard in her head, *One false move, dude, and I don't stop there.*

But Chad remained frozen in place. She pulled with her fingers and turned the small cut in his shirt into a tear, as if he'd snagged something and was too cheap, lazy, or broke to get another shirt.

On Duane she cut and ripped the sleeves off his T-shirt, making him looking even more dangerous and powerful.

Richie reached out and messed up Carla's hair, a move that seemed to surprise them both but was an improvement. He smiled carefully. Carla's laugh broke the last hesitancy. She grabbed Melissa's rag and smeared a streak of grease down her husband's nose despite his protests.

"Too slow, Kyle," Melissa teased him.

In moments they were all getting into it.

Standard issue Glocks were traded out at the small arsenal set up in the back of the hangar. Richie waited until she took one of the Colt M1911s with its big-hammer .45 rounds. Then he selected a nasty-looking Russian Grach that shot the smaller 9mm rounds but carried twice the number her choice did. Together, they'd be formidable combination.

Duane dug up a wood file and scuffed up everyone's boots.

It was a good moment.

Maybe she did have a role here.

It was dinnertime when they finally broke off to step back and see what they'd done. They stood together

outside the partly open hangar doors, the sun now shining in the front to reveal the nose of the *Tin Goose*.

Richie wrapped Melissa in his arms, because he
was just that proud of her. It had taken a long, sweaty
day, but now both they and their operation looked thoroughly disreputable.

One of the shiny-new Toyota Forerunner SUVs
had been replaced by a ten-year old Ford F-250 Crew
Cab. Chad added some wear and tear with judicious
use of a crowbar and a sledgehammer. Massive, black,
battered, and still with tinted glass—it looked down-
right evil.

A pile of old rusting car chassis and parts that had
been dragged out into the field behind the hangar were
dragged back in and shoved into the corners, adding to
the disreputable air of the place.

Richie himself had spent most of the day high in the
peak of the hangar with Duane, where the temperature
rose another twenty degrees, and also out on the roof
using tall wobbly ladders. There was enough new security in external cameras to make their battered hangar
look like Fort Knox. Not big or obvious, but to trained
eyes the gear was completely top end.

"They have to think that we invested in security
no matter how broke we are," Melissa had explained.
"Otherwise we'll just get the crap runs. We want them
to take us seriously but not think that we're horning in
on their business."

Richie concurred that was the line they had to walk.

Along with Kyle and Carla, Melissa had given the
plane a fast paint job—they laid down the base coat and
she dressed it with swirling strokes and spatter. The *Tin*

Goose was now a mottled smoky gray that would be harder to spot aloft than the plain-white paint job it had previously sported. Flecks of the color were spattered over her legs and arms.

He hoped to be able to drag her into a shower soon to help wash them off.

A hand-painted sign out front advertised:
Moore Aviation
Cargo Air Charters
Sea and land—Discreet, secure.
Contact within.

The team gathered in front of their hangar and observed what they'd done. Now they really did look like what they said they were.

Richie hugged her again. "You did great, Ace."

"It's a good start." Melissa was all smiles, but he could see that she still had a lot more in that amazing head of hers.

She turned to Chad and Duane. "I have a job for you two."

They stood like side-by-side mismatched twins, arms crossed over their chests, Chad's wheat-colored hair and Duane's dark. Duane offered one of his silent nods. Chad was scowling about something as if he was mad at Melissa for taking charge. But that didn't make any sense; she'd been absolutely right with every step so far.

"We need advertising and you guys are it."

Duane offered a grunt for her to continue.

"We can't find the people we want with big ads or flyers. You guys are headed out to find the worst dives and most marginal restaurants. Play cards, drink, brag a little too much. Get word out onto the street that we're here."

"Yeah, that will be a real burden for you two." Richie could see them both cracking smiles at the idea.

Chad punched Duane happily on the shoulder. "Bets on who takes home the hottest chick. Twenty bucks says I can—"

"I don't care about that crap," Melissa cut them off.

Crap? She still cracked Richie up every time she said something like that. Such a strong woman with such gentle language—it was a shock in the rough-spoken world of The Unit.

"I care about you getting our name out there. You're operators; focus."

No one else seemed to react, but Richie caught the edge in her tone. It would have sounded normal coming from anyone else, but from Melissa Moore the mild-mannered Canadian, from his Ilsa, it was a barbed slice. She might as well be calling Chad and Duane incompetent boobs by the way she'd said it.

Richie glanced at Carla, but she wasn't reacting as if anything unusual was going on.

Perhaps he was imagining it.

"Go already."

They headed for the battered pickup.

"No, take the Forerunner. The contrast of the high-end vehicle and your low-end actions might help spread the word faster."

Again the slice, again no other reactions. But he knew he wasn't imagining a thing.

As soon as they were gone, he could feel her tension ease. She even wiped at her forehead as if she'd been doing something hard and was glad it was over.

"And what's on the list for us, oh grand chess master?" Kyle spoke easily.

"Call Fred. Tell him that we want a cargo out of Colombia into Venezuela. Legal, but barely, would be best."

"When?" Kyle was pulling out a cell phone.

"We four take off at last light, in about three hours. Back at sunrise. Best advertising is getting the *Tin Goose* aloft and looking busy."

Kyle got busy on the phone, Carla leaning in to eavesdrop.

Richie guided Melissa aside.

"You okay?"

Her brittle "sure," told Richie that he wasn't going to get anywhere in that direction. He searched for another topic; he seemed to be doing that a lot around Melissa. She had very carefully constructed walls that he wasn't having much luck breaching. There were other things he wasn't having much luck with.

"I had rather hoped to get some time alone with you tonight, rather than flying to Colombia and back."

That softened her. She slid her arms around his neck and rested her forehead against his.

His hands landed around her waist and again it was the most natural gesture, right in a way that only electronics or computer code had ever been. There was a biologic synchronicity between them that was undeniable.

"That sounds lovely," she whispered. And he could feel the exhaustion sag through her.

"But it's not going to happen." He managed to not make it a question. Barely, but he knew she was right.

"It's not. But…" She left him hanging.

"What?"

"I could really use some room service and a shower."

Richie pulled her in closer until they were pressed hard together.

She clung to him and he never wanted to let go.

"I'll scrub your back," he whispered into her ear.

———∿∿∿———

Melissa had been bracing herself for some horrid dive of a hotel to fit their new image. The Bahamas had promised luxury, even if they'd had the opportunity taken away at the last moment. The Aruban hotel had also been very nice, but all they'd done was sleep. Images of climbing into a mold-stained shower stall barely wide enough for one was not how she wanted it to be.

She'd almost begged off, but Richie would know that there was nothing else they could do on the plane or in the hangar. And she didn't want to avoid him. She just wanted…

Kyle pulled the battered pickup right back up to the same beautiful hotel where she'd first met the team.

"What?"

"No one," Carla said from the driver's seat, "said that drug runners were smart about how they spent their money when they have it."

From the backseat, Melissa lunged forward so that she could reach around the front seat and grab Carla by the shoulders. She shook her with the sheer joy of it.

"If you were back here, I'd kiss you."

"Save it for Richie."

Okay, Melissa knew they were being obvious, but still she wanted to hug Carla for being so thoughtful.

They parked the truck and headed for the elevators.

"Nope." Carla tugged on Kyle's arm. "You and I are eating in the restaurant."

"But I need a show—" he tried to protest.

"Deal with it." Carla winked at her.

Melissa pictured the suite—with Kyle and Carla sitting out in the main room pretending they couldn't hear anything—and Melissa decided that she'd found yet another reason to like the Wild Woman.

Richie didn't attack her in the elevator, but he didn't let go of her hand either, instead holding it so tightly that she wasn't sure if she could escape even if she wanted to.

Down the hall…nothing.

Through the door…still nothing.

Was she going to have to be the one to—

The moment she was through the door and the lock had snicked into place, Richie slammed her back against the cool wooden surface.

She was hot, sweaty but not the good kind, covered in flecks of paint, and Richie was proving that he didn't care. They shared a lip-lock while his hands, his very agile Delta-trained hands, removed her clothes. Unsure quite how it happened, she was leaning naked against the hotel room door, not a sock or panties to her name, when everything came to a sudden stop.

Her eyes slowly refocused, and there was Richie. Still fully clothed. A step away from her. He was looking down the length of her body and swallowing hard.

"What? Why did you stop?"

"I—It shouldn't be like this."

"Like what? Me naked and you still fully clothed?" She never had modesty issues, they never lasted long in the Army anyway, but his look was unnerving her.

"No, that's not it."

She waited. When he didn't explain further, or even reach out to touch her, she fought against the desire to cover herself.

"Richieee," she warned him.

Still nothing.

"Use your words."

"Sorry." He shook his head, then shook it again. "I can't get over that you're so…" He scrubbed at his face, then looked her in the eyes. "You're gorgeous."

Melissa didn't want to feel charmed or pleased or surprised; she wanted sex. Yet Richie was charming her. She'd never wielded sex as power, but that she had a power over Richie was…interesting. She didn't intend to do anything with it unless… "Are you planning on doing something about it anytime soon?"

He grinned and swept her up in his arms faster than she could squeak out her surprise. He swept her through one of the doors and kicked it shut without slowing.

A king-size bed dominated the room. A wall of windows looked down on Lake Maracaibo and the city's waterfront. But Richie walked right past the bed and into the bathroom before setting her back on her feet.

An oversized glass-walled shower enclosure, a separate tub, bright tiles, and the same stunning view over the waterfront. The hotel was the tallest building in this direction, so there was no reason to curtain the window, but she still felt terribly exposed. After all, her clothes weren't merely in the bedroom; they were scattered on the floor just inside the suite's door. If someone came back unexpectedly, she didn't want that.

"I should really go and get…" Her voice dried up in her throat when she turned.

Richie had stripped down and moved into the shower. He was starting the shower and had a hand held out into the spray to test the temperature.

So simple a gesture. Thoughtlessly kind.

Men were never like that.

Richie was.

She watched him through the glass as he adjusted the final temperature.

"C'mon in. The water's fine now."

That wasn't the only thing that was fine. There was also Richie Goldman. There was no way to think of him as just the brain on seeing him unclothed. Long, lean muscle sculpted him from heel to shoulders. The simplest action—reaching for soap and a washcloth— rippled across his back.

"I promised to scrub your back."

The heat that had been building between them since… since the first moment they'd met…had been super-charged by their tussle in the back of the Twin Otter. And despite that, Richie had recalled an idle promise to scrub her back.

She stepped into the shower on autopilot, with no control of her flight path. Her next actions were out of her control; her body had taken over and she had no inclination to turn it aside.

—◆◆◆—

Richie turned with the soapy washcloth in his hand and was again struck by beauty of the woman before him. He'd had his fair share of attractive women climb into his bed, but he'd never been with one who shone like the sun.

Not merely her hair or her fabulous body. Every time he looked into her shining blue eyes, there was a joy there, a connection that he'd never found anywhere else.

Even now her smile lit up.

Then, as slowly as a runway model, she turned her back on him, spinning once through the spray until her hair darkened and her body sparkled.

Melissa from the back was its own miracle. Women, even the most fit, had a softness to them. It wasn't that Melissa was hard-edged, but that impossible fitness demanded by being a Unit operator reshaped into the female form was astonishing. Her curves weren't just womanly, they were powerfully so.

"Are you going to stare all day, or is *Señor* Drug Runner going to finally deliver on one of his promises?"

A pilot's proper response to the control tower once cleared for takeoff wasn't to get on the radio, but rather to shove the throttles forward and get the heck off their runway.

Richie raised his washcloth and began to rub it against her shoulders. The shock through his fingertips was no less than on that first contact sitting on the couch when he'd brushed his hand over her shoulder. Before it had been her shirt that separated them; now it was a washcloth.

He reached back his other hand and soaped it up, then he placed both hands on her shoulders. With one, he scrubbed; with the other, he explored and massaged.

Melissa braced her arms against the stall's glass wall and hung her head. He found knotted muscles in her shoulders and forced them to release. He scrubbed at her braced arms until they were clear of airplane paint. He knelt and did the same to her legs.

When she turned and leaned back against the glass it looked as if she was suspended in midair. He continued up her front, appreciating every single curve as he went. Studying what his earlier desperation had not allowed time to implant in his memory. Shudders ran up through her frame as he massaged and caressed.

"You still haven't kissed me." Her voice was practically a whimper. Richie had never made a woman whimper before.

"Sure I did," he teased her. "Up against the suite door."

"That was forever ago." Her whine of protest made him feel so…he didn't know what. Like he was more powerful than he knew he was. She was obviously teasing, but she implied that he alone held her happiness in his soapy hands.

When she opened her mouth to continue her complaint, he leaned his body against her and kissed her hard and deep. The sensation of skin to skin slammed against him as brutally as any training blow that had knocked the wind out of him.

But again, that impossible familiarity that couldn't possibly exist after less than a week. That sense of known, of belonging, shouldn't be possible with someone he'd known such a short time. But it was there, so deep, so pure that he couldn't imagine ever having wanted someone else. Or anyone else again, not after he'd found this feeling.

He kept her pinned to the glass as he dug one hand up into her soaked hair and the other cupped that spectacular form that her gluteus maximus muscles had made of her behind. He pressed himself against her. This time he was the one who groaned first.

Not during his very first time with a girl named Cindy, which had been awkward and over too fast, nor the second a year later with her sister, which had been utterly fantastic and had turned into a much longer relationship, had he felt anything like this, and he hadn't even entered her yet.

And with that thought, he couldn't wait any longer.

He'd dropped a foil packet in the soap dish when he entered the shower. He rolled the protection on while he kept Melissa in place with a kiss.

There was no need to ask. No need to whisper her name as a question. Nothing had ever been so right in his life. Not flying, not joining Delta, not serving with his team.

He lifted her hips and took her against the thick glass.

The moment he entered her, the careful, thoughtful version of himself that he knew so well slipped away. Instead he drove into her, held her hard, and kissed her harder.

They didn't rise together, a soft, gentle coupling in time with the waves on the sea. They simply flew. Fuel at max, temperatures at redline. There was no grace, no gentleness, not even thought. And his Ice Queen melted against him and gave back tenfold everything he gave to her.

It was chaotic, a distant part of Richie noted. It wasn't the right way to court his lovely Ilsa.

But the man who had Melissa Moore wrapped around him didn't give a good goddamn. He didn't care about taking her somewhere special. He didn't wonder if he was being too rough or too gentle—the latter something he'd actually been accused of.

He wanted her and he took her.

She lay her head back against the glass, both legs about his hips.

He buried his face against the base of her neck and kept driving ahead long after she cried out the first time, or even the second.

When he found his release, it was an internal explosion that locked his entire body rigid as the energy throbbed and rushed out of him. He held her tight as the shudders coursed through both of them.

He'd never been like this with a woman before. Never simply taken with no thought beyond himself. He kept his face buried against Melissa's neck as she continued to buck and shudder.

There was a place inside him that wanted to weep there against her neck. That somehow knew he'd found a place of perfection.

"What the hell did I do right?" His voice was heavy and rough to his own ears.

"Oh." Melissa brushed her hands through his hair, her arms still clamped about his neck, her voice little more than a breathy gasp. "I could make a long, long list."

"I meant to be here with you. It's the best place I've *ever* been." He raised his head just enough to kiss where his forehead had rested against her shoulder and then leaned his head there once again. He kept one hand cupped behind her to support her, as both of her legs were about his waist, and ran the other from her breast, down to hip, out along powerful thigh, and back.

He felt the shift. It was tiny, infinitesimal, but with their current embrace, there was no mistaking it. A sliver of ice had appeared and he didn't understand it.

———※———

Melissa felt as if she was fracturing inside her head.

Melissa The Cat, Richie's Ilsa, could purr for months over what they just done. Richie was the best lover she'd ever had by far, and not just the incredible foreplay of the soapy massage.

She'd been fully aware of his own surprise when the warrior had been unleashed. Her only surprise was that the considerate guy had let him loose at all. That guy was every woman's dream of a thoughtful, caring man.

Then there was the man she'd thought was the soldier, the dangerous and confident Delta operator with the hint of green in his eyes.

There was a true warrior hidden deep within Richie Goldman, and he was a devastating lover. His raw power and need all the stronger because of the contrast with the man Richie chose to be—because there was no question that every decision Richie made in his life was conscious. Except perhaps unleashing the breathtaking lover on her.

And while Melissa The Cat was thrilled to find such a one, Melissa Moore wasn't interested in anything deeper. The sex was great, but Richie had returned and still nuzzled against her neck and said that it was the best place he'd ever been.

That *she* was the best place he'd ever been.

If it was still the nameless warrior, she'd know it was just the sex and she'd be fine with it. But it wasn't; it was Richie, and he wasn't just talking about the sex.

He'd obviously sensed the shift in her, for which she was sorrier than she'd expected. But he didn't let her go. Instead he sat down carefully on the shower stall floor without breaking their connection, she still straddling him with her legs around his waist, her breasts pressed hard against his chest. The shower's warm spray pattered over them as if washing away all sins. If only it was so easy.

"Hey, lover." She brushed a hand down his smooth cheek and kissed him lightly.

"Hey," he responded, but kept his eyes averted.

"Look at me."

And that simply, with no evasion, he did. His light brown eyes looked at her as if she was far more special than she really was.

"Maybe you should stop looking at me." There wasn't need there, but rather a knowing. As if he knew more about her than she did herself.

Rather than stopping, he smiled softly and brushed his lips over hers. "I'm so sorry."

"If you're apologizing for the best sex of my life, I'm gonna smack you, Richie Goldman." Crap! She hadn't meant to say that.

"I wasn't." Then he blinked in surprise and whispered, "The best of your life?"

"Yes, damn you!" She *really* hadn't meant to say that…even if it was true.

"Cool!"

And there was her geek.

"I have to admit that it wasn't the best of my life." His tone might have been joking but she couldn't tell. She seemed to be a complete sucker for Richie's straight lines.

She tried to pull away to see him better, but his arms were still wrapped tightly around her back. If she wasn't his best, at least he should have the decency not to point it out. She shoved again, but he didn't let go.

"You were better than that," he explained happily, clearly enjoying his own sense of humor. "I don't even remember anyone else. How could I when you so over-shadowed every one of them?"

Melissa made a raspberry sound of disbelief. "Such a smooth talker." Except Richie wasn't. Not the mild-mannered genius, who was always frank and forthright. Nor the wild lover, who didn't speak at all. Maybe he was just trying to confuse her. She certainly hoped so, because if he was speaking truth, she was in far deeper water than she had any interest in.

He leaned in to nuzzle her neck again but she tugged on the back of his hair to keep him looking at her.

"Then what are you apologizing for?"

"For whoever hurt you so badly that you'd freeze up in my arms after what we just did together." No joke this time. No merry twinkle. No half laugh at his own wit. Instead she was facing the soldier who was angry on her behalf. He could speak and he was pissed. More than that, if she read him right, Richie was equally furious in his own way.

No one except her brother had ever thought to be angry on her behalf. And absolutely no lover.

Unable to face his eyes any longer, she pulled his

head back against her shoulder and tried to ignore how right it felt to hold him so close.

Melissa knew she wasn't merely in over her head. She was down deep in a blue hole without even a scuba tank.

—◦◦◦—

"What the fuck!" Chad's shout rang about the bathroom. He was holding aloft Melissa's bra, and his face was suffused red with his fury.

Richie did what he could to hide Melissa's nakedness, at least her back was to Chad. She kept trying to twist to see what was going on, but Richie wouldn't let her turn.

"God damn you to hell, bitch. I—"

"Get out!" Richie bellowed it so loud that Melissa covered her ears. His own hurt as his shout rang inside the shower enclosure.

"Out!" Richie shouted again, and Chad strode out, still clutching Melissa's bra in his fist.

Richie scrambled to his feet, then pointed at the stall and barked out a command, "You, stay!"

He was halfway to the door when he heard Melissa call his name. He turned to look, and she was pointing at him, at his nakedness.

He grabbed a towel and wrapped it around his waist as he stormed out of the bathroom, closing the door and then the bedroom door behind him.

Chad had turned to face him in the middle of the suite's living room.

"Don't you see what she is, man?" Chad's whisper came out as a hiss.

He waved her bra again.

"I've seen a thousand like her. I've *been* with a thousand like her."

"Like what?" Richie was impressed that he managed to keep his voice low and even.

"You saw her today, just like Carla said. The way she took over at the hangar, she wants to rule this team and won't accept anything less. And you she's just using to fuck her way onto the team. She's so easy that she practically spread her legs for you the second she picked you out of the crowd. Leaning back against you *oh-so-cute* when Fred showed up. In just four days, she's spread herself for you. She's a goddamn—"

Richie knew what the next word was.

Apparently so did his fist as it shot out and crashed into Chad's jaw.

It was like punching a goddamn rock; his head barely moved and Richie's hand stung like hell.

"I'm telling you—"

"Out!" Richie got right up in his face.

When Chad started to speak again, Richie slammed a blow into Chad's solar plexus, which had the advantage of being softer than his jaw, though it had about as much effect. If it came to a fight, the next step would be bone-breaking on both their parts—Delta training wasn't big on fisticuffs.

Chad glared at him, then up over Richie's shoulder.

Melissa. Of course she wouldn't stay put when told—she was Delta.

"Out. Now." Richie kept it soft and low this time.

Chad didn't say a goddamn word, just turned for the door.

"Leave her clothes here." The words grated hard enough in his throat to hurt.

Chad looked down at his hands, dashed Melissa's bra onto the carpet, then stormed out without turning. The slam of the hotel door must have echoed down the hall and at least two floors above and below.

"I don't think he likes me much."

Richie turned. He would have appreciated the skimpiness of the hotel towel at any other time, but at the moment he had another problem.

What the hell was wrong with Chad? This wasn't some fit of jealousy. Chad had been on the verge of calling Melissa a whore.

Please god, don't let her have heard that.

He twisted back to stare at the door as if he could see what was going on with Chad.

Sure, it had been fast between he and Melissa.

But it had felt so right.

And something that felt that right couldn't be wrong. Could it?

Chapter 11

THE FLIGHT TO COLOMBIA WAS SILENT. MELISSA COULD feel Richie thinking, but he wasn't volunteering anything, not a word.

She'd followed as quickly as she could but missed what they said to each other. She'd opened the door only to see the massive blow he delivered to Chad's chin. Despite being twice Richie's size, having his right leg behind him by chance was the only thing that kept Chad upright. The second blow had winded him so badly that he had tried to speak but didn't have control of his lungs. He was lucky that Richie hadn't killed him with the power of that blow.

And Richie hadn't spoken a word since.

It was her fault. She never should have fraternized with a team member. But Kyle and Carla did. And Richie had felt...perfect. She didn't have another word for.

She glanced at him again, but he was wholly focused on the flight.

His natural state was nerd, only flipping into warrior when called for. Now he was gone beyond the veil and she didn't know if that side of him could even speak.

Kyle and Carla had tried asking him some questions, but he hadn't answered them either. Carla had made a patting motion for patience and Melissa could only hope that it would be enough.

In Colombia, Agent Fred had arranged for two pallets of condoms to be waiting for them.

"Condoms?"

"With the collapse of oil prices, Venezuela is broke," Fred had explained. "They also top the South American charts for HIV and teen pregnancy. Abortion is illegal, so condoms are a rare, expensive, and highly sought-after import. Over seven hundred dollars a box on the black market. I've got a guy in Maracaibo who will take delivery and promised to undercut the competition by a third. The fact that he'll make a fortune I can't help, but at least it will help some people in the city."

"Technically legal, black market, and helpful. You done good for a spook," Melissa teased him, hoping to get a rise out of Richie.

Though he'd stood nearby, not a word.

The flight back had been even quieter.

After landing back in Maracaibo, everyone was still so tired that the hotel seemed like too much trouble. Besides, it was just now sunrise and they hadn't posted a phone number. They had to be at the hangar, at least during daylight hours.

Chad and Duane rolled in shortly after they'd handed off the shipment of condoms. The two of them looked as awful as she felt. Chad's dirty look was acid. Surprising herself, she flipped him the finger and then turned her back on him.

They tossed down blankets on the hangar's concrete floor for padding and passed out in the cool shade inside. Kyle took first watch. Melissa had made sure that she was on the side of Richie away from Chad before she collapsed.

The loud roar of the rare jet climbing out of Maracaibo didn't wake her for more than a second or two.

But the approach of a heavy truck engine had her and everyone else rolling to their feet. A glance at her watch showed she'd slept barely three hours. Midmorning.

Melissa slapped her hip to check that her weapon was there. It had been a relief when Duane had opened the weapon's cache; she'd felt naked without one. She'd drawn the Colt M1911. She had two spare magazines in her pants' thigh pocket and a battered but very service-able M16 tucked under the edge of her blanket. They were almost as ubiquitous as the AK-47 on the black market, so it was reasonable that she would have one.

They'd also carefully paired their weapons by power and capacity, so that subteams could unleash the widest variety of attack if needed. She and Richie, Kyle and Carla, Duane and Chad.

The truck stopped and a heavy fist pounded against the steel door. Carla and Kyle moved to either side, she and Richie moved up to the door, and Duane and Chad lay down behind the SUV and the truck so that they could shoot under them or roll into the open as needed.

Melissa propped her weapon on the inside of the door behind a handy angle in the ironwork so that it would be close to hand. She then cracked the door open with Richie out of sight just past the inside edge of the door-jamb. He had his rifle shouldered.

"Mornin', y'all," a big male voice boomed into the hangar before she could even see who stood out in the bright sunlight. "I'm looking to charter that purty little plane of yours we saw flittin' down out of the sky this morning. Took me a bit to find you, let me just say."

Melissa glanced over at Richie.

"Jackson, Mississippi," he whispered. "Moved around a bit, but he sounds authentic."

The man was as she expected once she could see him: fifties, overweight but fighting it, going to bald. Rumpled khakis, worn loafers, and a loud Hawaiian shirt. He mopped at his brow with a white handkerchief. It was as if he was a stereotype of himself.

A woman stood close behind him and couldn't have been a much greater contrast. She was a narrow woman, like she'd been caught in a giant vise and squeezed. She was native but dressed in black designer slacks with a sharp crease, practical but expensive flats, and a simple, white, Ann Taylor blouse that offset her dark skin. Wraparound shades had not been tucked up into her long dark hair—which was pulled back into a severe ponytail making her face appear even narrower—but instead kept her eyes hidden despite the hangar's shadows. Her leather portfolio, as slim as she was, made it so that she'd have looked in place at a Miami business meeting, but not in a rusting Maracaibo hangar.

The man shifted in surprise when Melissa shoved the doors wide enough apart so that they could see each other clearly. Richie leaned against the frame, so his rifle was still out of sight in his hand, but his handgun was on clear display. Then Carla and Kyle moved into view, farther back in the shadows but still carrying their rifles.

"I caught me a fish, a big one," the man continued in the face of Melissa's continued silence, obviously so surprised that he was trying to pretend none of it was happening. "Gotta get her to my guy in Miami. He always mounts my big catches."

"We don't normally carry such cargo." Richie stood up just enough for his rifle to show, though he didn't raise it.

The fish-guy was big, but Richie felt bigger. Not that he was taller, but that he looked so dangerous that he simply took up more space. Melissa had never seen Richie looking this way—a third variation. This was completely the Unit operator, as if he'd wholly shed his charming side. She hoped not. Though he was speaking, which meant that Richie's sharp mind was in full gear when he was in this mode.

"Afraid y'all was gonna say that." The big man put on a sad face but then continued jovially despite how often his wide eyes tracked down to Richie's rifle. "That's why I brought my expediter. She said she would take care of any little problems." He eyed the alleyway between hangars carefully as if finally considering his lines of retreat.

The woman pulled a single sheet of paper from her portfolio and held it out to Melissa.

She took it with her right hand, keeping her left free in case she needed to grab the Colt. Old trick, fill up your adversary's hands, and then attack. She was too well trained to fall for that one.

"This"—the woman's voice was as smooth and classy as her attire—"is a contract for immediate flight to Miami, including deadhead return. I have left the fee blank…for the moment."

"We don't—"

Melissa cut Richie off with a hand sign. She inspected the woman more closely; then she leaned out past the doors to look both directions along the hangar alleyway. With Richie at the door, Duane would have his eye on the camera feeds from outside, and he'd called out no warning.

No one else was in their dusty corner of the hangar area. The truck was a flatbed with a large crate strapped to it; the driver had not climbed down but sat with both hands visible on the wheel. Nowhere for other people to hide unless they were already in place in other hangars.

Life is risk, the trainers used to say. *You don't win an engagement from an armchair*.

"Let's see the box."

"Absolutely." The big man clapped his hands together and turned for the truck. "Now we're getting somewhere."

But it was the woman that Melissa was watching. The careful nod of acquiescence—an assessing moment—before she too turned toward the truck.

"What?" Richie whispered. "We don't want to be flying fish to Miami." His first words addressed directly to her since the hotel room.

"I don't think that's what she's about."

But when they reached the truck—Kyle and Carla rolling up to take clearly military stances with Chad and Duane remaining hidden—and pulled back the tarp, she saw the man had spoken accurately.

"That's one damn big fish," Kyle observed.

He was right. One meter of sword and three more of fish; it was a monster. Blue above, silver below, the swordfish lay in a deep bed of ice.

"My baby is eleven hundred and three pounds," the big man crowed. "Not a record by a long ways, but a record for this old boy, I can tell ya. I have pictures, but my man will want to see it before it dries out."

"Richie." She'd get even with him for giving her the silent treatment. "Check it. I want to know exactly what we would be carrying."

He groaned but pulled out a flashlight. First, he opened its mouth and bent down to inspect its gullet. She didn't see any signs that it had been sliced open and packed with drugs—of course, that could be on the underside.

Apparently satisfied with what he could see, Richie began shoving his hands and arms deep into the fishy ice to make sure the crate had no false bottom.

The guy hovered, clearly anxious about his fish—probably too thoroughly real to be an act.

But the woman stood back, cool and sleek.

Melissa jumped back off the truck and waved over Carla but had her hold one step back as Melissa moved up to the expeditor.

"Miami, one fish, deadhead return. One passenger, I assume." Melissa waved her hand at the fisherman who was now handing Richie his pole case for inspection.

Richie opened it and checked inside. "A Daiwa Saltiga 6500H on a Melton pole. Sweet."

It looked as if the fisherman had just died and gone to heaven. The two of them rambled off into some fishing tackle nerdvana. Not a word to her or anyone else on the team, but he was glad to talk fishing. Her first instinct had been right; she should have pushed him out of the plane over the Everglades and fed him to the alligators or crocs or whichever got to him first.

The expediter woman didn't answer right away. Instead she turned her head to inspect the four of them. The tilt of her head said that she hadn't missed the hangar's security cameras either.

"May I see your plane?"

Melissa nodded.

Carla was looking at her strangely, but Melissa led the woman inside. Without comment, she circled the plane and the two SUVs. At Melissa's signal, Chad and Duane stepped sufficiently out of the shadows to be seen. Like Carla and Kyle, they held onto their rifles so that those were in plain view as well.

Melissa snagged her own from where she'd propped it against the back of the door as she passed by and slung it over her shoulder.

The woman finished her brief tour and returned to where Melissa stood by the narrow opening between the hangar doors.

"There will be two passengers," was all the woman said. "I'll come back on the deadhead return with you."

"Twenty thousand." Melissa kept her tone casual. But she wanted to dance around, pump her fist in the air, and yell, "Bingo!" No mere expediter would ever waste the time to fly the route back and forth. This was an inspection trip for Moore Aviation. She'd been ready for weeks of waiting for a contact, already had several more steps she'd thought of during last night's "condom" flight. And here she was on the second day.

"Ten thousand," the woman countered.

"A Lear would cost him thirty-five, minimum. Plus five for stinking up the cabin with his fish."

"Twelve."

"Seventeen."

"Fifteen."

"U.S. Cash."

"Half before."

"Half after." Melissa closed the deal.

The woman reached into her portfolio again and handed across an envelope.

Melissa handed both the envelope—which she'd just bet already had seventy-five hundred-dollar bills in it—and the contract to Carla as if it was her job to deal with such things.

"Take care of these."

Carla studied her a moment, then guessed Melissa's intent correctly. She riffled the envelope, then pulled out a lighter and set the one-page contract on fire.

"We depart in ten minutes," the woman said crisply and stepped back into the sunlight.

"What the hell, Moore?" Chad came up as Duane slipped outside to keep an eye on the truck with Kyle and Richie. The heat of anger still burned in his voice. "A fucking fish?"

Carla spun to look at her. Clearly the light bulb had just gone on for her. "This isn't about the fish."

"Nope," Melissa agreed and turned to prep the plane for flight, leaving Chad to grind his teeth all he wanted. It was about the expediter.

—◆—

Richie had been worried about U.S. Customs pulling up a report on their plane when they landed in Miami and finding that it was listed as stolen from the Coast Guard. But they didn't, so Vito Corello must have taken care of that somehow.

It ended up being an uneventful five-hour flight to Miami, getting a fish through customs, refueling, and five hours back.

Mr. Fish—no names were ever offered and none were ever given—checked his fish about every three minutes for the whole flight up and gave a jovial farewell in Miami.

The expediter remained absorbed in the paperwork in her portfolio or on her equally slim tablet computer for the long hours—or at least she appeared to be. Richie suspected that she didn't miss a single thing in the whole flight—not a course correction or an altitude adjustment.

Duane sat quietly in the rearmost seat, guarding their backs while he and Melissa flew. The other three had remained behind in Venezuela.

Once back in Maracaibo, the woman had wordlessly handed a second envelope to Melissa and walked away, declining the offer of a ride.

It was sunset as they gathered once more in the hangar. A last flight struggled aloft through the hot Maracaibo twilight. The hangar smelled of rust and hot engines.

"Great, so we just made the CIA fifteen grand," Chad complained. "What else did we do?"

"Only eight grand," Richie estimated. "After fuel, landing fees, and ten hours operating time allocated to the Twin Otter's next service, it's only eight grand. Maybe eighty-five hundred, and that doesn't account for the pilot's time which—"

"And we achieved what?" Chad aimed the question at Melissa like a dagger.

Richie was about to step in between them, but Melissa never gave him a chance.

She went toe to toe with him. "Because, asshole…"

So much for the polite Canadian, Richie thought. Melissa angry was an impressive sight and once again, her Delta-ness, which slipped out of mind so easily when looking at the beautiful woman, stood front and center and her name was Fury.

"That woman is not just an expediter of fish. Haven't you ever heard of a test? We just had a test and got paid for it. The next load will smell less and be worth far more."

Something Richie hadn't figured out until they were well aloft, but Melissa had seen at first glance. Melissa wasn't a phony; she was too good. And she'd told him that she knew Colonel Gibson—he wasn't the sort of person that people knew about unless he wanted them to. During his own passage through the Commander's Review Board at Delta Selection, the man hadn't spoken a single word.

Chad shook his head like a bull balking a step before a red cape, his face going dangerously blank.

Carla swept an arm through Melissa's and tugged her back out into the fading sunlight, probably because it was clear the Melissa and Chad were gearing up to go head to head, a very bad thing between Delta operators.

All Richie had seen when the man and woman had arrived was an idiot who'd spent fifteen hundred dollars on a fishing pole that wasn't significantly different from a two-hundred-dollar one. A true pro might notice the difference, but likely not their rich boy from Jackson, Mississippi. And if he was a true pro, he'd probably be fishing with the Shimano Stella 10000…not that Richie had ever fished, but he'd read an interesting review while waiting for his last physical.

And then to spend fifteen grand on an airplane to ferry the fish to Miami. You couldn't even mount a saltwater fish's actual skin. What the taxidermists did was cast a mold and build a hand-painted fiberglass copy for the guy's wall, which was…nuts. Richie's own family was very well-off, Dad was a top salesman, had the plane (mostly paid for by IBM), and they lived in the nicest neighborhood Poughkeepsie had to offer. But they weren't stupid about it.

Then Richie refocused on what had just happened here.

"Hey, Duane."

When his friend had joined him to help stow the plane, Richie whispered to him, "What's up with Chad?"

Duane readied himself to lean into one of the landing struts to roll the plane back into the hangar. "Woman gives him an itch."

"Well I don't want him asking her to scratch it." Even as he said it, he knew he was wrong, was missing something. But Richie still didn't want Chad anywhere near her.

"Different kind of itch, buddy. More the kind between the shoulder blades." Duane slapped Richie right on that spot. "I don't see it, but you know Chad and women. Let's get this plane put away. Hungry and tired doesn't begin to describe it."

Chad's opinion surprised Richie to no end; it wasn't at all what he thought was going on. But the jealousy angle hadn't fit after the confrontation at the hotel. He'd thought about nothing else for the whole flight to Colombia and back, barely remembered the flight, and was just glad he hadn't crashed them while he'd been so distracted.

But this? It made perfect sense…even if it didn't make any sense at all.

He tried to see where Carla and Melissa had gone, but they were out of sight.

It was foolish to ignore that kind of itch coming from a Unit operator, but Carla's reaction was quite the opposite. Carla had clearly decided to befriend Melissa, and based on Carla's initial reaction, it wasn't because Melissa was also a woman.

Richie trusted Carla implicitly, but he also trusted Chad just as completely.

But Chad's opinion that Melissa was trying to take over? It didn't make any sense at all. Which left Richie having no idea what to think.

Damn it! He was right back where he'd spent the whole flight, chasing his own tail in circles and feeling stupider than when he started. On top of that, he'd punched one of his teammates in anger. That too was new territory for him. Neither the Richie Goldman that he knew nor a Unit operator functioned from a place of anger.

Chad strolled by him and Richie stopped him.

"Sorry for the, uh…" Richie rubbed his own chin.

"Nothing but a love tap, bro. Sorry for busting up your fun."

Richie shrugged.

But he could see that Chad was still on the lookout.

Until he figured out what to think, Richie would be as well.

———— ∿∿ ————

"Why did you stop me?" Melissa barked at Carla as she was escorted around the end of the hangar and out onto the dry grassy lot beyond the hangars.

The grasses were brown, the bushes low, and the dirt showed through in bare patches. It was about as attractive as the worst sections of Fort Bragg, which was a pretty low standard. Fort Bragg—the home of The Unit among many others—was generally acknowledged as one of the ugliest Army bases anywhere.

"Because I don't know how good a fighter you are, but I'll bet Chad is better."

Melissa tried to jerk her arm free, but Carla was far stronger than she appeared.

"Look." Carla towed Melissa right along by her arm. "I don't know what's going on with you two, but Chad is the most lethal fighter we've got. He didn't earn the nickname The Reaper by being Mister Nice Guy."

It rankled. It was another thing that Melissa knew she wasn't. She wasn't the best shot or the most dangerous fighter or the super-geek or... "What the heck am I doing here, Carla?"

"How the hell would I know? Someone decided you were supposed to be here on this team and—"

"Gibson."

Carla stopped cold as if she was the one who was suddenly Elsa the Ice Queen and now frozen in place.

"He's a Delta Colonel."

"Michael"—Carla blinked like an owl—"Gibson. Damn the man."

"He's the one who saved me and helped recover my brother's body five years ago; I only just found that out during OTC graduation. He's the reason I went Army and eventually Delta, though I didn't know it was him." Yet another thing she hadn't had time to think about yet. That list of things she hadn't had time to absorb was getting longer by the second. Gibson, the new team, Chad hating her, stolen planes, drug running, and that mixed look of need and wonder in Richie's eyes that had felt like a miracle but now was nowhere to be seen.

"And Gibson is the one who sent you to join our team?"

"Uh-huh."

"Did he say why?"

Melissa lowered the tone of her voice. "'I have recommended that you be assigned to our top South American team.' That's all he gave me. And he said he was sorry he hadn't been able to save my brother, who was dead the moment he fell into that crevasse."

Carla let go of Melissa arm and strode away, kicking her way through the thick clumps of grasses but clearly headed in no particular direction. Then she kicked her way back.

Melissa was tempted to follow her. She could think of several things she wanted to kick right about now.

"Well, he always was a deep one. If he sent you to us, there must be a reason."

"Because tall, blond Canadians blend in so well with South American drug runners?"

"I'm guessing that's not it." Carla's half smile showed in the distant runway lights that were finally overtaking the last of the day's light. "So what's special about you?"

"Nothing. Trust me on that. I'm a good enough soldier to make The Unit, which has to say something."

"Says a lot," Carla agreed, which helped Melissa to calm down a little.

"But they never gave me a specialty. I often led the

teams, but not the way Kyle does—he makes it look so damn easy that I often can't see him doing it. The primary attribute the training cadre always mentioned was that I was the *second* woman to make Delta. And just so you know, I totally despised Carla Effing Anderson the entire time."

Carla's laugh was bright and merry. "God but you are Canadian. From now on it's Carla Fucking Anderson to you."

Melissa rolled it around in her head for a moment before replying, "I don't know if that's going to work for me."

Carla's repeated laughter made her feel a little better. "No specialization, huh?"

"Not that I know about. Not breacher, not sniper, not candlestick maker."

"Well then, my friend"—Carla slipped her hand around Melissa's waist as if they'd been friends forever, or maybe sisters—"we'll just have to wait and see what we discover. At least we know one thing."

"What's that?" They started strolling back to the hangar arm in arm.

"You're the face of this charter company from now on. You picked up on that woman way ahead of any of us; I was on the verge of booting her narrow ass. And you did that negotiation perfectly; you couldn't have played it better. That was well done. Really well done."

Melissa felt a little like the Incredible Hulk, flickering back and forth between the Ice Queen and a Delta Force heroine.

It was both hopeful and giddy…and a little nauseating.

Then it registered how completely that was a Richie image. Oh god, the man was rubbing off on her.

"What's up with you and Chad?" Not Richie's most subtle approach, but the angry heat between Chad and Melissa at dinner—now that he knew what it was—was palpable.

"Can't we just drop it?" Melissa had flopped back on the bed the moment they got to the new hotel.

Kyle had decided that Melissa had been right and they needed to look a little more desperate. They'd shifted to a sunbaked hotel close by the airport.

Melissa looked as exhausted as Richie felt. The overnight into Colombia and then Miami and back, a busy day on top of a busy night. That was at least one thing that SEALs got right: *The only easy day was yesterday.* An unofficial motto that spoke pure truth.

She lay there with one arm flung over her eyes. In sharp contrast to the Bahamian resort, the cheap bedspread that might have once been white but was now an uneven beige made Melissa look washed-out rather than vibrant. The whole hotel felt that way and had been chosen for that reason. No chair, desk, or phone. A bed, a spot to drop luggage, and a couple of cheap lamps with battered shades.

"Uh, sure." Maybe dropping the topic was best. "Do you want a shower?" That should be a safe subject change. When she didn't respond, he considered whether or not to offer to wash her back again. Would that be a good move or a bad one? He glanced into the bathroom and decided it was more on the bad side; the shower was the kind you used flip-flops in.

"I'd rather kill Chad Hawkins."

"Whoa!" Richie had one foot in the bathroom but turned back to face Melissa. "Say that again."

"Oh, come on, Richie. He's a complete bastard. Surely you guys have seen that?"

Was that her angle? Was that the itch that Chad had felt? If Chad was right, then she really might be a threat to him...but that didn't work in Richie's head any better than the jealousy angle.

"Are you here to break up this team?" He could feel his voice hardening, his stance shifting as if readying for a sparring match. Sometimes you just asked the damned question.

She uncovered her eyes and raised her head enough to stare at him. "You've got to be kidding me."

"About what?"

"You're going to stand there and defend that asshole? Just yesterday you planted a punch on his jaw that would have killed most men."

"He's saved my life a half dozen times." But that Melissa said "asshole" rather than "jerk" only emphasized how completely she believed what she was saying.

"And how many times have you done the same for him?"

Richie shrugged. "About the same. It all works that way in the field. You'll see. Once we get back in the field, everything will be fine."

"No, it won't, Richie." Melissa sat up.

The geometry of the room placed them almost knee to knee. He could so easily lean down and kiss her. Lose himself in—

"I go out in the field with him and I'm going to catch

a bullet in my brainpan just like a training dummy. You check it out. It will match his gun."

"Shit, Melissa. You can't think he'd actually do that."

She buried her face in her hands for a long moment. Then she dropped her hands in her lap but didn't look up.

He waited her out.

"No. I suppose he wouldn't, but I sure wouldn't put it past him to nudge me out in front of someone else's shot. I'm too tired to deal with this. I'm going to sleep now." And she moved to the far side of the bed, close beside the yellowing wall that might have once been blue. She curled up with her back to him, and Richie stood there at a complete loss.

Everything made sense when he was alone with Melissa, but those times never lasted more than moments. Right now, not even that was working. And even just today, he, Chad, and Duane had worked together easily, shifting the plane back into the hangar and making sure it was all ready for an immediate flight if needed.

It was when they all came together that everything came apart.

He was missing something.

Something basic. Simple.

The kind of thing that Melissa would see.

Except she didn't. There were actually many things Melissa didn't see. She didn't see how amazing she was. She'd picked up multi-engine piloting so fast that he'd felt like a klutz beside her. Melissa The Cat had handled Mr. Fish Man and his expediter so smoothly that it should be taught in a Delta class.

She greeted Richie with a warmth that astonished him every time.

Or was Chad right and that just another game she was playing?

Did Melissa Moore's true identity begin and end as Elsa the Ice Queen? Had her heart died along with her brother on that icy mountain top?

Had she even had a brother?

He didn't know what to think.

Richie wanted to lie down beside her. Pull her into his arms and just hold her—protect her from whatever demons were chasing her.

But then he remembered Chad's anger. He'd never seen Chad angry. Not the moment he'd killed the guards for trying to stop them at the Bolivian coca plantation. Not even when they'd taken out murderers or rapists during their first mission as a team.

Grim? Sure.

Pissed? Not until Richie had faced off against him in the hotel. Though it wasn't until the airplane hangar that Richie understood why Chad was acting the way he'd been.

Richie didn't know what he was in the middle of, but he didn't like it. As quietly as he could, he slipped out of the room. Down the hall, he found Duane's room and tapped dit-dah-dit lightly on the door for *R*.

"Yo."

Richie entered slowly, then waited for Duane to confirm that it hadn't been a trap and reholster his weapon.

He took one look at Richie's face, then moved over to the far side of the bed and hooked a thumb beside him. Richie kicked off his boots and lay down on top of the covers.

Despite the long flights, he didn't go to sleep for a long time.

And despite all of his thinking, he ended up feeling dumber, not smarter, by the time he was done with it.

Chapter 12

"THREE DAYS." CARLA WAS DOING ONE OF HER RAGE-around-the-hangar things. "Three days and that bitch hasn't reappeared. And do we have a way to reach out to her? I ask you. No!"

Melissa watched her. Not caring. Not moving. She'd found a corner and stayed in it except when she was doing calisthenics to avoid losing her mind.

When Richie had walked away, Melissa had known she was screwed. She really was the Ice Queen inside.

She'd started taking long walks at night, despite the dangers of the Maracaibo streets after dark. But each time she'd returned to the room, he hadn't come back, wasn't there waiting for her. When a knock had finally sounded on the hotel room door the third night, she'd been far too angry to answer.

By then the Ice Queen was fully in place and would stay there until she could figure out how to get out of this outfit—if she could make it out alive. Maybe she'd stay frozen forever.

Perhaps she'd join Mutt and Jeff wherever they'd been assigned to. It was possible she'd been wrong to join The Unit in the first place. Even that thought just made for a colder core anchored deep in her chest.

All she knew was that this team was broken and she wanted no part of it.

Only Carla still tried to break through Melissa's ice

shield. Melissa felt bad about rebuffing her, but it was
easier to keep her shields up against everyone. It made it
easier to ignore Richie's confused looks. He'd be palling
around with Chad and Duane, then he'd look her direction and go all quiet and sad.

Not her problem.

She wasn't the one who'd walked away.

Unable to stand Carla's continuing rant, which
echoed off the hard steel walls of the hangar until she
thought her head was going to explode, Melissa stepped
out through the doors into the blast of sunlight. The heat
was a hammer blow after the cool interior of the hangar.

She almost plowed into the expediter who was standing just a few feet beyond the opening. This time she
had switched her wardrobe like a negative of her prior
self—pristine-white slacks and a black top that flowed
loosely over her narrow frame despite the fine tailoring.
The sunglasses and portfolio were still firmly in place.

"Your teammate is a very passionate woman," the
expediter said as Carla's rant continued, mostly muffled
by the barely parted hangar doors.

"She is," Melissa agreed. An effort to move the woman
a little farther from the door didn't succeed. Melissa
reviewed what she could recall of Carla's rant; she was
fairly sure that nothing critical had been revealed.

"She does not seem to like me very much."

Melissa did some quick thinking about how to fix
that. "It's, uh, just that times are a little tight. One
swordfish doesn't support this operation for long. We
had hoped for something more."

"And if I were to suggest a delivery to the Bahamas?"

Melissa cringed and at the same time tried not to hope

too hard. It was obvious that the expediter had found their arrest record. So that was probably a good sign. She'd been checking them out. Still, being rearrested by the Royal Defence troops would not go well.

"It wouldn't be my first choice."

The expediter nodded as if checking off the answer on her list and moved to the next topic. "Your plane's tail number has an interesting history."

"It does." Melissa decided to brazen this one out. If she denied any knowledge that it once belonged to a dead Venezuelan drug lord before it had been captured and impounded by the U.S. Coast Guard, she would look stupid and in over her head. But no one had told her exactly what information the USCG had released.

"Your Coast Guard has it labeled as 'stolen' in their database."

The woman wasn't a minor player. Not if she had someone on the inside who could check secure databases for her. So The Unit's mission was looking better even if the team itself was a shambles.

"Yet the FAA simply lists it as belonging to Melissa Moore—a former U.S. Army sergeant discharged for gun running—who I can only assume is you."

Melissa nodded and tried to think of where to go with that.

"It was more gun smuggling," Richie said, moving up from behind Melissa. "She was only the point of acquisition. Others did the actual transport." He left the sentence open-ended, implying that he'd been the actual smuggler. Then he slipped a hand around her waist and kissed her on the cheek.

She was surprised, even shocked. But before she

could even think not to show anything, her body had already reacted—leaning into Richie and giving out a soft sigh. Was it her evasion training—the second letter of her SERE course—or was it…

Think later! Focus on now.

The tail end of Carla's latest rant was still winding down in the background, which meant that Richie hadn't been sent out to look for her.

Melissa wanted to believe that Richie had come looking for her because… *Because you're imagining things, Melissa. He was merely playing the role; he'd noticed you leave and then heard voices.* She hoped that Richie at least had a good explanation of their aircraft's origin.

He made a hand sign that looked like a payoff. "I had a friend make a little change in the aircraft's official record. As long as it isn't the Coast Guard itself checking ownership, we're clean."

Melissa had forgotten all about the Aruban Customs official.

The expediter nodded again. Another check on her list. Then she offered her first-ever smile. "Shall we go inside and appease your friend?"

"Do we get a name this time?"

"Analie Sala. I look forward to doing business with you."

--- ⁓⁓⁓ ---

Richie rather enjoyed watching Carla choke mid-sentence when the three of them entered the hangar. It wasn't easy to fluster her, but she just stood there for several seconds with her jaw down; then she blushed so fiercely that even her naturally dusky skin colored deeply.

He did wish that he'd managed to find Melissa alone. Who knew that a team he was so close to could be such a hindrance? In the hangar, they were always together. At meals, Melissa had taken to eating elsewhere, and the few times Richie had started to follow, Chad always seemed to have a question for him until she was out of sight. His various attempts to knock on her hotel door had elicited no response. There'd been no light shining under the door anyway. He'd hesitated to use his own key to go in and confront her.

So when she'd left the hangar alone, he'd followed her as quickly as he could while avoiding Chad's attention, just in case he had something else to ask. And found her with the expediter. Which was great news, except that it totally sucked.

He'd stepped into the copilot-business-partner-lover role easily, and the way Melissa had melted against him had almost stopped his heart. She simply felt so right that Chad had to be wrong about her.

Introductions were finishing. Once again he'd have to get Melissa alone later.

And once again, Melissa was being magnificent in her role as the boss of their crew.

"The cargo"—Ms. Sala of course never specified exactly what it was—"needs to be moved tonight."

Richie looked at the coordinates that Ms. Sala had provided and let out a low whistle. They were headed up the Orinoco River, deep into the Amazonian rainforest.

"Maybe we'll get to see an Orinoco crocodile."

Melissa looked at him strangely. So did the expediter.

"They're very rare now. It would be great to see one."

The laugh that went around the group seemed to ease

the last of the tensions—even the expediter joined in. He hadn't been trying to be funny, but it seemed to have worked anyway.

On everyone except Chad and Melissa.

———

"I don't want to talk about it." Melissa didn't like the feeling of everyone sitting so close behind them on the Twin Otter for such a private conversation. She and Richie were the only two on the headset intercom and there wasn't a chance that their voices could be heard over the roaring of the dual Pratt & Whitney turboprop engines and the heavy wind noise of their flight. But still, everyone was right there just a few feet behind them.

Hell, Richie was right there next to her, less than two feet away as they turned south out of Maracaibo and headed toward the Orinoco River.

"Tough."

She twisted to look at Richie, at least what little she could see of him. He was flying copilot in the right-hand seat but had the controls. He'd become the lead pilot for the team; how had she ended up in his seat now?

Because she'd been so pissed at him, she hadn't cared and had simply taken the seat without thinking.

She'd kept her hands in her lap and off the flight control yoke. They were headed south over deep jungle. The setting sun was to the west, shining in through his side window, and made him little more than a silhouette.

For days he'd been the odd nerd—sad but nerd.

Now she was flying with the Unit operator. One who had found his voice.

"O-kay," she said carefully.

"I hate being apart from you." That was pure Richie.

"Your choice." And she was so numb that she no longer knew how she felt about that.

"Can we mark that off as I was being really, really stupid when I walked out of the hotel room?"

She considered that for several miles. "No, I don't think so."

"Crud! I was afraid of that."

A Unit operator who said *crud!* Richie the warrior would never say such a thing. It was just as bad as her thinking "Effing." They were a sad pair.

"Okay, I've been thinking."

Not a big fucking surprise, but she didn't say it out loud. She was surprised though, by her internal language. She wasn't merely ticked off—No! She was royally pissed and hurt, and the chill inside her was seeking a target. If she could, she'd freeze Richie's ass from here to eternity. It was better to keep her mouth shut.

"Carla is the smartest woman about people I've ever met before you. And she really likes you."

"She warms up pretty easily."

"Wrong! You have no idea how wrong." Richie was shaking his head. "Not even a little bit close. We were a full week into Delta Selection before she spoke the first time to Kyle, like three words. I don't think she said another word before the final hike, even to him. It wasn't until our second or third month together in the Operator Training Course that she spoke about anything other than the training. She's the ultimate outsider."

Melissa couldn't imagine such a thing. And if that woman had lacked a voice, she'd certainly found it now. Carla was at such complete ease with the team, and they with her. Melissa had circled back a few times to observe them during meals where she'd felt so unwelcome. There was no hesitancy, no caution, all of them visibly far more at ease without Melissa's own disruptive presence. They all teased each other, but they also really listened to one another.

Carla had spotted her once, hiding back among the market stalls, nodded slightly acknowledging Melissa's choice, and returned to the conversation without giving any sign to the others of Melissa's nearby presence.

This was the outsider who spoke to no one?

"Not no one. She's the center of—"

"No one," Richie insisted. "She's the center of the group *now*, but not back then. Yet when we compared notes, she's the only one who picked five for five."

There was no need to explain. It had been the last questionnaire of hundreds they'd had to complete during Delta Selection. After the forty-mile rucksack march but before the Commander's Review Board, they had each been required to list the candidates they would want to serve with—in order. Three out of the five Melissa had put at the top of her list had made it into OTC. And Carla had somehow picked five for five.

"On top of that, we all chose her as Number Two," Richie continued, "because Kyle was simply the best. He chose her as Number One."

Melissa remembered the same comparison among her fellow graduates. She'd rated a pair of Number Ones, a couple of Twos, and a Five. Carla really was that good.

"Carla saw us more clearly than any of us saw ourselves. I'm stupid about people; I'm aware of that blank spot. To compensate, I rely on others."

This was Richie the brain boy in full regalia. But she could hear what it was costing him to reveal these truths about himself.

As the sun set, the *Tin Goose* reached the far southern shore of Lake Maracaibo. Soon thick, dark jungle was rolling along beneath the plane. They continued a long way in silence before he spoke again.

"I just wanted to say I'm sorry for doubting your motives. I should have listened to Carla." A few more miles. "I hope that my screwup isn't permanent."

"What about Chad?"

"I don't know. I've given it a lot of thought, about three days' worth, and I still don't know. But what I feel for you just can't be imagined. And then I saw that you looked as miserable as I felt. I don't think the finest actress could do that."

She rested her hands on the control yoke for the first time in the flight. Melissa hadn't wanted the connection to Richie that it gave her, but now she did. He flew with a smooth confidence; after so many flights in the last week, the big plane felt normal. Familiar.

"Are you feeling what I am?" he continued. "I couldn't ever get you alone to ask, and you wouldn't answer your door—though I guess I can't blame you for that. Probably just as well, because I finally realized that the question was irrelevant. I found what I feel, which is so right when I'm with you that nothing else matters."

As apologies went, it was a pretty good one.

But somehow having *Carla* be her recommendation to a lover grated on her nerves. She understood this was Richie. But...

"Next time, Richie?"

"Yes?"

"Try trusting your own judgment."

He didn't answer. She could hear him thinking, his thoughts were churning so hard.

Without another word, they slipped down through the last of the fading daylight. The Upper Orinoco River, which formed the border between Colombia and Venezuela, spread out before them in a low valley bordered with thick trees that towered above the water.

The silence was almost surreal as the big engines slowed to a near idle. There was the motor grind of ailerons and flaps extending until the big plane was flying slower than a car went on the interstate. The only remaining sound: the wind rushing over the wings. The plane's floats skipped just once and then settled into the water with a bright *Shhhhhhush*.

A flashlight winked several times on the western, Colombian bank. Richie kicked the tail rudder and revved the engine enough to head them into shore.

Melissa brushed at her eyes to keep the sudden moisture from turning into tears.

Damn Richie for being right; even the Ice Queen couldn't fake how she felt about him. No matter how hard she'd been trying.

Chapter 13

THE TEAM EASED OUT OF THE PLANE FULLY ARMED but kept their weapons aimed at the ground. First off, Richie tied a rope from the float to a handy banana tree so that the plane didn't drift off the narrow sandy beach without them. The long wing practically touched the thicker ceiba and Para nut trunks that clustered tightly along the river. He then stayed low, hoping the angle might help him see more.

The silence of the Upper Orinoco River was almost shattering after Maracaibo and the flight. There was a bird cry that must have been a parrot from high up in the forest. An answering call sounded from the other side of the river, perhaps a hundred meters away, and then silence.

It was dark beneath the jungle canopy, though the evening still brightened the river itself. A fish little bigger than his hand leapt out of the water and splashed back in, leaving a wide ring of ripples on the surface that flowed lazily away to the north. No way to tell if it was leaping to catch a fly or streaking out of its natural element to escape a predator still lurking below the surface.

Several men moved forward out of the buttressed tree trunks. They were a mixed band: mostly native dark but a pair as light-skinned as himself. He took that as a good sign that his own team didn't look too out of place.

He took a closer look at the Delta team assembling in

the fading light. The days of being stuck waiting in the
hangar had been good for them. They looked dirty and
disheveled. Duane had even more oil and grease on his
shirt than Melissa had initially placed there. Carla's hair
was a mess from lack of care. Kyle slumped with exhaustion, which Richie finally figured out had to be an act.
Which probably meant that Carla's hair was an act as well.

Chad remained aboard, their surprise asset hidden
inside the cabin's shadows.

And then Melissa opened the pilot's door, stepped
down onto the float, then over to the beach. She shone
golden in the last of the day's light. In boots, cargo camo
pants, and a thin white sleeveless tank top that clung
to her figure—hell, practically showed every stitch and
seam in her bra—she was a hard right cross to his libido.
How in the world had he been dumb enough to stay
away from this woman?

She hadn't said anything else after remarking on his
lame-o apology. That was an acceptance, wasn't it? He
couldn't be sure.

Had it been his turn to speak? He didn't think so. But
if it had been, had he now blown it again and…

Richie focused on the other men as the last of them
filtered out onto the narrow beach. Seven, but grouped
closely—close enough to be the target of a single sweep
of his AK-47 if needed. That meant that even if they
were skilled fighters, they had no formal training. Or it
meant that there were others waiting back in the trees
and this group were staying in an easily identifiable
clump in case it turned into a firefight.

Two of the men labored forward, each carrying a box
heavy enough to make them stagger.

Kyle shifted forward, which caused Duane to move farther right to have a better angle on covering him. Kyle flicked on a light.

"*Libros?*" Kyle asked in Spanish. Books. The name of the latest James Patterson novel was displayed boldly on the sides.

"We no going to label it 'Illegal drugs,' *hombre*," one of the men answered in a Spanish far rougher than Kyle's. He looked and spoke like a street tough, Brazilian by his underlying Portuguese accent. He had an Uzi submachine gun that might have dated back to Venezuelan coup attempts in the 1990s, two handguns, a long knife, and a bandolier like an Old West gunslinger, ridiculously filled with single rounds rather than the magazines that would actually be useful in a prolonged firefight.

"I see what's in the boxes before they go on the plane," Kyle insisted.

"That no the deal."

"Then we fly away and your shipment rots on the sand right here."

There was grumbling but the boxes were finally propped on the edge of the cargo deck. Kyle pulled out a big military knife. It looked old and heavily worn, apparently from age, but Richie knew it was from long practice and heavy usage. The gesture was also right out of the handbook: "Find an excuse to wield your weapon in the enemy's presence. It will make you more respected, more accepted, and more prepared."

Kyle slit the lids and shone his flashlight without resheathing the blade.

Richie eased forward enough to look in. Neat white

bricks of powder: four by eight by one point five inches. Standard kilo bag. Packed in even layers. He estimated the box size.

"Fifty kilos each box," he whispered to Kyle. "If there aren't any false fillers."

Kyle poked a finger down the corner of the box and nodded. Cocaine bricks all the way to the bottom.

"If it's pure, that's five to fifteen million dollars on the street if sold by the gram. Half that wholesale by the uncut brick."

"*Hombre* smart. Way pure."

"Where's it going?"

One of the white men handed over a scrap of paper with coordinates on it and Kyle handed it to Richie.

He held it up to capture the last of the daylight rather than risk dazzling his eyes with a flashlight. He estimated as well as he could without a map. "Beach outside of Cancún," was his best guess.

The man confirmed it with a nod.

Kyle closed the box lids and shoved them deeper into the cargo bay in agreement.

"We need a guarantee." The first man grabbed Melissa around the waist. "We keep her until you return. Maybe we have some fun together while we wait, eh, *senorita*?"

"Not the deal," Kyle said evenly before Richie could draw.

Kyle could talk them down…or else a lot of people were going to die in the next minute. They were not keeping Melissa.

"She's one of the pilots."

The man grunted, "Then we keep this one." He shoved Melissa away.

When the man reached for Carla, Melissa spun smoothly, pulled her Colt handgun, and shoved the barrel hard under the man's chin, grabbing him by his bandolier close by his throat so that he couldn't move away.

"Didn't you hear the man?" Her voice was as smooth as Kyle's and about a thousand degrees chillier. "It's not the deal."

None of them had seen Melissa in a military conflict yet, but the move didn't surprise Richie at all. Melissa was a Unit operator; it fit her so perfectly.

When the man made a grab for his own weapon, Melissa pulled the trigger.

There was a crash and boom of the big .45 round that seemed to shake the jungle itself. The back of the man's head disappeared into the darkness out over the river.

The jungle screamed. Every animal in the vicinity crying out and beating their way aloft or racing deeper into the jungle.

Fish broke the surface, feeding on the unexpected bounty.

Chad popped the top hatch on the Twin Otter's passenger compartment and stood up in it like a gun turret. From over the top of the high fuselage, he aimed his massive M240 machine gun down at the group.

The tableau remained frozen until Melissa let go of the man's cartridge belt.

He keeled over backward, landing half-in, half-out of the water.

Melissa holstered her sidearm, "Now, who's the real *jefe* here?"

Richie blinked in surprise. How had she figured that out?

The other of the two white men, not the one with the coordinates, stepped forward from the back of the group.

"You belie your fine looks, *senorita*," the man said in British English, though his native tongue might be Dutch. "Such a pretty woman should not have such violence as well."

Richie flicked off his AK-47's safety—an intentionally loud sound in the quieting jungle.

"Interesting," the man said without looking his way. Then he moved over to the body lying partly in the river. He kicked the bottom of the dead man's boots hard enough to set the body adrift. It passed between the pontoon floats of the Twin Otter and continued north.

Richie wanted to keep an eye on it, see if an Orinoco crocodile was going to surface for the free meal, but he didn't have the luxury at the moment. It was too dark to see much anyway.

"If you leave no one behind"—the leader returned to face Melissa—"then I send four with you."

"Two," she countered as if she hadn't just killed a man. Some people didn't deserve to live, but he was the first man she'd ever killed who wasn't shooting at her—even if he had been reaching for a weapon. Like everything else, she'd think about it later.

"Three."

"Two!" If Melissa was going to be the front woman for this outfit, she was going to act like it—hard-ass and frozen to the core. "It's all the open seats I have on the plane, and I won't have some trigger-happy *idiota* like that one tumbling about in the back of the plane if I have to do any hard maneuvering."

Now to up the stakes to show she had equal power in this negotiation.

"And I return your *two* men to Maracaibo. How they get back to you is their problem."

He nodded and countered with, "You will turn off all of your radios. If my men see you turn them on before the delivery is complete, they will shoot every one of your companions in-flight, starting with the woman you have just defended."

"Understood." Melissa knew if they needed the radio before the delivery, their cover would be blown and she'd have to trust the four Delta operators to take out the two guards before they could get off a shot.

"Payment at Maracaibo," he continued the round.

"Payment on delivery or we don't offload the product," Melissa countered.

He nodded. Obviously he'd been testing her, even if it was a simple one. No desperate American drug-running team would ever let go of the product without getting their grubby hands on the cash they were owed. And she'd bet that no drug seller would release his product without up-front payment as well, no matter what the shipping arrangement might be.

"And I need a thousand gallons of avgas waiting within a hundred miles of the drop-off. And we get the fuel before we make the delivery."

"A barge will be waiting two miles due west of the northern lighthouse on Cozumel." He had anticipated the need. Not their first time doing this.

She decided to push for every penny she could. The

hundred-thousand-dollar fee promised by Analie Sala would easily cover the extra three-grand expense, but…

"And the fuel comes out of your share."

He grimaced but acquiesced when he saw her expression. "Deal."

In under ten minutes, the team, the drugs, and two heavily armed drug smugglers were all aboard. In moments, Richie had them skidding fast across the surface of the Orinoco. Melissa made sure that she and Richie were the only two on the intercom. He sat left seat this time, as he should be, and lifted them off the water.

"Now how do we deliver the drugs without delivering the drugs?" Melissa couldn't figure out that part of it, but there was no way she was going to be a part of actually delivering more drugs to the U.S. markets.

"Not our problem."

"Not our problem?" Melissa would have shrieked at him if not for the two nasty pieces of work sitting back in the cabin. Their "escorts" looked dangerous enough to make Chad look mild.

"Nope!"

But this time she caught Richie's tone. The pleased-with-himself nerd was back. She'd feared that the last few days had beat it out of him, and she was very relieved to be wrong. Too relieved. As if she actually cared about…

Abort!

"So, whose problem is it, if it isn't ours?" She did her best to match his easy tone, and then she knew. "Fred's."

"Yep! Take the controls, would you?"

When she did, Richie pulled out a small radio and kept it to one side so that no one behind them would be able to see it. He tapped out a quick message and hit send. An acknowledgement flashed back and he tucked the radio back into a thigh pocket.

He returned his hands to the controls and they flew, with both of their hands on the interconnected wheels, comfortable until they were approaching the Venezuelan coastline.

Melissa couldn't stop the smile. This is why she'd signed up with Delta. Go where no one else could and make a difference. She didn't know quite what that looked like at the moment, but she could feel when she was in the groove.

Together they eased down within a hundred feet of the ocean waves. The next thousand miles were going to be seven hours of hard work. It would take everything they both had to avoid U.S. and Mexican patrols. The Venezuelans weren't doing much about patrolling their own air and sea lanes, one of the reasons they were such a prime smuggling route.

A hundred miles to sea, they were probably clear of any Venezuelan patrol that might actually care. For the next nine hundred, it would be the random patrols of the U.S. Navy to which even Fred Smith said he had no access. So it was up to them not to surprise any warships.

"No pressure," Richie commented drily.

Melissa didn't laugh in return; she still didn't feel much like laughing. But she did allow herself to smile in the dark. Perhaps it was a little grimly, but she really did like Richie.

Another hundred miles and then he asked softly, "Are you okay? After, you know, the guy from Macapá?"

Leave it to Richie to know Brazilian regional dialects. And she liked Richie just a little more for asking.

"Not my first rodeo."

Richie answered with a waiting silence. How was it that he didn't trust himself about people? With only the one notable exception, he'd judged her moods perfectly. And that one time was because he hadn't listened to himself.

"I was forward deployed with the 101st Airborne," she finally offered. "I was embedded with the ground teams to frisk and question women. Every now and then, they weren't women beneath the robes but men in hiding. If they were dressed to hide, we knew they were Taliban, Al Qaeda, or worse. They would also be heavily armed. It was close a couple of times, but I was always faster than they were."

"You were good back there. Damn good," Richie remarked a few miles later.

And Melissa felt good. Normally a kill gave her the shakes, but this time it hadn't. The man had been the worst sort. He'd rubbed his erection against Melissa's ass the moment he'd grabbed her, and his hand had been headed south into her pants even as they stood there in front of everyone. Drug runner, street thug, and rapist.

And then he'd made to grab Carla.

Melissa would put up with some things, but he didn't get to do that to Carla. Taking him out had been a relief, not a strain. What was it about Carla that commanded such instant loyalty? It wasn't just her who felt that way; the whole team had surged a step forward in the moment before Melissa had pulled the trigger. And it wasn't about protecting "the female" either. If anything, they were scared of the Wild Woman at times...except for the unflappable Mister Kyle.

Kyle had offered her the barest nod in support of her action. His hand signals had the team shifting and ready for imminent combat. Melissa had earned respect for her skills with various teams in the past but had never truly belonged. Probably due to the fact that she was embedded much farther forward than most women. In the heart of the crisis, Kyle had indicated she was on a roll and to go with it.

She still didn't belong here, but she also was no longer ready to send a "Get me out of here!" signal up the chain of command. With the exception of Chad. The two of them were going to have to have it out and real soon now...just not on a plane filled with drugs and two gunsels.

Over the next hours of the flight she and Richie spooked themselves half a dozen times on ships. Who knew the Gulf was such a busy place? Whether they were fishermen, container ships, or Navy frigates, they didn't hang around to ask.

Oddly, the most useful tool was a radar detector for cars that Richie had mounted on top of the dash. It would start to complain and chirp at even the least refracted bits of signal from a ship's radar. Mounted on a swivel base with aluminum foil to either side, they could twist it back and forth to determine the direction of the radar's source and then turn the other way.

"Pretty slick, Richie."

"Thanks."

And she could feel herself falling back into a

comfortable place with Richie. Except with him, a comfortable place was also very uncomfortable.

The sex, what there'd been of it, had been fantastic. If she ever needed someone to think something through, it was Richie. She just wished there had been more opportunity to find out exactly what he had thought up.

The guy was decent and handsome and smart.

And he was also Delta, not just in her unit but on her team. That last fact was also placing immense strain on an operation that had apparently been functioning just fine. She didn't know how many teams from The Unit were operating in South America, but Colonel Gibson had called this the top team, and only six months out of OTC themselves. They'd been operating at an amazing level prior to her arrival.

Having a relationship with Richie was wrong on so many levels even aside from the military code.

This was a situation right out of *The American President*. The moment when the political activist describes the possibility of a relationship with the President as, "This has catastrophe written all over it."

The heroine's sister had responded with pretty much the list of positives that had just rolled through Melissa's head—except for the Delta part—and asked if maybe the heroine was overreacting. But there was something about the President being a better-than-average dancer.

"Do you dance?"

"Three left feet," Richie replied.

"Well, that's a relief at least."

When Richie asked why, she ignored him and paid attention to the flight.

And she was going to stop trying to understand her life by using movie metaphors someday real soon now.

—~~~—

It was shortly past two a.m. when they found the fuel barge easily enough, floating off Cozumel in a light swell. Richie landed the *Tin Goose* and taxied up to the craft. After seven hours aloft, he wanted to get out and stretch his legs, but seeing the demeanor of the two men aboard the barge, he didn't think that was such a good idea. He decided to stay right at the controls just in case.

The two guards who had flown with them squatted in the cargo bay door with their rifles at the ready. The rest of the Delta team was also poised on high alert.

"Lesson number one," he whispered to Melissa over the headset intercom, "don't trust anyone in this business." They each pulled aside one earmuff so that they could hear what else was going on around them but could still hear each other easily.

"Good advice. But since we're in the business now, what does that mean about you?"

"Me?" Richie placed a hand on his chest in shock. "Oh, I'm trustworthy."

"But you just said—" and then she cut herself off and groaned.

"Also, everything I say is a lie."

"I get it. I get it."

Richie bit down on his tongue. He was always doing that—driving a joke's point home past reason.

"What's lesson number two?"

"Uh…" Richie scrambled for something funny but wasn't hitting on anything. "Number two is…trust *you* no matter what." It sounded overblown, but it just sort of came out that way.

Lit only by the refueling work lights on the barge filtering in through the square windows of the passenger cabin, she turned in slow motion to inspect him.

"I know, weird isn't it? Now that I've said it out loud, I think that it's a good rule."

"You don't know me, Richie."

"I know plenty."

"Like what?"

"Like you survived Delta Selection and OTC. That the silent Colonel who didn't say jack to me but scared Kyle no end passed you through to our team. We've been doing well, very well. That means that he saw you adding something we could be doing even better. That counts."

"I guess."

"And the fact that I couldn't ever want to be with anyone else means I'd better trust you."

"About that."

Richie managed to keep his mouth shut and wait. It was hard. For something to do, he checked the fuel gauges. They were taking forever to fill the tanks. They must have the slowest pumps on the planet.

"We had sex just twice—"

"Barely. I recall promising you hours of attention. And we keep being rudely interrupted."

"And I recall you punching out your friend in my defense."

He had, hadn't he? Though *punching out* was a bit of an exaggeration based on Chad's nonreaction when Richie's fist had bounced off Chad's chin.

"I didn't ask for that."

"Didn't have to."

"That's not the point…"

Richie's attention drifted before Melissa completed the thought. The point was that a hand-cranked pump would fill their tanks faster.

Richie heard her ask if he was listening, which he wasn't.

He twisted in his seat to look back into the main cabin. He snapped his fingers to get Duane's attention and then raised a hand to his forehead as if shading it from the sun to look somewhere and pumped his fist for hurry.

The Delta team flooded out the door past the two guards they'd picked up in the heart of the Orinoco.

Melissa had caught the signal as well and yanked out her sidearm. She was on the side away from the barge, so she turned to cover the two drug runners in the rear.

Richie cracked open his pilot-side door and looked down at the barge.

There'd been two workers visible at the pumps. Now there were four men lying facedown and a stack of weapons with Kyle and Carla over them.

"Crank that pump up," Richie called out, and Duane slammed the controls onto high.

Chad had once again popped open the top hatch on the cabin for the best view. "Vessel, running fast. About three miles out. Farside of the barge, right where we couldn't see because of the work lights they were shining at us."

"Damn. If they have anything more serious than a BB gun, we don't have time to get clear."

"On it," Kyle shouted. "Get your engines cranking anyway."

Richie spun back to the plane's controls. Melissa was still sighting her weapon down the length of the cabin at the two drug runners.

"Anything from them?"

"No. If I'm reading them right, they're weren't expecting a welcoming party either."

"Okay, keep an eye, but start reading me the hot engine restart checklist." It was certainly the last time he would ever fully shut them down while on a mission.

"While we're still fueling?"

"Go figure." He eyed the fuel gauges, which were now moving much more rapidly. But a thousand gallons didn't flow in an instant.

She read and he worked the boost pumps and battery switches. And tried not to think about the boat that was approaching.

If it was the U.S. Coast Guard, it would blow their carefully prepared cover with the drug-runner guards.

"They just dowsed their lights," Chad called out. "Estimate arrival in two minutes."

"I'm guessing they aren't the Coast Guard," Melissa remarked between instructions of "Bus Tie Switch Normal" and "Flap Handle Up."

Richie pulled the flap handle into the up position, "Nope! So they're bad guys."

"Have I mentioned—Fuel Levers Off—how much I love my new job?" Melissa's tone was drier than a Fort Bragg rifle range.

"It does have its moments."

He heard a splash and glanced out the window over

his shoulder. A couple of large boards had been tossed over the side.

"*Nadar! Rápido!*" Kyle shouted out.

"*Tiburones!*" was the panicked reply.

Richie wouldn't want to go swimming among the sharks either, but since they were only a few kilometers off a major Caribbean tourist beach, he expected it wasn't likely a problem.

Kyle unslung his rifle and pointed it at the complaining man's head. He and his three companions went over the side.

"What are our buddies doing?" Richie asked as he turned back to watch the engine temperatures climb and stabilize.

"In the doorway. Guns ready but aimed high. Still on our side for the moment."

"One minute." Kyle had walked along the barge and shouted across at Richie's door, barely clear of the propeller spinning to life. "How's the fuel?"

"Don't ask. Keep pumping."

"You get another thirty seconds, maybe forty. When I shout, you lay down the hammer," and Kyle was gone.

"Should we tell him that the Twin Otter doesn't have a hammer?" Melissa's tone was wry. A turboshaft engine didn't simply engage. And the large propellers took time to spin up and more time to bite the air.

"No, let's not spoil his fun."

"Wonder what he has cooked up."

Richie appreciated Melissa's perfectly calm tone. She was definitely Delta down to the core. He wanted to turn and see what the rest of the team was up to, but he didn't have time to dare; he'd simply trust that the rest of the team was on it. At the moment his job was to get through the next two minutes of the start-up list in under thirty seconds.

"Skip that. Next," he started saying as Melissa read instructions first from the After-Start Checks then the Run-up Checks.

In moments, she too was editing the list as she went.

Somewhere in the blur, there was a loud rattle of fuel hoses being unlocked and a hand double-slapped on the plane's hull hard enough for the sound to echo in the cockpit.

Richie advanced the throttles before he even heard the shout to go and then prayed that they hadn't missed anything critical.

A glance showed Duane tossing the dual hoses back onto the barge; it might have been a trick of the light but the hoses appeared to still be pumping liquid fountains of Jet A fuel. Duane jumped off the barge and onto one of the aircraft's pontoon floats as the plane started moving. Kyle and Carla must already be aboard; he certainly hoped so.

The *Tin Goose* moved fitfully across the waves as he unfeathered the props and the engines hesitated under the sudden load change, a deepening of their whining pitch.

Then, as Kyle's shouts became more urgent, Richie called for Melissa to douse all of the interior cabin lights; only the instrument panel lights remained on. The exterior running lights had been switched off before they had even left the Orinoco. They'd landed in Cozumel with only the briefest flash of landing lights so that he could see the waves, but he wanted to be invisible.

The props bit into the wind and dragged the plane forward and away from the barge, but the first hundred feet went by at an agonizingly slow pace.

"We'll take off low, and then bank hard to lose them."

"If we get off the water," Melissa offered, again in that dry tone that he couldn't tell whether was fun or serious, at least not without seeing her face.

"I'm always an optimist," Richie declared as he begged the plane for more speed. At max throttle they were a full thirty seconds from stand-still to flight, thirty-five with a full fuel load. He considered trying to zigzag while still on the surface, but that would only waste speed and delay their takeoff. Besides, he needed to stay in the furrow between the waves to get safely airborne; at a meter high these waves were big enough that he wasn't sure if he could take off across them.

"Not a lot of ways to hide sixty feet of airplane in the open," Melissa's tone wasn't as calm as a moment before.

"Mind reader." Takeoff should be possible around sixty knots, roughly seventy miles an hour.

"Forty," Melissa read off. "Forty-five."

Richie glanced at the gauges—still a hundred gallons from full. But that wasn't the worry any longer. Now he was worried about someone firing an incendiary round into the nine hundred gallons they had managed to load into their belly tanks.

"Fifty."

Kyle moved up between the seats and clapped Richie on the shoulder.

"How are we doing up here?"

"Just peachy," Melissa answered for him. "Fifty-five."

The *Tin Goose* was starting to skip on the waves.

"Duane wants you to start out with a bank to the right and then straight out," Kyle shouted loud enough to be easily heard through Richie's headphones. "Climb hard."

"Sixty," Melissa called out then answered Kyle. "But that will just make us more of a target."

"Sure will," Kyle answered pleasantly. "But there will be advantages."

Richie rode it up until she called, "Sixty-five," then popped the wheel to break the last of the surface tension. With the floats finally free of the water, even if only by inches, they gained speed rapidly. If he'd guessed correctly what was going on, Kyle was only half-right.

Richie banked briefly to the right then flew straight out, but went for speed rather than altitude.

"Hang on!" someone shouted and the night sky lit up like a searchlight. The cabin was flooded daylight bright. Momentarily dazzled, he had to trust to simply not moving the controls even though his instincts were telling him they were rolling to the right. It was a common problem among pilots. When you couldn't see, your inner ear insisted that being aloft in a flying tin can was just wrong and it would do its best to correct. A lot of early pilot training was on trusting your instruments over your instincts.

The problem was that at the moment he couldn't see the instruments or the horizon due to the blinding flash and his instincts were screaming in panic.

Then the shock wave slammed into them.

"Shock wave!" Melissa shouted as stall alarms rang out.

The barge's explosion behind them was now moving the air forward faster than they were flying and the wings lost all lift.

"Lights," he shouted as he struggled to maintain flight. It didn't matter who saw them now.

"Melissa—" he cried out just as she hit the landing lights.

The waves were less than five feet below them and the plane was tipped thirty degrees to the left. He had overcompensated on not overcompensating.

He wrenched the wings level, skipped off the top of a wave with a spine-jarring slam, two waves, three…and he was back aloft.

Speed had been the right choice over altitude—if he'd climbed and been moving slowly when the shock wave hit, they'd have tumbled out of the sky and they'd all be dying in the ocean right now.

"Well." Melissa blew out a breath. "That was fun. What's next?"

Kyle barked out a laugh.

Richie saw him slap her on the shoulder. "Good job, you two. Damn good. Glad to have you aboard."

Melissa killed the big landing lights.

Richie turned the plane so that they could see the barge.

A fire still roared aloft from the barge like a warning beacon. Additional explosions rocked the craft as it breached more fuel drums.

And now Richie could see why Duane had said to bank right at takeoff. A large Zodiac had passed close alongside the stern of the barge, looking to circle it and follow the line of the plane's takeoff. Duane had rigged the explosion so that the initial blast had shot out sideways and ripped right through the passing Zodiac. If they had circled around the bow of the barge, the Zodiac could have followed and been merely shaken.

"Any guesses who they were?" Past tense was the proper one in this case.

"The four boys swimming for Cozumel"—Kyle pointed toward the darkened island—"might have said something about Sinaloa still being mad at the Venezuelans."

"Imagine that. Because of our little drug war?" Starting that war had still been one of the coolest things Richie had ever done.

"How's our fuel?"

"Let's see. We're ten minutes' flight to the delivery point. If the delivery goes as smoothly as the refueling did…"

Melissa burst out laughing, a bright, merry sound that he'd never get tired of. He hadn't meant to be funny, but he supposed it was. He'd just been thinking that their use of fuel both to find and land at the barge had been very efficient.

Richie looked at the gauges and ran some rough calculations in his head and then tried to think of how to make Melissa laugh again.

"Well." He turned to Kyle and tried for his own best Humphrey Bogart voice. "I think it would be good if Ilsa here started praying for tailwinds."

Richie just kept making her laugh. It was one of the things Melissa liked best about him. Somewhere over the last five years, she'd forgotten what laughing felt like. Her brother's direct connection to her funny bone was another piece that had been cut out of her without her even noticing—until Sergeant Richie Goldman had found a way to tickle it.

Up out of Cozumel, it seemed but moments before they were sidling up to a beach a handful of miles north of Cancún in the heart of Yum Balam Reserve. A wide sandy beach backed by the pitch black of a towering palm jungle.

"You know what this reminds me of?"

"Yeah," Richie answered pleasantly but without quite the fervor she'd expected. At night it could easily have been Cat Island in the Bahamas. With a little perspective, the image of their arrest struck her as fairly amusing. Apparently not Richie.

Melissa remembered how Richie's hand had felt as it had traced ever so lightly between her bare breasts…the moment before they were arrested. She'd have preferred a little more enthusiasm on his part as she was having troubles with her emotions at the moment. Too little time for tenderness while afloat in the Bahamas. Interrupted need in the Maracaibo hotel. Shutting each other out for three days because Richie was dumb enough to listen to Chad.

Okay, maybe she could have not reacted by totally shutting him out too. Bad decision.

Cat Island had been a good memory. If she could choose a reset to any point in whatever this was between them, that would be it.

"You promised me things at that resort." She tried to make it funny, but it still didn't come out right. She ran down the pre-landing checklist, almost none of which could be applied. No caution lights, control tower briefings, landing lights, or even a "fasten seat belt" sign. She couldn't think how to fix this. There was nothing for her to say.

Richie twisted them back and forth as he descended slowly. They were only fifty feet up according to the altimeter. The light of the moon off the waves looked about right for fifty feet. The descent was so slow it was almost painful.

"I know that I owe you," he spoke carefully. "I'll have to fix that."

"I was just teasing you."

"Oh. I missed that."

This time she caught the tension in his voice. Richie was so unflappable that all of her internal alarms finally sounded off. "What?"

"Sandbars," he muttered just as the floats kissed the waves with a bright hiss.

She swallowed hard and strained forward against her harness to see if she could see anything other than the dark water and moonlight reflected off low waves. She hadn't thought about sandbars—there hadn't been any near Clearwater, at least not that Vito Corello had used for training. If they caught a sandbar at night along this unknown shore while moving at landing speed, the plane would stop, nose over, and they would be in a one-plane accident at seventy miles an hour. She and Richie wore full harnesses, but the rest of the team only had lap belts. A hard crash would not end well for any of them.

And she'd just been a self-centered bitch, whining because Richie wasn't delivering on his sexual promises? Dumb! Maybe she and Carla were more alike than she'd considered—a very uncomfortable thought. Even if she was starting to like Carla, it didn't mean that she wanted to be like the Wild Woman.

Her attempt to whisper an apology didn't make it past the choke point in her throat until they'd slid down to taxiing speed.

"This doesn't make any sense." Richie was also leaning forward to stare out the windshield, but he was looking toward the beach.

"Us?" No. The mission. *Stay focused, girl.*

"This delivery. A hundred kilos when we can carry a thousand."

"Another test?"

"Maybe."

Melissa thought about it and decided that no matter what Richie might think of his instincts about people, he was Delta. Forcing herself to look away from the beach and her own attempts to see sandbars in the dark, she twisted to face Carla, who sat in the front-most seat of the passenger cabin. Melissa held out her right hand as if she held a pistol and then slapped at her right wrist with her left hand—the signal for "enemy."

Richie eyed the beach as he taxied fifty feet offshore. Why was this giving him such an itch? Far worse than the barge.

He wasn't afraid of the U.S. authorities. If it was them, they would try to make an arrest, which would then be up to Fred Smith to straighten out. If it was the Mexican Federales, they were more inclined to shoot first and ask later, but his radar detector hadn't picked up anything during their approach except for the Cancún airport.

He wasn't worried about their safety…particularly— not any more than was normal for a Delta mission.

Richie was worried about…

He raised a fist for the team in the cabin to see and held it there, signaling "freeze."

Melissa's signal for "enemy" had been correct, but he was guessing that it wasn't their enemy.

There were two separate blinks of flashlights from under the verge of the trees, showing him where to beach—about two hundred meters apart along the shore. One was in the same pattern used by the drug runners along the Orinoco. The second one wasn't.

Richie tried not to smile as he turned the *Tin Goose* and idled through the light waves toward the first set of lights.

Rather than beaching the plane as he'd originally planned, he turned parallel to the shore, close enough that the water was probably less than two feet deep. The waves were perhaps a foot high, so they started making a lazy side-to-side roll that would make everyone seasick soon. But he wasn't going to be here that long.

With the engines still running but the props feathered, he held his fist out with his forearm vertical and double-pumped for "hurry!"

It went down exactly as he'd anticipated.

Men rushed down the sand and into the shallow water as someone threw open the rear hatch on the plane. Six of them moving in a pack, rifles at the ready. A plastic five-gallon bucket was tossed in and moments later the two boxes of cocaine were handed out. They'd now been paid. And if the hundred thousand that Analie Sala had promised was the standard one-tenth share for their leg, there'd be a million dollars U.S. in that bucket.

The drugs would quintuple in price as they made their journey from Cancún, across the U.S. border, and finally into the cities, but their leg of the smuggling operation was complete and paid for.

The group that had flashed the correct signal was less than five steps back toward the beach when the firefight began.

Richie had never let the plane come to a true stop nor slid the engines fully to idle.

"Props now," he shouted at Melissa and he reached up to the overhead power levers and eased them back up as fast as the engines would take it. Their hands brushed on the side-by-side controls, almost as if they were holding hands. A heady feeling considering what was going on up and down the beach.

—◦◦◦—

Melissa had to admire how cool and steady Richie was being as mayhem lit up the night sky.

She tried to look everywhere at once while Richie was getting them the hell away from it all.

The second group—the ones with the wrong signal from two hundred meters down the beach—were firing wildly at the men who'd taken delivery of the drugs. Blinding muzzle flashes of heavy automatic fire must be heaving a lot of lead into the air. There were one or two reverberating *Thunks!* that sounded like they'd hit the *Tin Goose's* wings.

Like most thugs, and most soldiers for that matter,

there was a lot of shooting but less care for accurate aiming. It was one of the unique things about Delta, making every single shot count, even in combat situations. Even the general ranks of the U.S. Army fired over two hundred thousand rounds per kill in Afghanistan. Delta averaged under five, and three of those were planned on every one.

In the rear cabin, the two guards from the Orinoco were crouched in the rear hatchway and now spraying fire at the ones racing down the beach to steal the delivery.

One way or another, the drugs were going to go to market.

"Richie?" He'd known that. So why had he delivered the—

"Watch down the beach. If I'm right—"

And she saw it. The dim flash of a heavily suppressed single shot. And a second later, one of the two men carrying the drugs ashore dropped into the surf. A moment later, the one carrying the other box was down. Others in the group that had taken the delivery were too busy returning fire up the beach at the gang that was trying to hijack the drugs to notice. Then one of the intended recipients did and plunged back into the surf.

Each person who touched the drugs elicited another shot from the sniper down the beach. Far down the beach. This wasn't the cover man for one of the two teams; this was a trained pro, dug in a kilometer away.

"One of Fred's people?"

"What?" Richie had been wholly focused on getting them out of there. They were most of the way up to flight speed. "Was I right?"

He was. He'd anticipated exactly how it would go down,

readjusting the plan they'd discussed the moment he'd seen the second flashing signal. Maybe even before that.

It was only now that Melissa understood what had happened.

Richie had signaled Fred Smith of their expected time and place of delivery. Fred had filtered that information out to a rival gang who'd arrived to make a grab for the drugs. In the ensuing firefight, no one would notice that a trained American sniper would be the one who won final possession of the shipment. The Delta team had completed their assignment, delivering under harrowing conditions with the drug runners they had onboard as eyewitnesses.

The gunsels!

Melissa twisted around again and saw that the two gunsels were still firing toward the beach from the rear cargo hatch.

"Carla!" Melissa shouted to get her teammate's attention at the far end of the cabin. Then she drew a three-sided box in the air for "Door" and pumped out a "Hurry." They couldn't take off safely with the cargo doors open.

By the time they were skipping off the wave tops, Melissa felt the heavy slam of the closing doors. Then they were up and headed back out to sea.

The beach was on Melissa's side.

The few still standing from the group that had taken receipt of the shipment were retreating up the beach. By their bright muzzle flashes, she could see that none of them were carrying heavy boxes of drugs.

The second group, the ones who were trying to hijack the drugs, were scattered and running themselves.

It was hard to tell, but she thought she saw a shadow from the first group crossing the moonlit sands back toward the drugs. A bright flash down the beach and a second and a half later—the time it would take a 7.62mm sniper round to cross the kilometer-long distance—the shadow collapsed to the beach.

Yep, the drugs were still in the surf. And Fred's sniper would make sure they stayed there.

"Neat solution," Melissa observed once they were well clear.

"Rather pleased with it myself," Richie said lazily as if it was all in a day's work.

"But what do I tell Ms. Sala?" All they'd done was intercepted an infinitesimal percentage of the drug trade. A hundred kilos would never be missed except by the gang that had paid a million dollars for it.

"Don't worry about Analie Sala."

Melissa could hear that Richie already had it figured out. She raced to get there herself before he spoke again.

"If the delivery never reached the next tier of distributors, that's not our—"

"Because," she cut Richie off, "we've already been paid in full, as has Ms. Sala." The Venezuelan cartel didn't care if the drugs reached America; they only cared that they were paid. "Moore Aviation is about to be very popular with their Venezuelan contacts."

"It is."

"Now, Richie Goldman, you have something else to worry about."

"Oh?" And he did sound a little worried, because he clearly couldn't think of what it might be. She enjoyed outsmarting his genius with something so simple.

Melissa watched the darkness out the broad windshield. No longer carrying any contraband and finally heading south, they flew at a comfortable five hundred feet above the waves. She'd never flown that low in her life until last week, and now it felt like a luxuriously safe altitude.

"What?" Richie was clearly churning trying to come up with something that he'd missed in all of his careful planning.

She left him to stew awhile longer. Melissa let her mind wander. Richie was handsome, smart, and promised to be a fantastic lover. Watching him fly and solve the problems of the mission on the go had been electrifying.

But there was a moment that had been more powerful than almost anything that had happened the whole week. More powerful than him punching out that asshole Chad.

It was back in the Orinoco. She'd stepped way over the line of reasonable risk when she'd gunned down that thug. There had been an awful moment when she was certain she had just gotten the entire team killed. She imagined a top-secret report titled, "Recent OTC grad gets entire team eliminated in less than seven days."

The tension had ridden on a cusp, and then Richie had made the smallest sound, flipping the safety on his rifle into the firing position. It had said clearly, "I will die to defend this woman."

That tiny act had tipped the balance of the entire dynamic between The Unit's team and the drug smugglers. But that wasn't what had ultimately mattered to her.

It was the statement he'd made that had been so special.

Melissa knew it was stupid, insane, and totally ridiculous. She'd known Richie for one week. One week today as a matter of fact. The sun was just breaking the horizon over Cuba and they'd be arriving in Maracaibo at almost the same moment she had seven days ago.

He was a geek, the ultimate tech, and a warrior on her own team.

And as dumb as it was, her frozen heart hadn't merely thawed in his presence; it had beat as if it had never been frozen in the first place.

She wanted to bury her face in her hands. She wanted to get out of the plane and dance—if they weren't in flight. She wanted...

"Oh," Richie finally put the pieces together. "My promise. Trust me, I'll be taking care of that just as soon as we can find more than a dozen minutes of quiet."

And she knew he would because not living up to his promises simply wouldn't compute for Richie—his integrity reigned absolute.

Melissa had known for a hard and cold fact that it would never happen to her. But it had. She'd gone and fallen in love. And with Unit operator Richie Goldman. That was something she'd have to get over real soon.

Chapter 14

No CUSTOMS OFFICIAL MET THEM AS THEY PULLED UP
to the Maracaibo hangar, running mostly on fumes. He
was probably happily counting a few-hundred-dollar
payoff in some corner office.

What did await them was Analie Sala and two more
gunmen. She was all in black despite the midmorning
heat that was already cooking Richie's brain. He'd only
been awake for…thirty hours. And flying for the last
dozen of it.

The team deplaned very carefully. Richie and Melissa
held back at the cockpit doors. They wouldn't have good
flexibility if gunfire came their way, but they momentarily commanded the high ground. Looking down at the
others, Richie didn't want to give that up.

Ms. Sala stood calmly as the two teams of four
gunmen each faced off. The differences were very
distinct. The drug runners were edgy, hands shifting
on weapons, feet never in optimal position as they
constantly shifted. In contrast, each Delta operator
was dead calm, unmoving, up on their toes, and ready
to leap into action. It wouldn't even be necessary to
focus on faces or attire to know who to target if the
need arose; their body language was target enough to a
Delta-honed eye.

It didn't come to that. Ms. Sala waved for one of the
men to open the bucket. When it was opened, she pulled

out ten neat stacks of bills and handed them to Carla, then signaled for the bucket to be closed.

A low rumble in the distance drew Richie's attention to the head of the alleyway between the long row of rusting hangars. A fuel truck lumbered its way toward them. No one was hiding their rifles or sidearms. Carla had turned to slip the money into a small backpack so that it was out of sight.

No one spoke while the plane was fueled. No one moved, except to stay out of the way of the fuel truck operator…who was very careful not to look at any of them. He was pumping much faster than those Sinaloa members on the barge off Cozumel.

Richie signaled Melissa and they eased down, out of the front doors, to join the group after the fuel truck finished and was backing up the length of the alleyway.

"I hear there were problems." Ms. Sala was the first to finally break the silence.

"A few." Melissa stepped forward easily and Richie shifted into a support position that offered a clear range of fire. "Nothing we couldn't manage."

The two women squared off: the slim, dark professional and the tall, white-blond wonder. By sheer contrast, Analie Sala's sleek build and immaculate grooming should have made Melissa look large or overblown, but it didn't. Melissa instead stood like a shining beacon of health and beauty and made the Mexican expediter look diminished. Richie tried to cast them, but it wasn't working. Emma Frost versus Mystique from the *X-Men* didn't work. Tasha Yar versus B'Elanna Torres, if he was willing to mix *Star Trek* series, didn't cut it either. Even going to Kim Basinger as *Batman's*

Vicki Vale versus Halle Berry's Catwoman didn't get him there.

Melissa was…too vibrantly alive.

He was left to wonder at that while the two women silently assessed one another. It took Richie a bit before it clicked.

"You're the one who tipped off Sinaloa about the fueling barge." He pointed an accusing finger at Analie Sala.

"Of course," Melissa agreed smoothly as the others startled. "That much made perfect sense. If we couldn't handle them, you would have been paid through back channels anyway and we'd be *lost at sea*."

Ms. Sala nodded silently.

Richie noticed the reaction of the two guards who had also flown with them. They didn't like the idea that they'd been deemed expendable. *It's the world you chose, guys,* Richie thought at them.

"Did you set us up on the beach as well?" Richie decided to play dumb to keep the suspicions away from the Delta team.

"No," Ms. Sala said slowly. Then she turned to the two men who'd flown with them. "Tell me."

The men spilled out their account. It was scattered and included only about a quarter of what had actually happened—though they did reasonably well for untrained observers. Delta training taught you to see more than anyone else and process it quickly and logically enough to eradicate aggressors before they tried to do the same to you. What her two men delivered to Ms. Sala was confused and included not one word about the sniper operating from farther down the beach.

"Shot our plane too," Richie remembered.

"Show me."

It took a minute, but they found three holes, two in the wing and a long crease close above Melissa's window. Had the shot been a foot lower, an infinitesimal amount on a wild shot at a distance, it would have punched the windshield and caught Melissa square in the face.

Richie's gut twisted. He'd taxied the plane to keep Melissa out of the line of fire. Instead he was the one who'd turned her into harm's way. *Lesson here, Richie: The woman can take care of herself.* And she was doing a fine job of it at the moment. She was doing a good job of protecting them all at the moment.

"Richie?" Kyle called over.

"Huh? What?"

"Could you and Chad check where those bullets went? Make sure we didn't get anything structural."

"Roger that."

Then Kyle stepped up to the power position in close support of Melissa, and Carla and Duane took the opportunity to drop back a defensive step. Richie knew if Melissa was safe anywhere, it was beside Kyle.

They went inside the hangar together and pulled out a ladder so that they could get up to the wing.

"That is one cool lady," Chad said as he scrabbled around in the toolbox.

"Yeah, she's amazing." Richie was pleased that Chad was finally warming up to Melissa. "See. She's okay despite what you—"

"I was talking about Ms. Dark, Sleek, and Sexy Analie Sala. Woman's name is even fun to say."

"You weren't planning to…"

"Depends on whether opportunity presents itself.

And me, I'm a big fan of creating opportunity." Then Chad's voice darkened. "I still don't trust your bitch."

Richie's arm was back before he even knew it, and Chad had his hands up and was backpedaling.

"Whoa there, little brother. Man, she's got you in a twist."

Too far away for a punch, Richie simply dove at him.

There was a horrendous crash from inside the hangar. It sounded like their entire spare parts rack had just been dumped onto the concrete. The noise continued with huge crashes and bangs that made Melissa wince and tuck up her shoulders against the noise.

Analie was safely in her air-conditioned SUV and the four thugs were gone with her. They were only about halfway up the hangar alley, so she tried to look casual as she hurried into the hangar. It took her sun-blasted eyes a moment to adjust to the shadowed darkness. The others were piling in behind her as they hit the same problem.

It took her almost as long again to make sense of the scene as it did for her eyes to adjust. Richie and Chad were grappling on the floor, and Richie was playing for keeps. It was all Chad could do to defend himself, as it was clear he didn't want to hurt Richie.

Richie was a formidable fighter when he was roused. Whatever had set him off had been enough that Chad could barely manage a defensive battle.

Even as she watched, Richie heaved Chad, who was twice his size, into the tool chest, knocking it to the floor with a massive crash that sent wrenches and screwdrivers scattering in every direction. Richie the true warrior was as awe-inspiring a fighter as he'd been a lover.

Duane and Kyle tried wading in and were almost kneecapped by a viciously swung hammer.

Melissa pulled out her sidearm. She considered shooting Chad, but instead aimed for the big wooden post in the corner of the hangar.

The crash and boom of the big Colt M1911 shattered the air and reverberated off the steel roof and walls.

Duane and Kyle did dive-and-rolls coming up with their sidearms aimed at her chest.

Chad and Richie froze in place, Richie with a solid grip on one of Chad's ears and Chad in midcurse as he tried to find a way to break Richie's hold but still protect himself from Richie's next blow. For two men who could kill with a single strike, they looked practically comical in the abruptly freeze-frame positions.

Carla stood quietly beside Melissa with her arms crossed.

She was the first to break the silence with, "Are you boys done?"

Chad twisted his head enough to look at Melissa despite Richie's firm hold on his ear.

"Bitch!" His voice was low and nasty.

Melissa decided shooting him would have been the right choice, but she'd already holstered her sidearm and Kyle and Duane hadn't yet, so she left well enough alone.

And that's when Richie's fist caught the point of Chad's chin and sent him tumbling into the pile of rusted-out car parts that lined the back of the hangar.

A part of Melissa wanted to shout, "One for the home team." But most of her wanted to go back to OTC graduation and be assigned to join Mutt and Jeff on the Arabian Peninsula.

———

Richie saw Carla coming his way and knew he was in the shitter. But all she did was hold out a hand as an offer to help him get back to his feet.

She wasn't gentle as she grabbed his hand, which was throbbing from hitting Chad, crunching down on his fingers hard as she helped him up. Richie managed not to cry out, though Carla was Delta strong and proving it.

Then she stepped over an interlaced pile of pry bars and chisels and grabbed Chad by the ear. Chad cried out, "Ow! Ow! Ow!"—which satisfied Richie no end while he massaged his bruised and now battered fingers—as she guided him to his feet. As soon as she let go, Chad clamped a protective hand over his ear and hissed in pain. Richie wished he'd ripped the damn thing off when he'd had the chance. It would serve him right.

"Who's going to start?"

Richie ignored Carla and glared at Chad. "You try calling Melissa a bitch or whore again, and I'll take you down permanently, Chad. And don't think Q the nerd can't do it. I went through the same fucking training you did." Richie knew he'd never been so goddamn angry in his life. It was a tidal surge inside him that made him wish he'd clawed Chad's eyes out.

Chad gave him the evil eye in return. He was bleeding from a half dozen cuts where they'd slammed each other into anything they could find. Blood was dribbling out of his blond hair, coloring it dark red before it ran down his temple.

"What? No scoff this time? No rubbing your chin and calling it a love tap?" Richie spit out the words and was surprised when he spit some blood along with it. When had that happened? He wasn't feeling anything. *Adrenal surge,* some part of his training informed him. In a full-on adrenaline high he could lose a leg and not feel it. He glanced down but saw that he had two legs and both were still attached. He rubbed his hand along his own jaw but still felt nothing except for a couple of teeth that were wobbly.

"Because of name-calling, Richie?" Carla looked up at him. "Really?"

She shared a look with Melissa that Richie couldn't catch before turning to Chad.

"Care to explain?"

Chad just glowered at her.

Kyle stepped up behind Carla and rested his hands on her shoulders, anchoring her in place.

"Well, Chad," he said in that commanding voice— which at the moment made Richie want to turn on him as well, "we've heard Richie's complaint, and we've also heard him swear for perhaps the first time in his life. Now you either explain yourself or you and I are going to have some issues."

Melissa wasn't sure if she'd ever truly understood Kyle's role here until that moment. His adjustments had always been minor, his comments soft-spoken. Now he stood inside the dim hangar and all authority centered on him. He was judge, jury, and executioner, and there was no question about his ability to fulfill all three roles to their limit—he didn't wield power; he was power.

Watching him stand and wait out Chad's sullen silence, she also finally understood what there was between Kyle and Carla. And she could see that it was deep. She wanted that. All of a sudden, she wanted it badly.

When she couldn't stand it any longer, Melissa finally broke Chad's sullen silence. "He's had it in for me since day one."

Kyle nodded. "We're all aware of that. He—"

"She went right after Richie!" Chad shouted, then spit out a mouthful of blood that splatted audibly on the concrete before continuing. "You saw it. She went right for him from that first moment."

"And I went for her," Richie said evenly.

Melissa was impressed. Richie still looked like the magnificent—if a little battered—fighter, yet he was speaking calmly. Was the nerd integrating with his inner warrior?

"No, Little Brother. You don't get it. I know her type. Hell, how do you think I get the women I do? She was just looking for the easiest way *in* on our team and saw you with your jaw dropped down, easy pickings."

Richie kicked aside some of the metal scrap scattered across the hangar floor, which hurt Melissa's ears because it was so loud in the strained-to-the-limit tension. He moved up until he was right in Chad's face.

"And I went for her," Richie repeated.

"She's just using you, bro. You're just too naive to see it."

Richie's fist went back all over again, but Duane caught it.

She hadn't noticed Duane moving into position, his silence extending beyond merely not speaking. But he was right where he was most needed. And Duane was at least as strong as Chad; Richie's fist might as well have been trapped in concrete.

Chad didn't take advantage of it as Melissa expected.

Instead he hung his head and rubbed his jaw as if it hurt like hell. Then he mumbled, "Someone had to look out for you."

"Say what?"

Carla might not have heard it, but Melissa had, and it rooted her to the concrete as surely as Duane's grasp had trapped Richie's fist. No one had ever needed to "look out" for her since her brother. She'd never actually needed him to either; she'd always been the driven one in their family, but he'd liked saying it and she'd let him. Chad didn't get such a pass.

Melissa stepped around Kyle and Carla until she was right at the edge of Chad's personal space, close enough to be an easy target, far enough away that she'd have time to react if he attacked.

"You've given me all this shit to *protect* Richie?"

Chad nodded and then winced as if his head was really hurting. Wouldn't surprise her; Richie's punch had landed square and true.

"Did you ever think that just maybe Richie could protect himself?"

Chad rubbed his ear thoughtfully. "Think I found that out. Doesn't mean he was ready for your act. I'm just trying to protect the little shit."

Melissa stared into Chad's bright blue eyes for the longest time, until she became aware of her own reflection there. Chad hadn't been pissed because of his failure to sweep her off her feet. He'd been doing what he thought was right to protect his teammate.

Then she heard Kyle grunt out an acknowledgment.

Melissa turned to him. "What?"

He side-glanced at Carla and then looked away quickly before his wife noticed. "Uh, Chad can be very demonstrative when his sense of loyalty is offended." He swallowed hard as if at the memory of someone choking him. There was a story there that Melissa would bet Carla didn't know, and would never find out.

Chad might be dangerous, but he was also loyal—the self-proclaimed guardian of the team. Finally, his reactions to her made sense and, in that moment, became nonthreatening but also deeply disappointing. Far from being welcomed to the team, she was seen as a threat.

And now that she knew Richie, the team's reactions of surprise at Richie's animation and ease toward her made sense. Richie wasn't the sort to approach a woman on his own or speak out in her defense. And yet he had, repeatedly, surprising them all.

For her.

Melissa felt around inside. Her fear of Chad indeed was gone…as was any other feeling.

"I am not," she addressed him matter-of-factly, "some *lobo,* some she-wolf, who must be guarded against."

Then she turned to Richie.

"Nor am I some weak *femenino* who needs protecting. I'm a god damn Delta operator and have spent enough sweat and blood to prove it."

Then she turned and walked to the hangar door.

Behind her, she could hear Kyle's start speaking, his tone was preemptory—the closest she'd heard to a tone of command since her arrival. His disapproval was thick in every word.

"Analie Sala has *invited* us to shift our base of operations. We leave in four hours. I expect the plane to be serviced and all of this mess to be cleaned up and packed aboard along with your personal gear."

And Melissa stepped out into the late-morning sunshine and began walking off the field and toward the hotel.

Chad had been against her for all of the wrong reasons.

And Richie hadn't trusted his own feelings except to pound his teammate to protect the weak female. His apology, that she'd thought was sufficient at the time, wasn't. He was constantly overcompensating for the one thing that she knew was real—that she cared for him. That she… Melissa couldn't bring herself to even think it. It was better if Richie never knew.

She hadn't said what had been in her heart, partly because she didn't like the answer that was buried deep down inside her. *Did either of you ever think that maybe how I feel about Richie was as real as it gets?*

No, she didn't like that question at all.

Chapter 15

THEY WORKED IN SILENCE AS THEY CLEANED UP THE hangar. Richie caught sight of his reflection in one of the pickup truck's mirrors. Black and blue was already spreading along the side of his face and a deep ache had formed behind it. His left shoulder hurt like mad every time he twisted to that side.

Chad sported a black eye and a split lip. His distinct limp had worsened with the effort of cleaning up the hangar. Only Duane had stayed to help them. Kyle and Carla had taken the Forerunner to fetch their gear from the hotel.

When they finally finished reorganizing the tools and spares and had loaded them on the plane, they took the beater pickup to fetch their own gear. He and Chad took the front; Duane sat in the back of the crew cab. The pressure of the silence built even though it was a short drive. Finally Richie couldn't stand it anymore.

"Chad?"

"Uh-huh."

"We okay?"

"Never weren't."

That was a relief.

"You and Melissa?" Duane's question rumbled out of the back.

Chad's silence was long enough that they'd reached the hotel before he answered. He finally shrugged then cursed softly against some pain and rubbed his shoulder.

"Up to her now."

Richie nodded. That was good.

"Doesn't strike me as the forgiving type though."

Richie thought about her final comment as she was leaving. He'd been protecting her from unjust accusations, just like he would any other team member, hadn't he? Even as he thought it, he felt a pinch.

Nope.

Sure, he'd lay down his life for any one of his teammates. He'd rather take a bullet than see one of them take it. That was a given in a close-knit military unit—they'd even been lectured on it by Army psychologists at various stages of training. Being the guilty survivor sucked beyond imagining while your buddy lay there dying. He'd served more with the bridge-and-road crews of the 82nd's Eagle Battalion than the explosive ordnance disposal guys, so he'd only lost a couple buddies when he was in theater. The attrition rate on the EOD teams was horrific.

But with Melissa it was more than that. He'd lay down his life for her if she merely asked it of him.

What was that? It wasn't something that was in any of their training manuals.

They pulled up as Kyle and Carla were pulling out of the parking lot. They paused and rolled down facing windows.

"You seen Melissa?" Kyle's question struck fear into Richie's heart. What if she'd…gone?

He could only shake his head no.

Kyle looked worried. And beyond Kyle in the

passenger seat, Carla's look was fulminating. If Melissa had left, his ass was grass. They drove off.

Richie raced inside to grab his gear and was about to rush back to the truck and the airport when he had an idea.

He didn't bother knocking this time but instead used his key—this place was too primitive for cards—to enter the room he and Melissa had originally taken together but never shared.

And then he froze.

The black hole of the barrel on Melissa's Colt M1911 was centered on his forehead.

"Should have knocked first." Richie did his best not to move any muscles except those he needed to speak.

Melissa was slow on lowering the gun. Her gear was packed, a simple duffel at her feet. She wore the scuffed boots and camo pants that the whole team had adopted as their standard paramilitary look. Her other hand was clutched about the silly doubloon medallion that dangled over her black T-shirt. He couldn't tell if she was holding on to it or about to yank it off and throw it away.

Her eyes looked haunted.

He had the sudden feeling that she'd been sitting in exactly this position the whole time he'd been cleaning up the hangar and packing the plane. Was she waiting for something, or was she deciding whether or not to get on a flight to Fort Bragg for reassignment?

"You okay?" He couldn't read her expression at all.

"I should be asking you." She stared at his face. "You're the one who took on The Reaper."

Richie grimaced and then wished he hadn't because his jaw still stung. "I'll heal soon enough."

She nodded a few times in acknowledgment. "You two okay? You and Chad?"

"Yeah, we're fine."

Melissa dropped her hands into her lap and studied them.

Richie resisted the urge to kneel before them and grab hold. He didn't know if she was drifting away from him or already flown. He heard Chad down the hall telling Duane to hurry up his ass. Richie let the room door swing shut to buy them a few more moments.

Asking the next question would be horrible, but he evaluated it and decided that not knowing the answer was worse.

"Are we okay?" Richie managed.

"You're something really special, Richie Goldman." Melissa rose to her feet, shouldering her duffel as she did so. In the small room, they were now standing just a foot apart.

"But…" he offered because he knew it was over. That he'd blown it with the most amazing woman he'd ever met. Is this what it felt like to be shot, to be the one who caught the round rather than the one who was left standing? The pain was far worse than anything Chad had handed out to him earlier.

She studied him with those infinitely blue eyes.

He could hear Chad and Duane coming down the hall, Chad calling out Richie's name.

"We never get time do we?" Melissa's tone was still unreadable.

He shook his head and ignored the twinges of the ill-considered too-fast motion.

A fist thumped on the door. "Ass in gear, buddy. Time to rock."

Melissa didn't look away.

"Hang on," Richie managed without turning, but it came out as a croak, his throat tight before the pending verdict. He managed a deep breath, seeking calm. And he found it in Melissa's soft scent of icy mountains and warm fires. Whatever other craziness was happening, she was still his Ilsa. Even if she wasn't anymore. Perhaps especially then as Bogey hadn't gotten his Ilsa either. He hadn't liked that ending to the movie.

"Please," he whispered. "Say that we're okay."

"Do something for me, Richie."

"Anything!" That elicited a small smile.

She patted his cheek, the unbruised side, and smiled a bit sadly as she said, "Don't worry so much."

That reference back to their first meeting warned him that their universe had just had its timeline reset all the way back to the beginning as surely as if they had a time machine.

But the soft kiss before she moved by him to open the door gave him reason to hope that this new future still stood a chance.

"The airfield is very unique for the approaching." The pilot that Analie Sala had sent to meet them spoke nervously, as he had from the first moment he'd come aboard. He was in Melissa's seat and she hated that. Hated the loss of control.

She readjusted her headset and crouched between the two pilot seats so that she could see what Richie and Claude Mura—a small Japanese man with a distinct French accent—were seeing.

"You will be making the use of this unique approach and departure route every time you come to this place and you will stay very low for the last fifty miles."

They'd been dodging the jungle's treetops for over twenty minutes.

"See? The river? How she bends there?"

Melissa tried to rise up to see where he was pointing and banged her head on the Twin Otter's low ceiling for the tenth time in this flight alone. They'd left the Orinoco behind five miles ago, flying up the Río Atabapo, which now took a hard turn to the east.

"Go southwest here."

They made the turn, the last of the setting sun blasting into the cockpit. The horizon was a blaze of orange beneath an indigo-dark sky. Experience told her that in minutes it would be too dark to see where they were landing.

"If you go due west," Claude continued hurriedly, "you will pass over Inírida. *Erreur grave, oui?* The military, they have many units there because of FARC."

Melissa would bet they were flying for the FARC, which made it good advice. The Marxist guerillas of Colombia had been at war with the various national governments since the early 1960s. By the 1970s they were using kidnap and ransom, and illegal mining to finance their operations. Since the 1980s, the bulk of their income had shifted to the massive flow of cocaine out of the country. Whether an ideology existed at all anymore was an unknown.

"See, there." Claude pointed excitedly and Melissa again banged her head on the plane's low ceiling.

A tap on her shoulder and she turned to see Chad was close behind her. He had a plastic bin of assorted parts that must weigh close to a hundred pounds though he moved it like it weighed ten. He waved her aside and he slid it into place close between the pilots' seats. He'd made a seat for her so that she could learn what she needed to in order to support the team.

He watched her steadily for a long moment.

At her careful nod, he returned the same in kind before moving back to his seat.

Maybe Richie hadn't been lying when he said that he and Chad were okay. She'd cautiously take this plastic bin seat as a peace offering…and see where the future led.

She was now sitting at about the same height as Richie and Claude and could easily pick out what Claude had been pointing out.

The jungle was a low roll in this region. Rather than brutal ridges and carved canyons, the contour of the treetops indicated that a pleasantly rolling set of hills lay somewhere under the green canopy. There were signs of water everywhere, crisscrossing rivers and streams that glinted through the lush foliage.

They had left the land of *tepui*—vertically-sided mesas with their amazing waterfalls—to the east. Here there was little above the roof of the jungle, except for the trio of abrupt, unforested hills straight ahead of them.

Out of seemingly nowhere, two great mounds of black stone rose five hundred meters above the roof of the jungle and soared up into the sky. Close beside them, a third rose to half again the height. The Río Inírida twisted around their base, reflecting their dark images on its smooth-flowing water. The jungle didn't climb the steep faces of the three peaks; rather it slammed into the sides and could go no farther.

"Those are seriously weird."

"You must fly through the Cerros de Mavecure. Between Pajarito and Mono, the Little Bird and the Monkey. They are the tall one and the middle one. You must always do this at night. If you do it in the day, we would have already been shot down, even with the special permission of Analie Sala. Also, do not try to land if you are not expected. This is tonight's frequency." He dialed it into the radio and transmitted just one word, *Ibis*. "Never leave without first finding that night's frequency and what bird is the password."

They flew down into the saddle between the two hills that towered above them.

Melissa had never had the luxury of watching Richie fly without being observed herself. He had become so natural in the seat that it was hard to credit that a week ago neither of them had ever flown such a large or complex aircraft. His motions were assured and steady. He didn't even look as he reached up to tweak one of the prop controls.

He was the consummate professional trained to a level that few ever achieved. She knew that because it was a level she'd had to fight to achieve herself. She might feel a little less put out if he didn't make it look so easy right at this particular moment.

His face was awash in the ruddy glow of the last of the sunset, making him about the handsomest man she'd ever seen. And she knew that she was biased now, but she didn't care. He wasn't some museum exhibit that was all facade and little substance like most guys.

The beautiful outer shell was only enhanced by the inner man.

"There." Claude forced her attention back to the line of flight.

They had crossed over the saddle between the twin peaks and were once again facing the boundless jungle.

"See those lights?"

And she did. Of the oddest things to find in the middle of the Colombian jungle, airport glide slope VASI lights would have been high on her list. Visual approach slope indicators were paired lights that were designed so that when you were at the right descent angle you could see red lights shining above white lights. If you saw double white, you were too high. You saw red over red, you were about to fly into the ground and be dead. "Red is dead" had been repeated a thousand times by every pilot ever trained.

It was especially strange to find the lights here because—

"Where the heck is the runway?"

——

Richie wanted to know exactly the same thing. All he could see was the darkness of the forest canopy.

He spotted a second set of the lights fifty meters to the right, still lost in the darkness of the trees.

Even as he watched, they were shifting to white over white, they were too high.

"No!" Claude shouted. "There is no missed approach allowed on this field. Go down! Now!"

Richie hesitated just a moment, not trusting the man.

Then Melissa pinched the back of his arm sharply,

forcing him to jerk his arm forward to get clear of the pain. That shoved the wheel forward and forced him to nose down.

Between Melissa's reinforcement and Claude's panicked tone, Richie started pulling power and setting flaps as if they were actually on final approach to a runway he couldn't see. He was only peripherally aware of Melissa reading down through the checklist for him as he did each task.

"Claude, there is nothing but trees."

"Trust me, *mon ami*. It will be *aéroport* when you need it to be. Just stay between the lights and on the glide path no matter what. Our lives depends on it."

So Richie continued his descent toward the dark jungle canopy.

"Do I at least get landing lights?"

"Not yet. I will turn them on when you can have them."

Richie considered apologizing to Melissa because he was about to kill her deep in the Amazon rain forest in a place their bodies would never be found.

"Are we going in on water or land?" He didn't even know why he bothered asking; they were going into the trees.

"Land."

He lowered the wheels, flipped off the yaw damper, and double-checked that the propeller's controls were full forward.

Richie kept to the glide path, terrified each time he saw even the least bit of incorrect color in the lights. It was pure nerve that had him diving into the jungle. That and the suspicion that they'd be shot down if he didn't.

Delta had taught him plenty about how to handle a

crisis—stay loose, stay flexible, accept the moment, and find a way to take advantage of it.

They hadn't taught him shit about killing his entire team.

He was nearly on top of the glide path lights themselves when Claude flipped on the landing lights. A runway of hard-packed earth appeared not twenty feet below him. He flared the plane hard, dumped power, and got them down alive by some miracle he hoped he never had to repeat.

The runway was in good condition and he dropped speed quickly. The only light was his landing lights reflecting off the dirt. He could see shadows that might have been trees to either side, but beneath their overarching branches was a full airport.

"Where the hell are we?" Melissa voice was soft with wonder.

"You just swore." He glanced over at her and could see that she was bending down and forward, craning to look upward. Then he looked up himself. "Holy shit!"

Chapter 16

MELISSA TRIED TO TAKE IN THE SCALE OF IT ALL AS Richie taxied the plane following Claude's directions. The runway was crowded to either side by towering trees. Somewhere far above in the darkness, the trees' crowns probably merged, hiding the runway from view. Any final hints of the last of the sunset were gone.

From the air would be nothing but jungle. Jungle with a big hole at one end where planes must follow glide path lights if they didn't want to crash. The entire field was hidden except for that one, slanted opening in the trees.

Beneath the jungle canopy lay a small city. She closed her eyes, rubbed them, shook her head, and tried clicking her heels together three times. It didn't change anything as Richie turned the plane and they taxied to a stop at a place indicated by an actual ground controller signaling with a pair of light sticks, as if they'd just landed at USCG Air Station Clearwater.

In moments the entire team had tumbled out and simply stood and gawked. Even Richie slipping his hand around her waist and pulling her against his side didn't help her feel any more grounded.

On their side of the runway was a long line of parked airplanes. On the opposite side, winding between the trunks of the canopy giants of jungle trees, lay a softly lit tent city for a hundred people or more. But it wasn't some slipshod huddle of individual tents. One big canopy tent with open sides covered a long chow line with dozens of picnic tables, most of them filled with people eating their dinner. Maybe the population was closer to two hundred. Next to it was a wooden structure with a broad thatched roof. Rows of chairs and benches were spread around card tables or gathered around a big screen TV, currently showing Bruce Willis dying hard. A small tent sported a large blue-and-white *H*, marking it as a medical tent. Farther along were large tents that appeared to be barracks housing.

Richie pointed upward and Melissa squinted up into the darkness.

High across the entire runway, great nets had been suspended. Leafy vines were filling in the camo nets.

"They've been here a while," she whispered into the strange silence of the night.

The *Tin Goose* was now parked in a line with a dozen other planes. There were several small craft, but most were at least twin engine. A trio of Beech King Airs and a Cessna twin were all about half the size of their Twin Otter. Their plane was the second biggest on this side of the packed dirt field, looking particularly oversized and clumsy compared to a pair of sleek small business jets. A midsized, four-engine jet was parked at the farthest end.

She pointed the jets out to Richie and pretended she was a radio announcer. "When your drugs absolutely, positively have to be there overnight."

"They're slick. But they all land at around a hundred and fifty miles an hour, we just landed at sixty. I'll pass."

"You did it great, Richie."

"I don't know, Ilsa."

Why did she feel goofy every time he called her that?
She and Ingrid Bergman had nothing in common except
for some weird connection deep in Richie's mind. It
should make her scoff, but instead she was charmed.

"I wouldn't want to try doing that again or the *Tin
Goose* just might end up on the other side of this field."

She followed the direction Richie had indicated.

On the other side of the field were more aircraft, or
perhaps large piles of aircraft would be more accurate.
A DC-3 fuselage rested belly-flat on the ground with its
engines and most of the wings missing. A pair of small
Cessna 152 fuselages rested right where its engines
were supposed to be. The tail section of a midsize jet
lay crossways against a much smaller de Havilland
Caribou but there was no sign of the rest of the plane.
An Albatross, the big flying boat they'd practiced on
in front of the USCG offices, towered over most of the
other wreckage, but it had only one wing.

The far side of the field was a drug-runners' scrap
yard. All the planes that hadn't succeeded on the passage Richie had just flown.

At first it appeared to be a haphazard arrangement,
but it was a little too neat and some of the windows had
cheery lights shining from the inside even if engines or
whole wings were missing. Private residences?

As her eyes grew used to the dim lighting under the
trees, she could begin to see the activity of the operation. On their side of the field there were forklifts and
golf carts running about with cargo or supplies for different planes.

On the far side, beyond the line of wrecks, workers

shuffled back and forth, some moving fast on an errand, some apparently just going about their lives.

A heavy-duty ATV drove up, dragging a trailer with a large, plastic fuel tank.

"*Gasolina?*" the female driver asked him. She was dressed rough: khakis, boots, and a button-down shirt that wasn't buttoned up very far.

"I'll take some of what she's selling," Chad whispered to Richie from close behind Melissa.

"*Para aviones?*" Richie asked the woman, because regular gasoline would be a problem. The *Tin Goose* used jet fuel.

She looked at him like he was an idiot and waved a hand down the line. Right, he was in a line of planes. "Do you have enough to get back to the city before you refuel? Say yes, because we charge *un cojón* if you buy fuel here on the jungle strip."

"*Si, gracias.*"

Melissa would wager Richie was just as glad not having to pay for fuel with one of his nuts.

The fueler drove off without any other reply except a look that Melissa would rather the woman hadn't given to Richie.

"Damn it, Richie," Chad protested. "A woman looks like that and you just let her drive away?"

"But we don't need the fuel."

"That's not the point I—" Chad slapped him on the shoulder in what appeared to be a friendly enough fashion. "Never mind, buddy."

Melissa appreciated the newly revealed aspect of Richie's tunnel vision. He hadn't even noticed that the woman was particularly attractive or had been eyeing him.

"Hallo," a man called as he approached from along the line of parked planes. It was the tall, white man with the British accent who had said he was in charge when they had picked up the first delivery along the Orinoco. "Welcome to our little operation."

He shook hands all around and then came to stop in front of her.

"Niklas Pederson." He did the whole holding-her-hand-too-long thing that so many guys thought was charming. His face was oddly round when compared to his lean frame, making him look like a bobblehead doll of himself.

"Melissa Moore," she responded, "and I'll take my hand back unless you want Richie, my senior pilot, to shoot you."

He kept both her hand and his smile. "I would not suggest that. I am very well protected here." He nodded behind them. She didn't bother to look.

Instead, she heard Richie pull his sidearm. "I'll start with something they won't mind, like your balls." His MP-443 Grach swung into her peripheral vision, aimed at Niklas's crotch. Whether that was her warrior or he was just being a soldier following her lead, she didn't care. The effect was the same.

She made no comment.

Niklas raised an eyebrow, like a bad imitation of Spock on his round face.

Richie snapped the fingers of his free hand, and she heard the rest of the team shift into action. In moments there were a series of grunts, bodies slamming to hard earth, and the clatter of weapons being disarmed with a slippery drop of magazines and the sharp clack of cleared chambers.

Not a single shot was fired.

Melissa didn't look away from the man's eyes for a moment.

Niklas released her hand without any further comment.

Richie reholstered his sidearm, indicating that there were no longer any threats.

"We're here to fly, Mr. Pederson. But it's been a very long day, starting with the booby trap set by your Ms. Sala and then some question as to who would take final possession of the delivery. Are you going to keep screwing around, or are you going to tell us where we can get some sleep?"

His voice remained calm and smooth as if he was a hotel concierge, not a drug merchant who had just lost the first round of a power game. "We have reserved the DC-3 for your exclusive use. I hope that you find the accommodations comfortable. We work at night here and they're serving breakfast right now." He waved his hand toward the mess tent where others were gathering.

She nodded her acceptance. Not a problem; Delta was used to nighttime operations.

"Your team will be flying tomorrow night. I hope that you all join me for dinner at oh-five-hundred. I will be in my office." He waved a hand toward a plane parked at the far end of the field. Pederson stalked off without further pleasantries.

"Walks like you just rammed a stick up his butt," Carla observed from close beside her.

"Nice job on that," Kyle agreed.

"Girl's got some moxie," Chad rumbled and Duane offered an "Uh-huh," in reply.

"Hard not to be impressed." Richie was looking downfield. "He has a BAe 146-100 for a private office."

Carla just rolled her eyes in exasperation and Melissa tried not to giggle; it was so typically Richie to be having a different conversation from everyone around him.

"Can you imagine piloting that blind through the opening in the jungle?" Richie was on a roll. "That's a four-engine, seventy-seat, regional jet that could load up to seventy passengers and all of their baggage. It's good at short-field operations, typically under four thousand feet, depending on the load of course. But still, it can—"

Melissa couldn't stand it any longer; he was just too cute. She grabbed him and pulled him into a kiss. Caught mid-sentence, it didn't take him but a moment to shift them straight into a mid-kiss. Quick response to changing circumstances—another Delta trait to appreciate.

"Is that the secret to get a kiss like that?" Chad asked, though she could barely hear him through the buzzing in her ears. "Just be a total fucking dweeb? Really?"

Melissa pulled back enough to look Richie in the face because at the rate of climb that kiss was taking, they were going to be making love very shortly, right here along the runway. As a distraction, she struggled to answer Chad, surprised by his sudden approachability.

"It works on him. It helps that Richie actually is a total nerd."

"No, he isn't."

Oh no. Was he still going to put down everything she did?

"He's a total fucking nerd…or he will be soon if we can get you two somewhere private."

Oh. Maybe Chad's attitude was shifting. Then she noticed how brightly Richie blushed. Despite that, her warrior kept his hands tight around her waist and

Melissa was forced to agree with Chad's assessment, definitely something she looked forward to very soon.

"Let's go." Kyle changed the topic and reached out to pop open the Twin Otter's baggage compartment and pull out his duffel.

Richie glanced across the runway and then blushed a little brighter.

"What?"

"Oh." He smiled at her hungrily. "I was just wondering if there were any private quarters on our DC-3."

⁓⁓⁓

The team entered the inside of the crashed DC-3's fuselage through the rear cargo door. Richie expected to find any empty cargo bay and some bedrolls.

Instead, the inside had been totally renovated from whatever disreputable past it might have had when it was still operational. The interior was six feet wide, the same high, and about thirty long. It was filled with a scattering of couches and chairs of fine-furniture quality, and they looked upscale and inviting. The interior of the fuselage had been painted a warm gold and the deck had been planked with a dark hardwood. It was beyond comfortable. He'd have to rate it as luxurious, better than either the Bahamian resort or the first Maracaibo hotel, despite the fuselage's seven-foot diameter.

And if he didn't get Melissa down on one of those couches very soon, he was going to blow a blood vessel.

"Cozy." Chad dumped his bag on the floor. "I'm starving. Who else wants to get some food?"

As fast as they'd arrived, they were departing again. Richie couldn't remember the last time he'd eaten and started to follow even if that wasn't what his body was thinking.

He was a step from the door back onto the packed dirt, but Carla was now blocking his way.

"We'll bring you back something in a couple hours," Carla declared. Then she closed the cargo door in his face with a heavy clang. Then the clunk and thud of the door interlock being thrown, latching the door safely for flight.

He had to stare at the door for a long moment before he figured out what had just happened. He was in a room, alone with Melissa—an extremely comfortable room.

About time!

Richie almost gave out a joyous whoop as he turned to her, except he was alone in the DC-3's cabin. Couches, chairs, small fold-up tables…and no Meli—

Then he spotted the doorway to the cockpit. Except the partition wall was a couple yards closer than it should have been.

The doorway stood open but the area beyond was too dim to see clearly.

He moved forward cautiously and peered in.

The console and steering yokes were still in place, but the pilot's chairs had been removed. The broad windshields were curtained with a rich green velvet. The insides of the metal hull—sides and ceiling—had been finished in deeply-grained Parota wood with natural variation from tan to a walnut red brown, creating a nest of pure luxury. Drug runners had way too much money.

A king-size mattress filled all but a few inches of the cockpit. By the light of a small brass lantern, the dark

blue sheets were fresh and shiny with a satin sheen—
which draped so perfectly over the body lying between
them that he could see every outline. There wasn't a
single one of those perfect curves that was interrupted
by the least scrap of clothing. He could see the tiny
lump of the doubloon perched between the exquisite
mounds of her breasts.

Melissa. No, this wasn't Melissa Moore from Canada.
Nor Melissa The Cat, Delta Force operator.

This was his Ilsa, watching him through sparkling
blue eyes, her sunshine hair spread across the dark
pillow. It was where she belonged, in this impossible
nest of pure luxury.

He tried to speak, but his throat had gone dry.

It was barely an autonomic motion as he closed the
cockpit door and began undressing. He knelt on the bed
and looked down at her.

How had he ever ended up with someone so beautiful?

"Are you planning to touch me anytime soon?"

She shifted beneath the thin sheet which offered him
new shapes and terrain to admire.

———◦◦◦———

Richie reached out so slowly to touch her that she
thought she'd scream before he closed the gap. He didn't
reach for crotch or breast, but instead rested his hand on
her waist at the first rise of her hip, exactly where it had
been minutes ago as she'd kissed him beside the parked
Tin Goose.

Then he leaned down and, nudging the medallion
aside, rested his ear between her breasts.

The intimacy of the simple gesture through the thin

sheet was incredible—the only contact, his hand on her waist and his ear over pounding heart.

That's what he was doing, listening to her heart. She'd wager that he was memorizing the sound of every valve opening and closing and how the blood rushed through and probably the oxygen content as it did so and—it was leaving her breathless.

She brushed a hand through his hair as he lay there and listened. This wasn't about sex, not any longer. If he had come in and jumped her as she'd been hoping, it would have been...might have been. But he lay there and listened to her heart until she too could feel it changing and shifting.

And it was doing it in ways she wasn't ready for.

With the least twist beneath the covers, she shifted his mouth to her breast and his hand from her hip to between her legs.

Then more than her heart shifted.

Richie also shifted, right out of the gentle nerd.

In moments he had her pinned beneath the sheets. His hand and mouth suddenly hard against her. Not brutal or painful—oh god no—they felt way too good for that. He was suddenly so intense that it overwhelmed her senses.

He used the slickness of the sheet to stoke and entice. Had she been a frozen glacier at the heart of the Antarctic ice shield, she'd still have melted. She didn't go from frozen to thawed. She went from impatient to ecstatic.

But the warrior didn't merely take as he had in the shower. The nameless warrior coaxed her reactions forth. She had never been so controlled yet had no desire to escape. Her body's least reaction was noticed, enhanced until she was shivering with the power of it.

Richie's gentlest caresses demanded response. His focus so complete that she could probably drop a flash-bang down his shorts and he wouldn't notice—if he'd been wearing shorts.

Judging perfectly when she was on the edge of mad-ness, he slid the sheet off her. Then instead of finally taking her and giving them both the release she so des-perately wanted, he rocked back on his heels and studied her once again.

"I'm not some sculpture to be admired."

He nodded once, but still didn't move.

She almost called his name, but something made her hesitate. If she did, would the warrior remain, or would Richie reappear? She really needed the warrior right now. She needed to feel this man needing her as desperately as she needed him.

As if reading her mind, he slid on some protection and spread her legs with the lightest brush of fin-gertips on thigh. A growl sounded deep in his throat and echoed about the inside of the DC-3's finely fin-ished interior.

Then he was on her. In the shower he'd taken her with a desperate need; now he revealed a desperate need to please—no—to satisfy her.

The warrior didn't have to prove he was the best lover; he simply was. He took her on an upward flight that including barrel rolls, Immelmann turns, and soar-ing climbs without a single stall in between. She'd heard about people who couldn't remember a traumatic acci-dent or even the weeks leading up to it. If she forgot a single second of this ride, she was going to take her psyche out and shoot it.

At first she was able to give back as good as she got. But Richie ultimately overwhelmed her until all she could do was hang on and go for the ride. Her cry and his groan roared into the cabin space, and she didn't care if everyone in the whole airfield could hear it through the plane's hull.

When she thought she had no more to give, that's when Richie slid into her and expanded her horizons exponentially. When their peaks slammed through her, there was silence in the cabin. Too big for words, it was also too for any sound. Nothing to distract from the pure pleasure.

When he finally had eased them both back to a soft landing, Richie rolled them over so that she lay on the beautiful, perfect chest of his.

With a happy sigh he held her tightly against him and knew that he'd been right; this *was* the best place she'd ever been as well.

"So, Richard," she put on her best Ingrid Bergman voice. "Instead of Bogey's line, 'We'll always have Paris,' we'll be able to say, 'Well, sweetheart, we'll always have the cockpit of that smashed DC-3 in the drug-runner's camp in a hole in the Venezuelan jungle.'"

Richie's grunt of amusement told her that the warrior was still in place. Or perhaps it was Melissa The Cat's immense sexual prowess.

She liked that idea, soldier to soldier.

Well, perhaps it was time she took on this operator lying prone beneath her.

She started with nuzzling his neck and worked her

way down to explore that wonderful chest. By the time her breasts were over his hips, Richie groaned with returning need.

His recovery time was spectacular, though his speech centers still lagged far behind.

Conquering the warrior was almost as much fun as being conquered by him. Each time he tried to touch her, she brushed aside his hands. Ilsa was the one in control here—as powerful as Bergman should have been if she'd truly wanted her Rick—she orchestrated every sensation. Melissa tasted and teased and stroked until the mighty warrior had his hands fisted hard in the sheets and his body writhed at her merest action.

When she finally took him in, finished him off, and pinned him with her body until he was completely spent, he could do no more than shudder and moan.

Melissa remained straddled over Richie's hips and watched him. He reached up to brush a hand over her cheek, down to press the doubloon lightly against her breastbone for a moment, then he slipped toward sleep.

"No longer a welcher," she whispered softly so as not to disturb. He had just delivered on his promise times ten.

He slid into an even deeper sleep, every last bit of him finally relaxing.

She, in turn, had never felt more awake in her life.

Chapter 17

"I'VE SEEN THAT LOOK IN THE MIRROR BEFORE." CARLA'S greeting when Melissa slipped out of the DC-3's rear door would have made her jump if she didn't feel so kindly toward the world at large. "That's a good look."

"I—" she opened her mouth and then had no idea what she was going to say. She was spared further foolishness by the Gulfstream jet on the far side of the runway whining to life. She hoped it didn't wake Richie. Actually, at the moment, she doubted that anything—other than a call to arms—had any chance of disturbing him.

It taxied down the center of the runway until it reached the far end. Then with a sleek roar of engines, it bolted down the runway, keeping its nose down longer than she expected; then with a quick motion, the plane shot skyward.

She could see the moment it disappeared through the jungle's canopy, still invisible in the night. One moment she was looking at the hot exhaust of the twin jet engines, and the next it blinked out as the plane moved out of the narrow view afforded by the hole in the jungle's canopy.

"Richie will be sorry he missed seeing that."

"He'll have his chance. This is a busy place." Carla slipped an arm through Melissa's and they set out walking together like two friends strolling down a city sidewalk. "Perhaps you missed the other two departures and three arrivals while you were occupied."

"Hmm." She had, but could only offer a happy hum of satisfaction.

"So talk."

Melissa laughed.

"Care to let me in on the joke?"

"I don't even know where to begin." She waved a hand at the line of shattered aircraft that lined this section of the field. Most of them looked like the battered toys of a particularly rough three-year-old. "This place, you, Richie, me."

"Well, that's specific," Carla teased.

"See, there. That's part of it. Here I am walking arm in arm with Carla Effing Anderson. As recently as a week ago I'd have laid down a month's pay that would never ever happen under any circumstances."

"Ouch! Is my reputation that bad?" She didn't sound the least contrite.

"No, it's that good."

"Just imagine the poor woman who has to follow both of our acts."

Melissa had to laugh again at that. Carla had a point.

A bright buzzing noise was building. They'd reached the end of the jungle runway closest to the VASI glide path lights. The lights blinked on and moments later not one or two, but three small planes zipped in through the jungle canopy. This was a busy location.

"Useful load?" Carla asked, shifting to Unit operator with as little sign as changing a topic—all one integrated whole for her. For Melissa it felt as if she was still split a dozen ways: soldier, lover, pilot, friend to Carla, placater of Chad…

The newly arrived Cessnas were planes Melissa knew,

far better than the *Tin Goose*. "They're all Cessna 182s. They're the slightly bigger twin brother of the planes I earned my license in. A pilot plus fuel leaves them about eight hundred pounds useful load. Three planes together can move over a ton." She watched how they each hit the runway and wallowed toward the parking side of the runway. "And I'd say these were all coming in heavy."

"Interesting." Carla began leading her down the line toward the new arrivals, though she still kept their pace nonchalant. "So, other than despising my merest existence, what is the rest of the joke?" Carla asked as she slid effortlessly back across topics.

Melissa looked up at the jungle canopy. There was little stray light here on the ground, so it would be wholly invisible from above. It was an elegant piece of design work.

"Five years ago I was designing museum exhibits, I had a brother, and our hobby was rock and ice climbing. I always thought I'd find another climber or artist someday. I'd get a houseboat near my parents in West Bay. Kids, job at the museum, everything so normal."

"And now you're a Unit operator in a jungle fortress that is the heart of a major drug-running operation and you're in love with a soldier named Richie Goldman."

"Right."

Carla paused and looked at her. The woman on the fueling ATV drove by, her headlights casting enough light for Melissa to see Carla's expression clearly.

"What? What did I miss?"

Carla still simply waited, forcing Melissa to review what had just been said. Then she found it.

"In love with…" Melissa listened to how her own voice said it. No hint of surprise. Nor alarm. "Huh."

"As I said, I know that look."

"I thought you meant the sex."

Carla shook her head. "That's what I wanted to think it was as well when it happened to me. Guess what. It's not."

"I'm seeing that." And it wasn't freaking her out, which was almost as interesting as the thought itself.

"You seem much cooler about this than I was."

"What did you put Kyle through?"

Carla grimaced and started walking again.

Melissa had thought it was avoidance until they were approaching the Cessnas at the same moment as a small team of workers and a forklift.

"I'll just say that I come by the Wild Woman moniker honestly. Kyle and I had pretty spectacular fight over that one, almost shattered the team on our first week in the field."

"Whereas Melissa The Cat sneaks up on love, or rather has it sneak up on her."

"Apparently." Carla guided them past the trio of parked Cessnas. Then stopped and turned as if to pay more attention to Melissa. But Melissa knew her attention was really on assessing whatever was going on behind them.

Which was just as well; Melissa couldn't assess squat at the moment.

She was in love with Richie Goldman.

Even as a flat statement inside her head, it was no surprise; it was simple truth. "How did I trade in some gentle artist on a soldier turned drug runner?"

"Just lucky I guess." Carla's comment did make her feel lucky. How many men were there like Richie on the planet? Easy answer. One.

"You two, lend a hand," a team foreman called them over. Since a closer look was exactly what they wanted, Melissa was glad to lend a hand, though she and Carla were both smart enough to show what would be a typical reluctance, until the moment the foreman rested a hand on his sidearm.

The plane's interior had been stripped inside with only the pilot's seat remaining. Plastic garbage bags had been piled on the deck. The first one she picked up was heavy, about the same as a training rucksack, so forty to fifty pounds. She was careful to show more effort than it actually took a trained Delta operator.

Through the plastic she could feel the lumpy balls that had to be cocaine paste. If paste was flying in and purified cocaine was flying out, that meant that this was more than a shipping center; it was also a purification processing plant.

That would explain both the efforts to keep it hidden and the casual elegance that had been applied to such objects as the broken DC-3. This single shipment alone would be worth over ten million once processed, twice that if delivered directly to America or Europe. This operation would be awash in cash. If they had a shipment this size just once a week, a half billion dollars would flow through this site. She'd wager they had a lot more frequent deliveries than that.

In a matter of minutes, the three planes were empty, refueled, and back in the air.

She and Carla were left standing alone not far from the *Tin Goose*.

"Interesting."

Melissa kept an eye on where the loaded forklift went.

It crossed the field, circled behind the pile of wrecked planes, and past some tents before disappearing under the jungle canopy.

They continued down the row of parked aircraft, finally arriving at the last plane, parked at the very start of the runway. It was the sleek BAe 146 that belonged to Niklas Pederson. The high-wing, four-engine jet looked ready to leap for the skies at a moment's notice.

It also was circled by five heavily armed men—at least those were the only ones she could see.

"Apparently," Melissa observed, "Mr. Pederson likes his privacy."

One of the men cocked his head in the way that someone did when listening to a radio earpiece. Then he started walking toward them.

"They're observant."

The guard kept his M16 pointed at the dirt, but he was carrying the weapon rather than merely having it slung. Faster reaction time which implied better training.

"Mr. Pederson invites you to join him." The man nodded toward the folded-down stairs at the nose of the plane without looking away from them. Good training.

She'd rather not be inside Pederson's protective perimeter without the rest of the team, but it looked as if that choice had already been taken away from them—the guard's polite request hadn't sounded particularly optional.

A glance at Carla, a shared shrug, and Melissa indicated for the guard to lead the way. They had to meet with Pederson at some point; sooner was always better.

———

"You look pretty damn pleased with yourself."

Richie opened one eye and spotted Chad's smiling face. He opened the other and spotted Duane's. Kyle was leaning on their shoulders from behind and grinning down at him.

"I think he looks entirely too comfortable, don't you agree, boys?"

"He does, Mister Kyle."

Richie tried to make sense of the change. Just a moment ago, the most beautiful woman he'd ever been with had been naked and straddled over him in a luxurious hideaway. Her head thrown back in ecstasy as he'd emptied himself into her.

He hadn't closed his eyes for more than an instant or two, and now the tiny compartment was crowded with his three team members. And no sign of Melissa.

"What did you do with her?"

"She's long gone, buddy. Not *gone* gone," Chad added at Richie's flinch. "Just been off with Carla for the last hour. You've got to get with the program."

He pulled on his watch. They weren't kidding; several hours had passed. It was nearing midnight.

"I think he's been lying around too much." Kyle grinned, then slapped Chad and Duane on the shoulders. "Roust him, boys."

"No, wait!" But there was nothing Richie could do against the three of them. In seconds they had stripped the sheet clear, hauled him out of the bed, and dragged him through the DC-3's cabin before they dumped him out the rear cargo door and onto the dirt naked except for his watch.

"Goddamn it! At least give me my clothes."

"No!" A woman's voice sounded from behind him. The ATV fueler had stopped her vehicle along the dirt path that separated the wrecked planes from the chow tent. "*Por favor no.*"

"You heard the *bella dama*," Chad shrugged pleasantly that he was helpless before such a request.

Richie dove back through the door and tackled Chad who just howled with laughter as the two of them landed on a couch.

"Oh, I knew you always wanted me, Richie. But the *señora* is much more what I want."

Richie didn't give a damn about Chad, but he did manage to grab the clothes that Kyle was holding. By the time Richie was dressed, neither Chad nor the *señora* ATV driver were in sight.

"Fine." He finished tying his boots. "Where's Melissa?"

"In Niklas Pederson's plane."

"Shit!" Didn't they get how goddamn dangerous the man was? Richie wouldn't put it past him to try and lock them up in his aeronautical cave. Hadn't they seen the way he'd looked at Melissa and refused to let go of her hand even after Richie threatened to shoot off the man's balls? He shoved out the door and hustled diagonally across the field and toward the big jet. He could hear Duane and Kyle running to catch up with him.

The first guard who tried to stop him hit the ground with a heavy thud, and no weapons—Richie had relieved him of them. He heard Kyle and Duane behind him engage the other guards, didn't bother turning to see because he didn't need to. They were trusting his instincts and following his lead, because that's what a Delta team did.

Richie aimed the Ruger .44 Magnum Super Blackhawk revolver that he'd stripped off the first guard right between the eyes of the guard at the base of the stairs.

"Move," was all he had to say and the guy bolted.

He was up the stairs into the forward end of the cabin with Duane and Kyle close behind him.

Then he stumbled to a stop.

With a quick scan he located:

Three individuals—two known friendlies, one unknown status.

Possible hides—couch arm, two chairs, closed cockpit door, closed door at rear of aircraft.

All hands—weapons free and visible.

Armament—visible, Carla's and Melissa's sidearms. Hidden, no discernible signs indicating anything such as abnormal hand positions or shifted cushions.

He made a back-and-forth slice with the rifle he'd grabbed without letting the Ruger's aim at Niklas Pederson shift by even a degree. The gesture sent Duane to the cockpit and Kyle to check out the back of the plane.

The main cabin made their accommodations aboard the retrofitted DC-3 look like a shantytown shack. Deep-pile blue carpet, now with a line of Kyle's dirt-red footprints down the center of the aisle.

The cabin was filled with exotic woods, rich leather, glass tables, and golden—check that—actual gold fixtures. He was standing amid a small cluster of luxurious armchairs. The next section of the cabin included a deep couch to either side, one with Melissa and Carla sitting at ease upon it and across the aisle another one with Pederson. Beyond that, close by the rear cabin door Kyle had entered was a dining table of black ebony wood with room for a dozen, narrowed enough to fit neatly in the ten-foot width of the cabin without looking cramped.

Duane slapped an All Clear against his shoulder.

Kyle returned from the rear cabin, escorting a sleepy-looking Analie Sala in a plush robe, the white offsetting her dark skin. She looked exotic and was having trouble keeping the untied robe closed as she stumbled forward. Sala apparently didn't wear much when she slept.

Some remote part of Richie thought how much Chad would be sorry to miss such a sight. Then he figured that Chad was seeing plenty at the moment.

———⟲⟲⟲———

"Ah," Pederson said softly. "I suppose that I shall need some new guards."

"At least better-caliber ones," Carla agreed.

Melissa couldn't speak.

Her warrior stood at the entrance to the plane, his own weapons still slung on. He brandished the firearms she'd cataloged as belonging to the guards…liberated in his rush to reach her. He bore a Ruger 44 and an Imbel IA2—which was only supposed to be in the hands of the Brazilian military, though she'd been trained on one during the Delta OTC. There was a fire and a rage still burning in his dark eyes. She was in no danger, but he hadn't known that and he'd come hunting for her.

She waved him forward and he stalked into the cabin. When she'd coaxed him close enough that she could grab the front of this shirt, she pulled him down and kissed him. Despite being in full combat mode, it was as gentle and tender as the man behind the kiss.

"Good morning," she whispered.

"Uh…huh." That, however, was her warrior.

"Sit." She scooted down the couch, up against Carla. Kyle had dropped Analie onto the couch beside Niklas before perching on the arm of the sofa next to Carla. Duane stood back by the cockpit, his rifle turned toward the open front stairs.

Richie surveyed the situation once, then sat, resting the butt of the Imbel on the floor but keeping the Ruger in his hand.

"If"—Melissa waved toward Duane and Kyle, both with rifles poised—"you don't want any actual deaths, you'll want to call off your guards before they come back with reinforcements."

Niklas reached for his radio. "Julio?" A pause. "Julio?"

"I may have left him in the dirt," Richie grunted out.

Niklas grimaced. "Miguel?"

"*Sí?*"

"All secure here. Set up a perimeter."

"I must see you are not under duress."

"One man only," Melissa warned him.

Niklas relayed the message.

The guard who had been standing at the bottom of the stairs when she and Carla had boarded came cautiously into the cabin. He inspected the situation carefully then shook his head no. He sent a particularly nasty look at Richie.

"I guess you didn't treat him very well either."

Richie shrugged. Definitely not.

"Excuse me a moment." Pederson rose to his feet.

"They are not going to believe so easily I am not under duress." He walked down the aisle, giving Duane a wide and careful berth. Then he walked off the plane with Miguel.

Duane shuffled forward to overhear if they were plotting. Instead, what he repeated from them sounded clean, "See? I am not a captive. They are new, unused to our rules. This once we shall not hold that against them." Then Duane was backing off from the door as Pederson returned.

The man settled into the couch elegantly, as if bred to such situations.

"You make good on your deliveries. You are not afraid of force. You do not hesitate. I find these admirable traits. I also find myself reluctant to trust them. Your American DEA has tried similar infiltration tactics in other places."

Melissa didn't bother to answer; she simply pointed at Analie Sala still wrapped in her bathrobe. She was the voice Pederson would trust, not theirs.

"I am able to account for you and your pilot." Analie nodded. "Smuggling and arms trafficking. The rest of you have a very murky past."

"Estevan," Carla said flatly. "Bolívar Estevan."

She gained the full attention of Niklas and Analie, though Melissa didn't understand why the dead prior owner of their Twin Otter was such a powerful talisman.

"We were working for him, freelance you might say."

Freelance? No shit. Carla had tried to kill Estevan and Kyle had succeeded.

"And how," Niklas asked, "was Bolívar killed and you were not?"

"His daughter had recently been freed from kidnapping. She was a pretty woman and had been"—Carla looked particularly grim—"used. Hard. Upon her unexpected release, we were her trusted escort to the hospital. Then Sinaloa took out Señor Bolívar's operation and put us out of work."

It was perfect. Information that only an insider could know. And there was no questioning Carla's deep anger at the events. It made her sound even more loyal to the family, though the root cause was obvious to Melissa.

"That was six months ago," Analie commented.

"Six months of total suck," Kyle responded. "We worked the coca fields for most of it."

"You heard of the disasters in Bolivia?"

"What disasters?" Kyle leaned forward with a casual interest.

Analie raised an eyebrow and dropped the topic, but Richie had told Melissa all about it. Ten percent of the Bolivian production lost to a 747 spreading great swaths of defoliant with pinpoint accuracy at a dozen coca fields—all mapped by this group of Delta. They hadn't heard of the "disaster"; they were the disaster.

"And how did you come to team up?"

"After six months of total suck," Kyle answered, "we were back in Maracaibo trying to find work. We hooked up with these two who were in a similar boat. They had a plane; we had muscle. Seemed like a good idea at the time."

"I see two people who have stolen Estevan's plane from a Coast Guard station. I see four more who worked for Estevan. All American military trained. All who happened to meet in Maracaibo. I don't like coincidences."

Kyle shrugged. "Doesn't mean they don't happen."

"I suggest," Pederson rejoined the conversation, "that you need a better answer than that." He raised his radio.

Richie lifted the Ruger, aimed it at the center of Pederson's forehead, and pulled the trigger. Pederson barely blinked.

Then Richie whispered softly, "What the hell?"

Melissa broke her eye contact with Pederson to look over at Richie. With a quick flick, Richie opened the cylinder, then turned it for her to see. No bullets. He didn't even bother looking down at the Imbel rifle, simply flicked the magazine release. The magazine hit the carpet with an empty clatter.

It took less than a heartbeat for Richie, Duane, and Kyle to drop their confiscated weapons and pull their own.

Pederson lowered his radio and held his hands out. "It is no matter. I simply wanted to delay any gunplay until we'd had a little chat."

Duane did a flash check out the aircraft's forward door. He pulled back in and held his hand high with his fingers shaped like a fake gun, then he pumped it three times. Three rifles. If he could see three, that meant there were more around. The windows were curtained, but the location of the couch would be well-known and Miguel had seen them perched there. Gunmen outside the plane, perhaps even ones down in the cargo bay ready to fire upward, could easily target the couch positions.

Melissa decided against moving as that would display fear. She'd bank on Pederson not wanting to damage his plane. She tipped her head to indicate that the next move was his.

His smile was chilly. "Dayana is making sure that your blond friend is also, shall we say, well occupied. Now would anyone care to explain the coincidence?"

Delta had done many things to Melissa, one of which was instilling a sense of absolute calm in a crisis situation. The worse the situation, the calmer she felt. So she didn't leap into the silence; instead she did her best to look like she was considering her best answer while really hoping someone else had a plausible one.

"That would be my doing," Duane finally rumbled.

Melissa again didn't turn, forcing Pederson to keep watching her. *I have perfect confidence in my crew,* was the message she wanted to get across to him.

"We were looking for work. Then Melissa and Mr. Doofus there…"

She assumed he meant Richie and did her best to suppress a smile at Duane offering a tease to his teammate in the middle of the situation. It said much about how close they all were.

"…showed up in a plane with the tail number of our former boss. Didn't even change it. I tracked them down. Turns out that Chad and Mr. Doofus had served on a couple of missions together. Some interagency crap. We were all broke, so we threw in together."

It was the longest speech she'd ever heard from Duane. By the looks that briefly crossed the others' faces when she did glance aside, it was the longest they'd ever heard as well.

Pederson turned to Analie, awaiting her analysis of the situation.

After a long moment, she shrugged. "It fits. No one except his personal guards or Sinaloa would know about

Estevan's daughter. If they were Sinaloa, they wouldn't have been out of work. It is clear that while those two"—Analie indicated Richie and Melissa herself—"know the plane, it is equally clear that the other four know next to nothing about aircraft."

Pederson nodded, accepting his expediter's assessment. Then he turned to them with a big smile.

"*Bueno!* All is forgiven. We pay one million per ton for delivery to Honduras or Mexico, two million for direct to the U.S., plus an extra half million for danger pay if you cross into U.S. territorial waters. You will have secure refueling in Maracaibo, so you can make the big crossing if you wish to try for it. After you deliver, your plane will be clean and may enter the U.S. properly for refueling."

Melissa nodded and leaned forward to shake Pederson's hand.

Analie also leaned in to proffer her hand, a little faster than Pederson. Melissa shook with both in turn.

With the extended range tanks, the *Tin Goose* could carry their full crew plus a ton and a half.

"The U.S. works just fine for us."

Chapter 18

IT WAS NINE IN THE MORNING AS RICHIE WALKED along the trail that led from the bathing stream back to the jungle airfield close beside Melissa and marveled at how many changes it was possible to become comfortable with and how quickly they could occur.

After three weeks of flying every other day, he could land through the opening of the jungle airstrip without even breaking a sweat. Living the alternate days beneath the jungle's canopy now felt as normal as the barracks at Fort Bragg.

And sleeping, flying, and keeping fit with Melissa Moore had become as natural as breathing. He'd seen it before. His parents, Kyle and Carla, and… Okay, he couldn't think of anyone else offhand, but he'd seen it. But to feel the miracle of being together? That was a life-changer. His first thought each day: Where was Melissa? And to discover that the answer as often as not was "in his arms" was a joy he'd never expected for himself.

What had been an awkward, uncertain, and occasionally painful first week of having her on the team had settled into a well-oiled, Delta Force drug-running machine.

True to his word, Pederson kept the money flowing into the offshore account that he had set up for them. And Fred Smith kept funneling the funds out to make it look real.

The deliveries themselves always made it to land because Moore Aviation delivered. Of course with added electronic markers and drone surveillance—Richie often wondered if the FAA was in on the latter, he'd guess not—the shipments always seemed to go astray over the next few days.

A truck blew a tire in Milwaukee, because a female sniper on loan from the Hostage Rescue Team had shot it. A DEA agent, dressed as a state cop, pulled over to "assist," and found the load of drugs because he "just happened" to be a K-9 officer and his dog alerted to the truck.

A boat went under a bridge in Natchez, Mississippi, and never came out the other side.

Shortly after delivery, a Houston gang was jumped by another Houston gang—one they'd never heard of and would never hear of again, but were all crack shots.

The victories were kept out of the news, even though ten tons of cocaine had hit the ports without ever making it to the streets. Their system had to break at some point, but Richie figured they were good for another week at least.

Meanwhile, he'd appreciate the routine they'd fallen into.

He and Melissa had run their normal 10K, four laps of the airfield, then went down to the stream that served as the local bathing pool. There were a few more private pools farther upstream. Most of the Americans and Europeans, and there were any number of them in a variety of positions, gravitated to these. But by this time of the morning, their privacy was guaranteed because most of the camp had gone to sleep—except for those overseeing the purification, drying, and packaging process. The drug lab's operation was staffed twenty-four hours a day.

And none of them could get near it. Not even Chad, who was still shacking up with the sultry Dayana, had found a way in to view the operation.

But they knew where it was, and Chad had managed to get a photo of the exterior.

"Well, that solves that, like anyone cares," Fred Smith had complained when they met briefly during an Alabama refueling stop. "Tail number HK-1707X was a Colombian DC-6 cargo plane lost without a trace in that region in 1978 along with three crew members. Probably been a drug lab ever since." He'd then suggested that they just firebomb the place out of existence.

"There's a small city here," Melissa muttered as they wandered back from bathing together, restarting the whole non-argument.

They often made love at the quiet pool, but not today. It was like one of Chad's itches—the pressure was building—Richie just didn't know from where.

And no one had come up with a comfortable solution about the several hundred people working in this city under the trees. Pilots, cook staff, servants to the wealthy, mechanics, chemists, accountants, satellite comm technicians who worked in a concrete bunker… It was an incredible operation.

"Fred's patience is wearing thin," Richie continued the never-ending discussion. They had to keep reminding him of all of the drug-dealer channels that they were rolling up in the U.S. at the moment because of the delivery information that the team was supplying.

"I'm on the verge of agreeing with him."

"Civilians," Richie said what had been said a thousand times as the trail bent around a towering Para nut tree several meters across. Most of these people were just workers trying to do the best they could.

"Damn them!" Melissa's curse told him just how frustrated she was getting when she ducked into the last cluster of chupa-chupa fruit trees.

They came out of the trail. A sweeping view of the whole complex was visible from the slight crest at the end of the field.

He rested a hand on Melissa's arm to stop her just where the trail broke clear of the chupa-chupa. They hadn't even been holding hands, which said almost as much about their mutual distraction as not making love at the pool.

"What?"

Richie looked out at the field, the working aircraft down one side, the broken ones down the other used for housing. Behind those, the tents protecting chow lines, spares, machine shop, extra sleeping quarters. Barely visible deep in the trees beyond that, the fat fuselage of the crashed DC-6 turned into a drug lab.

When they normally would have returned—roughly an hour later than now, because there were some things about Melissa that were absolutely not worth rushing—the entire camp would have been asleep. A few guards and the drug processing operation were the only activity during the long, hot days.

"What is it, Richie?"

"Something's different. What is it?"

"Why are you asking me? You're the systems genius."

"Just do me a favor and look."

He watched her rather than looking at the airfield. He'd hoped that her gaze might jump to the incongruity, but it didn't. A Unit operator's attention was trained to find the break in patterns, terrorist versus hostage were distinctly different. A trained militia fighter moved and reacted completely differently from the civilians they were trying to hide among. It became more difficult when the hostages were also military, but The Unit trained for that as well.

But Melissa's gaze started at one edge of the camp and swept to the other.

A forklift making a delivery of cocaine paste drove to the rear cargo door of the DC-6. A dozen guards were active, four around the lab, two lounging atop the communications bunker, and six others roving the rest of the compound and airfield.

If it had been Richie's operation, he'd also have had a few snipers high in the trees. The jungle offered any number of good hides, so it would be impossible to check them all.

In frustration, the team had risked breaking out some of their high-end infrared scopes to scan the canopy… and found nothing.

That wasn't quite precise. They'd found any number of monkeys, a family of sloths, and a pair of jaguars. Outside of the class Mammalia they'd also found an astonishing number of parrots and other birds. But no perched snipers. It was the first flaw he'd seen in Pederson's whole operation.

Melissa finished her scan without even an unexpected eye blink.

But the itch wasn't going away.

"Kiss me."

She eyed him sideways.

"C'mon, pretty lady. Kiss me."

———✻———

Melissa was sure they'd never kissed so publicly. They were effectively on a display pedestal above one end of the field, even if there weren't many people active at this hour. Paused as they were, they'd already drawn the attention of a couple of the roving guards who were down this end of the field. And it was certainly something that Richie had never asked for.

"Weren't you all worried about something just a moment ago?"

"I was."

"And now you want me to kiss you?"

"I do."

Would she ever understand this man? "What changed?"

He shrugged and pulled her against him. Hard. Almost brutally.

She offered a brief kiss and received raw heat in return. She melted against him. Richie always did that to her, gave her his complete and perfect attention. He always did, but she'd long ago learned to expect far less from men. Though Richie was slowly convincing her there was an alternative—one she thoroughly enjoyed.

His hands started to rove and for a moment she forgot where she was, lost in the intense sensations that his slightest touch evoked. But when his hand slipped under her shirt and began traveling upward, she blinked her eyes in surprise and remembered they were standing on a slight rise, exposed to the whole field.

Over Richie's shoulder, she could see that they had the interest of three of the nearer guards.

"Richie," she managed to mumble against his kiss, just as his hand cupped her breast. After their swim she hadn't pulled her sports bra back on because it was sweaty from the run. Instead, she'd wrapped it in her towel.

"Mmmm," he made a very contented male sound as he stroked her.

"Richie!" She managed a harsh whisper when he shifted down to nuzzle her neck.

This time it might have been a contented noise or it might have been a snarl of irritation at her attempts to interrupt him.

A fourth guard wandered over to the base of the trail as if they were enjoying the show.

"Hey!"

He shifted one of his legs behind her knees, taking her to the ground. She landed hard in the red dirt and he landed atop her.

This time he clamped his mouth where his hand had just been, coaxing her to arch her bare breast up against him as he lifted her T-shirt.

"No. God damn it!"

He winked at her. "So hit me."

She couldn't believe it. Had the dichotomy of Richie the Geek versus Richie the Warrior that she'd always found so captivating and charming been a lie all along? No. He was up to something, but she had no idea what.

Melissa fisted him in the ribs and he didn't slacken his attack on her breast for a moment.

"No!" he whispered sharply and drove his hand down between her legs and grabbed her hard enough that it almost hurt. "Make it real."

She hauled back and delivered a right cross to his chin that sent him tumbling off her and into a tree hard enough that she heard the *klonk* of his thick skull smacking the wood.

"Didn't have to make it *that* real," he mumbled as he cradled his head.

His painful pinch had made her apply more force than she'd intended. Melissa rolled to her feet. If it was looking real that he needed…she kicked a cloud of the red dirt at his face.

She aimed a kick at his ass. The Delta training that had taught him to roll away when blinded caused her to catch him sharply in the kidneys instead.

"Ole, señorita!"

"En los cojones!"

"De neuvo!"

"In the balls! Again! Again!"

They'd gathered quite a crowd.

Melissa turned to stare down at Pederson's people.

The jeers and cheers increased. And they were looking…

She yanked her shirt back down. Being careful to make sure she caught the padded muscle of his butt this time, she kicked Richie once more in the ass. Shoving through the crowd of guards, she stalked down the field toward the DC-3 where the rest of the team would be bedding down.

Behind her she could hear that fucking male solidarity thing that she hated so much. Every military unit she'd ever served in had just been a bad variation of the old boys' club.

Which she knew was exactly what Richie had been counting on.

"*Oh amigo,*" she heard behind her. The guards really were that predictable.

She hoped that was the advantage Richie had sought, but it was disgusting.

She was halfway back to the plane, blessing that The Unit *was* different, when she figured it was safe to look back. Melissa shook her hair loose then bent down to retie her boot. Glancing sideways through the shield of her hair, she saw Richie still sitting on the ground with his head hung down—she hadn't hit him *that* hard, though she did feel bad about the boot to the kidneys. Seven guards were circled about him, giving him sympathy and commiseration for being beaten up by a woman.

Bonding, exactly as Richie had intended. It was a maneuver worthy of Chad. Another example of how his brain used another person's skill set as his own. And half the time he didn't see how brilliant he was.

She rose and stalked over to the DC-3 and ran head-on into Carla—would have fallen back on her butt if Carla hadn't grabbed her arm.

"You're all red."

Melissa looked down at her shirt and pants. She was coated with dirt. Brushing at it did no good. Everywhere she'd touched the dirt, or Richie had touched her after they'd hit the ground, was red. There was a particularly rude palm print on her crotch that she was finally able to brush enough off to blur what it was.

Carla was grinning at her.

"Well," Melissa offered a reluctant smile in return. "You should see the other guy."

"What happened?"

Melissa peeked over the nose of the plane back toward Richie. The guards had turned the event into a major rest break. Several of them were now sitting atop the hill with Richie and they appeared to be chatting back and forth.

Carla peeked around the fuselage close beside her.

"He wanted the guards' sympathy, so he pretended he was going to rape me."

"He did what?" Carla spun to face her, a dark anger seething to the surface. "I'll fucking castrate the bastard. He used you to get their sympathy? I'll stake him to a fire ant hill and coat his balls with honey."

"Carla?"

She sputtered to a halt long enough for Melissa to get a word in edgewise.

"He warned me first. He pushed a bit when I didn't get it right away because I didn't expect him to try something so sneaky. It's not like him."

Carla blinked at that and dropped her tone from murderous to merely vitriolic. "No, it isn't. But what does the bastard have to be sneaky about?"

"I'm not sure. He said that something wasn't right. We came out of the jungle and he froze like an Irish Setter on point. He attacked me to get the guard's attention and, by my beating him up, he made sure he won their sympathy."

The anger Carla had been displaying so vividly a moment before was blanked off her face and replaced in a single instant by an intently focused Delta operator. No wonder she was called Wild Woman; she'd made the mood change with no sign of transition at all.

"The way you are with people, that's what Richie has with systems only way more."

"I kind of got that," Melissa agreed sarcastically.

"No, you don't. It's like you or I but times a hundred. He'll see a shift hours ahead of when it could possibly be detected, yet he does. The fact that he used you to get to the guards either means that he has magically turned into something that he isn't—I still can't believe that he thought of that—or it's a big change and has him spooked."

"Before that he said he couldn't see something and asked me to look for him."

"Shit," Carla said softly and now looked at Melissa through narrowed eyes.

"What?"

"He really trusts you. I don't mean just a little. I'll bet he was watching you and not the field."

Melissa nodded. "When I finished my survey—and I didn't see crap by the way—he *was* looking at me."

"He was watching your reactions, trusting your training to focus on what was out of sync, even if you didn't notice."

"But I didn't see anything."

"How long after that did he attack you?"

"Seconds."

"Shit!" This time Carla's curse was far more emphatic. "Come on." She grabbed Melissa's arm and dragged her toward the entry of their DC-3 living quarters.

Melissa stumbled along behind, a sense of alarm building. What if…? She wanted to rush back to the end of the field. Richie was alone with half of the shift's guards. He needed support. Defense. He wasn't capable of... No! He was Delta. He was the most capable man she'd ever met. So she sent a quick prayer that he wasn't in over his head and followed Carla.

Kyle, Chad, and Duane were sitting on either side of the narrow aisle, playing Truco.

"Where's Dayana?" Carla asked Chad in the most casual way, again going through a mercurial shift from operator on the hunt to idly curious.

"She pulled a day shift at the lab."

"Bummer."

Chad shrugged and started to return to the game.

Duane tapped him on the arm, which also alerted Kyle. Then Duane looked at Carla and nodded.

"We're clean." Duane was their breacher, their master of explosives, but he was also their backup tech. He and Richie swept the DC-3's cabin for bugs and made sure there were no hidden microphones on each return to the plane.

Carla shifted back to Delta operator. "Tell them."

So Melissa told them. About his alert, exactly what she'd seen about who was posted where from her scan of the field, and the fake attack that Richie had staged to attract the guards' attention.

"Your right knuckles are redder than your left," Kyle observed. Just the sort of thing Richie would have said.

She looked down and saw they were far redder. She flexed her fingers and they hurt—from punching Richie with all the force she could muster while lying flat on her back. The only men who'd ever grabbed her hard between her legs uninvited were such jerks that maybe she had unleashed more than she'd intended.

"It had to look convincing." She did her best to shake

off the last feelings of the violation. He'd known exactly how to make her angry. Knew her far too well and she wasn't feeling very comfortable about that either. A good pilot, an amazing lover, and an open window into her heart that was so wide she didn't know what to do with it.

She could see the team start preparing themselves. Most of it was mental because there wasn't much physical to do; all of the flight crews that served the jungle strip were armed at all times. They had their plane's service parts tucked into a small shed they'd been offered close behind the plane. Their extra weapons and ammunition were stowed and locked in the plane's small baggage hold. Their duffel bags held nothing that they couldn't afford to lose.

But Duane checked a small bag that he'd slipped under a chair on the DC-3. Kyle tested the voltage on his small radio. Chad simply checked his knife and sidearm.

Kyle looked up at her. "So what the hell did he see?"

Melissa didn't have a clue.

Chapter 19

RICHIE RUBBED AT HIS JAW AGAIN. IT DIDN'T REALLY hurt *that* much—thank goodness he'd had her mostly pinned to the ground, making it harder to really drive the blow home—but he was getting good sympathy points. It had been hard to get the reaction he'd wanted out of Melissa. He'd had to pretend he was that jerk Drill Sergeant back in Basic who was always trying to manhandle female recruits no matter how many times he got slapped.

Richie had discovered just what kind of a soldier he was going to be during the fourth week of Basic. Despite the risks, he took down his own Drill Sergeant in the middle of an attempted rape and delivered him gagged to the base commander's office wearing a sign that said, "I am a serial rapist." It was written and signed in the man's own hand, photographs attached, and he'd been duct taped to the commander's chair in the middle of the night. No one knew who tied him there, least of all the Sergeant.

That had made it clear to Richie that he himself cared about justice, not about being acknowledged for it. Something he'd learned four years later was a required Delta trait.

It wasn't until the Commander's Review Board at the end of Delta Selection when they had questioned him about it that Richie knew he'd been identified at all. As far as he knew, only the Private he'd rescued had known it was him. That the Drill had gone to Leavenworth Penitentiary to finish out his military career and a lot longer besides had made it all the more satisfying—once word got out that he was under investigation, a lot of women had stepped forward.

Richie had needed Melissa's reaction to be authentic, and he felt awful that it had worked. It would have been so much easier if she'd figured out he was playacting a few beats faster—and probably less painful for him. But it had been convincing.

The guards had thought it amusing that he'd been beaten up. And by a woman.

Jerks! was all he could think.

But if anyone knew what was going on around the base, it would be the guards. He'd gone to some trouble to befriend several of them over the last few weeks.

"Hey, Jose, can you help me roll this oil drum closer to the plane?"

"No hay problema, campañero!"

"Marco, is that a Steyr AUG? Cool! I've never fired one of those."

Marco had taken it with him when he deserted the Ecuadorian Jungle Infantry Brigade.

Richie had considered trying a few lines about women, like Chad would have, but knew he couldn't pull it off, so he'd stayed technical because Q was a technical boy. It had worked well enough.

But how to get information out of them now? *What's going on here that I'm being too damn stupid to see?* didn't seem like the best ploy. So he kept them engaged, built a whole scenario of how he just couldn't control himself around Melissa, which was pretty much the truth. She was like a drug he couldn't get enough of. The quiet Canadian turned Unit operator. The beautiful woman who could fly like a dream and take him down with a hard right cross when he deserved it. And most of all the woman who responded to him so strongly that he was constantly dumbfounded and unable to speak in her presence.

Vasco dropped down to sit beside him. "That *señorita,* she sure knows how to walk." All of them had admired the effects of Melissa's fury as she'd stalked away. Only Richie had caught the shift when she'd abruptly squatted to retie a boot that hadn't come untied—and inspected him through that stunning fall of bright hair still glistening with the water of their morning swim. When she stood back up, there'd been a hurry to her stride that hadn't been there before she'd squatted down. On cue, she'd rushed to get the rest of the team.

"She does have an amazing walk," Richie agreed.

"You pissed her off pretty good, *amigo.*"

He had.

Richie didn't make a big deal of it, doing his best to shrug it off as if it was the woman's problem. He surveyed the camp further. He still couldn't see what had shifted. One part of his mind he kept focused on the idle chatter among the guards. Some pulled out cigarettes, resting their rifles against a handy tree. Others dropped down and made a show of checking their boots—hard to blame them, the guards were kept circulating on long shifts with next to no breaks.

Another part of his mind he kept waiting for one

guard or another's eyes to shift. Perhaps they were aware of something that wasn't visible.

And he let his eyes drift lazily over the camp. He knew if he concentrated, he wouldn't see whatever had caught his subconscious, but if he kept sweeping, he might stumble on it again. The morning light dappled down through the canopy to light the whole field. A great shaft of a sunbeam through the flight passage struck the line of parked planes like a searchlight.

Over by the drug lab, he recognized Dayana and her ever-present ATV. She was hauling some chemicals around for the cocaine processing. No sign of Chad.

Along the "town" side of the field, there was almost no one moving about. The chow tent was dark; everyone should be asleep during the daylight hours. The five aircrews that were on site had bedded down for the day. The only activity was by the DC-3 that had been assigned to Moore Aviation's team. He spotted Carla and Melissa assessing him over the nose cone several times, then ducking out of sight. He kept an eye out for other activity there, but didn't see any. At least the team was alerted; now if he only knew what to tell them.

The "itch" feeling hadn't gone away, but he'd seen no further evidence to alarm him in any way.

On the airport side of the field sat the *Tin Goose*, a trio of the small short-haulers, one of the sleek Gulfstream twin jets, and Pederson's big BAe 146. Even as he watched, Analie Sala descended the stairs and began circling the plane.

Richie was losing the guards' attention. Soon they'd be drifting back to their duties. He needed to hold them until he figured out what was going on. Time to try channeling Chad even if it wasn't going to work.

"Now there's a sleek outfit." Even at this distance Analie's slenderness stood out.

"Don't go sniffing there, *hombre*," Vasco chided him.

"Why not? Pederson doesn't scare me."

Maybe faux-Chad did work, at least on other guys.

"Pederson doesn't scare anyone," Jose agreed. "That *loba*, she eat you alive."

She-wolf, huh? "What's her story, anyway?" Though the plane rested several hundred yards away, it was easy to see how she moved—like a knife. Not a wasted motion or gesture, the ultimate woman of business. Dangerous business, yet her motions weren't military or even militia. If she was a fighter, it was very well masked.

"No one knows." Vasco shrugged. "She shows up, assesses, and hires your ass or not. Doesn't care if you drool or cower when she goes by. Cold bitch."

Marco hadn't said a word. Of them all, he'd been the only one to remain standing, his rifle slung over his shoulder and his eyes roving.

"I think Marco has a sweet spot for *la loba*." Sounded like a tease Chad would make.

"I'd be glad to mount that bitch," Vasco whispered, "if I thought I could live through it."

"Might be worth it anyway." Jose pushed to his feet.

She was moving about the BAe jet, checking it over carefully.

"Do they ever fly that anywhere?"

"No. It stays put. But always ready to go. She does a full check twice a day."

Richie watched her. Analie Sala wasn't just doing

a perfunctory preflight inspection. She moved like a pilot inspecting the craft she was about to trust her life to. Richie had seen the change in Melissa as they both became familiar with the *Tin Goose*. She'd transitioned from overly cautious about checking every detail and carefully following the checklist to the letter, to absolute surety of her actions and her familiarity with the craft.

If Analie was a pilot, it had made her the perfect person to assess and recruit people for a drug-running operation. It certainly would explain her insistence on being on the "swordfish to Miami" flight.

"I guess it's nice to have your home always ready to go."

Marco scoffed, speaking for the first time. "It is what is in her belly that makes her so special."

At first Richie assumed he was talking about Analie's belly, but he couldn't quite make sense of the comment.

"It's her insurance policy. Thirteen tons, highest grade."

Thirteen tons of pure cocaine in the jet's cargo hold. Three hundred million delivered, over a billion dollars on the street. "One heck of an insurance policy."

"She's a machine," Marco agreed.

But he wasn't looking toward Analie. Instead, he was continuing to scan the field. All of the others were gazing toward Analie and fantasizing about the woman and the billion dollars.

Except Marco wasn't scanning randomly. He was looking at the lab.

A forklift was parked and waiting for the next pallet of outbound product by the front hatch. A pair of guards were lounging by the rear hatch—no smoking around the volatile chemicals used in cocaine processing, but they looked bored enough that they probably wished they were allowed.

Dayana's ATV was parked midway between the hatches, where the wing had once been attached, before it had been ripped off during the DC-6's final, fatal descent into the jungle.

Except there was nothing near to where she'd parked. No opening for chemicals to be delivered or product moved. It was as if she was parked along a blank wall of a warehouse far from the nearest entrance or exit.

Richie hadn't been inside the fuselage turned lab, but he'd bet that she was directly outside the heart of the lab process itself, right at the center of the wreck.

Marco's attention had shifted back over to Pederson's plane as the conversation turned to bantering about what it would be like to spread Analie Sala inside that beautifully appointed aircraft, especially knowing there was a billion dollars of cocaine stored in the hold beneath her sleek ass.

Everyone agreed that Pederson was a *muy afortunado hombre*.

Richie was the only one who saw Dayana raise back into view as she stood up from where she'd been squatting between the lab and her ATV. She surveyed the area quickly up and down the line. Definitely acting as if she wasn't supposed to be there.

Richie was careful not to have his face turned in her direction, but rather watched her sidelong while facing up the field.

She surveyed him and the cluster of guards still gathered around him. Then climbed back aboard the ATV.

What could she have picked up there beside the processing lab?

No, what had she left there beside lab? That was the right question. By how quickly she was moving away, there seemed only one likely answer.

The Delta team wasn't the only undercover operator on the site.

That was it! That's where the pattern had broken. The most normal thing in this whole crazy place, Dayana scooting around the jungle airfield on her ATV. It made her a familiar face to everyone, gave her broad access to everything. Except he'd never seen anyone near that part of the lab's fuselage before.

It was time to get the team and get them out of here.

Fast.

Before Dayana, or whoever she really was, blew up the lab and all hell broke loose.

Richie was wondering how to extract himself from among the guards when he spotted something bright on the move. If he hadn't been perched as high as he was and looking in just the right direction, he wouldn't have seen it.

From the DC-3 where the team was staying, he could just pick out the brilliant shine of Melissa's hair…and she was moving toward the lab.

He slapped his thigh. No radio.

Dayana was driving the ATV from the lab, around the back of the chow tent, and crossing the field down beyond the farthest planes. She stopped at the first one. She was too far away for him to tell if she was refueling the plane, or doing something more nefarious.

Either way, this really didn't look good.

"I'd better go face the music, *mis amigos,*" he told the guards.

"Just make sure it isn't organ music for your funeral."

"*Si!* You know what kind of music to show her." Jose made a hip-pumping motion that earned him a round of jeers.

Several of them thumped Richie on the back in a friendly fashion. These guys didn't deserve to get caught in whatever was coming. And he'd bet it was coming soon.

He pulled Marco aside.

Chapter 20

MELISSA MOVED FROM COVER TO COVER: FAST, QUIET, and smooth.

Duane slipped along close behind her with Chad bringing up the rear.

Kyle and Carla would wait one more minute, and then casually stroll toward Richie. Extract him if he needed help.

Melissa was running the other way, not because she'd remembered anything, but she'd watched Richie out of one of the DC-3 windows. All of the guards had been looking toward Analie Sala as she did her routine inspection of the BAe 146. But Richie had been looking in the opposite direction; he was looking toward the drug lab—not right at it, but she'd wager that's where his attention was focused. He'd found his "itch," and she was going to check it out.

She, Chad, and Duane had walked normally into the chow tent, as if hoping to scrounge a snack, and then gone straight out the back. There they'd almost been run over by Dayana's ATV. Chad's tap on Melissa's shoulder for her to get down was the only thing that had saved her from being spotted.

Halfway from chow hall to drug lab, they all three squatted in a thick patch of young banana trees until Dayana was well clear. The ATV sounded like it was crossing the field.

The lab was quiet.

A glance through a gap in the leaves up the low hill.

Richie getting to his feet. He stood out among the guards because he was the only one not wearing a rifle. He had one hand clenched to the center of his chest. The other was in a fist, stretched out straight in front of him.

Chad tapped an "All Clear" and they were moving again.

Kyle and Carla were headed his way, holding hands and looking as if they were out for a pre-bedtime stroll. The guards were dispersing.

And if Melissa had seen Richie's signal, she had ignored it and kept moving toward the lab.

He dismissed any thoughts of warning Marco to get his men out of here and into the jungle. Richie had enough problems, so he slapped Marco on the shoulder and headed down the hill to intercept Kyle and Carla.

Dayana and her ATV had moved on to the second Cessna and had stopped there again.

The old itch between the shoulder blades was turning into a sharp burn.

As Richie descended the hill, he glanced over at Analie Sala.

She too had frozen in place close beside her plane's nose. She would be aware of every nuance of the operation…and she wasn't watching Richie and the cluster of guards dispersing back to their patrols. Analie clearly knew something was wrong but she too wasn't sure what.

Then she moved ever so casually up to the nose wheel of the big BAe 146. She kicked the wheel chock away from the front tire. The blocks of wood ahead of and behind the wheel kept the plane in place when it was parked. The only reason to move the chock was if you were planning to move the plane.

None of the guards headed in her direction; they actually made a wide sweep well clear around her and her plane. They were only too glad to avoid Analie Sala despite their libidinous talk just moments before.

When she slipped the small cover off the pitot tube—the tiny air intake that was necessary for many of a plane's instruments to run properly—Richie's internal alarms went on full loud.

He did his best to make it look completely casual, a mere chance meeting, as he hurried up to Kyle and Carla.

"Melissa is walking into a bomb rigged against the lab. And Dayana appears to be disabling the planes all down the row."

"Nice greeting," Kyle cursed.

He was on the verge of repeating himself when Carla rolled her eyes at him.

Oh.

"Friendliest I've got at the moment. Or should I tell you about the billion dollars of cocaine sitting in the hold of the BAe 146 that Analie Sala is preparing for flight."

Neither one turned to look at Sala; they'd been too well trained for that.

"Time?"

Richie hadn't particularly researched the BAe 146. He should have. He should have done it the moment he'd first seen it parked here on the jungle airstrip. But there was no Wi-Fi in the heart of the Colombian jungle. The only comm gear was inside the concrete bunker close to the lab. The trees had blocked satellite windows except once, which had opened briefly when an NSA bird had lined up from the DC-3 through the entry hole in the jungle canopy three days ago. So he made his best estimate.

"Three minutes, maybe four, cold start to takeoff." He risked a glance. Analie Sala was nowhere in sight, but the wheel chocks had been pulled back from the main wheels as well. The front and rear ladders were closed.

"I have to go get Melissa."

Kyle blocked him.

"I have—"

"No. You need to prep the plane. It's our only way out. Hey, Miguel," Kyle cut Richie off before he could protest and called amiably to one of the patrolling guards. "Got a question for you, *amigo*." He headed over to join Miguel and in moments they were both crossing to the "town" side of the field.

Richie was going to chase, but Carla snagged a casual hand around his arm—and vised down on the deep radial nerve on the back of his forearm with a grasp of steel.

"Why don't you walk with me, Richie? A woman hates to be left alone in a strange place."

"Okay," he managed to gasp through the hot fire burning up the length of his arm.

She eased off, enough that he could walk and think, but not enough that he'd be in any way tempted to make a break for it. She turned them toward the planes and he turned with her to avoid any further agony.

"Chad's Dayana and Analie Sala are in cahoots with

Pederson?" Carla mused. "And they seem to be shutting down the operation? I find that quite unexpected."

"Something has Analie spooked. I could see it."

"But if she isn't the one shutting down the operation…" Carla eased off further and Richie risked a deep breath that he desperately needed. "…then who is?"

They cut around the back of the Gulfstream jet at the same moment that Dayana came down the line along the rear of the planes.

Carla waved a cheerful hello as a distraction.

Richie had a sudden idea of what was really happening.

He took Dayana off the ATV with a flying body tackle that had her pinned facedown in the dirt with one arm twisted up behind her back and the one holding a Glock 17 pinned under his knee.

—~~~—

Melissa eased up to the middle of the lab's fuselage and leaned her back flat against the metal of the hull. It was green with a thin layer of moss and cool to the touch. The windows were all blocked, at least on this side—no way to see what was going on inside.

Chad and Duane moved in beside her, weapons raised and facing in either direction.

She could see the hill, but Richie and the guards were gone from it. She estimated angles. The last she'd seen of Richie he'd been standing up there, his clenched fist aimed…right toward where she was squatting.

Didn't mean anything. It didn't match any standard military hand sign.

Well, it was past time to do a little exploring.

But Melissa had seen Richie use that hand sign recently; she just couldn't place where.

She raised a hand to signal Chad and Duane to move out; they'd start with the receiving cargo door at the rear of the fuselage.

Then the memory slammed in and she froze in place.

Chad and Duane were looking at her strangely. She clenched her hand into a fist as a hold signal.

Then closed her eyes so as not to lose the image.

Richie had been...

In imitation Melissa clenched one fist to her chest and inadvertently grabbed her four escudo gold doubloon medallion.

Not inadvertent. Richie did nothing by accident.

He'd been showing her the image as well as he could.

The doubloon.

The dive on Cat Island.

She and Richie. Side by side. Blue, red, white, yellow, gray. The colors vibrant...through that water of the reef. In diving, a clenched fist was aimed at danger as a warning—on that dive it was a moray eel hiding in a hole in the reef. She'd spotted it first and held her fist toward the eel. Richie had made a fist of his own and aimed it at the same spot to confirm the sighting and warn the guide.

The military hand signal for danger was a slashing motion across the throat; not a gesture he could make while surrounded by a circle of Pederson's guards.

Instead he'd clutched their shared doubloon and pointed his fist...right here.

Danger. The lab.

"We're in trouble," she whispered to Chad and Duane. "Find it."

Richie leveraged the Glock 17 out of Dayana's pinned hand.

"Who are—" he started to ask but was cut off.

"Let her up. Move nice and slow." Marco. He had his Steyr AUG raised to his shoulder, safety off but finger outside the trigger guard. It was pointed at Richie's head. Carla was close enough to Richie that she'd have no chance to act.

"Nice and slow, Marco," Richie agreed pleasantly. He pushed off Dayana clumsily, as if nervous. Planted a knee in the small of her back which kept her in place.

He used the distraction of her grunt to swing up Dayana's Glock 17 and shoot Marco twice in the face. He placed a third, a security shot, in his heart even though he was already keeling over backward.

Three gunshots shattered the late-morning silence of the jungle.

Melissa could see the guards at either end of the plane going on alert, leaving their posts to hurry toward the sound.

The jungle roared awake with shrieks and cries. Great flocks of birds swooped out of the trees, momentarily clustering in the great open airspace above the runway, then disappearing upward through the canopy.

A wild tapir grunted and raced through the undergrowth not five feet away. The weirdly shaped pig-like animal was panicked—she was sure Richie could provide her with chapter and verse on it. She just hoped that the five-hundred-pound beast didn't run into them. It didn't, disappearing from sight as quickly as it had appeared.

Chad and Duane were poised to race back the way they'd come, but Melissa knew they had to find what was going on here at the lab as well, and this was their one chance.

She surveyed the immediate area.

A set of ATV tracks was clear in the dirt, undisturbed except by their passage and the tapir's.

A set of footprints that weren't any of theirs.

That led to—

She tapped Duane's shoulder and pointed.

It took him only a second or two to see it.

He squatted low and gently lifted a banana leaf that was resting against the drug lab's hull. It hadn't broken or been torn; it was cut.

"God damn it!" Dayana was cursing.

Richie kept her pinned in place and pressed the Glock back against the base of her skull.

She struggled briefly, but stopped when Carla placed her own weapon against the woman's temple.

"Start explaining," Richie would wager she was a rival drug-running gang.

"You just shot my ride out of here."

"I'm heartbroken."

The high whine of an APU finally broke through the noise of the panicked jungle animals. The BAe 146's Auxiliary Power Unit was started first and would be used by Analie to start the four big jet engines as soon as it was supplying enough power.

"She's leaving!" Dayana sounded livid with anger. "You can't let her get away."

Richie wished Melissa was here. Something wasn't jiving and he wanted her to tell him what it was.

"We've got company arriving in twenty seconds," Carla said mildly.

"I agree that Analie Sala can't get away, but why are *you* saying it?"

Dayana stopped struggling and tried to look at him sideways from where her face was pressed in the dirt.

"Why?" Richie prompted her.

"You aren't drug runners," Dayana managed.

"Answer the question."

"If you are, I'm dead anyway." Dayana switched from liquid Spanish to British-accented English. "I'm NCA."

Melissa looked over Duane's shoulder and then wished she hadn't. A large package was nestled against the hull. A timer was counting down in bright red numbers.

"What is this, a *Mission Impossible* movie?"

"No," Duane offered cautiously. "That's definitely a bomb. It's going to shatter this lab in one minute-fifty."

Melissa's training had her setting a countdown timer on her watch even while her mind churned.

"Can you disable it?"

Duane studied it carefully for five achingly long seconds. "Probably not in time."

"This was Richie's danger signal."

"What danger signal?" Chad and Duane asked in unison.

"Long story. Flashbangs." She held out a hand.

Chad slapped one into her palm.

She made three chopping motions: right, middle, and left over the fuselage. Then, three fingers, two… She grabbed the pin, pulled it, and heaved hers over the top of the DC-6's fuselage to land on the other side. Chad and Duane mimicked her actions, angling their throws toward either end of the plane.

With a harmless *krump!* loud enough to deafen anyone on that side and blinding bright flashes, it should scare any workers out of the lab. Hopefully driving them well clear of the coming explosion.

"Let's move," she called out. "Weapons free."

At one minute-forty, they stayed low and started moving fast.

At one minute-thirty-nine, the flashbangs rocked the jungle.

Fifty feet later, they caught up with Kyle.

No explanation needed.

One look at them and he spun on his heel to fall in at point position.

"NCA?" Carla asked blankly.

"National Crime Agency," Richie told her. "Britain's version of the DEA and the ATF combined." Then he had a sickening thought? "Was Marco—"

"Just what he said, Ecuadorian Army deserter. I hooked up with him to get in here and he was my way back out. Who the hell are you?" He'd give her spunk points for arguing from her current position of her face planted in the dirt.

"U.S. Special Forces" which wasn't wholly accurate as they were Special *Operations* Forces, not Green Berets. But it was close enough. The Unit never revealed their presence, ever. He let her up carefully as Carla backed off enough to keep them covered.

"Ten seconds to company," Carla reminded him.

Dayana moved carefully to a kneeling position, "Marco was an Ecuadoran Army pilot." She waved a hand at one of the small Cessnas.

"Five," Carla whispered.

Richie wondered if he could trust Dayana, or if he was about to get shot in the back. Chad had chosen her and Chad might enjoy women, but he wasn't stupid about them.

He dropped the Glock into Dayana's hand. "Both of you. Down in the dirt. Prone firing position, aimed into the jungle."

They both spun and dropped the moment before the first guards rounded the low body of the Gulfstream jet. He'd swung his own rifle to his shoulder and was kneeling between them, one knee still on Dayana's back just in case.

"Shooter! In the woods!" He had to shout to be heard over the loud whine of the BAe's engines all cranking up the scale toward full heat. "They got Marco and I think they went west. Cutting around toward the lab. *Rápido!*"

The guards raced right by them, plunging into the jungle.

The moment they were clear, he looked back at Carla. "We have to get to the Twin Otter and stop Analie from taking off."

"No!" Dayana grabbed his arm. "You can't."

He stopped to stare at her. Glanced at the track of the ATV. She'd already visited the Twin Otter. She'd planted a bomb on the *Tin Goose*.

"Disarm it!" He demanded, but she was already shaking her head. Her expression said that she wasn't arguing; she was saying it couldn't be done. "How long?"

"Two minutes."

―⁓―

Melissa hit the field with one minute to go. They were huddled close by the nose of the DC-3.

Kyle raised his fist for Hold Position. Chad and Duane dropped to kneel behind her. One would be watching her flank, another the rear. Kyle lay in the dirt two steps in front of her, peeking under the nose of the grounded DC-3 for a wider field of view.

The hundreds of residents of the jungle town had filtered out of the tents and their quarters among the shattered planes converted into private apartments.

She considered firing a long stream of bullets close in front of them to scare them back, farther from the lab that was about to go up. Chase them to safety. But a brief hail of gunfire wouldn't do the job and it would attract all of the wrong kind of attention their way.

"Duane," she called over her shoulder.

"Yo!"

"Blow the DC-3 on a fifteen-second timer."

"Big or little?" He unslung the small bag he'd had over his shoulder since her first warning aboard the DC-3. She could feel him working close behind her.

"*Muy grande!*"

"*Si, señorita*. Ready in five."

She counted five seconds, felt the slap on her shoulder, reached forward, and slapped Kyle's heel in turn.

No neat two-by-two formation. The four of them lined up and sprinted across the open field toward the *Tin Goose*.

———

Richie reached the *Tin Goose* at the same instant Melissa did. He stole a moment long enough to squeeze her shoulder. The sense of connection that rushed through him and the smile that lit her face told him that she understo—

Across the field the DC-3 blew up in a towering column of fire and a cloud of smoke. He could see the civilians tumbled back by the force of the explosion.

Then the crowd broke and sprinted off down the length of the runway, racing away from the burning DC-3 and the lab as well.

"Can I cook or what?" Melissa grinned at him.

"Hot shit, lady!"

"Lab in"—she glanced down at her watch—"another twenty seconds."

He checked his own. "*Tin Goose* in one minute-twenty. We need our weapons."

"Not the *Goose*!"

"File a complaint with the British government." He pointed a finger at Dayana. "She slid a charge into the fuel tank. Can't get it back."

Melissa grimaced at her. "Well, now you make perfect sense. Should have seen it, but you're very good."

Richie glanced between them as like acknowledged like. He still didn't see it at all, but if Melissa did, then it must be true.

Carla had already unlocked the rear baggage compartment.

They'd come to the jungle airstrip heavy…and been adding to their armament with each trip. Kyle raced to the small shed where they'd stored the plane's spare parts and placed a large ammunition cache. He came back out with two heavy bags, passing them off to Duane and Chad, before coming back with two more.

Richie looked down the row toward the BAe 146. Whoever was piloting rode the controls forward hard. The engines awoke with a deep-throated roar that drowned out all other sounds.

It also sent a blast of intense heat straight back into the trees. They must have expected to tow the jet out onto the field before starting the engines, and certainly before hitting full throttle.

The jungle burst into a towering wall of flame.

A figure came stumbling out of the jungle, his body burning brightly, his mouth open in a scream though there was no way to hear it over the jet engines' roar.

One of the guards, still carrying his rifle. They had all been racing through the jungle to find the fictitious shooter. Richie didn't have time for sympathy. And even if he had, the guards' main job was to make sure that that workers didn't run away into the jungle. His sympathy level was set very low for them anyway.

The lab went up in a bright bloom—an inferno that shot up fifty feet into the air. Melissa could barely hear the explosion, adding only a basso roll to the much closer

BAe 146's roaring engines. The size of the charge had looked plenty big over Duane's shoulder.

A whole section of the fuselage, perhaps ten feet square, shot a dozen feet into the air. A blinding wave of light shot to either side. Then one of the chemicals inside the lab must have breached its container.

The entire top half of the fuselage lifted as a single piece ten stories into the jungle before shattering and cascading back into the pillar of fire that erupted into the jungle's high canopy.

Analie Sala's jet began rolling down the runway.

Melissa shouldered a rifle—an M-16 she'd grabbed out of the baggage compartment—aimed at the pilot's window on the BAe 146, and spotted a dim figure inside leaning forward to see the exploding lab.

Melissa fired.

And the round bounced off the glass. Armored glass.

A dark, narrow face twisted to look out at her. Analie Sala. She'd expected Pederson.

"C'mon, bitch!"

She fired three more shots around the window, hoping that Sala hadn't armored the whole cockpit, but the jet kept accelerating. More shots at the wing tanks, but by now the angle was bad and the distance long.

Then Sala was aloft and flying out the hole in the canopy.

Over the jet's fading thunder, she heard a lot of shouts.

The civilians' panic as they raced away from the series of explosions.

The guards as they stumbled out of the fire on this side of the field lit by Sala's departing jet.

Then Pederson came running across the compound. He wore underwear and one shoe.

"Analie!" he shouted up at the departing plane. "Analie!"

Kyle raced over and grabbed him just as Richie grabbed Melissa's arm.

"Got a plane to catch, Ilsa." Richie grinned at her as they raced away from the ticking *Tin Goose*.

"We do?" Melissa was feeling a little dense and a lot charmed. Racing with her lover hand in hand through the heart of a battlefield was impossibly crazy for a girl with a frozen heart to imagine. So her heart must not be frozen at all.

They dodged around the little Cessna; it wasn't big enough to carry their whole crew, even without Dayana or Pederson.

Behind them, the farthest plane in the line exploded in a ball of fire, which then set off a large secondary explosion as the fuel tanks were breached.

"Dayana only left two planes untouched."

Melissa stumbled to a halt as the second plane they'd left behind them blew up.

The Gulfstream G250 was sixty-plus feet of sleek twinjet. It looked fast sitting on the ground.

"Who's flying it?"

She didn't like the way Richie was grinning at her.

The team set up a secure perimeter as Melissa raced along close behind him and shouted out the checklist.

Richie did his best to figure out what each instruction meant. He'd never flown a jet, but how different could it really be?

Not very. Because if it was very, then they were dead and that just wasn't an option.

The timer on his watch beeped.

He spun around, tackled Melissa, and pinned her to the ground with his body over hers.

"What the—" was all she managed before the *Tin Goose* blew up like a Roman candle. The fuel tanks deep in the hull breached separately in a cascading set of explosions that shredded the Twin Otter. Shrapnel whistled by over their heads, some of it pinging off the Gulfstream's hull, but the Cessna between them took most of the abuse.

"Let's hope nothing critical was hit here," he whispered to Melissa, not letting her up yet.

"Just my pride."

"I'm sorry," he tried to apologize. "I know I shouldn't have. But I needed you to react and—"

"Richie!" Melissa cut him off.

"Yes?"

"Get off me, save our lives, and we're square. Okay?"

"You're the best woman ever!"

"Thanks. Get off me!"

"Oh, right. Sorry." He levered himself up. "What's next on the list?"

She grabbed his shirt collar and pulled him in, spending a precious second on a kiss.

"That's one," she said, ending the kiss as fast as it began. "Two. Remove wheel chocks."

He dove and rolled under the low plane to pull them from the farside wheel as she pulled the nearer ones.

There was sporadic gunfire.

He couldn't waste time looking up to see what the targets might be. It wasn't until they were in the cockpit and going through the cold-start checklists that he managed a peek. People were storming toward them to board the plane. The Gulfstream could carry a dozen safely. There were six Delta, Dayana, and Pederson. Each of the Delta had at least eighty pounds of weapons and ammo. And he had no time to check what was in the cargo hold. It was official; they were full.

The team laid down warning shots to brush the crowds back, and it was working for the moment.

There was another booming explosion, muffled by the Gulfstream's hull, and a blast momentarily blinded him through the windshield.

"I spotted a large propane tank behind the chow tent. That must be it," Melissa informed him between APU start and temperature range targets, which he managed to find despite the bright dots and blotches swimming across his vision.

He flipped open the small pilot window when he had the engines up to temperature.

"Now! Now! Now!" Richie shouted it as loud as he could.

The team tumbled toward the plane. He could feel it shift on its shock absorbers as each person dove aboard.

"Go! Go! Go!" Kyle shouted from the back.

There were red lights, green lights, and a half a hundred switches that Richie didn't recognize. It didn't just have a yoke like a steering wheel. There was also a control beside him that looked like a helicopter's cyclic, a joystick with a bulbous head covered in switches. For all he knew, it was a *Star Trek* auto-destruct switch, so he didn't touch it and prayed that he wouldn't need to.

But he knew what throttles looked like and he

rammed the two large silver levers in the center of the console forward as fast as he dared.

In moments they were rolling and people who had run out onto the runway were diving aside to get out of his way.

To the left were the ongoing explosions of the drug lab and chow tent. A fire had formed and was sweeping toward the tents and wrecked planes of the living quarters.

"The DC-3?" Richie was very fond of that plane.

"Sorry," Melissa replied, "I had Duane blow it up."

"Oh." He didn't know quite how he felt about that. There were memories there that…

"Don't worry, Richie. We'll make some new memories in the future. That's a promise."

He wanted to look over at her, acknowledge it somehow, but there wasn't time. And there was a tightness in his throat that he couldn't speak past.

To their right was a line of burning planes blown up by Dayana, the British NCA operative, and a wall of the jungle alight in two places directly behind where the BAe 146 and the Gulfstream each had been parked.

Melissa was the sort of woman that a man made promises to.

And that was an awfully big thought for an awfully small moment because straight ahead was a wall of tree trunks a hundred feet high and a dozen feet across.

Above them was a wall of massive trunks and tangled branches. Above that was a hole that looked far too small to slip this huge plane through.

As he raced past the *Tin Goose*, he sent a thank-you its way and was glad that he didn't have time to look over at its shredded remains. He also wished that's what he was flying. Wished it was just he and his Ilsa, off seeking adventure.

Melissa was reading aloud take-off speeds and rates of climb. He managed to locate his speed in the bewildering array of instruments spread across the dash.

It was a glass cockpit, with way too many display screens and each mode buttons all around them. Hardly a single decent, familiar, round-dial readout anywhere.

So he watched the number that he understood, ignored everything else, pulled back on the yoke when he dared, and climbed for a hole that his radar—at least that's what he guessed it was—was telling him, "No way!" in loud alert tones and red flashing proximity alarms.

"Gear up," Melissa called as she toggled the switch. He felt the hum and *thunk* through the fuselage as the wheels retracted. That would improve his speed and control.

Leaving the wheels down wouldn't have helped anything anyway; they were far past landing again if he didn't make it.

The jet kept accelerating. They were already faster than the top speed of the *Tin Goose* and he didn't dare trying to slow down to give himself more time to maneuver. He always flew the Twin Otter through the entry of the jungle airstrip as slowly as he dared. He was going three times faster than that already.

The hole was coming at them so fast.

Tops of trees so close below.

Canopy close above.

Jungle ahead.

"Climb. Climb! Climb!" The last was a shout begging the plane to lift for him.

They raced toward the narrow opening at over two hundred miles an hour and accelerating.

—⁓—

The Gulfstream burst out into the midday sunlight.

Melissa felt as if she'd been reborn.

She could practically feel the shards of her past self falling away, tumbling slowly down toward the jungle.

And she looked over at Richie, he was side-lit by the sun streaming into the cockpit.

He looked…magnificent. Nerd, genius, warrior, and jet pilot. No one else could have jumped from a sixty-year-old turboprop to a ten-year-old jet and gotten them out alive.

Richie had just saved her life. And the lives of the whole team. He was right; it was a matter of give-and-take and it felt amazing.

He was circling over the hole in the jungle. The fire had climbed up and burned away the canopy from both sides. The whole airfield was exposed to the sky.

She figured out the radio and called Agent Fred Smith.

"Do you still have that 747 around?"

"Sure, it's parked at…well, I can't tell you that, but it's not far away. What do you—"

She cut him off. "Load it with water. There's a fire at the location we gave you. It wants putting out."

"You burned it? That's great. Why would I want to stop it?"

"Because you want an intel team on the ground there. There are also pilots with plenty of delivery information, a communications bunker, and a load of civilians still on the ground and none of them are going anywhere."

"Okay, I've got the 747 on the move. I'll get a ground team in right behind it. Did you take down the whole operation?"

She didn't answer. Instead she looked at Richie.

He shook his head without speaking.

Analie Sala had gotten away.

"Pederson would know where she's going, wouldn't he?" Richie asked her.

Melissa considered going back into the cabin and beating Analie's destination out of Pederson. But she wasn't so sure.

Melissa thought about it and became even less sure. "Remember the interview aboard the BAe 146? She was the one sleeping in the cabin at the rear of the plane when we raided it. She was the first one to lean forward to shake hands on the deal even before Pederson did."

"Huh!" Richie agreed. "That means she left Pederson to run around camp in his underwear because he'd been in someone else's bed rather than hers, as we always assumed."

"He was the front, but she was the brains. That's why she flew that stupid swordfish job with us; she didn't trust anyone else's judgment. I'd wager that she didn't trust Pederson with her next hidey-hole."

Richie was nodding in agreement. "So how do we find her?"

"You want me to do the thinking for both of us?"

"That's my Ilsa. You do the thinking, and I'll do my best not to crash this jet in the meantime."

Analie Sala had played her cards so close that it was hard to imagine what she was thinking. Her jet was capable of reaching North or South America, but not Africa. But maybe, just maybe...

"Head north."

Richie didn't ask why. He simply trusted her and turned the jet.

Then Melissa started studying the console in front of her.

Chapter 21

RICHIE DID HIS BEST TO FLY BY THE SEAT OF HIS PANTS, because Melissa was doing something that kept scrambling the screens in front of him. Every time he thought he had figured out something, there would be a blink and the information was gone. She was using that joystick control which must be the display commander. Hopefully it didn't also have a James Bond ejection seat switch or he was in trouble.

Airspeed here—then over there. Engine temperature—not quite redline but gone before he could see if it was stable or getting worse.

He took to watching out the window.

They were already over the mountains of the Venezuelan coast. This bird was fast. Minutes later they flew over Maracaibo and then were out over the Caribbean. Still no midsized jet out ahead of them. No air traffic at all except for one of the rare commercial jets climbing out of Maracaibo airport.

He'd been staring out at the water for a while when the console finally stopped changing and Melissa spoke very proudly over the intercom.

"There's the bitch, Richie. Go get her."

He had to blink at the screen several times before it made sense. It was a radar sweep. And ahead of them, way ahead of them, there was a little blip. He looked out the front windshield. Still nothing but water.

"How can you be sure?"

"Straight line flight from her hole in the jungle to Honduras. She needs to refinance and she has a billion dollars of cocaine in her hold. She's headed to the drug capital of Central America, Honduras, in a straight line. She'll offload there and then rebuild her operation somewhere that we'll never find. You've got to stop her."

"Any brilliant suggestions? We're moving at Mach 0.85, which is almost six hundred miles an hour. We can't exactly open the door and shoot her down." Over the mountains, the land turned semiarid, and then in a flash they were over the intense blue of the deep ocean. "How about calling Fred?"

"I did that."

"I didn't hear you do it."

"I switched you out of the circuit. I figured you were a little busy flying. Didn't want to distract you from keeping us alive."

"Oh." Richie tried to think of something more intelligent to say, but repeating, "Oh," was all he managed. "What did Fred have to say?"

"No assets that can get here in time. Panama we have a lot of assets, but none that can beat her now; it took me too long to find her. In Honduras we only have a small helicopter group. There's a British frigate now turning for Honduras, but they're half a day out; closest U.S. Coast Guard vessel is a couple hours behind it. We're the only asset that can get to her before she lands. I don't want her to land; she's far too slippery."

He was already moving at very close to the Never Exceed speed, which was a little faster than Analie's plane could do. He corrected his course and kept crawling up to her, closer and closer.

Richie looked over his other shoulder and saw the rest of the team sprawled out in the cabin. Carla came forward when she saw him looking back.

"What's the plan?"

Richie pulled back the ear of his headset so that he could hear her.

"Ilsa The Cat here wants me to take on Analie, jet to jet."

"No other assets in the area," Melissa explained quickly. "She's on the ground in an hour and fifteen, then she's gone. I was worried that she'd put the plane on autopilot and parachute out, but I don't see her doing that with a billion dollars of cocaine in her plane's cargo hold."

Carla slapped Richie on the shoulder. "Get me close and I'll shoot her down."

"We can't exactly open the door at six hundred miles an hour."

That silenced Carla for all of about five seconds. "You'll figure it out, Q. You always do."

Richie grimaced. "Great! Thanks for the big help."

—ᴡᴡ—

Melissa held on to her seat as Analie Sala's plane came into view. The Gulfstream was faster, but not much. It had been an agonizing forty-five-minute chase, with no one coming up with any brilliant ideas on how to avoid this. Both planes were at thirty thousand feet. The idea of shooting out a window and catastrophically depressurizing the plane had been the best they'd come up with.

Except for one. And now that they'd come to the moment, Melissa really didn't like it, even though she was the one who'd thought it up.

"Richie. It was stupid. We've got to come up with something else."

"My Ilsa doesn't have stupid ideas. We're approaching from her six. Just like Vito The Priest said, she'll never think to look directly behind her until it's too late."

"Your confidence is charming. But this has got to be an exception. Six-hundred-mile-an-hour bumper cars?"

Richie shrugged. "I want her down as badly as you do. A third of the cocaine that reaches U.S. soil came through that camp. Pederson said they'd been in operation for seven years. She gets set up again, you know that she'll be even harder to find."

Melissa had tried flying the jet for a few minutes but didn't like the feel of it. It felt as if they were constantly on the edge of tripping and tumbling out of the sky. If she was going to trust anyone, it would be Richie's steady hand and sharp mind.

"Okay, Richie. Do it."

"Wish I could kiss you first."

"Later. Just as often as you want."

"That's a deal, sweetheart." He put on his best Bogey for her. If he had any doubts, he wasn't showing them to her.

She watched him take a deep breath, then another, and another as they drew closer and closer to Analie's plane.

The risk of what they were about to do was insane. The chances of surviving it were… She'd rather not try to calculate that.

But there was a question that wanted asking. Needed

asking. Something she needed to know just in case there wasn't a "later."

"Richie?"

He turned to look at her for a moment, but she wasn't even sure he recognized her. He turned back to stare at the plane now just a few hundred yards off their nose.

She knew the look.

The warrior was in complete control.

Melissa's question was going to have to wait.

Damn it!

———※———

Richie tapped the high tail of the airplane in front of him by flying right over it and then lowering the Gulfstream's nose onto it as hard as he dared.

It didn't turn out to be much of a tap but it must have shuddered up the length of Sala's airframe.

She twisted her plane to the left and Richie followed. He had the feel of the Gulfstream now. Could stay like glue right on the tail of the bigger, less maneuverable jet.

As soon as it settled, he whacked it again, much more sharply this time.

Again. The pilot corrected hard and he hung close.

Time was ticking.

No sign of the shore yet, but it wouldn't be far now.

He flew up alongside the big jet, so that he could see the pilot. He pointed down. As if to say, *You land the plane where I want, or I will land it for you.*

With a twist of the controls, the pilot sent her far larger jet sharply into his path.

A twist, a pull, right rudder. He dodged the maneuver.

Out of options, he circled behind once more.

This time he hammered his nose down on the other plane's tail. A whole side of it bent sharply.

He heard a scream. Metal or human. It all sounded the same.

The big plane started a spiraling descent. One side of its tail section bent completely out of shape.

He followed it down. The pilot managed a partial recovery.

He drove in and bashed the other side of the tail control surface. Again the crunch and scream. The Gulfstream shuddered from the abuse.

Sala twisted and fought the controls, but the aircraft was now beyond help and going down hard.

He pulled up to watch her final descent.

Except the Gulfstream didn't pull up. It struggled; it wallowed.

He glanced back. The wings looked intact. He couldn't see the rear-mounted engines despite what someone had told him to do at another time in another world.

He tried the controls again. The problem wasn't the plane; it was the controls. He'd crippled the nose of his own plane where all of the wires and everything ran from the cockpit back to the control surfaces. The plane could still fly, but he could only barely control it.

Sala's big jet tumbled into the ocean, shattering against the hard waves. Huge chunks flailed off in different directions. Wing, engine, tail, a luxury couch, bales upon bales of cocaine.

Richie didn't have a moment to howl in triumph.

He heard a Mayday. From the downed plane? Impossible. From his? Didn't matter.

He pulled power. Extended flaps. Held up the nose and fought the twisting descent.

Pilot like he was in a floatplane. With a single pontoon made of a smooth fuselage. Low wings were bad. The ocean was rough.

Waves six feet. Maybe ten. More than the Twin Otter could handle.

Not in the Twin Otter. In a jet.

Didn't matter. Same tactics.

He aimed down the furrow of the waves.

Land high on the slope of one wave, and glide down its face like a surfboard, riding it right into the trough. Bleeding speed.

Nose high.

A hundred feet.

Fifty.

Stall warning.

Time the wave.

Time it.

Now!

Chapter 22

WITH CHAD'S HELP, MELISSA DRAGGED A DAZED Richie into the raft. The Gulfstream had two rafts and the team had managed to deploy both. There were plenty of bangs and bruises, but they had all made it. Richie was the most battered and dazed of them all. Chad laid him along the bottom of the raft with his head in Melissa's lap. Then he gave her a nod that she gathered was his final acceptance of her role on the team. She returned the silent acknowledgment.

She held Richie close against her; Carla and Duane were also in this raft. Chad clambered across to join Kyle, who had Dayana and Pederson in the other one. The Gulfstream G250 was slipping beneath the waves and shattered pieces of the bigger BAe 146 were scattered everywhere, sinking a piece at a time.

She could hear Kyle and Dayana debating who got Pederson. Melissa knew that the British frigate would be here in just a few hours—they were the closest when she radioed her Mayday—and that would answer that question.

Melissa couldn't tell if Chad was more bummed that he wouldn't be accompanying Dayana after the American ship caught up with the Brits or that he hadn't found her out before the final escape. The two of them were talking about military exchange programs. Or their next leave. But Melissa would bet it was never going to happen. They'd had their fun and they were done with it, or soon would be.

Melissa didn't want "a moment" or "some fun."

Richie was coming around but didn't speak. Instead, he held on to her tighter and tighter until she could barely breathe. It was the best feeling of her life. She wanted to wake every day with this man in her arms.

They'd serve together and fight side by side. And someday they'd—

"You had a question?" Richie mumbled in her arms.

"Did I?" She was impressed that he remembered.

"You did."

"Well, you did say I was supposed to do the thinking for you."

Richie nodded. "I like giving that task to the smartest one in the relationship." Not a chance that was her. Yet maybe it was in some ways. Carla had complimented her again on her clear and accurate perceptions of people. Richie might be the genius, but Melissa knew she was smart about people.

"Does that make you Ilsa and me Rick?" Melissa teased him.

"Anything you want." Richie snuggled his face against her belly. "As long as I don't have to put you on a plane for Lisbon. I like having you in Casablanca."

Duane kept his silence. Carla was working the radio with the USCG frigate.

"Not going anywhere without you," Melissa agreed.

There was a sharp spit of silenced gunfire which made her jump.

"What was that?" Richie struggled up, but then dropped back into her lap with a grunt. He was battered in a dozen spots and possibly concussed by the crash landing.

Melissa looked over at the other raft.

Chad and Kyle had brought over most of their weapons and ammo when they'd deplaned. They were taking turns shooting at the water.

She looked around. Floating all around them were one-kilo bags of cocaine from the shattered BAe 146. Each one they shot quickly flooded and sank.

Kyle noticed her attention. "Don't want these floating ashore anywhere. Nothing else to do while we wait."

Duane strapped a knife to one of the oars and began stabbing bags. Pederson groaned with each kilo of cocaine that sank out of sight. The guys started tallying their "kills" in hundred-thousand-dollar-per-kilo increments to rub it in.

"Any sign of Analie?"

Kyle nodded grimly and Melissa returned her attention to the beautiful man still lying in her lap.

"I think," Richie mumbled against her belly, "that I'd better keep being Rick. I just don't think wearing a dress is my style. Sure wouldn't mind seeing you in one someday though."

"We'll see," Melissa teased him. "But no more showing off my breasts to a bunch of drug-runner guards, okay?"

"I can work with that."

"Bro," Duane grumbled. "Way too much mush. Just kiss the woman and tell her."

"Tell me what?" She looked at Duane.

He pointed for her to look at Richie.

She did. "Tell me what?"

Richie looked at Duane for a long moment, then back at her.

"Tell me what?" she demanded with about as much imagination as a one-track Amazonian parrot…but she knew what. It was what she'd wanted to say just before Richie crashed them into Sala's jet.

"Ilsa."

"Yes, Richie?" She brushed a hand over his face unable to believe how good it felt to do so.

"This looks like the beginning of a beautiful friendship."

"What?" Melissa thumped the side of her fist down on his chest and he grunted when she nailed him on the medallion. "That's what you have to say to—"

He laughed as he dragged her down to lie on him at the bottom of the raft and kissed her. Kissed her like a promise that no one had ever made to her, and he warmed her all of the way through to the very center of her heart. So completely that she'd never be cold again.

To a background of silenced gunfire slaughtering kilo bags of cocaine, Richie whispered in her ear.

"Love you, Ilsa."

"Love you, Richie."

"And I do love looking at you, kid…in or out of your clothes. I look forward to doing it for as long as we both shall live."

She fisted his ribs hard enough to make him grunt, but not hard enough to interrupt the kiss he pulled her back into.

*Keep reading for an excerpt from the
explosive beginning to the Delta Force
series, nominated for a RITA Award:*

TARGET ENGAGED

CARLA ANDERSON ROLLED UP TO THE LOOMING STORM-
fence gate on her brother's midnight-blue Kawasaki
Ninja 1000 motorcycle. The pounding of the engine
against her sore butt emphasized every mile from Fort
Carson in Colorado Springs, Colorado, home of the 4th
Infantry and hopefully never again the home of Sergeant
Carla Anderson. The bike was all she had left of Clay,
other than a folded flag, and she was here to honor that.

If this was the correct "here."

A small guard post stood by the gate into a broad,
dusty compound. It looked deserted and she didn't see
even a camera.

This *was* Fort Bragg, North Carolina. She knew that
much. Two hundred and fifty square miles of military
installation, not counting the addition of the neighboring
Pope Army Airfield.

She'd gotten her Airborne parachute training here
and had never even known what was hidden in this
remote corner. Bragg was exactly the sort of place

where a tiny, elite unit of the U.S. military could disappear—in plain sight.

This back corner of the home of the 82nd Airborne was harder to find than it looked. What she could see of the compound through the fence definitely ranked "worst on base."

The setup was totally whacked.

Standing outside the fence at the guard post she could see a large, squat building across the compound. The gray concrete building was incongruously cheerful with bright pink roses along the front walkway—the only landscaping visible anywhere. More recent buildings—in better condition only because they were newer—ranged off to the right. She could breach the old fence in a dozen different places just in the hundred-yard span she could see before it disappeared into a clump of scrub and low trees drooping in the June heat.

Wholly indefensible.

There was no way that this could be the headquarters of the top combat unit in any country's military.

Unless this really was their home, in which case the indefensible fence—inde-fence-ible?—was a complete sham designed to fool a sucker. She'd stick with the main gate.

She peeled off her helmet and scrubbed at her long brown hair to get some air back into her scalp. Guys always went gaga over her hair, which was a useful distraction at times. She always wore it as long as her successive commanders allowed. Pushing the limits was one of her personal life policies.

She couldn't help herself. When there was a limit, Carla always had to see just how far it could be nudged.

Surprisingly far was usually the answer. Her hair had been at earlobe length in Basic. By the time she joined her first forward combat team, it brushed her jaw. Now it was down on her shoulders. It was actually something of a pain in the ass at this length—another couple inches before it could reliably ponytail—but she did like having the longest hair in the entire unit.

Carla called out a loud "Hello!" at the empty compound shimmering in the heat haze.

No response.

Using her boot in case the tall chain-link fence was electrified, she gave it a hard shake, making it rattle loudly in the dead air. Not even any birdsong in the oppressive midday heat.

A rangy man in his late forties or early fifties, his hair half gone to gray, wandered around from behind a small shack as if he just happened to be there by chance. He was dressed like any off-duty soldier: worn khaki pants, a black T-shirt, and scuffed Army boots. He slouched to a stop and tipped his head to study her from behind his Ray-Bans. He needed a haircut and a shave. This was not a soldier out to make a good first impression.

"Don't y'all get hot in that gear?" He nodded to indicate her riding leathers without raking his eyes down her frame, which was both unusual and appreciated.

"Only on warm days," she answered him. It was June in North Carolina. The temperature had crossed ninety hours ago and the air was humid enough to swim in, but complaining never got you anywhere.

"What do you need?"

So much for the pleasantries. "Looking for Delta."

"Never heard of it," the man replied with a negligent

shrug. But something about how he did it told her she was in the right place.

"Combat Applications Group?" Delta Force had many names, and they certainly lived to "apply combat" to a situation. No one on the planet did it better.

His next shrug was eloquent.

Delta Lesson Number One: *Folks on the inside of the wire didn't call it Delta Force. It was CAG or "The Unit."* She got it. Check. Still easier to think of it as Delta though.

She pulled out her orders and held them up. "Received a set of these. Says to show up here today."

"Let me see that."

"Let me through the gate and you can look at it as long as you want."

"Sass!" He made it an accusation.

"Nope. Just don't want them getting damaged or lost maybe by accident." She offered her blandest smile with that.

"They're that important to you, girlie?"

"Yep!"

He cracked what might have been the start of a grin, but it didn't get far on that grim face. Then he opened the gate and she idled the bike forward, scuffing her boots through the dust.

From this side she could see that the chain link was wholly intact. There was a five-meter swath of scorched earth inside the fence line. Through the heat haze, she could see both infrared and laser spy eyes down the length of the wire. And those were only the defenses she could see. So...a very *not* inde-fence-ible fence. Absolutely the right place.

When she went to hold out the orders, he waved them aside.

"Don't you want to see them?" This had to be the right place. She was the first woman in history to walk through The Unit's gates by order. A part of her wanted the man to acknowledge that. Any man. A Marine Corps marching band wouldn't have been out of order.

She wanted to stand again as she had on that very first day, raising her right hand. "I, Carla Anderson, do solemnly swear that I will support and defend the Constitution…"

She shoved that aside. The only man's acknowledgment she'd ever cared about was her big brother's, and he was gone.

The man just turned away and spoke to her over his shoulder as he closed the gate behind her bike. "Go ahead and check in. You're one of the last to arrive. We start in a couple hours"—as if it were a blasted dinner party. "And I already saw those orders when I signed them. Now put them away before someone else sees them and thinks you're still a soldier." He walked away.

She watched the man's retreating back. *He'd* signed her orders?

That was the notoriously hard-ass Colonel Charlie Brighton?

What the hell was the leader of the U.S. Army's Tier One asset doing manning the gate? Duh…assessing new applicants.

This place *was* whacked. Totally!

There were only three Tier One assets in the entire U.S. military. There was Navy's Special Warfare Development Group, DEVGRU, that the public thought was called SEAL Team Six—although it hadn't been named that for thirty years now. There was the Air Force's 24th STS—which pretty much no one on the outside had ever heard of. And there was the 1st Special Forces Operational Detachment—Delta—whose very existence was still denied by the Pentagon despite four decades of operations, several books, and a couple of seriously off-the-mark movies that were still fun to watch because Chuck Norris kicked ass even under the stupidest of circumstances.

Total Tier One women across all three teams? Zero.

About to be? One. Staff Sergeant First Class Carla Anderson.

Where did she need to go to check in? There was no signage. No drill sergeant hovering. No—

Delta Lesson Number Two: *You aren't in the Army anymore, sister*.

No longer a soldier, as the Colonel had said, at least not while on The Unit's side of the fence. On this side they weren't regular Army; they were "other."

If that meant she had to take care of herself, well, that was a lesson she'd learned long ago. Against stereotype, her well-bred, East Coast white-guy dad was the drunk. Her dirt-poor half Tennessee Cherokee, half Colorado settler mom, who'd passed her dusky skin and dark hair on to her daughter, had been a sober and serious woman. She'd also been a casualty of an Afghanistan dust-bowl IED while serving in the National Guard. Carla's big brother Clay now lay beside Mom in Arlington National Cemetery. Dead from a training accident. Except your average training accident didn't include a posthumous rank bump, a medal, and coming home in a sealed box— reportedly with no face.

Clay had flown helicopters in the Army's 160th SOAR with the famous Majors Beale and Henderson. Well, famous in the world of people who'd flown with the Special Operations Aviation Regiment, or their little sisters who'd begged for stories of them whenever big brothers were home on leave. Otherwise, totally invisible.

Clay had clearly died on a black op that she'd never be told a word of, so she didn't bother asking. Which was okay. He knew the risks, just as Mom had. Just as she herself had when she'd signed up the day of Clay's funeral, four years ago. She'd been on the front lines ever since and so far lived to tell about it.

Carla popped Clay's Ninja—which is how she still thought of it, even after riding it for four years—back into first and rolled it slowly up to the building with the pink roses. As good a place to start as any.

"Hey, check out this shit!"

Sergeant First Class Kyle Reeves looked out the window of the mess hall at the guy's call. Sergeant Ralph last-name-already-forgotten was 75th Rangers and too damn proud of it.

Though…damn! Ralphie was onto something.

Kyle would definitely check out *this shit*.

Babe on a hot bike, looking like she knew how to handle it.

Through the window, he inspected her lean length as she clambered off the machine. Army boots. So call her five-eight, a hundred and thirty, and every part that wasn't amazing curves looked like serious muscle. Hair the color of lush, dark caramel brushed her shoulders but moved like the finest silk, her skin permanently the color of the darkest tan. Women in magazines didn't look that hot. Those women always looked anorexic to him anyway, even the pinup babes displayed on Hesco barriers at forward operating bases up in the Hindu Kush, where he'd done too much of the last couple years.

This woman didn't look like that for a second. She looked powerful. And dangerous.

Her tight leathers revealed muscles made of pure soldier.

Ralph Something moseyed out of the mess-hall building where the hundred selectees were hanging out to await the start of the next testing class at sundown.

Well, Kyle sure wasn't going to pass up the opportunity for a closer look. Though seeing Ralph's attitude, Kyle hung back a bit so that he wouldn't be too closely associated with the dickhead.

Ralph had been spoiling for a fight ever since he'd found out he was one of the least experienced guys to show up for Delta Selection. He was from the 75th Ranger Regiment, but his deployments hadn't seen much action. Each of his attempts to brag for status had gotten him absolutely nowhere.

Most of the guys here were 75th Rangers, 82nd Airborne, or Green Beret Special Forces like himself. And most had seen a shitload of action, because that was the nature of the world at the moment. There were a couple SEALs who hadn't made SEAL Team Six and probably weren't going to make Delta, a dude from the Secret Service Hostage Rescue Team who wasn't going to last a day no matter how good a shot he was, and two guys who were regular Army.

The question of the moment though, who was she?

Her biking leathers were high-end, sewn in a jagged lightning-bolt pattern of yellow on smoke gray. It made her look like she was racing at full tilt while standing still. He imagined her hunched over her midnight-blue machine and hustling down the road at her Ninja's top speed—which was north of 150. He definitely had to see that one day.

Kyle blessed the inspiration on his last leave that had made him walk past the small Toyota pickup that had looked so practical and buy the wildfire-red Ducati Multistrada 1200 instead. Pity his bike was parked around the back of the barracks at the moment. Maybe they could do a little bonding over their rides. Her machine looked absolutely cherry.

Much like its rider.

Ralph walked right up to her with all his arrogant and stupid hanging out for everyone to see. The other soldiers began filtering outside to watch the show.

"Well, girlie, looks like you pulled into the wrong spot. This here is Delta territory."

Kyle thought about stopping Ralph, thought that someone should give the guy a good beating, but Dad had taught him control. He would take Ralph down if he got aggressive, but he really didn't want to be associated with the jerk, even by grabbing him back.

The woman turned to face them, then unzipped the front of her jacket in one of those long, slow movie moves. The sunlight shimmered across her hair as she gave it an "unthinking" toss. Wraparound dark glasses hid her eyes, adding to the mystery.

He could see what there was of Ralph's brain

imploding from lack of blood. He felt the effect himself despite standing a half-dozen paces farther back.

She wasn't hot; she sizzled. Her parting leathers revealed an Army green T-shirt and proof that the very nice contours suggested by her outer gear were completely genuine. Her curves weren't big—she had a lean build—but they were as pure woman as her shoulders and legs were pure soldier.

"There's a man who called me 'girlie' earlier." Her voice was smooth and seductive, not low and throaty, but rich and filled with nuance.

She sounded like one of those people who could hypnotize a Cobra, either the snake or the attack helicopter.

"*He's* a bird colonel. He can call me that if he wants. *You* aren't nothing but meat walking on sacred ground and wishing he belonged."

Kyle nodded to himself. The "girlie" got it in one.

"*You*"—she jabbed a finger into Sergeant Ralph Something's chest—"do not get 'girlie' privileges. *We* clear?"

"Oh, sweetheart, I can think of plenty of privileges that you'll want to be giving to—" His hand only made it halfway to stroking her hair.

If Kyle hadn't been Green Beret trained, he wouldn't have seen it because she moved so fast and clean.

"—*me!*" Ralph's voice shot upward on a sharp squeak.

The woman had Ralph's pinkie bent to the edge of dislocation and, before the man could react, had leveraged it behind his back and upward until old Ralph Something was perched on his toes trying to ease the pressure. With her free hand, she shoved against the middle of his back to send him stumbling out of control into the concrete wall of the mess hall with a loud *clonk* when his head hit.

Minimum force, maximum result. The Unit's way.

She eased off on his finger and old Ralph dropped to the dirt like a sack of potatoes. He didn't move much.

"Oops." She turned to face the crowd that had gathered.

She didn't even have to say, "Anyone else?" Her look said plenty.

Kyle began to applaud. He wasn't the only one, but he was in the minority. Most of the guys were doing a wait and see.

A couple looked pissed.

Everyone knew that the Marines' combat training had graduated a few women, but that was just jarheads on the ground.

This was Delta. The Unit was Tier One. A Special Mission Unit. They were supposed to be the one true bastion of male dominance. No one had warned them that a woman was coming in.

Just one woman, Kyle thought. The first one. How exceptional did that make her? Pretty damn was his guess. Even if she didn't last the first day, still pretty damn. And damn pretty. He'd bet on dark eyes behind her wraparound shades. She didn't take them off, so it was a bet he'd have to settle later on.

A couple corpsmen came over and carted Ralph Something away, even though he was already sitting up—just dazed with a bloody cut on his forehead.

The Deltas who'd come out to watch the show from a few buildings down didn't say a word before going back to whatever they'd been doing.

Kyle made a bet with himself that Ralph Something wouldn't be showing up at sundown's first roll call. They'd just lost the first one of the class and the selection process hadn't even begun. Or maybe it just had.

"Where's check-in?" Her voice really was as lush as her hair, and it took Kyle a moment to focus on the actual words.

He pointed at the next building over and received a nod of thanks.

That made watching her walk away in those tight leathers strictly a bonus.

Chapter 2

DAY EIGHT AND NO FORMATION UNTIL 0600 HOURS. Kyle felt like he'd been lazy and slept in. He did a rough head count. From the first day of 104 candidates, they were down by at least twenty-five.

Several hadn't made it through the day-one PT test, which hadn't even been hard. The only unusual part of the physical training test had been the amount of it. Most of these guys had been in advanced branches of the military—Special Forces, Special Ops, 82nd Airborne. How could these guys not have been prepared for a round of hard-core PT?

Sergeant Carla was one of only three regular Army. All three of them were still in. You had to be tough to think you could jump straight from Army to Delta without spending a couple tours in Special Operations or as a Special Forces Green Beret first.

He'd won his first-day bet with himself when he watched the Hostage Rescue Team dude nearly drown halfway through the hundred-meter swim in full clothes and boots toward the end of day one—without even a rifle in his hands. He'd panicked, grabbed for the boat moving along beside him, and voluntarily quit.

This was real, not a game. He should have known that before he walked through the gate. Sympathy level: zero.

The first day had cut six; the first week had cut about

twenty more. Half of those couldn't deal with the brutal physical workouts, and the other half couldn't deal with the rules. He could pick out another twenty he didn't think would survive much longer for that second reason. Sympathy level: same.

Delta Selection rules were oddly too simple for most. Life in other units of the U.S. military was about explicit orders that told you exactly what to wear, how to make your bed, where to be, and what to do.

Delta rules rarely lasted more than three sentences—for an entire day's exercise. Last night's bulletin board had said simply, "0600. No rucks." That meant no brutal hike with a heavy rucksack, at least not to start the day.

A lot of the guys had cheered when they'd seen that. Assessment Phase had been a week of escalating work-outs, lots of PT, and lots of heavy-duty hikes. First day had been an 0200 start, a full ruck, and eighteen miles along the roads of Fort Bragg. They'd also been told that there was an unspecified time limit to each hike, so they shouldn't dawdle.

Any drill sergeant worth his salt would have added something more. "…Dawdle like a little old ladies' knitting circle." Or "…like the lame weaklings we expect from the other services."

Not Delta. Just, "Don't dawdle."

Not real helpful.

Unlike Green Beret assessment and training, no instructor was hovering beside you, yelling at you to dig in and keep up. In Delta, if you lagged, a member of the testing cadre slipped up quietly beside you and asked if you wanted to voluntarily drop out. If not, they let you grind it out against a hidden clock that they never revealed. At times he wondered if the training cadre even knew what the time limits were or if only the sergeant major in charge knew the required maximums.

Whatever was coming, Kyle already knew it would be harder than the day before, heavy rucks on their shoulders or not. No cause to cheer or be depressed. Steady. Just like Dad had taught him.

Without preface, the cadre started calling roll as the sun cracked the horizon, and most guys pulled down their sunglasses. As each man was called, he stepped forward. Per standard practice, they were given a swatch of colored cloth with a number to pin to their uniform and then told to climb into truck number such-and-so.

Today his swatch was "Red 4," and that's all any instructor would call him by for the rest of the day. Truck 2 looked no different than the other two. Only three trucks. They were going to be sardined in by the time everyone was called.

He had looked for a pattern to their numbering but found none. That bothered several of the guys; made others a bit paranoid as they were certain it was a reflection on their prior day's success or failure. Kyle saw no pattern, decided it was a mind game, and stopped thinking about it. They clearly didn't need him to know, so he didn't worry about it.

He admitted to being pretty pleased when "Green 3" climbed into Truck 2 as well. The trainees filled the side benches of the truck as they climbed in, and Carla Anderson ended up directly across from him. She had kept to herself, ignored the subtle harassments, and put down the more obnoxious ones. In whatever direction the candidates would be dispersed through the day, he'd account starting out across from her as a good beginning.

It had become clear to him after day two that she could handle herself just fine. A brain-dead grunt had grabbed her ass and found himself head down in a toilet—not the flush kind, the slit-trench latrine kind. The aggressor hadn't been in the barracks that night; she had. No one said a word and everyone left her pretty much alone after that.

Kyle had been pleasantly surprised as Carla continued to survive each day. Woman was damn tough. She might keep to herself, but she gave a hundred percent. As often as not, she'd be on his heels at the end of each hike or exercise. He sure as hell knew where she was at all times, close and moving at full tilt. She pushed him hard and he appreciated the extra motivation.

Also, in this sea of guys, she was a sweet relief to look at, even if the "Don't Touch" sign was glowing bright above her head.

"Check it out," she said and nodded toward the rear of the truck. They were the first words she'd spoken directly to him since asking where to check in.

He turned to look. Damn, he'd been staring at her again. He really had to cut that out. Well, if she wasn't going to complain, maybe he'd just enjoy it while it lasted.

Out on the assembly ground, thirty guys were still standing at roll call when the Sergeant Major closed his clipboard.

The three trucks that the roll-called soldiers had climbed aboard started their engines but didn't move off. They weren't packed in any tighter than usual.

"Men." The Sergeant Major raised his voice.

Kyle could hear him clearly despite the rumbling.

"You have failed to achieve the times necessary on the hikes. We will be sending you back to your units with letters of praise. You are fine soldiers, but regrettably, you aren't what The Unit is looking for. Thank you all. Pack your gear. Transport arrives in fifteen minutes. Dismissed." The Sergeant Major snapped a salute that was returned sloppily by the shell-shocked soldiers left standing in the dirt.

"Shit!" Kyle knew a half dozen of these guys. Three were Green Berets from his own battalion, though none of his own company were here. They were damn fine soldiers.

The trucks dropped into low gear and moved off as the shock continued to ripple through those left behind. Several dropped to sit in the dirt. Others stood and wept openly. Most simply watched the trucks drive away with a look of desperate longing on their face.

"Harsh," Carla observed.

Kyle looked at her. No sign of pity in her face. No sign of fear that it might just as easily have been her left standing in the dirt. A number of the guys on the truck looked aghast at their narrow escape from such a brutal cut, a full third of their forces gone in a single moment.

Sergeant Carla Anderson wasn't worrying about being cut. She was facing what was right in front of her. Like a good soldier, she focused on what came next.

He was starting to learn that whatever it was, she'd hit it full force and be damned good at it. Few soldiers and, up till now, no women, ever truly impressed him.

Kyle gave her a grin across the jouncing bed of the

truck as it slammed into the now-familiar potholes along the road outside Delta's front gate.

"On the bright side, at least they'll be spared an opportunity for you to send more of them swimming in a latrine."

She smiled back. It was a good smile, the first one he'd seen cross her face. It was easy and lit her eyes as well. "At least I didn't break any bones. I guess I *was* being a little mellow. I was in a good mood that day."

He cringed in pretend fear. "Ooo, so scared."

"How little you know."

That was the most words he'd heard her say since her arrival, the guys seated to either side watching her in surprise.

Himself, he was under the sway of that hypnotic voice and wouldn't mind hearing a lot more of it. But it took a more than a pretty face and a bit of training to make Delta. So, show her that there was a deep end of the swimming hole.

"Will we be seeing you at the end…girlie?"

Her returned smile was wicked; wicked enough that he wondered if there might be a latrine swim in his own immediate future. If so, he wasn't going in alone.

"You'll be seeing me only if you're still here, tough guy."

Kyle laughed back. It was a good moment.

And Sergeant Carla Anderson, both the soldier and the woman, impressed the hell out of him.

About the Author

M. L. Buchman has over forty novels in print. His military romantic suspense books have been named Barnes & Noble and NPR "Top 5 of the Year" and twice *Booklist* "Top 10 of the Year," placing two titles on their "Top 101 Romances of the Last 10 Years" list. He has been nominated for the Reviewer's Choice Award for "Top 10 Romantic Suspense of 2014" by *RT Book Reviews* and for the prestigious RITA Award for Romantic Suspense. In addition to romance, he also writes thrillers, fantasy, and science fiction.

In among his career as a corporate project manager he has: rebuilt and single-handed a fifty-foot sailboat, both flown and jumped out of airplanes, designed and built two houses, and bicycled solo around the world.

He is now making his living as a full-time writer on the Oregon Coast with his beloved wife and is constantly amazed at what you can do with a degree in geophysics. You may keep up with his writing by subscribing to his newsletter at www.mlbuchman.com.

Devil and the Deep

The Deep Six

by Julie Ann Walker

New York Times and *USA Today* bestselling author

—⁓—

A flaming desire with earth-shattering repercussions...

Maddy Powers's life revolves around fund-raisers and charity events—but she can't forget the daring former SEAL and the scorching kiss they shared before he disappeared into the deep blue sea.

Bran Pallidino carries a dark secret behind his lady-killer eyes—one that keeps him from pursuing a serious relationship with Maddy. But when she's taken hostage, he enlists the men of Deep Six Salvage to embark on a dangerous mission to save Maddy.

As they fight her merciless kidnappers, they discover this isn't a simple hostage situation, but something far more sinister. Passion boils between Bran and Maddy, but what good is putting their hearts on the line if they don't survive the dawn?

—⁓—

Praise for *Hell or High Water*:

"Readers will be panting for the next in
the series." —*Publishers Weekly*

"Hot men, hot action, and hot temperatures
make for one hot romance!" —*BookPage*

For more Julie Ann Walker, visit:

www.sourcebooks.com

Hold Your Breath

Search & Rescue Book 1

by Katie Ruggle

In the remote wilderness of the Rocky Mountains, rescue groups—law enforcement, rescue divers, firefighters—are often the only hope for the lost, the sick, and the injured. But in a place this far off the map, trust is hard to come by and secrets can lead to murder.

That's why Callum, the surly and haunted leader of the close-knit Search and Rescue brotherhood, finds it so hard to let newcomer Louise "Lou" Sparks into his life. But when these rescue divers go face-to-face with a killer, Callum may find that more than his heart is on the line...

Look for the rest of the Search & Rescue series:

On His Watch (available only in ebook)
Fan the Flames
Gone Too Deep
In Safe Hands

For more Katie Ruggle, visit:

www.sourcebooks.com